CHRYSAL

CHRYSAL;

OR,

THE ADVENTURES OF A GUINEA.

BY

CHARLES JOHNSTONE

FOUR VOLUMES IN TWO

EDITED WITH AN INTRODUCTION AND NOTES

BY

KEVIN BOURQUE

VOL. II.

Kansas City:
VALANCOURT BOOKS
2011

Chrysal; or, The Adventures of a Guinea by Charles Johnstone
First four volume edition published 1764
First Valancourt Books edition 2011

Introduction and notes © 2011 by Kevin Bourque
This edition © 2011 by Valancourt Books

ISBN 978-1-934555-85-9

Published by Valancourt Books
Kansas City, Missouri

Composition by James D. Jenkins
Set in Dante MT

10 9 8 7 6 5 4 3 2 1

CONTENTS

Chrysal; or, The Adventures of a Guinea

Volume III

ADVERTISEMENT.

THE circumstances in which *The Adventures of a Guinea* fell into the hands of the Editor, as explained in the General Preface, accounts for this, and the former Additions to that Work.

The uncommon favour, with which the first Edition, imperfect as it was, was received, encouraged him to spare no pains for the recovery of the rest of the Manuscript: Though his success however in this attempt exceeded his expectations, fear of the prejudice, in general too justly, entertained against *Continuations*, prevented his publishing, in the Second Edition, any more of what he had recovered, than could be added without enhancing the price. But as the sale of so many numerous impressions, since that Addition, has entirely removed every shadow of such fear, he thinks it would be injustice to the Public to withhold the rest from them any longer.

As to the objection made to *Continuations*, that they are written after the first design is completed, and when the imagination is exhausted, it can by no means affect the following sheets, which are really *a Restitution of the Original*, not an Addition of any thing new; as will plainly appear to the judicious Reader, who will find the same scope of imagination, the same spirited freedom, and depth of remark in every period of these Volumes, which so eminently distinguished the former; and trace the genuine connection through the whole.

For one great disadvantage, which these Volumes lie under, Candour will make the just allowance, when the occasion of it is considered.

This is the Printing of these Parts, thus detached, and by themselves with only references to the places, where they follow in the Context of the former Volumes; by which means they lose the advantage of the general Fable, or as I may say, *Machine*, which so happily introduces and supports the whole, and of which no more could be recovered; all, but what was at first published, being cancelled by the Orthodoxy of the pretended Clergyman, into whose hands the Manuscript unfortunately fell, who spared no more than was indispensably necessary to open the design.*[1]

Had the Editor attended solely to his own interest, it would have suggested to him to have published this, as he did the former Edition, inserted regularly according to the Connection; as the established reputation of the Work would ensure the sale of the whole, even to those, who had before purchased the former Volumes. But this was an artifice he was incapable of using; and he chose to publish these Volumes in this manner, rather than incur the least suspicion of so mercenary a design. He hopes therefore, that a disadvantage occasioned by such a delicate disinterestedness will not be looked upon as a defect; and that the whole will be viewed together, before any part is accused of abruptness, or want of uniformity to the general design.

The absurdity, and injustice of levelling the general reproof of vice, against particular Persons, and tracing to real characters a work of mere imagination, are too glaring to require proof. Mr. *Addison*, in the instance he has given in one of his *Spectators*, of *the whole Duty of Man*, has shewn that the best book that ever was written (humanly speaking) is liable to be construed into a scandalous libel, by such a *Perversion*.[2]

The Editor of this Work has the satisfaction to see that whatever injurious attempts of that kind were at first made against it, they have not been able to prejudice it in the opinion of the Public, as appears from the great and continued demand for it, for so many years. Defamation may please the malignancy of Man for a day; but it must be merit that can stand the test of time. Such insinuations are long since forgot, because unsupported by truth; as will all of the same nature, which may be made against the Volumes now offered to the Public, while the merit of them shall remain for the entertainment and instruction of ages.

---

1 Johnstone's note: "See the general Preface" (1.7-15).
2 In the *Spectator* 568, Addison makes an example of a man who, while reading Richard Allestree's *The Whole Duty of Man* (1658), "had written the Names of several Persons in the Village at the Side of every Sin which is mention'd by that excellent Author; so that he had converted one of the best Books in the World into a Libel against the 'Squire, Church-wardens, Overseers of the Poor, and all other the most considerable Persons in the Parish."

VOLUME III, BOOK I

CHAPTER I

Introduction. *Chrysal* enters into a new service. His master finds an
ingenious excuse for returning home; but is unexpectedly stopped
short by the way. In the common course of business, *Chrysal* changes
his service: Character of his new master.

(*There being a war between* Spain *and* England, Chrysal *in the shape
of a* Doubloon *is presented by a* Spanish *governor to the captain of an*
English *man of war cruising off the coast of* Mexico, *in return for his
quitting his station to give him an opportunity of sending the treasure to*
Europe.)

"As this was a compliment of great consequence to the
Spaniards, the captain had been so handsomely considered for it,
that his desires were satisfied, and he only wished to be safe at
home to enjoy the wealth he had so happily acquired."[3]

However impatient though he might be to return, it was
necessary for him to find some pretence to justify a conduct
so contrary to his duty, the time appointed by his superiors for
continuing on that station, not being near expired.

But a proper knowledge of the world is never at a loss for
expedients. He immediately came to a right understanding with
the master of the ship,[4] who alarming him suddenly at midnight
with an account that her *stern-post* was loose, and the rest of the
officers between sleeping and waking formally signing his report
without examining, he *bore away* directly for home with an happy

---

3 Johnstone's note here directs the reader to 1.59, where this storyline begins.
4 KEY: "Lord H. Powlett." Harry Powlett (1720-94), naval officer, who on the
death of his brother Charles (see 1.58) in 1765 became Duke of Bolton. The chapter
refers to Powlett's actions on the gunship *Barfleur*. In 1755, when the *Barfleur* was
commanded to chase a ship southeast of the British fleet, Powlett lost sight of the
pursued ship and, after the ship's carpenter reported the stern-post dangerously
loose, returned to harbor. Powlett was court-martialed for separating from the
British fleet and returning to port without good reason; the events earned him
the sobriquet "Captain Sternpost," and he never again commanded a ship.

heart, anticipating in imagination the enjoyment of all those pleasures, which he had hitherto looked at with a longing eye from a distance.

When man, confiding in his own wisdom, quits the straight path to strike out a nearer to his wishes, he generally blunders into that which leads directly to disappointment. My master had not proceeded many days on his voyage, when he *fell in* one morning just at the dawn, with a mighty fleet,[5] from which it was impossible for him to escape. His anxiety made him instantly conclude them enemies. He cursed his fate in the bitterness of his soul, and leaving the care of the ship to his officers, pretended to be sick, and threw himself on his bed in agonies little short of despair. "Was it for this?" (exclaimed he, wringing his hands, and gnashing his teeth) "was it for this I betrayed my trust, and favoured the enemies whom I was sent to distress?—For this did I put my honour in the power of a venal wretch, and desert my station, in direct disobedience to my orders? But I am justly rewarded! I have stopped at nothing to gather wealth, and now I lose that and my liberty together. May every villain meet the same fate!"

But the severity of his distress lasted not long. As soon as it was clear day, the fleet which caused his fears was found to be *English*; the moment he was informed of which he recovered from his sickness, and putting the best face he could upon the matter went to wait upon the Admiral.

Though the fleet which the Admiral commanded was irresistibly superior to any that could possibly be opposed to it, he was so desirous of every addition of strength, that he received my master with evident pleasure; and never enquiring what had been the cause of his quitting his station, informed him whither they were going, and congratulated him on the opportunity he should have of making his fortune.

---

5 KEY: "Expedt. against the Havannah," confirmed by other keys. The British fleet ordered to attack Havana, the richest and largest settlement of New Spain, sailed from Portsmouth on March 5, 1762. According to the *Annual Register*, "the armament amounted to nineteen ships of the line; eighteen small vessels of war; and near one hundred and fifty transports, which conveyed about ten thousand land forces." In mid-August, after a forty-day siege, Havana surrendered to the British.

But this opportunity, promising as it might appear, had no temptations for my master, whose thoughts were turned another way. However, to carry off the chagrin which he could not conceal, he expressed his concern in the strongest terms at not being able to bear a part in so glorious an enterprize, and produced the *report* of the condition of his ship, by which she was represented to be incapable of service, the reason, as he alleged, for his having quitted his proper station. This instantly changed the whole scene. The Admiral, assuming all the consequence of his unbounded authority, answered with a supercilious look, that he would order the ship to be surveyed by the proper officers, and then turned away without deigning to take any farther notice of him.

As this was no more than my master had expected, his knowledge of the world, which brought him into the scrape, soon suggested the proper means for preventing any disagreeable consequences from it. Accordingly, when the *survey* was regularly made next morning, he was *honourably* acquitted; but the master of the ship was broke *for his error*,[6] and the other officers severely rebuked, for not having examined his report before they signed it.

In the course of these transactions, I changed my service for that of the Admiral's Agent for his own private affairs, who directly gave me to the Admiral in some dealings between them.

When I entered into the possession of my new master,[7] he was lolling in a listless manner on a sofa, in his *state-room*, where every art was exerted to counteract nature, and elude the mid-day heat, in one of the fiercest climates of the Torrid Zone.[8] A gown of thinnest silk hung loosely over his large limbs; the radiance of the sun was softened by shades of linen drawn before the open windows, and kept constantly wet to cool the air as it entered

6 Although Powlett's court-martial acquitted him of returning to port unjustifiably, and the ship's carpenter was dismissed as incompetent, "public opinion blamed Powlett as the real author of the carpenter's report" (DNB).
7 KEY: "Sir Geo. Pocock." Sir George Pocock (1706-92), Admiral of the British navy, who in 1762 was appointed naval commander of the British forces sent to attack Havana. Chrysal's attacks here may result from the several unsuccessful or abortive missions Pocock led in India against the French.
8 "The regions or zone between the tropicks" (Johnson).

through them; and every disagreeable savour was drowned in the most delicate perfumes.

The contrast between such magnificent luxury, and the condition of those whose numbers made his strength, shewed in the most glaring light the infatuation of vanity, in displaying such temptations to its own destruction, as the most implicit obedience to laws could hardly be supposed proof to.

The awkwardness with which my master bore his state shewing that it was not natural to him, I looked back to his past life to see by what illustrious actions he had risen to such an exalted station; but to my surprise discovered that the foundation of his fortune had been no more than a *phlegmatic indolence* and *servility of soul*, which induced his superiors to entrust power into his hands, without apprehension of its raising him to a consequence that might clash with their designs on any future occasion.

I see you are astonished that a person of such a turn should ever engage in active scenes, or be entrusted with the conduct of an enterprize so opposite to his disposition, as to make success improbable. To unexperienced reason such things must seem unaccountable; but the least acquaintance with the ways of man would soon reconcile you to greater absurdities. The *convenience* of the parent, not the *genius* of the child, is in general the only thing considered in the choice of a profession on which the success of life depends; and this is the reason why so few are eminent in things so easy to be eminent in; and when at length a person may have it in his power to quit a profession which he did not choose, it is too late for him to choose another, and therefore he plods on with habitual indifference, not knowing what else to do with himself.

This may remove your surprise as far as it concerns my master's first entering into, and continuing in such a way of life. As to his fitness for so difficult and important a command, that was the thing least thought of when it was entrusted to him. The *insignificancy* of his character, and his *servility* to his superiors pointed him out as the person proper for their purpose, as they not only made them secure that he would not go beyond their orders, but would also put it in their power to arrogate to themselves the merit of success, or lay the blame of miscarriage upon him; and for these great qualifications only did they choose him on this occasion to execute *the design of another*,[9] who had been guilty of the unpardonable crime of shewing that he knew more than themselves, and whose penetration and activity of soul might too probably have made him see through their designs, and push matters farther than was consistent with them.

CHAPTER II

Motives of the enterprize in which *Chrysal*'s master was engaged. In a private conference between him and his agent, some curious secrets, in a business not generally understood, are laid open, and a seeming contradiction naturally reconciled.

WHENEVER *England* is at war with any of her neighbours, the effects are felt to the extremities of the globe. The armament which my master now commanded was sent against one of the most important and wealthiest settlements of the *Spaniards* in that part of the world; not indeed with an ambitious design of annexing it to the state, or reimbursing any part of the expences of the war, but merely to distress the enemy by its destruction, and enrich those immediately employed in the conquest; the prospect of which, and the consequent schemes to accomplish it, so entirely engrossed the attention of them all, except my master, that they disregarded the difficulties, and ran so eagerly into the dangers of the attempt, though such and so many as were sufficient to have damped the

---

9 KEY: "Adml. Knowles." Sir Charles Knowles (d. 1777), naval officer and first baronet, who was second in command during a 1757 failed British attack on the French port of Rochefort. "The fiasco had cost £1 million and brought nothing but humiliation" (Szabo), and the question of who deserved blame prompted a heated pamphlet-war. In self-defense, Knowles published *The Conduct of Admiral Knowles on the Late Expedition Set in a True Light* (1758), which prompted Tobias Smollett, in a review for the *Critical Review*, to lambaste Knowles as stupid and inept, "an ignorant, assuming, officious, fribbling pretender; conceited as a peacock, obstinate as a mule, and mischievous as a monkey." Although the plan for the attack on Havana was based on his ideas, Knowles was penalized for his role at Rochefort, and "had no further active service in the English navy" (DNB). Some years earlier, Knowles had also been reprimanded for a failed attack on the Spanish treasure fleet (see 1.58, note 210).

ardour of any beings directed by reason, and not insensible to the first principle of human action, that his phlegmatic disposition was no impediment to their success, as it left them at liberty to pursue such measures as the instant occasion should shew to be expedient, without the delay of consulting him.—I say, "except my master;" for not all the cares of so extensive a command, all the hurry and bustle around him, could ever ruffle the characteristic stagnation of his mind.

He was just awoke from his noon-tide nap, when his Agent laid the bag *in which I was* upon his table, along with some papers. The chink of the gold instantly attracted his attention. "Eh!" (said he, rubbing his eyes and yawning) "what is it o'clock?"—And being told, "Aye!" (continued he, stretching and yawning again) "I thought I had overslept myself, I am so heavy! This climate is fit for nothing but sleeping."—Then rising languidly, "What papers are these?" (said he) "Did I not say I would not be troubled about business?"

"They are your own accounts, for the *out-sets*[10] of this expedition," (answered the Agent) "which if you please you had better look over now, as we shall have others to attend to soon. I am sorry to say it does not answer your expectations, but the people alleged that they had been made to pay so extravagantly for their *contracts*, that it was impossible for them to sink the quantities of the stores so low, as to be able to give you any thing on that account, so that all your profit is reduced to the one article of *short-tale*; and in this too every Captain must *go snacks*."[11]

"Not able to give me any thing!" (said the Admiral, who had been roused from his lethargic indifference, by the first mention of his own affairs) "They lie, the scoundrels; and I'll make them know it. The *sick-lists*[12] shew that they have sunk them with a vengeance, and beyond every degree of reason; and if they think that I'll connive at their murdering the men, without having any share in the profit, they shall find themselves damnably *out in their reckoning*; and therefore do you go directly to every Purser in the

---

10 Expenditures (OED).
11 Short-tale: short of the initial sum or numerical account. Go snacks: to divide up the profits (OED).
12 Official lists "of sick persons, esp. soldiers or sailors" (OED).

fleet, and order them to have a *survey* privately made of their worst stores, to produce when I call for it. I'll make them *come down*, and handsomely too, or they shall repent it."

"But, sir," (replied the Clerk) "is not there danger that they may discover the affair of the *short-tale*, in revenge for such an attack; and that they who made the contract with them may be so offended as to hinder your being ever employed again?"

"I care not!" (returned the Admiral, clapping his hands a-kimbo) "I care not for their being offended!—Not I! I don't desire to be employed. If I mind my *hits* this time, I shall be as rich as the best of them, and will stay at home, and take my ease, as well as they: and as to what you say of their discovering the affair of the *short-tale*, that only shews your ignorance. They would lose more by that, than I should, as they have made every thing so damn'd bad, and are paid for the whole complement. Besides, don't you consider whom they are to complain to? No! No! We shall hardly expose one another! Things hang together too close for that! One is as deep in the mud as the other is in the mire."

"But may not they spread stories abroad, which may injure your character with the public?"

"My character, do you say? Not in the least. Such stories affect only the *Clerks*, and such low people, whose *perquisites* those things are reputed to be, and who only appear in them; but that can't be said to injure them neither, for what Clerk ever had a character that could be injured! Hah! Hah! Hah! So that your care for character forsooth is quite unnecessary! Do what you will, you cannot suffer in that. All you have to do is to mind your business, and when you have got money, no one will enquire about your character."

"Then, sir I presume the account must stand open as it is, till we go back, to settle those affairs."

"Aye!—Or stay! You may leave it with me. It will amuse me to look it over when I have nothing else to do! And you may pay in whatever money you have got too. I can give you a receipt on account."

"That's right, sir," (said the Clerk turning back, as recollecting himself) "I should be glad to know what *poundage* you will require of the sutlers[13] for the provisions they shall take on shore. Several of them have applied to me to know."

"Only twenty shillings in the pound!" (answered the Admiral) "*Cent. per Cent.*[14] on the first cost."

"Perhaps, sir," (replied the Clerk) "You don't consider that the General will expect *his composition*[15] too."

"Well! and what is his composition to me? Let them give him as much more if they will. They can afford it well enough. They may charge as high as they please; their customers cannot help themselves. They must pay any price, rather than starve, since they have no-where else to go.

"But you need not give yourself any concern about this. The general and I have agreed to act in concert, and divide equally between us every profit that can be made, while we continue together, so that all you have to do is to meet *his private Agent*, and settle matters with him."

"I am very glad you have come to a good understanding with each other!" (said the Agent, applying equivocally to the Admiral, what he really meant of himself) "It would otherwise have been impossible to avoid disagreements, as your interests would have clashed in so many instances, than which nothing can be more dangerous in such affairs as ours, for fear of improper discoveries; but where all parties understand each other rightly, business goes on with pleasure and success."

These weighty matters being thus adjusted, the Agent withdrew, when my master walked a turn or two about his great cabin, and then opening the money-bag, and telling the contents, put a few pieces, *among which I was*, into his pocket, and locked up the rest in his strong box, after which he threw himself again on the sofa, to rest after the fatigue of so much business.

You seem at a loss how to reconcile the sentiments which my master discovered in this conference, with the luxury and magnificence of every thing about him. But they contradict not

---

13 "Men who sell provisions and liquour in a camp" (Johnson).
14 "A hundred for every hundred; interest equal in amount to the principal" (OED).
15 "The settling of a debt, liability, or claim, by some mutual arrangement" (OED).

each other in the least. In the transactions with his Agent, he shewed the genuine motions of his heart; but with the other he has nothing to do. They are entirely at the expence of public, though in a manner not obvious to every eye, being a kind of tax established by custom on the *Pursers* of men of war, under the appearance indeed of a *present* to their commanders, but in reality as a *bribe* for conniving at their impositions; and this tax it is that enables those commanders to live up to their rank which their just pay would never do: a striking instance of that wise œconomy, which *to save a penny lays a man under a necessity of stealing a pound.*

CHAPTER III

The behaviour of *Chrysal's* master on hearing an interesting piece of news, with his concise method of conducting an enterprize. *Chrysal* changes his service for that of a person of a very different character. An eloquent speech produces the usual effects of eloquence.

My master had not passed his time long in this agreeable manner, when the officer next to him in command[16] entered hastily, and told him in a transport of joy, that the man at his mast-head, had *made* the land.

"What land?" (said my master, unmoved at the news, or the manner in which it was delivered by the other, whose eyes flashed fire as he spoke) "What land does he *make?*"

"The place of our destination!"[17] (replied the officer): "I had just then taken an observation myself, and am convinced I am right."

"Well then," (returned my master) "if you are sure it is the place, here are your instructions. You are to lead the van, and cover

---

16 KEY: "Adml. Keppell." Augustus Keppel, Viscount Keppel (1725-86), commodore of the forces bound for Havana and second-in-command under Pocock. Later, at the end of the War of American Independence, he became First Lord of the Admiralty. During the period, he was "one of the most popular and best-regarded captains in the navy" (DNB); according to Admiral Edward Boscawen, there was "no better seaman than Keppel, few so good, and not a better officer." Keppel would later sit as a member of John Byng's court martial (see 2.108-17), and petitioned Parliament to intervene on Byng's behalf.

17 As indicated in one reader's annotations, "the Island of Cuba."

the landing, about which proper directions will be given by the General: When that is done you shall have farther orders."—Then swelling with the thought of his own consequence, and resolving to support his dignity by an uncommon effort of generosity, "Has the fellow who *made* the land" (said he) "been rewarded for his news?"

"Not yet" (answered the officer) "the moment I heard it, I ran up myself to the mast-head, and as soon as I was convinced it was true, flew to acquaint you. But I shall remember him, when I go back."

"And pray when you do, give him *this* in my name," (replied my master, putting his hand into his pocket, and reaching *me* to him); "the men's spirits must be kept up. We shall have warm work of it; warm work!"

"Glorious work!" (added the officer) "the trophies of your fame will now be established in the opposite extremities of the globe. Few attain such happiness."

"Aye!" (said the Admiral, puffing and sweating with the sense of his great achievements) "I have done something to be talked of in more places than one. I have endured the severities of various climates. But we must bear every thing in the service of our country! We must bear every thing without complaining."

"Have you any farther commands, sir?" (said the officer) "It is proper I should be on board. I see several of the ships have now made the signal of seeing land."

"Nothing more at this time" (answered the Admiral). "You have your orders, and will take the best method to execute them. If you should be at a loss at any time, you may apply to me. I shall be in my proper station *in the rear*, attentive to every thing that is doing."

My *new* master on this withdrew, leaving the Admiral to enjoy the contemplation of his own consequence, and keep himself cool till dinner.

If the indolence of my late master was inconsistent with his station, the activity of my present seemed to exceed the abilities of an human being. The moment he got to his own ship he made a signal for all the captains in his division, and the General, to come on board him; and then ordering his ship's crew to be called *aft*, he went to the *barricadoes*,[18] and waving his hat over his head, "Courage, my lads!" (said he) "the day is ours. The Admiral has given us leave to take yonder town with all the treasure in it, so that we have nothing to do now, but make our fortunes as fast as we can, for the place can never hold out against us. The Purser will give every brave fellow a can of punch[19] to drink prosperity to old *England*, and then we'll go about our business with spirit. We shall all be as rich as Jews. The place is paved with gold, which the lubberly *Dons*[20] have gathered for us. Old *England* forever is the word, and the day is ours."

This eloquent harangue had the effect that eloquence usually has, *it transported the hearers out of their senses.* They answered with three cheers, which made the welkin[21] ring, and then went skipping and dancing with joy to get their punch; a foretaste of their good fortune, which many of them would not have given up for all their expectations.

As they were going off, my master happened to see among the crowd the man who had first discovered the land, and calling to him, "Here, ship-mate," (said he, giving him a Doubloon) "here is something the Admiral has sent you for your good *look-out*; and take this also from me;" (giving him another) "and I hope to give you an hundred more for hoisting your colours on the top of yonder walls."

"Aye! noble Captain," (said the Sailor, shrugging his shoulders, and making his best bow) "and so I will, or it shall cost me a worse fall, than from the main-top gallant-mast-head, that is when the ship takes *a heel!*[22] I'll pull down proud *Spain* and clap old *England* in its place."

The spirit which my master shewed in every word and action interested me so far in his favour, that I was pleased at his not having parted with me on this occasion.

By this time the General and the Captains were come on board,

---

18 "Fortifications; bars; anything fixed to hinder entrance" (Johnson).

19 "Liquour made by mixing spirit with water, sugar, and the juice of lemons." A "cant word" (Johnson).

20 Lubberly: "lazy and bulky" (Johnson); Don: "a Spanish lord or gentleman" (OED).

21 The skies (OED).

22 Lurches or inclines to one side (OED).

and being shewn into the great cabin, "Good news, gentlemen," (said my master in ecstasy, shaking every one of them by the hand as they entered) "I bring you good news! Yonder is the object of our hopes, the place that is to make our fortunes, and crown us with glory, if it is not our own faults, for the Admiral has given us general orders to proceed in the best manner we can, and without losing time or opportunity in waiting to consult him on every occasion; so that if we fail the fault will be entirely ours, as I said before, as also will the glory of success."

This news filled them with all the highest spirits. They congratulated each other on a success of which they made no doubt; and having concerted the measures proper to be taken, returned to their ships to carry them into instant execution.

CHAPTER IV

A characteristic conference between *Chrysal*'s new master, and his friend the general. The general professes an uncommon motive for military ardour. An officer desires to speak with the general, the mention of whose name opens some secrets in the service. Account of the officer. An extraordinary instance of ignorance of the world. He signalizes[23] himself at the expence of his superiors, who reward him accordingly. The best qualifications for rising in the army, with reasons why things were otherwise under another commander.

As soon as the Captains were gone, my master turned to the General,[24] for whom he had a particular regard, and embracing him eagerly, "Now, my dearest friend" (said he) "you will have an opportunity not only of gaining such glory, as will add lustre to the

---

23 "To make eminent; to make remarkable" (Johnson).
24 KEY: "Lord Albemarle." George Keppel, Earl of Albemarle (1724-72), commander of the land forces sent to Havana and Augustus Keppel's elder brother. After Havana was conquered, he served as governor of Cuba, provoking "criticism from merchants who complained (with reason) that he imposed illegal taxes on them." Walpole characterized him as "ambitious, greedy, and a dextrous courtier," and Wolfe (see 1.307-13) thought him one of those "showy men who are seen in palaces and the courts of Kings," who "have a way of trifling with us poor soldiers that gives many honest, poor men high disgust" (DNB).

dignity of your birth, but also of acquiring a fortune to support that dignity properly. But what is the matter? You do not seem affected at the happy prospect! are you not well?"

"Well!" (answered the General, shrugging up his shoulders) "Yes, I am well enough as yet; but know not how long I shall continue so, in this damn'd place, the heat of which seems to have set you on fire."

"Damn'd place do you call it?" (replied my master, vexed to the soul at the manner in which the other spoke) "It will be a happy place for you, if it is not your own fault, a much happier place than where I suppose you wish to be, *gaming at the coffee-house, or cracking jests for your patron over a bottle.* But take care! The eyes of all your officers are upon you, and if they should observe this indifference it would ruin you for ever. They would directly attribute it to want of spirit, on the least suspicion of which your patron would cast you off with contempt and abhorrence, and never interest himself more in your behalf, and you know with what difficulties he obtained this command for you; so much indeed that gratitude to him should make you exert yourself if you had no other motive, as he in a manner staked his character for you. Come! stir! You will be in no danger. Your post exempts you from that. All you have to do is to appear animated, and alert; and give your orders with fire. Your officers are to encounter all the dangers."

"As for the dangers of war," (returned the General, stung by the implication in the latter part of what my master had said) "I disregard them as much as any man. But this damn'd climate is the thing. I hate the thought of fighting with an invisible enemy, of sucking in diseases and death with my breath; and then besides I hate all trouble so much too, that I would this moment give up the prospect of glory, which you seem so struck with, to be at home safe, and at my ease."

"But the prospect of gain! Would you give that up too? I have often heard you passionately lament your want of a fortune suitable to your rank, and now you have it in your power to acquire it. But if you miss this opportunity"—

"May I never get another!—No! No! I shall hardly give up that! I will not neglect any thing in my power to acquire a fortune! But what did you mean just now, by saying you'd go yourself in your long boat to head the men! Sure that is not necessary."

"Aye! And you must go too for this time! There is no possibility of dispensing with it. But this will be the only night you need stay on shore, or expose yourself to any danger. You may go on board every night after this, and sleep in quiet and safety; for there will be little or no danger by day. All the work must be done by night."

"My dearest friend, and if I may, I will. It is but saying that the night air does not agree with me, and no one will dare to mutter a word to the contrary."

"Come then! let us move! The men will do their duty with double spirits, when they see us in earnest. I am as desirous of making and enjoying a fortune as you can be; but would make it with as much credit as possible tho'; and to convince you that I consult your credit also, your cousin shall go with me, and give out whatever orders I see proper, as if they came immediately from you. Only do not you betray the contrary by your inattention. Consider what immense treasure there is in the place, and what a noble share of it will fall to you."

"Aye! Aye! Let us but once come to sharing the plunder, and I'll engage to be as alert and attentive as the best of you all. Never fear me at that work. No one shall get the start of me there. As you say I must stay on shore to-night though, I'll just see my *night-dress* put up ready, to take with me, with a *febrifuge*, two or three *juleps*, and some *ptisane* to guard against the worst,[25] and then I'll be with you; though I wish it were possible to avoid going on shore this night! There will be such hurry and confusion in landing the men, that I shall unavoidably put myself in an heat, and that is very dangerous in the night-air; but I'll take a purge[26] in the morning to carry it off."

"Prithee don't think of such things now. Your officers all expect you, and it is time you were with them, so remember the consequence, and exert yourself with spirit. The success of this affair will enable you to spend the rest of your life as you please."

The friends then embraced with ardour, and were just separating

---

25 Febrifuge: "any medicine serviceable in a fever" (Johnson). Julep: "a medicated drink used" as a "'comforting' or gently stimulating mixture" (OED). Ptisane: "a wholesome or medicinal drink" (OED).
26 "A medicine that evacuates the body by stool" (Johnson). A laxative (OED).

to attend the business of their different departments, when a subaltern officer desired to speak with the General. On hearing his name, "Did you not know that I am engaged?" (said the General, with an embarrassed air) "He must wait, till I am at leisure."

"Don't let me hinder you," (said my master) "I am just going."

"You do not, in the least. He can have no business with me, but what you may hear; and indeed what you must help me to extricate myself from; for I know he comes upon some scheme of *distinguishing* himself, that will only give me trouble."

"How can that be? If you do not approve of what he proposes, surely you have it in your power to reject it, without fear of giving him offence; or if, on the other hand, you think it practicable, and worth pursuing, I cannot suppose that any honour or advantage that can possibly accrue to him, can make you unwilling to carry it into execution."

"Most certainly not. The difficulty I am under is of a very different nature. The character of the man gives me reason to believe, that he will not propose any thing, which is not both practicable, and important; and as it is not in my power to reward his success, his doing any thing out of the common course of duty would involve me in the highest distress, both on account of the injustice to him, and the poor figure I must make myself on so flagrant a breach of my own public declaration, *that in the disposal of all preferments, I would pay due respect to seniority, where superior merit did not give a stronger claim.*"

"Well! and why should it not be in your power to fulfil that declaration?"

"My dearest friend, I blush to think of, much more to expose even to you the mortifying hardships laid upon me. The truth is, I have, since I made that declaration, another Officer, who was in his cradle since this has been in the army, and has never yet seen the face of an enemy, put upon me for the first preferment, by one whose directions I must not disobey, however detrimental to the service."

"That is a disagreeable circumstance, I own. But who is this Officer, your good opinion of whom gives you such apprehensions?"

"He is a military enthusiast, *who knows so little of the world, as to think of rising in the army by merit alone;* and with that view, not satisfied with doing his duty in the most signal manner, is always a volunteer, whenever he thinks any glory can be acquired; though his own particular experience, as well as general observation might have long since convinced him of the folly of such a thought. You must know him. This is he, who in that unlucky affair upon the coast of *France*, made a stand with the single company to which he belonged, (and which he had so attached to him by giving out of his own pocket to such as behaved well, a daily gratuity in addition to their pay, that they would follow him any where) to cover the embarkation of the troops,[27] while every Officer was shifting for himself, as he actually did in a great measure, till most of his little party was cut off, as it was a thousand to one, but they all must, unsupported as they were; though it appeared after, that if a proper force had been posted in that very place at first, or he reinforced in any time, the heavy loss, and disgrace suffered on that occasion, might have been prevented. But still that was reckoned no business of his; and therefore all the reward he got for his pains was to have two Officers, *who were not even in the action*, put over his head, and the company's money, which he had lost along with all his own baggage, *refused to be made good to him because he was a volunteer on that attack*. For (sorry I am to say it!) that is not the way to rise in the army now o'days. Where a man has not interest to push him forward, *being able to sing a good song*, or *pimp well*, or *having an handsome wife*, or *sister*, with a proper degree of humility, and complaisance, will avail him more than all the courage and

---

27 Perhaps Richard Howe, Earl Howe (1726-99), an extraordinarily capable and successful commander who served in the Jacobite Rising, the Seven Years War, and the American and French Revolutions. He would later rise to become First Lord of the Admiralty and Vice-Admiral of Great Britain, and "his achievements in fifty-nine years of active service in the navy were prodigious and must put him in the first rank of any of the naval commanders of any age" (DNB). The "unlucky affair upon the coast of *France*" may refer to an disastrous 1758 attack on the French coast at Saint-Malo. Howe saved many lives by efficiently re-embarking British forces, bravely waiting to lead the final evacuations himself: "in the midst of a fire that staggered the bravest seamen who managed the boats," reported the 1758 *Annual Register*, "Commodore Howe exhibited a noble example of intrepidity and fortitude, by ordering himself to be rowed in his own boat through the thickest of the fire, to encourage all that were engaged in that service, and to bring off as many men as his vessel could carry." Chrysal meets Howe's brothers William (who served with distinction during the siege of Havana) and George Augustus in Chapter XXI. See 2.82-87.

conduct in romance. In my patron's time[28] indeed things were not so. Brave himself, he expected that every man under him should be brave also; nor would let any recommendation compensate for the want of merit, in those who sought his favour; *as his own interest and honour were naturally, and inseparably connected with those of his country; and he was not lifted up to power, only to be the tool of a party; nor obliged to support himself in it, by intrigue, without any other view or motive than that of amassing its emoluments;* and therefore it has been the great misfortune of this officer, that he never served immediately under him."

CHAPTER V

Chrysal's master makes some close remarks on certain matters. The method which the general took to parry the officer. *Chrysal's* master makes up the affair. The general gives the officer an opportunity of distinguishing himself, which he does in a signal manner.

It is remarked that men seldom enquire into the causes of things, continually before their eyes. Habitual acquaintance prevents that curiosity, which is one of the strongest incentives to knowledge. They have always seen such things; and therefore have never enquired how they came to be so.

My master, who had long observed the fact, but never thought of the cause, was struck with what his friend said. After some pause, "I am afraid what you say is too true!" (said he) "and cannot help attributing it to a cause, not much to the credit of the commanders, who certainly would never discourage merit in others, were

---

28 KEY: "D. of Cumberland." Prince William Augustus, Duke of Cumberland (1721-65), younger son of King George II. Cumberland, who served as Commander-in-Chief of British forces from 1745 to 1757, was proclaimed a hero after subduing Jacobite rebels in 1746. His heretofore distinguished career, however, would end in disgrace with his signing of the Convention of Kloster-Zeven, in which Hanover effectively capitulated to France (see 2.350-52). Albemarle was Lord of the Bedchamber to Cumberland from 1746, and "his loyalty to his patron was fierce"; at Cumberland's death, Albemarle "culled the Duke's papers of politically sensitive materials," destroying everything the Duke "might have desired to keep concealed" (DNB).

they not conscious that they had not risen by it themselves; and therefore look upon it with an envious eye, as a reproach to them. Indeed, it can scarcely be expected, that *a General, who has spent his life in paying court to a minister, or favourite, or who was prefer'd only for his interest in Parliament*, should act otherwise. But what will you do with this officer? It will have an odd look, if you don't see him; at the same time, if he should propose any thing of real consequence, I am absolutely at a loss how to advise you to act."

"The only method, I can think of, is this. His temper is warm; and his notions of honour punctiliously high. I will therefore receive him with a distance, that I know will hurt his sensibility, and provoke him to say something, of which I may take advantage to break off the conference, without entering into the subject of his coming; for he speaks as boldly as he acts; and thinks it beneath him to soften his sentiments by any qualifying expression."

Accordingly the General ordered the officer to be admitted, and asking him slightly what was his business, "I come, Sir," (answered he) "to inform you that I have discovered a proper place for landing the troops, and formed a plan for that purpose."

"You have discovered, Sir!" (interrupted the General haughtily) "Pray when, and how did you make this notable discovery?"

"Just now, Sir!" (returned the Officer,) too intent upon the object he had in view to take notice of the manner of his reception. "The *transport*, in which I was, happening to *stretch away a-head*, I got out a boat, and have carefully reconnoitred a great part of the coast, in the thick of the enemy's fire."

"And pray, Sir," (interrupted the general again, determined not to let him explain himself) "Who gave you orders to reconnoitre in this manner?"

"No one, Sir!" (answered the officer warmly, and hurt at the manner, in which the General spoke) "I never wait for orders, to do any thing in which my own safety only is concerned, when I think it for the advantage of the service."

"When you think!" (retorted the General sternly) "I should be glad to know who has appointed you to judge of those things. At this rate the whole army will be generals by and bye; and every one will be out reconnoitring forsooth, when they should be at their posts; but I'll put a stop to such contempt of discipline, and make you know, that it is your duty to wait for orders, not to got rambling thus, whenever you please."—Saying which he called one of his *Aide de Camps*, and putting the Officer in arrest, sent him away bursting with indignation and resentment to his ship.

When he was gone, "I am very sorry" (said my master) "that your engagement to that other man laid you under a necessity of treating this Officer so harshly. I have conceived a very good opinion of him; he appeared to be actuated by true zeal; and spoke with a confidence, that shewed he was convinced of what he said; for which reason, I am resolved to reconnoitre that place myself, and don't doubt, but I shall find his account of it to be just."

"Nor do I, in the least. He has an head to plan, and an heart to execute the most important enterprize; and I am as sorry for what I have been forced to do as you. But as soon as I have it in my power to reward his merit, I'll give him every opportunity of displaying it, till when this affair will keep him out of the way."

I see you are anxious to know the sequel of this Officer's story. To avoid breaking the thread of my narrative with it, therefore, at another time I will conclude it here.

My master, as he said, went that very night and reconnoitred the place pointed out by the Officer, whose account of it proved so just, that he repaired to him directly, and enquiring into his plan for landing the troops, found it so judicious, that he immediately adopted the whole, and carried it into execution with success.

After some days, when the Officer's impatience of being idle thus in the midst of action, had in a great measure got the better of his resentment, and the severe loss sustained in the siege made the worth of men more attended to, my master attacked him on his *foible*, his passion for glory, and zeal for the service of his country, and prevailed on him to return to his duty, on the General's making an apology for what he had done, which he attributed to his anxiety, and apprehension of the enemy's being put on their guard by his reconnoitring in that daring manner; and to cancel the disgrace of the arrest, treated him with particular attention; and as he was now at liberty to do justice to his merit, (the other, who had been imposed upon him, being provided for) gave him the first opportunity he could of signalizing himself, which he did in a manner, that amply justified the opinion my master had conceived of him.

The affair was this. The General had resolved to make an attack upon the principal redoubt, that defended his fortress, and gave the command of it to him. The plan laid down by the General was that an Officer with a party of men should go from another post, just before the dawn to reconnoitre the redoubt, and if he found that the fire of the night had made the impression expected, a signal was to be given for this Officer to advance and make the attack. The other accordingly marched but missed his way, and falling in with a lesser redoubt mistook it for the object of his designation, and inconsiderately attacked it, upon which the signal was given for this Officer to proceed. The alarm had set the soldiers in the principal redoubt on their guard, which he perceiving before he came within their shot, and being sensible that his attempt could succeed only by surprise, by one of those instantaneous efforts of genius, which mark the true military character, he resolved, without a moment's hesitation that might discover his disappointment, to try a stratagem of his own, since that of the General had been frustrated by this mistake, and directed his march regularly toward the attack that was begun upon the lesser redoubt, as if he had been sent on purpose to support it.

Deceived by this feint, the Officer who commanded in the principal redoubt knowing the force there to be too weak to make resistance, sent the greater part of his own to their relief. This was what he had foreseen. He therefore continued his march slowly, till they had got beyond him; and then facing suddenly about, pushed with all speed for the redoubt, they had thus abandoned. The moment they saw this motion, they turned back, but the narrowness of the entrenchment, in which they were, prevented their making such expedition, and coming up in a body, as his men did on the plain, so that he entered with the very foremost man of them, and made himself master of the place, with inconsiderable loss.

The importance of this redoubt, the taking of which greatly facilitated the operations of the siege, enhanced the merit of the action. Nothing else was talked of in the army, where the fortune of this Officer was looked upon to be made. But no opportunity offered for promoting him during the remainder of the expedition, so that the only reward in the General's power to give him, was thanking him publicly at the head of the army, which he did in the strongest terms. Resolved however to be the instrument of his promotion, tho' he could not promote him himself, he represented him, on his return, in so advantageous a light to one,[29] *whose inclination it was known to be, and who from his office should have had it in his power to reward merit,* that he promised to do him justice.

But the delicacy of the Officer's sense of honour defeated these generous intentions. He would not accept of the preferment offered him, without having, at the same time, reparation for the injustice he had suffered, by an honorary rank superior to those, who had been put over him: and when this was refused, *for reasons of convenience,* insisted on quitting the service, in the permission for which, his patron did justice to his character in the most authentic manner, before he himself resigned an office, which he would hold no longer, than it was in his power to fulfil the declaration he had made on accepting it, *"that while he should be in that office, he would not only be a vigilant servant of the crown, but also a faithful trustee, for the honest claim of the brave, and deserving officer."*

CHAPTER VI

Chrysal accounts curiously for some interesting points of policy. He supports his reason for not entering into the particulars of the siege, by some remarks on war, more just perhaps than popular; and assigns a motive for courage, not likely to be meant by those who give it.

I HAVE been so particular in the story of this Officer, in order to give you some notion of matters, with which your manner of life has made you unacquainted. In his fate you see the consequence of a subaltern's striving to distinguish himself, by doing any thing more than his immediate duty.

This, however strange it may appear to you, who judge only from reason, is strictly consistent with the principles of modern

---

29 KEY: "Chas. Townshend." Charles Townshend (1725-67), who at the time of writing was probably either Secretary at War or a Lord of the Admiralty. See 1.101.

policy, which is calculated entirely for private convenience, without the least regard to public good. Every attempt of this kind is taken for an affront by his superiors, as implying a design of forcing them to promote him, and putting himself in competition with them for the good opinion of the public, and therefore discountenanced.

Indeed if it were otherwise, few men of fortune or interest would according to the present way of thinking go into the army at all, as *they could not expect to enjoy their ease, or shew a prudent regard to their safety*, without being subject to disgraceful comparisons from the *officious assiduity, or rashness* of every man, desperate in disposition or circumstances, who disregarded life, and all its pleasures, or had no way of being able to live, but by hazarding the loss of them.

In former times men entered into the profession of arms; with a certain prospect of honour and advantage, if they could merit them, and therefore exerted all their abilities of mind and body, in emulation for so tempting a prize; but now, every idler, who is unfit for any other business, *purchases* a commission in order *to live upon the pay*; and as he is sensible that no efforts of his own can procure an addition to that pay, by raising him to an higher tank, he is satisfied to enjoy his bargain as easily as he can, and do no more than he needs must to avoid losing it. And this will account to you for the difference between the *English* forces, now, and in those days. Nor is the case otherwise with those, who get into the army by interest. They depend solely upon the same interest to push them forward, and therefore give themselves no trouble to deserve promotion, which they are convinced no desert could procure them.—But to quit reflections not likely to be regarded, and return to my story.

You must not expect a minute detail of the progress of this enterprize. The operations of war are too confused to give pleasure to reason in the representation, too horrid not to give pain to humanity.

I see you think this too severe: but that is the effect of prejudice. When the victories, which have been blazoned highest, and reflected the greatest honour on those, who gained them, are stripped of the false colouring, laid only to dazzle, and deceive, and examined coolly, most of them will be found owing to some unforeseen accident, some lucky improvement of a blunder of the enemy, or else an obstinate perseverance in their own, after every boasted rule of art had been broke through, every resource of judgment exhausted in vain; and to have been attended by circumstances of such miser, and loss to victors as well as vanquished, as tarnished all their glory, and infinitely overbalanced every advantage possible to be gained by them. I shall therefore mention only such particulars, as may contribute to illustrate this picture of the heart of man.

The ardour shewn by the subaltern officers and private men in carrying on the siege, in which they suffered more from the inclemencies of a climate unnatural to them, and against which no proper provision had been made though they had been delayed to meet its fiercest fury, as well as from the diseases caused by the badness of every necessary of life,[30] than from all the efforts of the enemy, all the arts which the ingenuity of man has devised for the destruction of his own unhappy species, was impossible to be accounted for, from any other principle, than *disregard to a life destitute of every comfort and convenience that could endear it;* a remark, which to the humane wisdom of some may seem to justify the deficiency, and badness of every kind of provision too generally made for them on such occasions; while those, whose higher rank may be thought to animate them with a sense of honour, and ambitious hope, and who therefore may be thought not to want such incitements to desperation, enjoy a luxury scarce to be reconciled with the confusion of such an unsettled state: that neither of these motives though, powerful as they may be, in general, will always prevail over a foolish fondness for life, instances appear in every war.

---

30 During the protracted siege of Havana, thousands of men were lost to heat exhaustion and tropical disease.

CHAPTER VII

One of the captains under *Chrysal's* master behaves in an extraordinary manner, and vindicates himself as extraordinary. His crime is overlooked for prudential reasons, which he mistakes, and demands a trial. He meets his deserts.

As my master was attending one morning to the success of an attack which he had ordered to be made by some of *the men of war* under his command, upon a fort that principally obstructed the progress of the siege, he was surprised to see one of them not only notoriously make the most shameful delay in *bearing down*, but also the moment she came within reach of it, instead of joining in the attack begun by the others, put about and quit her station, without even attempting to do any thing.

Though the Captain of the ship[31] had drawn the general disesteem of the corps upon him by his arrogant behaviour, and by his morose treatment of his men and officers raised suspicions of his spirit, on this unerring maxim, that *cowardice is the inseparable companion of cruelty*, yet as he had those powerful motives to courage, *pride of family*, and *poverty*, and must know that the inevitable consequence of such a flagrant breach of duty must be a disgraceful death, if it could not be properly accounted for, my master concluded that some accident must have happened, which was the more probable, as the ship was the worst in the fleet, and therefore as soon as the affair was over made his signal to come on board, that he might learn what was the matter.

Though the first sight of him might have explained the whole, the fears of his heart being visible in every feature of his

---

31 KEY: "Captain Campbell." Probably James Campbell, Captain of the *Stirling Castle*. Contemporary accounts of the siege record that although the *Stirling Castle* had been ordered to lead the vanguard of ships bombarding El Morro, the principal fort of Havana, Campbell shirked his duty and lagged behind the other ships. For cowardice, Campbell was brought to a court-martial, and according to N. A. M. Rodger in *The Wooden World: An Anatomy of the Georgian Navy*, "was dismissed the service, and was probably lucky not to have been shot, considering the strength of naval opinion."

haggard face, my master disdained to aggravate his distress by an appearance of severity, and only asked him coolly the reason of his not having *borne down* the attack, with the same expedition as the other ships.

"Sir—Sir—Sir—" (faultered the trembling wretch, not sufficiently recovered from his fright to express the evasion he had prepared) "I—I—made all the expedition I possibly could."

"How can you have the confidence to say so," (returned my master) "when there were several of your sails, which you never *set*?"

"That was not my fault, Sir;" (replied the Captain, resuming his natural assurance) "How could I set them, when I had sent the *booms* ashore yesterday, by your orders?"[32]—

"The booms!" (interrupted my master with a look of the most contemptuous astonishment) "Can such ignorance be possible? Surely you must have known, that the booms meant in my orders, were those the boats are stowed on, which were to be sent ashore, that the men might not be hurt by the splinters in the attack, not those of your sails!"

"Very likely, Sir! It might have been so to be sure. But as the order was to send all my booms, without any such exception, I did not think I could justify disobeying them, on my own opinion."

"And pray, Sir, how can you justify your quitting your station, in the manner you did, when you at length made a shift to come up! was that in obedience to your orders too?"

"No, Sir! that was quite another thing. When I come up, I saw the other ships had suffered considerably, and as I thought they were sufficient for the purpose, I judged it best to save his Majesty's ship entrusted to my care, for another occasion. That was my reason, Sir."

"A very prudential one truly; but I believe you should add too, to save the Captain; for if I mistake not greatly, that was not the least object of your care."

"Very true, Sir! and with good reason too, let me tell you; as I know that the interest of my family which has promoted me thus

---

32 Campbell claimed his ship steadily fell behind the others because the captain had earlier "sent ashore most of the *Stirling Castle*'s sails, yards, and booms." See David Syrett, *The Siege and Capture of Havana*.

far, will not fail to raise me higher. Men of low birth, or whose
relations will not serve them, may set no value on their lives; but
that is not my case; I am akin to most of the nobility of my country,
who always stand by their own blood, where any preferment, or
advantage is to be gotten! Hem! ahem!".

"I know their interest full well," (retorted my master, scarce
able to suppress his indignation at such insolence) "and the
closeness with which they hang together; but take care that you
do not depend upon them too far."

Unabashed by the manner, in which this was said, the Captain
asked if he had any farther commands, and being answered in the
negative, marched off in triumph.

There are some crimes, in the punishment of which all men are
more than ordinarily severe, in order to prove their own exemption
from them. One of the first of these is cowardice, which though
often an involuntary defect of constitution, is justly reckoned a
crime in military men, from the consequences that may attend it,
and as it makes them unable to perform the duties of a profession,
which they should not have entered into, under a sense of such an
incapacity.

All the Captains present were for punishing the offender
instantly, in the most exemplary manner, for so flagrant a breach
of duty. But my master, much as he detested the crime, and was
provoked by the insolence, with which he strove to carry it off,
thought it better to overlook it for the present, than by bringing him
to justice, throw a disgrace upon the forces, that might encourage
the enemy to exert themselves, in hopes of more instances of the
kind.

But this moderation was disappointed by a common cause. In
a few days after, the Captain judging by himself, that nothing but
fear of giving offence to his great family, could have prevented his
being fallen upon directly (for notwithstanding his evasions he was
conscious of his crime) instead of improving that precious respite
to extenuate his guilt, by some meritorious action, presumed,
upon meeting some instances of contempt from the rest of his
chore, to demand the justification of a public trial, in order to be
formally acquitted, of what he thought they dared not convict him;
and also to escape being involved in any farther dangers, during

the expedition, as he knew the immediate consequence of such a demand must necessarily be suspending him from his command, till he should be tried, which he knew could not be, before the conclusion of the siege; and in this latter particular, his expectation was not deceived.

This directly put an end to the prudential reasons, that had hitherto saved him, and of which the successful progress of the siege had also greatly lessened the force. Accordingly, to end his story here, in a few words, the trial he desired was granted, the result of which was, that he was *broke* with infamy, in contempt of all his boasts, and menaces, of the power and resentment of his family and friends.

CHAPTER VIII

Chrysal accounts for the peculiar animosities, which some nations shew in war. A noble *Spaniard* is taken prisoner in a sally. He makes a proposal to the general which is accepted, and opens a prospect of peace. A brutal outrage disappoints his design, and embroils matters more than ever.

THERE is nothing suggests so disadvantageous an idea of mankind, as the more than brutal ferocity, with which they destroy each other, when quarrels between nations set the animosity of individuals free from those restraints of law, with which necessity has taught human prudence to enforce the observation of the general duties of social and moral life.

The animosity though is never seen in its most sanguine colours, but in wars between people of different modes of religion. In that revelation of the will of heaven, which should be the rule of the religion of *Christians*, the first precept in respect to the mutual intercourse between man and man, is brotherly love to each other.[33]

Such a precept bears intrinsic evidence of its divine origin. But still human perversion has dared to represent the breach of it as a duty of that revealed law, by confining the benefit of the

---

33 The Golden Rule or ethic of reciprocity: "Love your neighbor as yourself."

obligation to the profession of some particular opinions, and not only excluding the rest of mankind from the circle of general brotherhood, but also making it a merit to propagate those opinions, by the extirpation of all dissenting from them, who are held incapable of the favour of heaven, and therefore not entitled to the common rights of humanity.

Of all the people, who profess *Christianity*, the *Spaniards* are the most bigoted slaves to this narrow, and gross prejudice. With them, therefore, the natural animosity of war is heightened by religious abhorrence, against all who differ in opinion from them; and the laws, which more enlightened nations have mutually agreed in, to restrain its ravages, and facilitate the restitution of peace, are often broken through with a cruelty, disgraceful to the name of man.[34]

In a sally made one night by the besieged, a noble *Spaniard*, who had penetrated so far into the trenches, that it was impossible for him to get back, fell wounded into the hands of the *English*. The gallantry with which he had defended himself gained him respect from his enemies; and he was treated with that generous tenderness which brave men feel for each other.

Struck with a behaviour so different from what he expected, for he had been taught to look upon the *English* as enemies to mankind, and delighting in the most savage cruelty, he desired to be led to the Commander, to whom he said he had something of consequence to propose. Accordingly, as soon as his wounds were dressed, he was conducted to the General, with whom my master happened to be, and advancing to him with an air of dignity, "I am come, illustrious Chief," (said he) "to thank you for the humane and generous treatment I have received from your brave soldiers, which if known to my countrymen, would facilitate an accommodation between them and you, as dread of your power, raised, I am not convinced, by injurious misrepresentations, has hitherto principally prevented their listening to any terms from you. I speak not this from ignorance. My father is governor of the city. If you will let him know that I am your captive, he will directly

---

34 An example of the Black Legend of Spain, a trope common in literature of the sixteenth through the eighteenth centuries, in which the colonial activity of other European powers—such as Britain—is excused or celebrated in relation to the supposed ignorance, brutality, and religious fanaticism of Spain.

pay for me, whatever ransom you desire, and on my return I will faithfully remove the prejudices, which keep up their animosity against you, and by that means open the way to a reconciliation, till the pleasure of our Sovereigns shall restore peace to their subjects."

Such an offer required no arguments to enforce it. "The *English*" (answered the General) "never abuse the advantages they obtain in war. I desire no ransom for your liberty. You are free to return to your father, when you please; and if you can be the means of preventing the effusion of more blood, as you must be convinced that resistance is in vain, I shall think myself happy in having an opportunity to shew respect to all, whom you shall recommend to your friends, and deserving of it."

These words filled the benevolent heart of the *Spaniard* with joy. "I fly," (replied he, eagerly) "to execute a commission, in which there can be no difficulty. As you are brave, and faithful to your Sovereign, you will require no terms which brave men and good subjects ought not to comply with."

The General then prevailed upon him to take some refreshment, after which he and my master went with him to the head of the lines, where he dismissed him with every mark of respect, attended by an officer with *a flag of truce*, to bring back the Governor's answer.

But this pleasing prospect was soon overcast. The Officer and he had not advanced above half the way, between the trenches, and the town, where they were fired upon by a party of *Spaniards*, who lay in ambush among the ruins of some old buildings. At the first sound of their fire, the *Spaniard* rushed forward in order to put a stop to it, and the Officer waved his flag of truce over his head, but that sacred ensign afforded him no protection. They repeated their shot, and seeing him fall, ran up, and in despite of all the *Spaniard* could do, who received a mortal wound as he covered his body with his own, butchered him in the most barbarous manner, replying to his appeal to the law of nations,[35] violated thus in him, that *Heretics were excluded from the benefit of all laws.*

---

35 Killing prisoners of war was a violation of international law. See Emer de Vattel's *Law of Nations* (1758): "as soon as your enemy has laid down his arms and surrendered his person, you have no longer any right over his life."

The indignation, with which such an outrage fired the *English* forces, is not to be described. They vowed to exterminate a people, who were unworthy to live; and in the first madness of their rage were with difficulty restrained from attempting to *storm* the walls, before a breach should give them even a possibility of success.

The leaders did not fail to improve such a spirit. Every thing was pushed on with redoubled vigour; and war became more horrible, when blackened with a passion for revenge, which had taken such possession of the men, that it was some time before all the endeavours of their Officers could put a stop to their indulging it, and bring them back to that generous valour, which is their peculiar glory.

CHAPTER IX

Chrysal's attention is agreeably diverted by the appearance of a young *Spaniard*, who throws himself at the feet of his master to prefer an extraordinary request. The History of *Don Alphonso Guzman*, the young *Spaniard*.

I WAS relieved from the pain of attending to such scenes of horror, by an affair that shewed in a striking light the force of passions more natural to the heart of man.

As my master, who was the soul of the enterprize, was standing one night to see the effect of a battery which he had caused to be raised on an eminence, that commanded a particular quarter of the town; for not content with performing his own duty in his proper station by sea, he literally fulfilled his promise to his friend, the General, and directed the operations by land also in his name; a youth, who had made his escape from the garrison,[36] and advanced in the face of all their fire, though sufficient to terrify any being capable of terror, threw himself at his feet in agonies of distress.

My master, whose heart was warmed with that generous compassion, which is inseparable from true courage, was struck at the sight, and raising him from the ground, bade him declare the

---

36 KEY: "The whole of this story seems a Work of Imagination."

nature of his distress, and expect every assistance to which he was entitled by the sacred duties of humanity.

Encouraged by these words the youth raised his head, and fixing his eyes upon my master with a look inexpressibly supplicating, "O stop your fire, gracious Chief!" (said he pressing his lips passionately to the hand that had raised him, and on which he still hung) "stop your fire in that fatal direction, where it can hurt only innocence and virtue. That building, against which it is levelled, is not a part of the fortifications, the destruction of which can be of any service to you. It is a convent dedicated to the *Virgin Mother of God*, and at this time contains all that my soul holds dear, all that is beautiful and virtuous under heaven."

Though his youth, beauty, and distress interested every one present in the suppliant's favour, the nature of his suit must necessarily have prevented its success. But an accident saved him from the pain of being refused, the powder which was to serve the guns somehow catching fire, and destroying the greatest part of the battery, in the very instant he spoke.

Not all the horrors of such a scene could suppress the joy he felt at an event so favourable to his hopes. "Heaven has interfered!" (exclaimed he, in an ecstasy) "Heaven has interfered to save her; and man will not presume to oppose its pleasure."

The enthusiastic manner in which he said this, struck my master. "Restrain your passions for a few moments," (said he) "till I have leisure to attend more particularly to you; and then if you can convince me of the truth of what you say, your request shall be complied with. Far be it from me to hurt those helpless votaries of religion. *Britons* seek other objects of their valour."—He then gave the necessary orders for repairing the battery, and desiring the youth to follow him, went on board his ship, where he treated him with every mark of politeness and compassion.

As soon as they had taken some refreshment, my master made a sign to every one else to retire, and addressing himself to the youth in the most humane manner, desired to know who he was, and what motives could have induced him to run into such imminent danger in order to prefer a suit, of the success of which there was so little probability.

The youth for some moments hung down his head, abashed,

then with a sigh that seemed to burst his heart, "It is my duty, most generous Chief," (said he) "to give you the information you require, however painful the task may be to me; especially as your condescending to listen to the story of my misfortunes awakes an hope, that you will be moved by them to grant a request on which depends my life.

"My name is *Alphonso*. My father, *Don Pedro*, bears an honourable command in the forces which defend yonder city against your arms, but glories more in the honour of being descended from the noble family of *Guzman*, which has preserved its blood pure from every debasing mixture, since the beginning of time in the mountains of *Castile*,[37] and produced a race of heroes, whose fame has filled the world.

"When my father arrived at an age fit to bear arms, as none of the powers of *Europe* dared to provoke the wrath of *Spain*, disdaining a life of inglorious peace, he entered into the forces sent hither to reduce such of the rebellious natives, as still presumed to refuse submission to the monarch of the *Spanish* worlds, where he signalized himself so eminently, that at the end of seven years his merits were rewarded with a commission, signed by the Viceroy himself in the name of the King.

"Such a distinguished honour gave weight to the addresses which he had for some time paid to the only daughter of *Don Alonzo Garcias*, who was a native of *Arragon*,[38] and had been sent over by the King to fill the important office of Secretary to the Receiver of his Revenues.

"From this marriage, so honourable to both parties, I have the happiness to derive my birth, if it can be called an happiness to be born only to misfortunes.

"As I was the sole hope of two such illustrious houses, no pains were spared to give me an education suitable to my birth; the great exploits of my ancestors, the antiquity, and untainted nobility of my blood, were continually repeated to me to excite emulation, and inspire me with proper sentiments of honour. Such care

---

37 A region in central Spain, and formerly an autonomous medieval kingdom.
38 Also a former independent kingdom, Aragon, a region in northwest Spain, joined with Castile and Navarre to form the Kingdom of Spain.

seemed the surest means to procure happiness, but the wisdom of man strives in vain against the decrees of fate.

"In the neighbourhood of my father's house, there lived a merchant named *Don Antonio*, between whose family and ours there was the closest intimacy; an intimacy mutually advantageous, the countenance of a person of my father's consequence being an honour to his friend, who never omitted those returns of gratitude, which his wealth often gave him an opportunity of making.

"*Don Antonio* had an only daughter, whose being heiress to his great fortune was the least blessing heaven had bestowed upon her! O! my *Olivia*, shall I ever behold you more? May I yet raise my hopes so high as to think of calling you mine?"—

At these words a flood of tears choking his utterance, my master took the opportunity to go out, and give some orders to his officers; and on his return, the youth proceeded.

"*Don Antonio*'s daughter and I being nearly of the same age, the tender connection of infant fondness grew up between us, and improved with our ripening years. The attention of my father was too much engrossed by his military cares to take notice of our attachment, and my mother was so sensible of the many perfections of *Olivia*, that far from discouraging, she promoted it by every means in her power, dwelling continually on her praises, and suggesting to me such little offices of affection and respect as were suited to our ages, and most likely to make an impression on her tender heart.

"Nor did the father of *Olivia* (she had lost her mother in her infancy) shew any dissatisfaction at a passion which could not escape his notice; influenced most probably by a sense of the honour which he should derive from such an alliance.

"In this happy state we lived till I entered on my fifteenth year, when my father thought it proper for me to learn the art of war, in order to qualify me for such military promotions as I was entitled to by my birth, and for that purpose gave me notice to prepare myself to march with some troops, which were going to reinforce a garrison, in the most distant part of the kingdom.

"Though my heart glow'd with all the ambition and desire of glory, which my noble blood must naturally inspire, the thought of being separated from *Olivia* overbalanced every other consideration. In the first emotions of my soul therefore I threw myself at my father's feet, and rashly own'd my passion, imploring him as he regarded my life to make me happy in the possession of my love, before he attempted parting us, even for a moment.

"It is impossible to describe his rage on this unhappy discovery. Spurning me from him with his foot, 'Degenerate wretch!' (said he, when his wrath permitted him to speak) 'Degenerate wretch, to stain the honour of your blood by thinking of an alliance with the daughter of a person, of whose family you have no knowledge!'— (For in all the intercourse of intimacy, the father of *Olivia* had never discovered in what part of *Spain* he had been born; nor could the recital of illustrious pedigrees, the constant topic of discourse among the noble, ever incite him to an emulative mention of his own).—'Hence! Fly my sight this moment; nor ever presume to appear before me again, till you have conquered this disgraceful passion.'

"I knew the inflexibility of my father's temper too well to attempt making any reply, even would the fullness of my heart have permitted me. I retired therefore without speaking a word, and going to my mother, informed her of my distress, which she strove to alleviate by every expression of tenderness and consolation, promising to exert all her influence, as soon as the first heat of his wrath should be allayed, to prevail upon him to consent to my suit."

CHAPTER X

Continued. *Olivia's* father is taken up by the Inquisition, and herself put into a convent, on an *English* battery's firing, upon which, *Don Alphonso* comes in despair to *Chrysal's* master to make a very odd request, which he grants at length, and also promises him his assistance to obtain his mistress.

"THOUGH I received some encouragement from these assurances, I could not forbear going in the boding of my heart, to acquaint *Olivia* with what had happened, but in the most delicate terms. Her affliction was not less than mine. She saw the sincerity of my love, and in the tenderness of such a scene yielded to my entreaties, and plighted her faith to me by the most sacred vows.

"Comforted by the thought that she could not now be torn from me, I returned home, where I found my mother fulfilling her promise, and pleading with my father in my behalf. As their earnestness made them speak aloud, I could not resist the natural desire of listening to a debate of such importance to my hopes. She urged with all the strength of reason, the absurdity of thinking a family dishonoured by the admission of a female, and enforced her arguments with the examples even of Sovereigns; she insisted on the beauty, virtues, and fortune of *Olivia*, which made her worthy of the most honourable alliance; and concluded with saying how much better it would be for us all to have me married to a person, whose wealth would enable us to spend the remainder of our lives in plenty and happiness, than to continue struggling with every misery of poverty, merely to indulge a false ill-grounded pride.

"My father had listened to the former part of what she said with an appearance of attention, but the moment she mentioned his poverty, he lost all patience. 'Forbear, mean, mercenary woman!' (said he stamping his foot upon the ground with a violence that shook the house) 'Forbear to tempt my wrath by such base insinuations. Did ever a *Castilian* think poverty an hardship, or put riches in competition with his honour? Such sentiments may suit an *Arragonian*, but are beneath me. I see the source of the wretch's degeneracy! My blood never could have stooped to such meanness, had it not been mixed with yours.'

"Saying this, he flung out of the room, and finding me at the door, 'Mark me, thou disgrace to my blood!' (said he with a look that appalled my soul) 'If ever I hear more of this affair, I swear by the offended honour of all my ancestors, to sacrifice every one concerned in my being offered such an affront.'

"What I felt at hearing this dreadful denunciation may be easily conceived. I swooned away, nor recovered my senses till several hours after, when I found my mother weeping over me, in the bitterness of resentment and grief.

"As soon as she perceived that I was come to myself, she strove to comfort me, by repeating her former promises, to the accomplishment of which she was now farther impelled by her resentment of the reflections, which my father had thrown upon her country.

"But an unforeseen misfortune blasted all our hopes before she had time to make another effort.

"The father of *Olivia* having had occasion to go to *England*, on some affairs in the course of his extensive dealings, was so taken with the people of that country, that after his return, he never omitted any opportunity of vindicating them from the injurious aspersions of those who spoke only from prejudice, and without proper information.

"This attachment naturally raised the jealousy of the clergy; but as he confined his approbation merely to their moral and social virtues, without ever saying a word in vindication of their religious tenets, they contented themselves with cautioning him against misplacing his praise, and telling him, that *there could be no virtue where the true faith was not; and therefore those actions, with which he was dazzled, were no more than shining sins:* And they were thus mild in their reprehension, as he was remarkably punctual in the profession and practice of all the rites and doctrines prescribed by the holy church.

"But this lenity lasted not long. On the breaking out of the present war with *England*, some persons who envied the success with which his honest industry had been rewarded, raised a suspicion in the governor of his holding an improper correspondence with the enemy, to which his former regard for them seemed to give an appearance of probability.

"Bold in conscious innocence he denied the charge, nor could the strictest enquiry procure the least proof of it: But in the course of their search a discovery was unhappily made, that involved him in ruin, if possible, more dreadful; a number of books containing opinions contrary to the Catholic Faith being found in his possession concealed among some of his goods.

"In vain did he allege that they belonged not to, nor could possibly have been known of by him, the goods among which they had been concealed having been landed but a few days before out of an *English* ship, which had been taken by a *Spanish* man of war in her passage to one of their own colonies, where such books were openly allowed of, and sold to him unopened, as they still remained.

"But evident as the truth of this was, *the Holy Office*, to whose jurisdiction the affair belonged, would not admit of any such excuse. They instantly seized the unhappy man, and hurrying him away to their own prison, took possession of all his wealth, and forced his helpless daughter into yonder convent.

"This misfortune which deprived me of the wretch's poorest consolation, the liberty of complaining, drove me to despair. I pined in silence; and was beginning to meditate on laying down a life, that was become a burden to me, when my father calling me to him one morning, 'The time is come!' (said he smiling fiercely) 'that will prove the blood of *Guzman*. The evil genius of the *English* has prompted them to come, and seek their deaths here. The most noble Governor has not only promoted me this day to the command of a company in the forces destined for the defence of this city, but also in respect to my family, has appointed you to be my lieutenant. Let this arouse you to a sense of yourself! Consider what you owe to your country, and to your name! Every feebler passion flies at the manly voice of war.'

"Languid as my soul was, I could not hear this news, without joy, especially as it opened me a prospect of meeting honourably that death, which was now my only hope. Accordingly, as soon as the enemy appeared I courted danger with such eagerness, that my father in spite of all his magnanimity more than once desired me to restrain a courage, that arose to an excess.

"But even death itself is deaf to the wretch's call. Nothing material happened to me, till the battery, to which I came to you, opened upon the convent, when the thought of my *Olivia*'s danger of being buried in its ruins drove me to madness. I instantly flew thither, and imagining that such circumstances bore down all regard to rules calculated for times of peace, demanded entrance to convey the inhabitants to some place of safety: But what was my astonishment to hear, the Governor had given the strictest orders, that not a soul should be allowed to stir, committing to the immediate hand of heaven the protection of its peculiar votaries.

"Such inhumanity, for I can call it by no milder name, broke every bond of duty and allegiance. I abjured all farther connection with so cruelly insensible a monster; and recollecting the many exalted instances of true generosity which the unhappy father of *Olivia* had told me of the *English*, I resolved to apply myself to them, and try whether I could not obtain that safety for the beloved of my soul, which I could not hope from him, whose duty it was to protect her.

"This, most illustrious Chief, is the story of my misfortunes; the cause of that conduct which appeared so strange to you. If you grant my suit, you will be amply rewarded by the conscious approbation of your own mind. You will merit the blessing of heaven on your undertakings, by sparing the most perfect of its works! And may I presume to add! You will attach to you an heart that is incapable of deceit! Through every vicissitude of life will I attend your steps, the faithful servant of your fate."

The brightness of truth breaks through every cloud, and forces conviction. "I grant your request;" (said my master with a smile of consolation and encouragement) "The convent shall be spared. Nor is that all. If success crowns my hopes, I will also use every means in my power to restore your *Olivia* to your arms."

The joy which the youth felt on hearing these words, is not to be described. "O generous *Englishman!*" (said he throwing himself at my master's feet once more, and kissing them in rapture) "You must succeed! Heaven will prosper every enterprize conducted with such virtue."

CHAPTER XI

The fortunate effect of *Chrysal*'s master's sparing the convent. The mutual advantages to victors and vanquished of articles of capitulation. The only business of a general. *Chrysal*'s master performs his promise to *Alphonso*, into whose service *Chrysal* enters. *Alphonso* recovers his mistress, whose father is set at liberty by a piece of *fun* of some *English* sailors. Conclusion of the story of *Alphonso*. *Chrysal* changes his service.

ACCORDING to his promise, the next night when the battery was repaired, my master gave orders to direct the fire another way, where he soon found the reward of his generosity, one of the first bombs which was thrown setting fire to the principal magazine in the whole city, the blowing up of which overturned a considerable part of the fortifications.

Animated by this success to a degree of frenzy, the besiegers pushed on their attacks with such irresistible fury, under the directions of my master, (whose impetuosity bore down all obstacles and made amends, though at a dear expence of blood, as well for his own ignorance in a species of war foreign to that which he had been bred, as for that of those whose particular business it was) that *in spite of the accumulated havoc of war, and disease, of want, and blunders worse than all,* they at length overcame the obstinacy of the besieged, and compelled them to propose delivering up the city on terms, the establishing of which was readily agreed to on both sides, *as they saved the plunder from the soldiers, for the victorious Commanders*; at the same time that they protected the persons of the vanquished from licentious outrage.

The moment the garrison offered to capitulation, my master flew with the news to his friend the General, and embracing him in a transport of joy, "At length" (said he) "the moment is come, that makes our fortunes for ever. The city is our own. Go; and exert the plentitude of your authority, in making such terms as shall enable us to support the dignity of our birth and rank, without being any longer obliged to languish in slavish dependence on ministerial favour."

"That I will!" (answered the General) "that I will, my dearest friend! Doubt not my acquitting myself properly for the pleasing task! I have been long prepared for it. It was the sole motive for my soliciting the command, nor has any thing else entered into my thoughts since I obtained it, but making terms, and dividing the spoil; that is *devising how to swell our own shares upon the division.* I have calculated every thing to the greatest nicety, and will shew you such strokes as shall surprise you. *The only business of a General is to calculate contributions, and divide plunder."*

Though my master was sufficiently eager to acquire wealth, he could not approve of the profession of such sentiments. He hasted away therefore, without making any reply, to the place of action, to be ready in case of any accident, never thinking he had done any thing, while any thing remained for him to do.

Much as such scenes engrossed his attention, he did not forget his promise to the *Spanish* youth, but ordering him a guard of soldiers, bade him go, as soon as the gates should be delivered up, and secure the convent where his *Olivia* was confined, from any accident which might happen on such an occasion in spite of all their care, give him at the same time a purse of gold, *in which I was*, to answer any present necessities, with directions to apply to him again, if he should have any farther need of his assistance.

My new master did not want to have such a commission repeated. He kissed the hand of his benefactor in a rapture of gratitude, and encouraging the guard assigned him with the most liberal promises, flew, the moment the gates of the city were opened, to the convent, and demanded his *Olivia* with the peremptory voice of a conqueror, where the sight of the guard removed every objection, and she was instantly delivered to him.

The meeting of these young lovers was most affecting. They flew into each other's arms, and embracing in ecstasy too big for utterance, gave vent to the fullness of their hearts by a flood of tears.

Recovering himself at length, "Come, my *Olivia*," (said *Alphonso*, taking her hand) "let us leave this place. Let us go"—

"O whither" (interrupted she, starting wildly) "whither shall I go? I have no home; — no father to receive me."

"My home is yours;" (answered *Alphonso*, embracing her most tenderly) "We will go to the house of my father, who cannot persist in his cruelty, when he is informed how signally heaven has interfered in our favour, and there we will consult on the means proper for procuring the deliverance of *Antonio*. I have a protector among the conquerors, the most generous of mankind, who will not refuse his assistance on such an occasion."

These words comforted *Olivia* with an hope, for the accomplishment of which she was indebted to another cause.

The way from the convent to the house of *Alphonso*'s father leading them by the prison of the Inquisition, *Olivia* was so affected at the sight of it, that she swooned away in the arms of *Alphonso*. Such an accident naturally threw the whole company into an embarrassment, while they were in the midst of which, a body of *English* seamen, who had slipped away from their officers, and were roving about merely from curiosity, and without intention of doing mischief, but ready to join in any that should fall in their way, happening to come by, no sooner understood from the guard what was the matter, than looking at each other for some moments, as if waiting for the word of command, at length one of them cried out, "Hallo, boys! What say you? Shall we bail the gentlewoman's father? Mayhap there may be some of our countrymen in the bilboes³⁹ along with him! Damn my eyes and limbs, but it will be good *fun* to set them all free! I fancy the Inquisitors will not refuse our bail; if they do, I should be glad to pick a quarrel with them: I hate them mortally ever since I saw them roast some poor *Smouches*⁴⁰ at *Lisbon*, because they would not eat pork. Come! cheer away, my hearts of oak! All hands aloft, and to work."

These words were like fire given to a mine. He had scarce finished, when the thoughtless creatures without more ado ran to the prison, and while some of them were forcing in the gates, the rest mounting on each other's shoulders climbed over the walls.

The moment *Olivia*, now recovered from her swoon, saw the prison open, "Now is the time, *Alphonso!*" (said she) "Now is the time to set my father free."

The hint was sufficient. *Alphonso* turned directly to the guard, and perceiving by their looks that they were willing to assist him, "I go, my love!" (said he) "But where shall I leave you in safety till I return? Such a place cannot be fit for your delicacy."

"Speak not of leaving me!" (interrupted she eagerly) "I will go with you! No delicacy shall interfere with such a duty."

On her saying this, they all entered the prison, where the seamen were shouting, and skipping about like so many wild creatures, and setting all the prisoners at liberty wherever they sent.

The secrets of this prison-house are too horrid for description. I shall therefore draw a veil over them at this time, especially as another occasion will lead me into the same scenes again, when the representation will be more interesting.

No words can convey an idea of the tenderness of the meeting

---

39 "Stocks, or wooden sheckles for the feet, used for punishing offenders at sea" (Johnson).

40 Jews (OED).

between *Olivia* and her father, whom *Alphonso* and she readily found out. As soon as they had indulged the first transports of their joy, she informed him briefly how much they were both indebted to *Alphonso*, for their present happiness. Though her father was not at a loss for the motive of such generosity, he thought it not proper to take notice of it at that time. He embraced him tenderly, and besought heaven to reward his virtue.

"The happiness of serving those most dear to us" (said *Alphonso*, who had not the same command of his temper) "is its own reward. *Olivia* and her father have a right to every thing in my power. But let us leave this place, the sight of which appals my soul. Let us go to the house of my father."

"Lead on, my children!" (answered *Olivia*'s father) "I follow willingly; and not without hope of reconciling my friend to our general happiness."

When they went out of the prison, they found the sailors employed in executing a piece of justice exactly in their character. They had rambled all through the prison, without doing or designing mischief, till they came to the chamber in which were kept the instruments of torture, the sight of which incensed them to such a degree, that they instantly resolved to make the Inquisitors themselves feel the force of them in their turn; but they, apprehensive of what might happen, had prudently made their escape by a secret passage, as soon as the prison had been forced. Disappointed thus in their design, the sailors took all the horrid apparatus, with the habits, ensigns, books, &c. of the office, and piling them up in the court, set fire to the heap, concluding the exploit with three cheers for the honour of old *England*; after which they marched off in quest of more *fun*, as unconcerned as if nothing had happened.

When *Alphonso* arrived at his father's house, he found his mother just sinking under the weight of affliction. On hearing his voice, she started up, and running to him, "O my son! my son!" (exclaimed she, clasping him in her arms, and leaning her head upon his bosom) "Heaven has heard my prayers! I am not childless, though I am a widow."

"A widow!" (exclaimed *Alphonso*) "Forbid it, heaven! O my father!"

"Yes, *Alphonso!*" (continued she, raising her head from his bosom, which she had bedew'd with her tears) "Your father died, as he lived, with honour, fighting valiantly by the side of his General, in defence of his country. But what do I see?" (casting her eyes upon *Olivia*, her father, and the guard, whom her surprise had prevented her taking notice of before) "*Olivia! Antonio!*—And who are these strange men?—But alas, I know too well!—O! my son, art thou then a prisoner to the enemies who slew thy father?—Am I to lose thee again, the moment thou art returned?"

"No, my mother:" (answered he) "I am no prisoner! They are our protectors, given by the most generous of men, who has thus restored us to each other! O that my father were alive, to make our happiness complete."

"Since heaven has appointed otherwise," (said *Antonio*, going up to *Alphonso*'s mother, who was weeping with *Olivia*, on whose neck she had fallen) "it is our duty to submit to its pleasure. The circumstances of our lives make it improper for us to think of living any longer here. But that should not discourage us. The virtuous find an home every where! We will remove to the dominions of the *English*, where I have lodged in honest hands fortune sufficient to make our retreat happy. Under the protection of their laws, a man's mind is at liberty, and his wealth is secure. Mine was my only crime here; but I was aware of such an attack, and had removed it beyond the reach of those, who impiously made religion the pretext for depriving me of it. Were my friend *Don Pedro* living, I would have removed the objections which his high notions of honour made to an alliance with my family, and prevailed upon him to accompany us."*[41] These words comforted the mother of *Alphonso*, and made the lovers happy.

Every thing being thus settled, the guard was dismissed with professions of the highest gratitude to the generous Chief, which *Antonio* and *Alphonso* proposed waiting on him to pay in person, as soon as he should be more at leisure; and to reward the soldiers for their attendance, *Alphonso* gave them the purse of gold he had received from his benefactor, and *in which I was*; in the division

---

41 Johnstone's note: "The story of *Antonio* followed here, but was so blotted and imperfect in the M.S. that the *Editor* was obliged to omit it."

of which I fell to the lot of the serjeant who commanded them, who, looking upon me as an earnest of the vast treasures he was to receive as his share of the spoil, went away with an happy heart to join his fellows, who were now in full possession of the city.

CHAPTER XII

Chrysal makes some striking remarks on a state of absolute liberty. Disappointment of the hopes of the conquerors, with the natural consequences. *Chrysal's* master going to take a taste of the pleasures of affluence, is flammed[42] out of his treasure by a sutler, into whose service *Chrysal* enters.

THE conduct of man in such scenes as this, where he thinks himself at liberty to follow the instantaneous impulse of his own will, without apprehension of immediate punishment, shews the groundless vanity of those who boast so loudly of the excellency of his nature, and deny the necessity of coercive laws.

It is true, no people ever abused this liberty less than the *English*, who scorn to inflict upon others that oppression from which their laws protect themselves; as on the other hand, slaves, on a change of fortune, always prove the most imperious tyrants; but still the circumstances attending even the most moderate exertion of it are too shocking for dispassionate description, wherefore I shall waive the painful task.

As soon as some degree of order was established in the city, the victorious commanders proceeded to divide the spoil,[43] *a work for which they all shewed their capacity in the most remarkable manner,* the pittance which they thought proper to appoint for the share of each of the private men, who had literally borne the heat and burden of the day, being a trifle beneath the acceptance of any but a beggar who wanted a morsel of bread, and not *the fifty-thousandth part* of what the chief commanders, who comparatively had lived

---

42 "Deceived with a lye. Merely cant" (Johnson).

43 Pocock and Albemarle made their fortunes at Havana. The two of them alone claimed a third of the prize money plundered from the city, or £123,000 each, a sum met with criticism in England (DNB).

in luxury, and issued their orders from places of safety, modestly owned to have reserved for each of themselves.

Nor was the case of the inferior officers, who executed those orders, any better, their shares not being sufficient to defray the extraordinary expences which they had been at, to provide for the enterprize, much less the extraordinary expences of living, where the indispensable necessaries of life were subject to the most extraordinary impositions of an avaricious and arbitrary will; so that all they gained by their conquest was to exchange the dangers of war for the miseries of want.

This disappointment of the hopes which alone had supported their spirits through hardships almost beyond the power of nature to support, filled up the black list of the calamities which attended this enterprize, aggravating by despair the diseases to which the climate subjected the victors to such a degree, that their loss, after their conquest, exceeded many times that which they had suffered in the siege from so many combined causes.

To the truth of this representation, which to unexperienced speculation may appear too severely drawn, the wretched remains of the conquering army which returned to their exhausted country, bore a melancholy testimony.—But to quit these disagreeable reflections!

Such a treasure as I was (a greater much than he had ever been possessed of before!) raised the spirits of my master, the serjeant, so high, that he went directly to a sutler's tent to take a taste of the good living which he thought himself secure of, for the remainder of his days.

On his entering the tent, and asking what entertainment he could have, the sutler, ignorant of his wealth, answered with a curse, that he had none for such shabby fellows as he, and took him by the shoulder to thrust him out. Provoked by such an indignity to a person of his present consequence, my master turned upon him, and pulling *me* out of his pocket, demanded haughtily, why he might not have what he would pay for, as well as another?

The sight of the gold instantly changed the sutler's whole behaviour. "My worthy friend!" (said he, shaking the serjeant by the hand) "I beg your pardon. I actually did not perceive who I spoke to, I am so hurried about. But come along with me, and I'll make you amends. I have a nice leg of a fowl which was bespoke for your colonel; but *first come first served*, as the saying is, so here it is for you; and here is a bottle of wine as cool as if it came but this minute from *Iceland*."

My master was not proof against such an invitation. He *fell to*, without more ceremony, and when he had finished his feast, calling to know what he had to pay, the sutler answered, Two doubloons.

"Two doubloons?—Two devils!" (said the serjeant, staring at such a demand) "For a leg of an old hen, as black as hell, and lean as *Beelzebub*; and a bottle of rot-gut, sour cyder? No! no, friend! no such tricks for me. I am not to be *flammed* so neither."

"Why there it is now!" (answered the sutler, not much pleased with my master's looks) "The moment a man grows rich, he grows covetous. I received the same for the other leg of that very fowl this moment from an ensign, who by the same token left his laced waistcoat in pawn for half the money. But I will not fall out with you for such a trifle, as I expect more of your custom; so e'en give me what you please. You can't think one doubloon too much I am sure! But you shall make it up another time."

Such an argument could not be resisted. The serjeant threw *me* down upon the table with an air of grandeur, and went to consider how he should lay out to the best advantage, the treasures which he expected immediately to receive.

CHAPTER XIII

Character of *Chrysal's* new master. The right way not to suffer by making mistakes. A curious conversation between *Chrysal's* master and two persons of consequence lays open the secrets of some interesting affairs. He makes up a foolish dispute by a sensible toast.

I WAS now entered into a service, which opened to me so many various views of human folly, vice and wretchedness, as made the prospect painful.

The manner in which my new master got me into his possession, shewed his character in a light sufficiently strong. But I soon had the satisfaction of seeing that with all his address and imposition, he was himself no more than the tool of the impositions of superiors, who scarce left him the poorest gleanings to pick up, after all their plenteous harvest: the just and constant fate of all such wretches.

The continual hurry in which he was engaged, though he had falsely alleged it as an excuse for his treatment of my late master, the serjeant, was really sufficient to excuse any inadvertency or blunder, and must have caused many in any one, whose ideas were not settled in one certain course, out of which it was impossible to divert them, of which his customers, whose attentions were not so distracted, might be apt to take advantage. But I soon found that he was in no danger of that kind, all his thoughts having such an invariable bias to his own interest, that every mistake naturally fell to that side, for which upon detection his hurry was a ready and probable excuse.

The serjeant had scarce left him, when two persons entered, whom he received with every mark of the most obsequious ceremony and respect. One of them I directly knew to be my old master, the Admiral's Agent for *secret services*, as I soon found the other to be in the same important station with the General.

My master, who was not at a loss for the occasion of their visit, led them into the most private place in the tent, and setting before them a bottle of *his best*, proceeded to business. "Mr. Admiral, to your good health! Mr. General, my very hearty service to you!" (said he, filling a brimmer, and addressing each by the title of his master, as he shook them by the hand) "Here is a good conclusion of the campaign to us. I was impatient for your coming, to know how I should go on. Here have been several officers with me already, for credit on the score of their prize-money, for the length of the siege, and the dearness of every thing has not left them a penny, nor any thing to pawn for one. I have got as many clothes, and things of all kinds, as would serve to set up a *Monmouth-street*[44] merchant. If the place had held out but a few days longer, the poor devils must have done duty in *Buff*. Hah! hah! hah!"

"And the properest dress for them:" (returned *the Admiral*) "Who wants any clothes in such a climate as this? I am sure I go

---

44 A common location for merchants trading in secondhand clothing. The eponymous hero of *The Adventures of a Black Coat* (1760) is similarly sold to "a merchant in Monmouth-street."

naked half my time, though I keep under cover, and have nothing to do to heat me."

"Very true!" (answered my master) "But naked and hungry both are not quite so well; and when their moveables were all gone after their money, I don't know who would have supplied them."

"Then let them live on their allowance!" (said the General) "They who can't afford to pay for better, should be content with that."

"To die upon it, you should say;" (interrupted my master) "I am sure the stores laid in are such as no one can live upon, that has ever known what living was. For my part, I wonder the contractors were not ashamed to supply such wretched stuff of all kinds. They must have no conscience at all, who can do such things"—

"Conscience! hah! hah! hah! who ever heard a sutler speak of conscience before!" (said the Admiral) "And pray, my conscientious friend, what do you charge a bottle for this most excellent wine of yours?"

"For this wine?" (answered my master, palating it two or three times) "I charge for this wine only a *pistole*; and let me tell you, that is not so much, considering every thing. This Burgundy cost me five shillings a bottle, prime cost; and when you compute every expence, you'll find that my profit is nothing extraordinary; nothing at all in comparison of what others get."

"No! to be sure," (replied the General) "your conscience won't suffer you to do as they do! you are too good a man"—

"Too good a *Christian*, you should say;" (interrupted the Admiral) "as appears by your *baptizing* your wine so piously! hah! hah! hah! Pray what did the water cost, that is mixed with this same Burgundy? I hope that did not stand you in five shillings a bottle too? Hah! hah! hah!"

"It is very well, gentlemen!" (returned my master with a sneer) "You are pleased to be merry. But if I had not some way to make out matters, I could never pay the exorbitant taxes which are squeezed from me, by some people whom I shan't name. And so here's my service to you both once more! When you lower *your composition*, I'll lessen the quantity of water, and mend mine. Hah! hah! hah!"

"And so you had need," (said the General) "to make it drinkable: As it is, I wonder it does not poison every one that tastes it. When

I lived at the *Shakespear*,[45] we did not give worse than this to our company after they were dead drunk!"

"Worse than this!" (added the Admiral) "If you had given me half so bad, I should have broken your head with the bottle."

"Broken my head!" (returned the General) "fine words truly! When you were a blue-nosed[46] journeyman Barber, and used to come to me to beg broken victuals, and bottoms of bottles, you spoke in another tone."

"And when I was, Sir," (replied the Admiral) "I had a good trade, and never looked upon myself as upon a level with the pimp of a tavern"—

"And yet that pimping made you what you are now!" (retorted the General, rising up in a passion) "You forget perhaps how you begged of me to introduce your sister to the Admiral, by which means you got into his service! This is a fine return indeed."

"And you forget too," (said the Admiral starting from his seat, and catching at the bottle) "That it was that same sister of mine, who got you into the General's service, if you go to that; so that I think the obligation is equal."

"Gentlemen! dear gentlemen!" (interrupted my master, clapping an hand to each of their collars) "consider what you are doing! What will the world say of such a quarrel between gentlemen, who ought to agree like brothers. For shame! every body will laugh at you! Come! sit down, and be good friends, and I'll try if I have not one bottle of better wine, over which we'll make up all matters."—Then bringing it, and filling his glass, "Come, gentlemen," (continued he, shaking each of them by the hand) "I'll give you a toast that shall drown all animosity: Here is prosperity to pimping! it is the best trade going, and has made us all! Aye, and is practised too by people in every station, however they may affect to turn up their noses at it. So let us attend to our business, and not fall together by the ears for nothing, like a parcel of dogs about a bare bone. It signifies nothing what we have been;

---

45 The Shakespeare's-Head, a notorious tavern and brothel named for its sign, as described in *Covent-Garden: A Satire* (1756), "high raised above the Tavern door, t'invite each drunken rake and whore."
46 "Priggish, puritanical" (OED).

if we mind our *hits* now, we shall all be gentlemen as good as the best of them; and as well respected too."

The Admiral and General saw the force of what he said, and pledging his toast, shook hands, and were as good friends as ever.

CHAPTER XIV

Continued. The mysteries of agency; and convenience of a military government, with some curious notions of the genteelest ways of rising in life.

"WELL, gentlemen," (said my master, who was not pleased at their jests upon his liquor, because he could not deny the truth of them) "I hope that wine pleases you!"

"Aye!" (answered the Admiral) "this is *the right sort!* this is *the thing.* Give us this; and keep the other for officers, and such as are not used to better."

"And if it poisons them" (added the Admiral) "the public will have the fewer to pay. Now they have done the business, let them live or die as they can, we care not. That's nothing to us."

"Very true!" (said my master) "All we have to do is to make the most of them, while they do live; and therefore I should be glad to know, as I said before, how far I may venture to go with them, on the credit of their prize-money; for as the place was saved from being plundered by the articles of capitulation, they must all get money on their shares, whether they will or not; their necessities are such."

"So much the better for us who can buy their shares:" (answered the Admiral) "They'll give the better bargains. Their necessity is our gain."

"Aye?" (replied my master) "But I don't find they intend selling. All they propose is to mortgage."

"Then let them see who'll give them money:" (said the General) "No! no! no mortgages for us. An absolute sale, or nothing. We'll have no after reckonings; no *over-haling* accounts. As to their being unwilling to sell, we'll manage that matter with them. When you have got them sufficiently in your books, call for your money, and as it will be impossible for them to pay, apply to the commander in chief, who will oblige them to do you justice."

"Why! to be sure, that must do!" (answered my master) "But how far am I to trust them?"

"This will shew you!" (replied the General) "Here is the rate of all their shares. Look at the sum total. What noble fortunes that would have made for half a dozen reasonable men. It went to my heart to *fritter* it away among so many."

"This! this is the rate of their shares!" (said my master, not able to conceal his astonishment, when he looked at the paper which the other gave him) "Is it possible that this should be all?"

"Yes!" (returned the Admiral) "and too much for them too. More than most of them ever had before, or will make a good use of now."

"Why they'll mutiny, and cut all our throats!" (returned my master) "There are several of them who owe me almost as much as this already. I thought they would have ten times this sum at least. They'll certainly mutiny and cut all our throats."

"Don't you give yourself any trouble about their mutinying!" (said the General) "Do you mind your business, and leave us to take care of that. Their spirits will hardly be so high! if you have gone hand over head[47] and trusted them so far, you must abide by the loss. I thought I gave you a friendly caution about that before."

"And so," (returned my master) "I am not to go beyond this rate, you say?"

"Not a penny!" (answered the Admiral) "That is your rule. Whatever you can beat them down of that shall be your own."

"That is deducting five *per cent*. Agency!" (interposed the General) "and five or ten *per cent*. as you can make your bargain, for prompt-payment, for we will not appear to have any hand in the affair, farther than paying you the money. It must not be known that we are concerned in the least."

"You concerned!" (replied my master) "I don't understand you. Are you to be concerned with me in what I buy?"

"Not in the least," (returned the Admiral) "any farther than by employing you to act for us. You seem to mistake the matter

---

47 "Precipitately, hastily, rashly, recklessly" (OED).

entirely. You are to buy the shares for us, according to this rate, for which we will allow you a proper agency: And that is all the concern you are to have in the affair."

"But I suppose," (said my master) "I may buy on my own account if I please!"

"Buy on your own account!" (interrupted the General) "Such another word, and you shall neither sell nor buy any thing here. Are we not the Commander's agents; and do you think they will suffer us to be interloped upon? You may be very well content with the profits of your own business, without thinking to interfere in ours."

"I ask your pardon, gentlemen!" (said my master, who knew their power too well to dispute with them) "It was only a mistake. I by no means presume to interfere with you; and shall be proud to execute your orders, on whatever terms you think proper. I suppose though our former *composition* is to end. Provisions will now come in from every part, so that we can never think of keeping them up at the former prices."

"Can't you so?" (answered the General) "That shall be your own fault then; and your own loss too, I can tell you. Let provisions come in as they will, no one shall sell an ounce here without our permission, and that shall be on our own terms, you may be assured. Our hands are not tied up by laws. Ours is *a military government*, in which we can do what we please, without being accountable to any one. So you may go on as before."

"But gentlemen," (replied my master) "you should consider that the whole odium of this will fall upon me, as you do not appear in it, so that I shall lose my character forever."

"Your character! Hah! hah! hah!" (interrupted the General) "A sutler's character! I shall never be able to bear the word again! Pray, my good friend, what character had a sutler ever to lose, that would not be a greater loss to the finder? Come! here's my service to you. Go on with your business, and make money, and never fear suffering by the loss of your character. It is time for us to go and settle what taxes we shall lay upon the different kinds of merchandize, that shall be brought here. *Our duties* shall be paid, as well as those of any king of them all. This is our reign; and if we do not make the most of it, we have no one to blame but ourselves."

"And as rich as so many kings you will be;" (said my master) "if you can carry off things in the manner you say."

"As to our being rich!" (returned the Admiral) "that depends entirely upon our own management. Our principals indeed will be rich enough, which is all they care for; not what becomes of us, whom they would have do their business for nothing, or next to it. But they shall find themselves mistaken.

Every thing must go through our hands; and *gold in handling will stick to the fingers*, as the song says.[48] We shall feather our nests in spite of them. They cannot do without us; and will hardly be fond of calling us to too strict an account, for fear of our telling tales. To be sure, the great harvest will be theirs; but we will take toll."

"I don't doubt but you will," (said my master) "twice over for fear of mistake, as the miller does. Why you'll make such fortunes that you won't know what to do with yourselves."

"Never fear that!" (answered the General) "we shall not be at a loss. For my part, I design to buy a borough, and push my fortune in Parliament. That's the genteelest business a gentleman can follow now, and the readiest way of advancing in life, and making a family."

"Now I think otherwise;" (said the Admiral) "and that it is the most ungenteel way; such dirty jobs are required for every thing a man gets, that it is beneath a gentleman to do them. My scheme is to buy an *Irish Peerage* at once, and then live splendidly, without troubling myself about any thing. Or if I should grow tired of idleness, go into Parliament there, and turn *Patriot*, and make speeches for the good of my country."

"Both your schemes may be very good!" (said my master) "but my ambition is not so high as either, at least as yet. I will try to get a *contract*; and then I shall not fear making a fortune sufficient to do what you propose, or more if I choose it; without being

---

48 "The Miller," a popular song which satirized the corrupt noble classes in relation to the honest work of the miller. "If so happy a miller," it concludes, "who would be a king?" The line in question is "Gold in handling will stick to the fingers like meal."

sneered at for my folly. You may say what you will, but there is more to be got by a *contract* than by every other way; and therefore it is the genteelest in my opinion. How many *contractors* have I seen buy noblemen's fine houses, and members of Parliament's estates, with the profits of a single campaign? And so *My Lord*, and you most honourable *Mr. Member*, I am your humble servant."

"Honest *Mr. Contractor*," (replied both at the same time) "yours."

CHAPTER XV

Affecting consequences of carrying the foregoing schemes into execution; with the conclusion of the character and history of *Chrysal's* master. *Chrysal* changes his service.

As soon as this worthy pair had left my master, he set about his business of preying upon the necessaries of every one who came near him, with as much keenness as a vulture tears a carrion, and with as little feeling, or he could never have gone through with it.

The transactions I now saw are a pain to memory. For the first few days after their success, the officers, under the same intoxication with my late master, the serjeant, gave a loose to every kind of extravagance, to compensate to themselves for the wants and hardships they had suffered. But no sooner had they advanced near the limits prescribed to their credit, than the whole scene changed.

The first mention of the amount of their respective shares was like a clap of thunder bursting over their heads. Their astonishment for some time deprived them of their senses. But when they were able to make a proper enquiry, and found the case to be too true, their rage broke through all bounds, and rose almost to desperation. *The horrors of a jail, the cries of a starving family*, every aggravation of human misery stared them in the face, and made the very thought of returning to their native country too terrible to be endured. But there was no remedy. Those from whom alone it could proceed were too much interested to listen to their complaints; and instead of preventing, permitted their authority to be prostituted to complete their ruin, in the manner proposed by their agents, so that the unhappy victims were forced to submit to the terms imposed upon them.

The consequence of this, as I have said before, was that to drown reflection they spent whatever trifle remained to them on concluding the bargains, which sealed their ruin, in still greater excesses, and so precipitated the distress they feared.

As for the private men, the impositions they suffered were if possible still severer, (though from their insensibility perhaps not so severely felt) as the *management* of their affairs went through many more hands, every one of whom had a pull at them, down to the very lowest class of the harpies which prey upon an army, so that what remained to them was too trifling to be of any service even to the very few, who struggle with their necessities in order to save it.

I have not entered minutely into the particulars of this horrid scene. This slight sketch will give you a general notion of it, and that is as much as any humane heart can bear. Indeed no description could reach the truth. I shall therefore only just finish the outlines of my master's character, and then pass on to the occurrences in my next service.

The extortions to which he was himself forced to submit from those in authority, took off every shadow of shame (to conscience he had long been a stranger) and added double keenness to his natural propensity to extortion, by giving it what he thought the appearance of justice, and provoking him to wreak his resentment upon others, for what he suffered himself from those above his reach.

The opportunities for exerting his talents this way were infinite in a profession that is a mystery of iniquity too complicated to be unravelled, too black to be conceived, but upon experience, which he had acquired to the most consummate degree, in the gradual progression of his life.

A natural sharpness of genius, which ought to have been curbed not encouraged, had influenced his parents to bind him when very young to an attorney, under whom he learned, beside other valuable qualifications, the nice distinctions between law and justice, so as to know critically how far he could infringe upon the latter, without danger of getting within the reach of the former.

But encouraged by much success, he had at length unhappily happened to go too near those boundaries, and been obliged to quit that profession; after some common steps of descent from which, such as *bailiff's follower*,[49] *knight of the post*, and *bully to a bawdy-house*, he stopped in that of footman to a beau, from which the necessary arts of *prevaricating, lying,* and *evading disagreeable demands*, the qualifications of his former character, soon raised him to be his *gentleman*.

In this station he added to his stock of accomplishments, natural and acquired, *pimping, servility, adulation,* and *an absolute command of countenance*, on the strength of all which, together with some little money, the fruits of his honest industry, on his master's fixing his habitation in a jail, he set up a tavern, where his *second-hand politeness* and *cringing behaviour* soon brought him into business, that enabled him to live better than he could have any right to have expected, and would in time have procured him an independence.[50]

This success, which would have satisfied a reasonable person, only raised his ambition, and made him despise his business. Accordingly he commenced *wine-merchant*, as more suitable to a *gentleman*, in which profession he went on, *till his one-horse chaise, his country house, and kept mistress* would have brought him back to his primitive poverty, had not his knowledge of the world taught him how to secrete from his creditors, something to try his hand upon in some other way, when he pitched upon his present occupation of *a sutler*, in which this account of his life shews he was most eminently fitted to make a figure.

Thus qualified in himself, and supported by his employers, he proceeded making his bargains, with a success to which it may be thought no regard to honesty, no sense of compassion was the least impediment. He flattered, professed the highest respect and attachment, and pressed his goods upon his destined victims, with every insinuating art, till he got them into his snare, when he directly put on all the insolence of power, and made even ruin still more wretched by the cruelty with which he drove them to it, the

---

49 A hired thug who assisted deputies in serving warrants.
50 "A fortune which renders it unnecessary for the possessor to earn his living" (OED).

insensibility with which he treated them after. How often have I seen him refuse to trust a glass of what he called wine to cool his raging thirst, and comfort his fainting heart, the man whom but the day or two before he had cajoled into the excesses which drew him into that distress.

After some days of painful attention to such shocking scenes, I had the pleasure of being paid away to the captain of a merchant's ship, for some liquors, which he had the address to deceive the vigilance of the ruling powers, and all their emissaries, and convey *impost-free* to my master.

CHAPTER XVI

Chrysal's master swallows a pill, and pleads an important cause without success. A curious method of parrying one false oath by another, with the first oath taken by the master of a merchant-man.[51] He shews another instance of his skill in steering clear of perjury, but without his former success. His notion of conscience. *Chrysal* changes his service.

THE care which I knew to be taken to detect and punish this kind of *illicit* trade, made me wonder at first that it should even be attempted; but I soon found that the danger of such detection, when it depends solely on the confession of those concerned, however forceful the means made use of to extort that confession, is held at nought by a set of people, bred in the grossest ignorance of every principle of moral virtue, or religious obligation, and hardened by long habit into contempt of whatever clashes with their interest.

When I came into the possession of my new master, he was going to attend the two *great men*, whose conversation with the sutler I have just now related, in obedience to a summons sent him the moment he entered the harbour. The reception he met with was suited to their importance. He was obliged to wait a considerable time, before they were at leisure to see him; when being admitted to their presence, and having delivered in his bill of lading, and *taken his oath*, that he had no *private trade* on board, nor

51 "A ship of trade" (Johnson).

any thing which was not contained in that account; they informed him what *duties* he must pay on every article, before he should be permitted to land them.

My master, though he was sufficiently apprized of this before, affected surprise, and attempted to expostulate with them on the illegality and injustice of such a demand, alleging that the goods had been purchased at the highest prices in order to send a speedy and effectual supply to the troops, who were known to want them, so that there could be no advance made upon them, which could defray such additional duties; that his owners, not in the least suspecting any such, had given him no power to pay them; and that many of the commodities being of a perishable nature, must be damaged if not permitted to be landed directly, by which means not only the merchants would be great losers, but also the troops suffer severely for the want of common necessaries, which they could not otherwise be supplied with.

But all he could say had no effect. They did not even deign to make him any answer, farther than that they had authority for what they did, and expected obedience, not arguments, which they had not leisure to listen to.

Such a repulse, however unjust in itself, and personally offensive in the manner of it, was far from giving my master any concern. On the contrary, the difficulties which it threw upon the business of his owners, afforded him an opportunity of carrying on *his own private trade* to better advantage, which no oaths they could devise were able to put a stop to, as an instance or two of his conduct will shew.

Some suspicion having arisen of his commerce with the sutler, of which no direct proof could be obtained, he was summoned to appear before the tax-gatherers, *to acquit himself by his oath* of so heinous an offence.

The sutler, who knew the consequence of being convicted, and with all his knowledge of the world saw no possibility of avoiding it, gave himself up as ruined: But my master soon shewed him the convenience of a conscience trained to swearing; for calling upon him the morning they were to appear at the dread tribunal, and seeing him so cast down, "Cheer up, brother," (said he) "I'll bring you safe through this strait! By the virtue and contents of this book" (pulling one out of his pocket, and kissing it in form) "I will never swear that you have bought any thing from me; so throw off that sneaking, *Tyburn* look, and come along."

Such an assurance naturally gave the sutler some spirits; though he could not conceive how he meant to make it good; but a little time cleared up the mystery, and shewed him the force of a custom-house oath.

As soon as the two culprits appeared before their judges, the latter assuming all the dignity of their office, exaggerated the charge in the strongest colours, and administering the oath to my master, demanded in an authoritative tone, whether he had not sold *uncustomed* goods to the sutler, and to what amount; who not in the least disconcerted either by the question, or the manner in which it was put, "Why look ye, gentlemen," (answered he, turning the *quid* in his cheek, and pulling up his breeches at the hips, with both his hands) "as to that affair, by the virtue of my oath, *if I should swear that I sold him any, I should be forsworn*, and I'll always try to weather that point, if I can."

As there was no more than a general suspicion against the criminals, this answer satisfied the sagacity of their judges, and they were dismissed with flying colours.

When they were alone, "Well!" (said my master, shaking his friend by the hand) "I told you I'd bring you off. Let that be an example to you for the future. *None but fools convict themselves*; and *none but greater fools expect it*. I should have little business in the merchant's service, if I scrupled swallowing such a pill as that every day of my life! No! no! they must be cunning if they can make an oath that will stick in the throat of the captain of a merchant-man, even if he can't find an opening to steer through, as was the case here. We have a *salvo*[52] for such things. *The first oath we take as soon as we get into employment, is never to swear the truth to a custom-house-officer while we live; so that all the oaths they give us go for nothing.*"

But with all his cleverness, he sometimes failed of success. A lieutenant of a man of war happening as he was *rowing guard* one night to see a boat put off from our ship, pursued it in hopes of making some reprisals for all the extortions he and his brethren

---

52 "An exception; a reservation; an excuse" (Johnson).

daily suffered from every one concerned in trade, as he knew it must be a *smuggler*.

The hope of prize made the crew of the lieutenant's boat pull with such spirit, that they gained fast upon the *chase*, which the others seeing, and that it was impossible for them to get clear off, they threw their cargo overboard to disappoint their pursuers of their expected booty, and then ran the boat a-shore to save themselves from being taken, leaving her of course to the captors for their trouble, who towed her away in triumph.

The chief of the smugglers was my master's son, who in the account he gave him of the affair on his return, was proceeding to tell him the names of those who had been with him, when the father stopping him short, "Avast!" (said he) "coil up your tongue. I desire to hear no more of them. Have you a mind to make me forswear myself when I go to recover my boat? For have her again you know I must, as I can't get another here, nor carry on any business without one."

Accordingly next morning he made a public enquiry after his boat, which he pretended had been stolen from his ship's side, and finding her in the possession of the lieutenant, demanded to have her restored directly, and on his refusal had him summoned before the officers of the customs, who were judges in such affairs.

As he grounded his claim on her having been taken without his privity, and by persons unknown to him, he was put to the common test of an oath, Whether he knew who had been in her, when she was pursued by the captors. "By the virtue of *my oath*, Gentlemen" (answered he, without the least hesitation) "*I do not know one of them.*"

So *direct* an answer satisfied the judges, who were no ways concerned in the affair; but that was not the case with the lieutenant: "Hold, Sir!" (said he to my master, who was sheering off, laughing in his sleeve) "what is that you say?"

"I say," (answered my master, nothing disconcerted) "that I don't know *one* of them."

"*One of them!*" (returned the lieutenant, who instantly saw through his evasion) "but don't you know *any* of them though? Take care what you say! Perhaps I know more than you think I do!"

"Why as to that" (replied my master laughing) "I cannot say so much. Perhaps I may know some of them."

"How!" (interposed the judge, offended at an answer which he thought shewed a slight to his authority) "Did you not swear this moment that you did not know one of them?"

"No more do I!" (answered my master) "There were twelve in the boat, of whom I know only eleven; and sure in that case, I can safely swear I do not know *one*, that is *the twelfth* of them. Hah! hah! hah!"

"Take care, Sir," (replied the judge) "how you attempt to trifle in this manner before us again. You know the punishment of perjury, if you should be caught tripping."

"Never fear!" (said my master) "I know the *compass* of my conscience too well for that. I can steer as near that wind as another. *Thus! thus! and no nearer*, is my trim.[53] I'll never break an oath; but if I can give it the *go by*, at the *lee-side*[54] thus, by a double-meaning, I hope that's no offence."

Then turning to the lieutenant, "Well, Sir!" (continued he) "it seems *you have carried too much sail for me this trip! But if I meet you upon a wind again, mind your helm, or I may chance to fall aboard you.* However, since I can't have my boat cheaper, I must e'en come to your terms, so what do you ask for her?"

To this proposal the lieutenant made no objection: Setting therefore his price, "Zounds!" (said my master) "I believe you have no conscience at all, to ask a man so much, and for his own boat!"

At his mentioning *conscience*, all present set up a loud laugh, and repeated the word.

Nothing abash'd at which, "You may laugh as much as you please" (continued he) "but my notion of conscience is not to ask out of reason, for any thing one has to dispose of; and so, Sir, if you have a mind to part with the boat, I'll give you half of what you ask; and I should think even that too much, but that I want her, and do not know where to get another."

"And as I want to sell her, and do not know where to get another

---

53 Both "the nature, character, or manner of a person" and, in sailing, the proper balance of a ship (OED).

54 As opposed to "weather-side," "that side of any object," such as a ship, "which is turned away from the wind" (OED).

purchaser!" (answered the lieutenant) "you shall have her. Not that I think she comes very cheap to you upon the whole neither! You have sworn well for her at least."

"As to that matter," (replied my master) "that is my business, and not yours. Here is your money; and that is all you need care for."—Saying this, he paid him for the boat, and then walked off, without concern or shame.—I here quitted his service, of which I was heartily tired, and entered into that of the lieutenant.

CHAPTER XVII

Chrysal makes some reflections on the policy of imposing oaths of exculpation.[55] The proper method of preserving the validity of oaths, with the consequences of their being administered indiscriminately to all persons, and on all occasions. An uncommon lecture from a captain of a man of war to his officers, represents some polite amusements in an odd light.

I SEE you are shocked at such flagrant instances of profligacy, of bare-faced contempt of every thing most sacred and important. They certainly are a reproach to human nature; but that reproach must not be confined to those alone, who obviously incur it. They who from false principles of policy give the occasion, against the conviction of reason and experience, are at least equally guilty.

The impotency of man to resist temptation is such that he is taught to pray against it! Why then should those, who are entrusted with the care of directing his actions in the common intercourse of life, lay snares to lead him into it, which there is no probability of his avoiding?

Appealing to the attestation of the Deity is most certainly the highest assurance possible to be given by any being, who has a

---

55 On July 8, 1736, the *Grub-street Journal* complained that "the repeated Swearing, required by Law in all Branches of the Constitution, has taken away the Terror and Awe that should naturally accompany an Oath," and underscored custom-house oaths as particularly notorious for fraud: "Every Master of a Ship, upon coming into Port, is obliged by Act of Parliament to swear to the Quantity and Quality of the Cargoe; and scarce one Master in a thousand but is perjured on that Occasion; so that a Custom-House Oath is grown into a Proverb."

sense of his dependence on that Deity; nor should ever be given but on the most important occasions, and in the most solemn manner; nor accepted but from such as may be presumed to understand the nature of it.

In such circumstances it would never be violated. Man is not so desperately abandoned as to run with his eyes open into inexplicable perdition. But when that attestation is given lightly, for every trifle, when it is placed in opposition to interest, and demanded from such as cannot be supposed to know its consequence, the reverence which should be its guard is taken off, the violation becomes familiar, and of course the end, for which it is thus impiously and injudiciously prostituted, disappointed; and by that means the most sacred assurance of life rendered void, the bond of social confidence and safety broken.

The effects of this absurd policy of making the obligations of Religion the common test of truth on trivial occasions, and where interest is concerned, are more extensive than is generally imagined. The immediate wants of nature engross the attention of the greater part of mankind too much to let them see the congruity of moral virtue, however evident to exerted reason; wherefore the threats and promises of Religion were found necessary to enforce the practice of it: But as the accomplishment of those is placed at a distance, when they interfere with present enjoyments, their force wears off, the threats lose their terrors, and the promises are slighted by those, who look no farther than the instant moment; and this is the great source of that immorality and irreligion so prevalent in life, and which will never be corrected, *till legislators make oaths less common, prevent their interfering with the swearer's own interest,* (as in the instance which gave occasion to these reflections) *explain their nature before they are administered, and inflict instant punishment on their violation.*

My new master had but just returned on board, when the captain received orders to go and assist the operations of the war in another part of the world. The news raised every one's spirits. The sight of a place in which most of them had been guilty of excesses, which threw them into distress, and where all had been so wretchedly disappointed, was necessarily disagreeable; and consequently a removal to another, where a new object attracted their attention from such reflections, and awoke new hopes, however likely to end in the same manner as the former, gave them pleasure.

There was a decency in the behaviour of both men and officers in this ship, so very different from what I had seen in others, as to strike me with an agreeable surprise. But I was not long at a loss for the reason. As soon as the ship was under sail, the captain[56] summoned all his officers into the great cabin, and after some general instructions about their duty, "Gentlemen," (said he, addressing himself to my master, and another, who had been but lately appointed to his ship) "as we have never sailed together before, I must desire your attention to a few hints, which I always take the liberty to give in such circumstances.

"We are now shut up together in a prison, where the unavoidable inconveniences of our situation make all our care necessary to prevent its becoming insupportable to us. For this reason, the first thing I recommend to you is *not to game*. Beside the danger of disagreement when the passions are agitated by the vicissitudes of play, our pay is scarce sufficient for our support; so that the least loss must be distressing, the consequence of which must be general unhappiness, for who can see his companion miserable, without sharing in his misery?

"There is another thing, against which, though not commonly considered in this light, I must earnestly caution you, as inevitably throwing a gloom over that cheerfulness of mind, which is the greatest happiness of life, and to us must supply the place of every other happiness, and this is *the vice of profane cursing and swearing*, to the reproach of our service, too prevalent among us.

"There is no man, however hardened in this detestable habit, but knows it to be a crime, and feels a check from within every

---

56 In the notes of one reader, John Jervis (1735-1823), Earl of St Vincent, later First Lord of the Admiralty. His behavior, through a long career "marked by devotion to the navy," earned him a reputation as tough yet fair: "his belief in efficiency and discipline was absolute, his hatred of slackness and inefficiency vigorously expressed," yet he was also "ungrudging to zeal, skill, and courage, promoting those who showed such qualities," and "kind and generous" in private life (DNB). According to popular legend, General Wolfe asked Jervis to deliver his final words to his betrothed, Katherine Lowther (see 1.310-12). Another key, however, identifies this figure as Richard Howe (see 2.20).

time he is guilty of it, the repetition of which self-accusation sours his temper, and makes him dissatisfied with himself, and every person and thing about him. For the truth of this I appeal to unvaried experience. Who ever saw a man serenely cheerful, that was addicted to this vice? (I might say indeed to any vice, but as our situation precludes us from the practice of most others, I mention these only into which we may fall) for occasional mirth is a very different thing, and too often leads into consequences destructive of serenity of mind, especially when it is raised by means inconsistent with virtue.

"I do not speak of the effect which the practice of virtue has upon our resolution. The courage of a *Briton* can never be doubted; but still there is as much difference between that of a virtuous, and a vicious man, as of the same person when sober, or intoxicated with liquor. The former is uniform, steady, and attentive to improve every advantage, or remedy any misfortune; the other boisterous, headlong, and blinded with passion; for passion only can make a man face death, who in the cool moments of reflection is afraid to die. In a word, one is the courage of a man, the other the rashness of a brute.

"Against these two things therefore, *gaming* and *swearing*, I take the liberty to caution you, as a friend, who is sincerely desirous of your welfare; but there is another vice, in respect to which I do not think myself obliged to observe the same delicacy; and this is *drunkenness*, which is liable to be attended with such dangerous consequences in our situation in particular, for I think it unnecessary to mention any other, that I shall ever exert all the authority entrusted to me to suppress it, and therefore it is but just for me to declare, that no officer, who is once guilty of it under my command, shall ever do duty under me more.

"This, gentlemen, is what I had to say to you. The observation of these few hints will make us happy among ourselves, and respected by our men, without which it is impossible for us to be well obeyed by them; for heedless and profligate as they may appear, they are the severest critics on the conduct of their officers, and not only like people in higher stations, revere the virtues which they have not resolution to imitate; but also actually do imitate them in a great degree."

CHAPTER XVIII

The folly of a person's prostituting his character to please his company,
aggravated by the dangerous mistake of ridicule for applause. *Chrysal's*
master changes place with the chaplain, and preaches him an interesting
sermon, in which, among remarks more just than polite, he gives an
uncommon reason for the particular deformity of vice in women.

I HAVE already taken notice of the effect which the advice and
example of the captain had upon every one in the ship. The
officers lived like a family of brothers, and the men did their duty
with regularity and pleasure; but though all paid due respect to
what he said, it was impossible to work such an instantaneous
reformation, but that some of them would now and then jest
among themselves upon his conduct, as from comparison with
that of others in his rank, inconsistent with his character; and in
other respects indulge in the levities of discourse and behaviour
too general among persons not much accustomed to the rules of
rational conversation.

But whatever allowances the circumstances of their education
might claim for such sallies in the officers, the person who
transgressed most was certainly entitled to none. This was the
chaplain, who to avoid the imputation of being hypocritically
sanctified, ran into the opposite extreme.

The selfish vanity of man always takes pleasure in seeing any
person debase himself, by acting beneath his character, especially if
that character is such as appears to be placed in a more respectable
point of view than their own. The officers, who in general look
upon a chaplain as no better than lumber in a ship, and think he
is placed as a kind of check upon them, were pleased with this
prostitution, which he, by a common mistake of ridicule for
applause, gave still farther into, *imagining they laughed with him*,
when in reality *they laughed at him.*

But my master beheld the matter in another light; and taking an
opportunity one day, when the chaplain and he were by themselves

in the ward-room,[57] "I have observed with much concern, Sir," (said he) "that you are falling into an error, which I have known prove fatal to many gentlemen of your profession. This is departing from your character, in order to accommodate yourself to what you think the humour of your company. Believe me, sir, no man ever did so, who did not immediately fall into contempt with the very people, whose approbation he strove to purchase at so dear a rate. The greatest libertine despises a clergyman, who is a libertine; and the reason is plain. *You are set apart from the rest of mankind to perform the rites of Religion, and inculcate virtue by your precepts and example; and for this you are paid by the public, who expect that you should earn your wages, by doing your duty; and look upon those who do not, as no better than cheats.* This may appear an odd way of speaking, but it is true nevertheless.

"On the other hand, where a clergyman fulfils his duty, and enforces his preaching by his practice, though he may not absolutely reform all those with whom he converses, yet he will certainly work this good effect, that he will keep them in awe, and prevent their running into outrageous lengths of wickedness, at least in his presence. For whatever people may inconsiderately imagine, *no man ever acted in character who was not respected; no man ever acted out of character who was not despised.*

"Do but reflect a moment, in what light you yourself would look upon a lady, who should speak obscenely, swear, drink, and talk of fighting, and it will shew you the justice of this remark. For what makes these vices so particularly hateful in a woman, is not any thing in their nature particularly contradictory to the sex, more than ours, but because they are contrary to her character.

"I beg your pardon, Sir, for talking to you in this free manner, in respect to your conduct, which I am sensible concerns only yourself; but as the errors you have fallen into appear to have arisen merely from inadvertency, and mistake, I think it my duty to caution you against the danger of them, particularly in your present situation, with which I have had the opportunity of being much better acquainted, than you possibly can be. I was in the service long, very long, before you were born; and have been intimate with

---

57 "The mess-cabin of naval commissioned officers" (OED).

many chaplains, but never knew one who prostituted his character to humour his company, who was not neglected by them, when they had it in their power to have served him; as on the contrary, I have known many instances of those who have reaped the happy fruits of a regular, and virtuous conduct, by which they acquired an esteem, that proved the foundation of their fortune; and if all have not been equally successful, their disappointment must be attributed to some other cause.

"I would not by this be understood to advise you to a morose distance, and stiffness of behaviour, or asperity of reproof upon every occasion. They seldom, if ever, do good, in any situation; in yours they will certainly do hurt, by piquing false pride to act in opposition to them, without regard to the consequences. An obliging temper, and a uniformly decent conduct lead insensibly to imitation, where contradiction or direct admonition would be held impertinent. These hints are so obvious, that they may seem unnecessary; but it is want of attention to them which has made so many chaplains miscarry in life, and indeed has brought the very character into disrepute."

The chaplain, who wanted neither natural good sense, nor virtuous inclination, was struck with the justice and force of this rebuke. He thanked my master in the most ingenuous manner, and promised to regulate his future conduct by his advice. Such a change at first naturally exposed him to the merriment of his companions; but as my master took his part, and shewed them the injustice of such behaviour, it soon wore off, and he had the heart-felt satisfaction to find himself treated with friendly respect and confidence by those, whose gross familiarity had before often given him pain, as it evidently implied contempt.

CHAPTER XIX

Chrysal describes true compassion; and shews the general consequence of a man's acknowledging distress, with the reasons of it. *Chrysal's* master is prevailed upon by his captain to tell him the cause of his melancholy, which is removed by an act of uncommon generosity. *Chrysal* enters into a new service.

As the captain maintained the most friendly intercourse with his officers, he soon observed that my master laboured under some heavy distress of mind. This naturally raised his compassion, and *as real compassion never sees distress, which it is not desirous of alleviating*, he frequently took occasion, when they were by themselves, to turn his discourse upon such subjects as he thought might lead him to open himself; but finding that modesty, or a reserve contracted from long acquaintance with misfortune, and observation that *the knowledge of a man's being in distress always sinks him in the esteem of his companions, by cutting off their hopes of service from him, and alarming their apprehensions of his expecting assistance from them*, prevented his taking the hint, he resolved to break through forms, and ask him directly.

Seeing him therefore one day walking the quarter-deck, in a mood of deepest melancholy, he called him into the great cabin, and desiring him to sit down, after a little general chat, "I fear, Sir," (said he) "that something hangs upon your spirits. If it is proper to be communicated, let me know what it is, and depend upon every assistance in my power to make you easy. I ask not from idle or impertinent curiosity."

"Sir," (answered my master, struck with the manner in which he spoke) "I believe you above the influence of such motives, and shall therefore obey your kind commands without scruple. It is too true that I am unhappy; and I fear my unhappiness is too common. I have devoted my life to a profession in which I have served my country above forty years with fidelity; and I will take the liberty to say with some success: and now when my constitution is broken with wounds, fatigue, and change of climates, when nature calls for rest and refreshment, the only reward I have to expect is poverty, and its inseparable attendant, contempt. This, Sir, is the cause of my unhappiness; and such a cause, as I believe you will think to be a just one."

"Very true, Sir," (replied the captain) "it is a just one; and what must affect every man of spirit, and a generous way of thinking. But you should not yield to it too far! You are still in the vigour of life; and while the war continues, should look forward with hope. Though you have been unsuccessful hitherto, fortune may prove more kind."

"Alas, Sir," (returned my master) "I have been so long cheated by hope, that I now detest it. When I came out upon this last expedition, our force made me so confident of success, and I was so well acquainted with the wealth in the place, that I unhappily gave way to hope, and ran into expences, which though far from being unnecessary, were imprudent, and threaten now to involve me in ruin, on my return home, as it has been thought proper by our superiors to rate our service in the conquest, at so low a price."

"If that is the case then!" (said the captain) "do not return till matters mend. Whenever I am ordered home, I'll take care to get you removed into another ship. Your staying abroad on such an account is not inconsistent with the strictest honour, as you do it with an intention truly honest."

"Dear Sir," (answered my master) "that is very true. But I am precluded even from the wretched relief of a voluntary exile. I have a wife and children at home, the apprehension of whose distresses drives me to despair. It was to clothe and settle them in a little habitation, where they might enjoy the indispensable necessaries of life with some degree of comfort, that I anticipated my success, in the manner I mentioned; and now as that success has fallen so far short of what I thought just expectation, all the former savings of my life (savings from the very necessities of nature) will be torn away by the rapacious hands of merciless creditors, to make up the deficiency in the articles bought of themselves to discharge their demands, and my wretched family thrown upon the unfriendly world, without its being in my power to assist them. I must therefore return, and go into a jail to prevent their starving in the streets. What affected myself only, honest indignation enabled me to support. I have seen boys, whose ignorance I despised, and men whose principles I detested, preferred to command, while my services were overlooked; but as I had not the interest of the former, nor the *modish merit* of the latter, I bore my fate with patience. But to have those dearer to me than life exposed to misery is more than I can bear."

"Nor shall you bear it!" (replied the captain, who had feigned to cough to hide the sympathetic tear, that glistened in his eye) "Nor shall you bear it. How much is the debt that alarms you? I will advance it for you directly; and not that only, I will take upon me to make your merit (to which I am no stranger) known to your superiors, in such a light as shall not fail of just reward."

"O Sir!" (returned my master, as soon as the fullness of his heart gave him utterance) "How can I submit to obligations, to which it is impossible I should ever make any return?"

"All the return I desire" (answered the captain) "is your friendship. Speak! how much do you want? The Pacquet[58] is yet in sight. I will order a signal to be made for her, and give you a draught upon my agent."

"Good heaven!" (exclaimed my master) "Can there be such virtue in man?"

"Come! what is the sum?" (interrupted the captain, who wanted to shorten a conversation that began to be too affecting to him) "I shall think you doubt my sincerity if you hesitate to accept of my friendship."

"Such a doubt" (returned my master, whose heart a gush of tears had lightened) "would be a blacker crime than ever stained my soul! No! I receive your beneficence with humble gratitude, as from the hand of heaven, nor will mention any other return, but what must be made to that, till it shall be pleased to bless me with better ability."

Then pulling out his pocket-book, "Here is the account of what I owe" (continued he, giving him some papers, and a purse containing little more than his share of the price of the smuggler's boat): "And here is all my worldly wealth, which is no more than

---

58 A packet-boat, which sails "between two ports, originally for the conveyance of mail" (OED).

an assignment of my miserable prize-money, and these few pieces of gold, thrown by fortune in my way, mostly since our hands were tied up by the capitulation. For the balance I must be your debtor."

"For the balance!" (answered the captain, returning the purse, and the assignment) "No! you shall be my debtor (if you will call it so!) for the whole. It would be strange friendship to strip you of every thing you may want yourself"—

"Excuse me, Sir;" (interrupted my master, unable to suppress the delicacy, the dignity of honour) "I am not so low a wretch, as to accept of more than I indispensably want; and that for persons dearer to me than myself. If you will not permit me to make the debt as light as I can, it is impossible for me to receive your friendship, however essential to the happiness of my heart. I am sorry you should have entertained so mean an opinion of me."

"I have the highest opinion of you!" (replied the captain, who saw what pain he had given him) "and spoke in the warmth of my regard, without the most distant design of giving you offence. But you shall make your own terms, on this condition though, that if you have any occasion for money, you will apply to me with the freedom of a friend."

To such a proposal, it was impossible to refuse assenting. My master complied, and the captain taking the money, &c. from him, desired that he would order a signal to be made for the Pacquet, and write his letters, while he himself should draw a bill upon his agent.—The sentiments expressed by the captain made it a pleasure to me to pass into his service on this occasion.

As soon as the lieutenant went out, my new master walked a turn or two about his cabin, in the exalted happiness of conscious virtue; and then drawing a bill for considerably more than the lieutenant was to pay, he desired that he should be called; and when he entered, "I beg pardon" (said he) "for interrupting you, but it is to desire that you will present my compliments to your wife, and tell her I beg she will accept of a trifling present from me, which I have taken the liberty to include in the bill. Come! no words! In this I will not be contradicted."

"O Sir!" (answered the lieutenant, catching his hand, as he reached him the bill, and kissing it eagerly) "this is too much! My heart will burst."—Saying which, he went out of the cabin, in a silence more expressive of his soul, than all the flights of eloquence.

CHAPTER XX

History of a lieutenant of a man of war. A comparison between the rewards of merit, in the land and sea services; with a remarkable instance of a great man's remembering an old friend. The consequence of attempting to set up for a mender of manners, and of a man's not meeting an opportunity of making himself remarkable.

WHEN every thing was settled, and the Pacquet sailed, the lieutenant desired leave to wait upon my master; and as soon as he entered, "I come, Sir," (said he) "to pay you the thanks, which the fullness of my heart would not let me utter before. You have raised me to happiness from the lowest state of despair."

"Hold, my friend!" (answered my master taking his hand, and squeezing it tenderly) "Speak no more of it, I conjure you. I am abundantly overpaid for what I have done, by the pleasure of having served a man of merit; and shall think you repine at my happiness in being able to purchase that pleasure, if I ever hear the affair mentioned more."

To relieve the lieutenant, whom he saw oppressed with gratitude, he then changed the conversation to another subject, when the lieutenant shewed so much good sense, and solid judgment, that my master could not forbear expressing his astonishment, that such a man should have been so long unpromoted in the service.

"If you can have patience to hear the story of my life" (answered the lieutenant) "it will soon explain that difficulty to you. My father was an officer in the army, who was rewarded for the loss of a leg, and thirty years service, with the half-pay[59] of a captain of foot. As he had a wife and children to maintain and provide for, he retired to a cheap county, where he lived in the most rigid œconomy in hopes of saving, for he could not make any thing, being precluded

---

59 "A reduced allowance to an officer in the army or navy when not in actual service, or after retirement" (OED).

from every kind of industry, by the profession to which he had
devoted his youth.

"The first acquaintance a stranger gets in a country place is
the parson of the parish.[60] It was my father's happiness to fix his
habitation, where there was a clergyman who would have been a
valuable acquaintance in any place, and who was equally happy in
the acquisition of a rational acquaintance in him. The common
intercourse of neighbourhood was therefore soon improved
between them into the strongest friendship, in the intimacy of
which, as my father would often naturally mention his anxiety for
his children, his friend persuaded him to breed me, the eldest, to
the sea-service, in which he thought he himself might be able to
serve me, by his interest with several commanders, with whom
he had been acquainted formerly, when chaplain to a man of
war. 'That is the service!' (would the good man say, with pleasure
sparkling in his eyes) 'That is the service in which merit is never
disregarded. You would not have been laid aside after thirty years,
to pine upon five shillings a day, if you had been bred to the sea.
No! no! merit is all that is necessary there.'

"Such an argument was too flattering to my father's hopes
to be resisted. Though he felt the evil of not having been bred
to business himself, he was charmed at the thought of his son's
being placed in the way of rising to an higher sphere, and readily
assented to the advice of his friend, who not content with mere
advice, insisted on taking me home with him, and giving me
such an education as should qualify me to make a figure in the
profession to which he had directed me. 'If ever a man of merit in
the sea-service' (would he often say) 'fails of rising, it is for want
of having had a good education to found his hopes upon. A mere
seaman may work a ship, but an Admiral should be a scholar.'

"How well this reasoning was founded, experience daily shews;
though it would be ingratitude in me to arraign it, as the little taste
for letters which I acquired from his care, if it has not contributed
to my advancement, has at least enabled me to support the shock

---

60 KEY: "Bp. of Derry." There were several Bishops of Derry in the period, but
none seems to have served as "chaplain to a man of war." The connection, if any,
remains unclear.

of disappointment, as well as to avoid many evils into which I have seen others, who had not the same advantage, fall.

"At sixteen, (for he insisted that it was most wretched policy to turn a boy loose upon the world before he had come to the use of reason, and was well instructed in the principles of morality and religion, for the sake of gaining a couple of years advance): At sixteen, I say, I was sent to sea, provided with a chest of books, and mathematical instruments, and a good suit of clothes, not to discredit the recommendation which my best friend gave me to an Admiral,[61] with whom he had been most intimate, when a lieutenant; and whose readiness to serve him in any thing, he would not admit a doubt of.

"On my presenting my letter, the Admiral at first had forgot the name, but recollecting himself at length on my mentioning some circumstances which I had often heard my friend dwell upon with pleasure; 'Very true,' (said he) 'I remember him now. He made the best bowl of punch of any man in the navy.'

"This was all the notice the *great man* took of him, or of me on his account, except I should add, that on his captain's observing I should make a good figure on the quarter-deck, I was directly rated a midshipman; a favour for which I soon found I was indebted to

---

61 KEY: "Adml. Matthews." Thomas Mathews (1676-1751), described by Walpole as a "blustering," bullish figure; "I dare to say," states one letter, "Matthews believes that God lives upon beef and pudding, loves prize-fighting and bull-baiting, and drinks fog to the health of old England." Despite an eighteen-year absence from naval service, "an acute shortage of capable senior flag officers" led to his appointment as Commander-in-Chief in the Mediterranean in 1742 (DNB). At the 1744 Battle of Toulon, off the coast of France, Mathews commanded an unsuccessful attack on the combined Spanish and French fleet, then failed to give chase to the fleeing Spanish. An ensuing pamphlet-war debated whether blame lay with Mathews or with his captains, particularly Richard Lestock, who neglected to respond to Mathews's signals. Upon the decision to hold a parliamentary inquiry, the case ballooned into a major media and political event. Although public opinion largely sided with Mathews before the inquiry, his reputation was severely damaged by it. Lestock's evidence that Mathews "had been sloppy, reckless, and impatient" (DNB) was compounded by Mathews's own behavior at trial, where he came across as "a hot, brave, imperious, dull, confused fellow" (Walpole). As reported in the *Gentleman's Magazine,* on October 22, 1746, Mathews was found guilty and "was render'd incapable of serving in his majesty's royal navy for the future." The case, particularly Lestock's blameworthiness, is again alluded to in 2.114-15.

his caution of sending me well dressed, much more than to his interest.

"Though I felt this disappointment of my first hopes very severely, on my friend's account, as well as my own, I could not think of shocking him with the news, but saying in general terms that I had been well received, resolved to apply myself to my business, and try whether I could not deserve that favour, which he had failed to procure me.

"As I had been accustomed to conversation very different from that of those with whom alone I could now converse, I took every opportunity, when off duty, of running to my books. But the relief I found from this was for the present overbalanced by the general ridicule into which it drew me; especially as I not only avoided obscenity, swearing, and drinking myself, but had also been so imprudent as to rebuke others for them. I was immediately nick-named *the parson*, and avoided by every one in the ship.

"I need not describe to you the situation of a *petit* officer,[62] insulted by those below him, ridiculed by his equals, and looked down upon with contempt by his superiors, who forgot they were ever in his station themselves. I bore it for fifteen years, at the end of which time, having the good fortune to be sent to *London*, with a press-gang,[63] on purpose to mortify me, for I always disliked that particular duty more than any other in the service; on seeing an advertisement in the newspapers, that all who were qualified by their standing to be lieutenants in the navy, should attend to pass their examination, I offered myself without any other introduction, or interest, and was appointed to a ship.

"In this station I have now done my duty for five and twenty years, without reprehension; but as I have no *corporation-interest* to push me at home, none of the *modern polite accomplishments*, to recommend me to the favourites of fortune, whom I occasionally meet in the service, nor have ever had the good luck to find an opportunity of making myself remarkable, by any action of *eclat*, though in itself no more than a successful blunder, my uniform

---

62 "A minor or inferior officer" (OED).
63 "A crew that strolls about the streets to force men into naval service" (Johnson).

conduct and care have passed unnoticed, and I remain a lieutenant still."

The circumstances of this story affected my master in the strongest manner. He took the lieutenant by the hand, and desiring him not to despair, repeated his promise of using all his interest to serve him, of the success of which he had no reason to doubt.

Nothing particular happened during our voyage. One instance though of my master's conduct in his military capacity I cannot forbear mentioning, as it shews his character in the strongest light, which was, that he never interfered in the business of his officers, but if he happened to see any thing which he disapproved, instead of interposing his own authority publicly, and giving contrary orders, he always spoke privately to the officer on duty, and giving his direction under the appearance of advice, let the alteration proceed as immediately from him, by which means he spared him the pain of being found fault with before the men, and consequently lessened in their opinion.

This delicacy not only endeared him to them all, but also contributed greatly to advance the service. For as every officer knew that he should have the credit, or bear the blame of his own actions, they all exerted themselves with the utmost ardour; whereas on the contrary, where a captain is continually interfering, and leaving nothing for his officers to do, they grow careless of course, and do nothing, as they know he will arrogate to himself the merit of success; if they do not even take a malignant pleasure in any miscarriage, the blame of which they have so just an opportunity of throwing upon him.

CHAPTER XXI

An uncommon method of carrying on a war; with the danger of speaking
the truth too plainly, at an improper time. *Chrysal's* master meets his
brother. Some account of him. He represents certain matters in an
odd light. *Chrysal* enters into his service. Conclusion of his character.
Chrysal quits his service on an uncommon occasion, for one, from
which he passes in the usual course of business into that of the general.

WHEN we arrived at the place of our destination, we found the
shore covered with an extensive encampment, and every thing
wearing the appearance of the most active war.

The first thing my master[64] did was, of course, to wait upon
the General,[65] whose operations he was sent to assist. He met him
viewing an occasional fortification, which he had caused to be
raised to train his army to the method of making regular sieges
and attacks; and marking out a piece of ground to be sowed with
vegetables to correct the bad effects of the salt provisions, which
his men had lived upon in their passage thither, and preserve them
in health.

The account he received from my master of the heavy loss
sustained in the expedition from which he had just come, gave

---

64 KEY: "The character is here changed to Lord Howe." Chrysal's master in
this chapter is army officer William Howe (1729-1814), Viscount Howe, younger
brother of Richard (2.20) and George Augustus Howe (2.84). "A knowledgeable
and meticulous officer and a skilful commander" (DNB), Howe played important
roles in the battles for Quebec, Montreal and Havana, and would later be
Commander-in-Chief of British forces during the American Revolution. This
chapter is set in Nova Scotia, 1757, where British forces were preparing to attack
the French stronghold of Louisbourg.
65 KEY: "Lord Loudon." John Campbell (1705-82), Earl of Loudoun, "a
conscientious, but conspicuously unlucky, professional soldier," who in 1756
became Commander-in-Chief of British forces in North America. In 1757,
his attempt to capture Louisbourg "ended in ignominious failure" when
sufficient reinforcements failed to arrive from Britain in time. "While the bulk
of Loudoun's redcoats remained gathered at Halifax," French forces destroyed
Fort William Henry in New York. Although such disasters "stemmed partly from
Pitt's interference in his original plans," Loudoun was recalled and replaced in
December 1757.

him visible pleasure, as it seemed to set his own conduct, which was diametrically the reverse of that observed there, in the most advantageous light.

"I wonder" (said he, looking around him with an air of conscious exultation) "how officers can reconcile it to themselves to throw away the lives of their men in such a manner! For my part, I act upon very different principles. I take care not only to give my troops an insight into all the various branches of the military art, but also to keep them in such health as may enable them to reap the advantage of their experience. There is nothing so bad in war as precipitation. It was the sole cause of the late General's defeat and death."[66]

"Yes!" (interrupted an officer[67] who stood near, and had hearkened to him with evident impatience) "Delay is full as bad. Your troops want neither health nor experience to conquer every opposition they can possibly meet; and will accomplish the end they were sent upon before your cabbages are fit for them to eat, if you will but lead them against their enemies, and not give them time to retire with their effects into places, whither it is impossible for an army to pursue them; while your men waste their time and spirits in the foolish parade of mock battles and sieges, till they lose their ardour by delays which can answer no end, but that of protracting the war, and thereby lengthening a lucrative command."

Such an attack was quite unexpected, and struck the General with equal surprise and indignation, as it touched him in the tenderest part; however, dissembling his passion, of which he had an absolute command, "I would have you know, Sir," (said he)

---

66 The defeat of Major-General Edward Braddock. See 1.308.
67 KEY: "Ld. Chas. Hay." Lord Charles Hay (1700?-1760), who in 1757 was made Major-General and sent to join Loudon's forces in Halifax. After criticizing Loudoun for failing to attack Louisbourg, Hay "was arrested and placed aboard ship at Halifax and sent home in late 1758" (DNB) to be tried. The *Daily Advertiser*, on February 2, 1757, reported Hay was "accused of every military crime that an officer can be guilty of (except cowardice and desertion)." Samuel Johnson, who visited him while under arrest, thought him "a mighty pleasing man in conversation" (DNB), but when Hay died before sentence could be passed on him, Walpole wrote he was a madman who was "luckily dead, and has saved much trouble."

"that I think it the highest assurance in you to attempt censuring my conduct, who are sent merely to execute my orders. When I ask your opinion, it will be time enough for you to give it; till then, obedience, not advice, is what I expect from you. If I did not hold it beneath me to shew resentment to one so absolutely subject to my power, you should instantly find the effect of this insolence. But presume not on that protection any farther, as you regard your safety. No man provokes me with impunity."

"N-n-nor me!" (sputtered the officer, whose temper, hot as that of the General was cool, caught fire at the faintest shadow of offence, and flamed almost to madness, as soon as rage permitted him to articulate a word) "Nor m-m-me. I seek no p-p-protection but my sword, with which I will v-v-vindicate my own honour, and make good what I say.—Talk to m-m-me of safety, and im-p-p-punity!"

The affair now became serious, these words striking at the General's safety, as well as his honour, and convincing him that he must support his dignity by a vigorous effort. "What!" (retorted he, therefore, with a tone and air of offended authority) "Do you menace me too? I suppose you design to raise a mutiny in the army, but I'll prevent that."—Then turning to an officer who attended, "Take that madman away,"[68] (continued he) "and put him under a guard, till he recovers his reason. Such behaviour must not go unpunished."—Then addressing himself to my master with an affected unconcern, as above being moved by what had happened, while the other was led away speechless and convulsed with rage, he politely invited him to dinner, an honour, however, which my master declined accepting that day, as he was most impatient to see his brother,[69] who bore a principal command in the army under the General.

---

68 Hay seems to have suffered from bouts of insanity. "In November 1746 he was reported to be 'confined raving mad' and had been 'tied to his bed some time'" (DNB).

69 KEY: "late Lord Howe." George Augustus Howe (1724?-1758), Viscount Howe. Pitt named him second-in-command to attack the French fort of Ticonderoga. On the march to the stronghold, Howe's forces were ambushed, and as printed in the *Gentleman's Magazine* in August 1758, "his lordship was shot thro' the breast, and died instantly." The loss was deeply felt in Britain. The *Gentleman's Magazine* reported he was "universally beloved and respected throughout the whole army,"

The meeting of these brothers was truly affecting. The instinctive connection of nature had been indissolubly cemented between them by the sacred bond of friendship, founded on a sense of mutual virtue.

Actuated by the same principles, they had both devoted themselves to the profession of arms, in the different services of the land and sea, as if to avoid the jealousy of rivalship, each being determined to let no competitor take the lead of him in the road to honour.

Undebauched by affluence, and disdaining to waste his youth at home in luxury, when the cause of his country called for his assistance, the elder bravely came to seek for glory in these inhospitable wilds, with as much ardour as my master pursued it on his proper element, in order to earn honours which he might transmit to his own posterity, equal to those which his brother inherited from his illustrious ancestors.

When the tender enquiries of affection were reciprocally answered, my master gratified the curiosity of his brother with a particular account of his late dearly bought success, closing the black detail with some remarks on the different conduct of the General of this army, which were much to his advantage.

"Your reflections, my dearest brother," (answered the officer) "are most just, as things appear to you. But when you have had an opportunity of seeing farther, I fear you will find reason to change your sentiments, and that the *delay* here proceeds at bottom from the same principle with the *precipitation* which produced such terrible effects with you, and heaven grant it produce not as bad. Interest is the object every where; and *whether that is pursued by sacrificing the forces in rash and ill-conducted attempts, to gain an immediate* prize, *or by letting them melt away in inaction, to accumulate the* profits *of command*, makes no difference in the end.

"I would not be understood from this to justify the officer for arraigning the General's conduct, in so public and personal a manner. Such ungoverned warmth is inexcusable. Proper respect

the *Scots Magazine* commemorated "his robust soldier-like constitution, his bold enterprising spirit, and every other military accomplishment," and Wolfe mourned him as "the very best officer in the King's service," whose loss was "one of the greatest that could befall the nation" (DNB).

must be paid to those who bear authority, or the effect of that authority ceases; indeed it is not to them, but to him who delegates the authority, the respect is paid. A General at the head of an army represents his Sovereign in the plentitude of his power, and to suffer any slight to be shewn to his delegated character, were to betray the trust of that delegation.

"For this reason, I think his punishment was necessary, and *therefore* just; I wish I could add that it was equally so from the injustice, as from the circumstances of the accusation which occasioned it; but to any one who will not shut his eyes, it must appear beyond a doubt, that his great crime was speaking too much, and too plain truth; for with all our boasted care for the preservation of the men, their distresses are such as have not left me a penny in my pocket, for I cannot shut my hand where my heart is opened. In short, I am so sick of the whole scene, that I have solicited the command of a detached party, with which I hope to shew that the native bravery of *Britons*, when led with spirit, requires but little experience to enable them to conquer more formidable foes, than naked savages, led by a few wretched *Frenchmen*, in a condition not much better. I set out to-morrow morning, and think it a particular happiness that you have arrived time enough for me to have this interview with you."

The rest of their conversation is not necessary to be repeated, as it turned upon their own domestic concerns. This much only is but just for me to observe, that it shewed their conduct in the intercourse and relations of private life to be as amiable, as that in their public capacities was exalted; and proved that moral virtue is the best foundation for true heroism.—My master's brother having in the course of their conversation intimated his having some present occasion for money, I here entered into his service.

You may judge that I remained not long in the possession of my new master. His brother had no sooner left him, than he paid me away, among a large number of my fellows, to a merchant for some additions, which he thought it necessary to make at his own expence to the provisions made by the public for the support and comfort of his men, through the fatigues and inconveniences of a campaign in an uninhabited country.

The sentiments expressed by my master, in the effusion of

his soul to his brother, shewed his character in the justest light: I shall therefore only add, that as he acted from principles firmly established on the invariable basis of reason, there was no danger of his deviating from the paths in which he set out.

So bright a prospect made it a pain to me to quit his service so suddenly; but I have since met many mortifications of the same kind, my stay being always shortest in the best hands.

My continuance, though from another motive, was not much longer with my next master, the merchant, who in the common course of soliciting permission for a ship of his to sail with a cargo that must be ruined by delay, an embargo having been laid on all the shipping in the place,[70] in the unfathomable wisdom of the ruling powers, to promote some unintelligible plan of service, gave me to the General's clerk, from whom in the same course of business, I came into the service of the General.

---

70 On January 3, 1757, Loudoun instituted "a general embargo on all outward-bound ships in American colonial ports," hoping both to keep sufficient transports and troops on hand for the attack on Louisbourg, and to prevent the French from learning of preparations to attack. The measure was widely criticized in both America and in Britain, "and, in spite of the precaution, the French heard of the project. In the early spring, therefore, they sent a fleet and strong reinforcements to Louisbourg" (William Laird Clowes, *The Royal Navy: A History*).

VOLUME III, BOOK II

CHAPTER I

Chrysal's master makes some characteristic reflections. He is surprised at
the officer's refusing to make up matters; and gives a particular reason
for some people's rising in the world. An extraordinary personage
enters to him. Description of him. He gives a character of the native
Americans; and offers some interesting remarks on the return they
make to the treatment they meet with; and on the practice of forming
in the closet,[71] plans of operations for armies in the field. Odd reason
why the *Americans* are desirous of gold. *Chrysal* changes his service.

WHEN I entered into the possession of my new master, he was
waiting in his tent, with the most anxious impatience, for the return
of a person whom he had employed to mediate as of himself,
between him and the officer, whose presumption in daring to find
fault with the measures he had thought proper to punish in the
manner I just now mentioned.

His reflections on an affair that struck so dangerously at his
pride and avarice, the ruling passions of his heart, could not be
very agreeable; but the sight of the money gave them a more
pleasing turn. Having asked the clerk a few questions in the way
of business, and dismissed him, he took the purse, and weighing it
in his hand, "Aye!" (said he, with delight glistening in his eyes) "this
will do. This embargo was a lucky thought. Let who will complain
of the hinderance it is to the business of the public, it advances
mine; and that is all I care for. I came here to serve myself, and not
the public; and as there is neither plunder nor contributions to be
got by activity, I must try what I can do another way. I shewed my
dexterity at hunting Savages in the mountains of my own country;[72]
and have no desire to renew the chase here. It was necessary for

---

71 A "place of private study or secluded speculation; especially in reference to
mere theories as opposed to practical measures" (OED).
72 Born a Scot, Loudoun led "a regiment of loyal highlanders" during the 1745
Jacobite rising (DNB).

me then to do something that should make me remarkable, and gain favour with those who I saw must prevail in the end, and therefore I spared no trouble nor fatigue, neither friend nor foe, to convince them of my attachment; and in reward they have now given me this command, in conducting which I must use delay to reap the advantages of my former activity. *Fabius* saved *Rome* by delay;[73] let me but make my fortune by it, and I envy him not his fame. I prefer this sound" (chinking the purse) "to the empty noise of public acclamation, the shouts of a giddy mob, who bless and curse with the same breath, and without knowing why they do either. No! no! no! this is the music that charms my ear."

His meditations were broken off here, by the gentleman he waited for, who informed him that the officer would come to no terms of accommodation; nor even accept of his liberty till he should be acquitted by a court-martial,[74] and have justice done him for the affront offered to his honour.

Such an account was far from being agreeable to my master, who for obvious reasons wished to have every thing go on as quietly as possible. After some pause, "This is a damn'd affair," (said he) "but we must now e'en make the best we can of it. Who could have thought that a countryman of my own would have proved so refractory.[75] We have always been remarkable for hanging well together. *One and all* was the word, or we could never have done such great matters. If it is once found out, that we can be divided, we shall soon lose our consequence; and every man be reduced to *the poor prospect of depending on his own merit.* However, since he will not accept of his liberty here, he shall e'en go home a prisoner, and recover it there as well as he can. I am of the right side; and don't fear but my friends will bring me through more than this; especially as it is a national concern to us all alike. In the

73 Fabius Maximus, dictator of Rome, defeated Hannibal of the Carthaginians by avoiding and delaying pitched battles. The cost of maintaining the Carthaginian army in the field, over extended supply lines, and subsequent loss of Carthaginian morale saved Rome.

74 Hay demanded his own court martial, which sat from February through March 1760.

75 Hay, the son of the Marquess of Tweeddale, was also a Scot.

mean time, we must double our diligence to make hay while the sun shines."

The gentleman, who was in all his secrets, acknowledged the force of his reasoning; and was going to communicate to him some new strokes of management, when word was brought to my master that a person,[76] to whom he could not properly be denied, desired to see him.

There was something in the whole appearance of this person that struck me with the strongest curiosity the moment I saw him. His stature, above the common size of man,[77] was formed with the justest proportion, and denoted ability to execute the most difficult attempts, which the determined and enterprizing spirit that animated his looks could urge him to. His open countenance, in which humanity and reason attempered resolution, shewed the genuine workings of his soul; and his whole deportment was in the unaffected ease of natural liberty, above the hypocritical formality of studied rules of behaviour, devised only to deceive.

As soon as he entered, "I am come, Sir," (said he, throwing himself carelessly into a chair, and cutting short all that parade of ceremony, on the punctilious observation of which my master

---

76 KEY: "Sir Wm. Johnson." Sir William Johnson (1715?-74), first baronet, who came to America in 1738. His ties with the Mohawks through kinship and trade "created enormous potential influence among their fellow Six Nations Iroquois," who called him Warraghiyagey, or "he who does much business" (DNB). In 1755, General Edward Braddock (see 1.308) appointed Johnson to command an expedition against the French fort of Crown Point, and Johnson's combined British colonial and Mohawk forces would later defeat the French at the Battle of Lake George—an especially poignant triumph, as it followed Braddock's own defeat and death by only two months. The victory, combined with the exoticism of Johnson's family and exploits, made him a celebrity in the British press. "Major Gen. *Johnson*," reported the *Gentleman's Magazine* in September 1755, "is universally esteemed superior to any we have in our parts," both skilled in battle and beloved by the native people: "by his honest dealings with them in trade, his courage, which has often been successfully tried with them, and his courteous behaviour, he has so endeared himself to them, that they chose him one of their chief sachems or princes, and esteem him as their common father."

77 Johnson "was physically an imposing man." His contemporaries described him an "uncommonly tall, well made man: with a fine countenance;" and "a man of large size, with a pleasant face, piercing eyes, ready communication, and pleasing manners though sometimes very abrupt" (Fintan O'Toole, *White Savage: William Johnson and the Invention of America*).

prided himself not a little) "to receive your orders. It is time, I should join my people, who grow impatient, as the enemy have begun to stir; and I never choose to baulk their first ardour. There is nothing like taking men in the humour to fight; and before they have time to consider too much about it."

"I design, Sir," (answered my master, with a solemnity and affectation of politeness, which made the strongest contrast to the blunt freedom of the other) "to call a council of war very soon; at which I shall be glad of your assistance, to form a plan of operations for the campaign. When that is done, and all proper measures concerted, you shall set out. *Precipitation* is very dangerous, and directly contrary to the principles of the *regular art of war*, by which I mean to proceed. The Savages shall find some difference between my conduct, and that of my predecessors. They shan't surprise me on my march; nor draw me into an ambush, among woods and mountains."

"As to the art of war, Sir," (replied the other) "I know no more of it, than what heaven and common sense have taught me, which is to find out the enemy, and beat them as soon as I can, my plan for which is always directed by present circumstances; nor do I know how one can be formed to effect any other way."

"Your exploits have always been well executed:" (returned my master, with an air and tone of importance, as designing to say something that should raise him in the opinion of the other) "But you have hitherto acted rather in the low sphere of a *partisan*, than as a general. The duty of a general comprehends much more than what you mention, as you shall have an opportunity of learning before we take the field. I intend to go through a regular course of military operations to instruct my officers, and discipline the men. Your *heaven-taught* generals may beat the enemy; but that is the least part of the care and duty of a general now-a-days. The very least part."

"And pray, Sir, how much time will this course of operations take up?"

"I cannot exactly say; but not above a month or two, I imagine."

"A month or two! why, Sir, I hope we shall have done the most troublesome part of our work by that time; or else I do not know what may be the consequence. For, to be plain with you, these delays will never do with the *uncivilized Americans*, who judge of things only by common sense; and cannot be made to comprehend this way of carrying on a war, by lying still in a camp and doing nothing. They have formed very disadvantageous notions of the delays already made; and think a man who does not advance to fight his enemy is afraid of him; and therefore if they are not led to action directly, they will desert, so that if I stay a month or two here at school to learn a lesson I may never have occasion for, I must find other forces to put it in practice with."

"Cannot you devise any reason that may account for your staying, to their satisfaction?"

"Really, Sir, not I! I never was good at devising reasons, destitute of truth, in my life; and have entirely forgot the practice since I have conversed with the *Americans*, who are far from being such fools, as they are too generally thought to be. Though they have not the advantages of learning, they see by the light of natural reason through all the boasted wiles of policy; and as they never mean deceit themselves, detest it in others, however speciously disguised; nor ever place confidence a second time, where it has been once abused."

"How! the *Americans* never mean deceit! Surely you must know better! they are the most perfidious deceitful Savages that burden the earth; and it would be an advantage to the world, if the whole race of them was exterminated."

"Such of them as converse much with *civilized Europeans*, it is too true, learn many things from them, which are a disgrace to their own *Savage* nature, as you call it. But I speak of the general disposition of the people. Treat them with candour, probity, and tenderness, and they will return them tenfold, in all their intercourse with you; as on the other hand, they seldom fail to retort the contrary treatment with severe usury. Nor are they to be blamed. In all their dealings with the *Europeans*, they find themselves imposed upon in the grossest manner; in a manner not fit to be practised even with brutes. Their sensibility is quick, and their passions ungoverned; perhaps ungovernable: How then can it be wondered at that they make returns in kind, whenever they find opportunity, and become the most dangerous enemies? Whereas if those passions were attached by good treatment, they would be the most affectionate, steady, and careful friends. I speak from experience. I treat them as rational creatures; and they behave as such to me. I never deceive them; and they never deceive me. I do them all the good offices in my power; and they return them manifold. In short, I practise to them the behaviour which I wish to meet from them, and am never disappointed. All the evils which have been suffered from them have proceeded from the unhappy error of thinking ourselves possessed of a superiority over them, which nature, that is, heaven, has not given us. They are our fellow-creatures; and, in general, above our level, in the virtues which give real pre-eminence, however despicably we think of and injuriously we treat them."

"They are much obliged to your character of them at least; whatever others may be. And pray, Sir, what is it you would have me do, to preserve the good opinion of these most *virtuous people?*"

"I presume not, Sir, to say what is proper for you to do. All I desire is that you will dismiss me directly, in a capacity of making good my promises to my friends; and by the time you say you shall be ready to move with the army, I hope to give a good account of the enemy."

"That, Sir, I have no thought of. However, as you are so desirous of going, I shall not detain you. I'll form a plan of operations for you this very day."

"For me, Sir! I do not understand you. How can you know what will be proper or possible for me to do, at the distance of many hundred miles, in a country you are an utter stranger to. In *Europe*, where war, like a game of chess, is *played*, as I may say, entirely by art, that method of planning in the closet the operations of the field may do perhaps; but then it is necessary that each side should play the game by the same rules. A body of *Americans*, who know nothing of the art of war but fighting, might be apt to move so irregularly, as to disconcert the whole scheme of the *game*. Indeed, by what I can judge of the matter, that very method of planning the operations of a campaign is advantageous only to the general, as it prolongs the war, and consequently the emoluments of command, by tying up his hand from availing himself of any unforeseen circumstances in his favour. Whereas if armies were sent out only to fight, as formerly before the *improvements* in the art of war, the dispute would soon be decided, and even the vanquished better off than the victors are at present, whose riches and strength are so exhausted by this dilatory way of proceeding, that they are not the better for their success. I hope, Sir, you do not take offence at the plainness of my speech. I have so long been accustomed to converse with *Savages*, who speak just what they think, that I am become quite a stranger to that *dissimulation*, which is called *politeness*, among *civilized* nations; and must make use of words, in their original intention of conveying my thoughts."

"Not in the least, Sir! I like your free manner much. It is in the character of a soldier. I will order every thing to be got ready for you directly; and you shall go as soon as you please, at full liberty to act as you see proper."

"I hope, Sir, I shall not make a bad use of that liberty. And pray, among the other things, do not forget to order me some money."

"Money, Sir! What occasion can you possibly have for money, among *Savages*, who do not know the value of it?"

"Why really, Sir, that question is natural. But the matter is, the *Savages* who come among the *Europeans* see every thing governed by gold, in such a manner, that they have taken it into their heads we worship it; and therefore are become as eager for it as ourselves, in hopes of gaining an ascendancy over us, when they have got our god in their possession."

A conscious heart takes to itself more than was ever meant. The dry manner in which this was said touched my master to the quick, and made him not desire to pursue the conversation any farther with such a free speaker, nor have so nice an observer longer about him to pry into the motives of his actions. Giving him therefore the money he required, he wished him success with a forced politeness, and dismissed him to prepare for his departure.

It was a pleasure to me to change my service on this occasion; as the idea I had conceived of my new master, both from his appearance and conversation, promised me some variety, and my curiosity was heartily surfeited with the regular art of war.

CHAPTER II

The manner in which *Chrysal's* master was received by his subjects. Antiquated principles on which his authority was founded. His odd opinions and conduct in some important matters, with the consequences.

As soon as every thing was ready, my master set out for home, where he arrived without meeting any thing remarkable in his journey, as you may suppose, through uninhabited deserts.

The reception he met with from his people was the very reverse of what *Sovereigns* usually meet. They welcomed him with sincere joy and respect, which they expressed in the overflowing of their hearts, without ceremony or parade: I say, "Sovereigns," as he really enjoyed that power in its most rational sense, his will being a law to all around him, *because they always found it just and advantageous to them.*

Though the account which he gave my late master of his manner of treating his people shewed a just foundation for his power over them, I found that it depended not on that alone. His authority, like that of the first rulers of the earth, was founded also on the relations of nature, and supported by its strongest ties, he being literally the father of his subjects, the king of his own family.

To explain this it is necessary to inform you, that on his fixing his residence among these *uncivilized* nations, in order to gain an influence over them the more readily, he had laid aside all such rules of conduct as seemed to him to be contradictory to natural reason, and the public good, however forcibly enjoined for particular convenience.

Among these the chief was the custom of restraining the commerce between the sexes, and confining individuals to each other, after the desire which first brought them together had ceased; as he saw that the strongest passion which governs the human heart is that desire, (for his philosophy was not refined enough to suggest one thought of governing the passions) and as the continuation of the species depends entirely on the gratification of it, he held every opposition to it to be most criminal in itself, and detrimental to the public good, (properly the first object of every civil institution, and which can be promoted no way so effectually, as by promoting population) and therefore exerted all his influence to encourage that commerce, under such restrictions only, as were evidently necessary to procure the great end of it, the propagation of the species. He gave liberty to every man to converse with as many females as he pleased; and to quit them whenever he thought proper, provided they were not pregnant. To the women the former liberty could not be extended, as the use of it would defeat the design; or, where it had not immediately that effect, cause confusion, and prevent both paternal care, and filial duty, by the uncertainty of descent: But the latter instance they enjoyed equally with the men, being allowed to choose whom they liked; and if not pregnant, quit them at pleasure, for others, without reproach or shame; the offspring of all which connections were to remain with the fathers.

I shall not say whether reason originally suggested this system to him; or (as is often the case) whether he sought for reasons to support the dictates of inclination. Be it which it would, the effect was the same. His subjects increased in an uncommon degree; and he founded, like the patriarchs of old, an authority on the justest of all principles, voluntary consent, over a people inseparably linked to him, and to each other, by the strongest ties of nature, as being by this complicated commerce in the strictest sense one family; for disdaining to make laws for others, which he would not observe himself, (like too many of his brother legislators) he had enforced his precepts so powerfully by his example, that there was scarce an house in any of the tribes around him, from which he had not taken a temporary mate, and added a child of his to their number.[78]

---

78 Johnson had three children with Catherine Weisenberg, whom he called his wife although they were never officially married, and eight with his housekeeper, "sister of the Mohawk leader Joseph Brant" (DNB). Although Johnstone's account is undoubtedly hyperbolic, it typifies popular tellings of Johnson's domestic life. Local legend held that Warraghiyagey was "the father of a hundred children, mostly by native mothers, who were young squaws, or the wives of natives who thought it an honor to have them intimate with the distinguished king's agent" (Arthur Pound, *Johnson of the Mohawks*).

That his reception, as I have observed, should be most cordial from such subjects, is not to be wondered at. They flocked about him on his arrival, and hailing him with one voice by every tender relation of nature, brother, father, son, husband, shewed an affection too sublime to be expressed by formal rules, and impossible to be seen without sympathizing in it.

When this tribute was paid to nature, he called the elders of the people together, and distributing among them the presents which he had received for that purpose, gave them an account of the mighty army sent by his Sovereign against the enemy, and proposed to them to assist its operations.

There required not many arguments to confirm their confidence, in one who had never deceived them. They readily and sincerely assented to his proposal, and sending to invite all their neighbours to join them, separated to make the very little preparations necessary for persons who were strangers to luxury, and knew no wants but those of nature.

CHAPTER III

Chrysal describes his master's habitation and family. He makes an uncommon progress. The manner in which he found the females of his household engaged. Remarks on *finery*. Account of their amusements, with the manner in which they usually ended. The method by which *Chrysal's* master kept peace in his family.

As soon as my master had thus concluded the business of his public character, he retired to devote a few minutes to his domestic concerns.

His habitation was built on an eminence by the side of a rivulet, the banks of which were covered with a number of neat little cottages, inhabited by the females of his present family; for instead of attempting to prevent their quitting him for other men, as inclination led them, he not only always dismissed them with presents in the most friendly manner, but also kept up an intercourse of regard with them and their successive husbands, every one of whom he attached to himself in the strongest manner, being particularly ready on all occasions to do them every good office in his power.

In these cottages they bred up their children, and enjoyed from his care all the necessaries of life with more convenience and comfort than they could possibly have experienced among their own people, unembittered by any of those jealousies and feuds which such a situation might seem to threaten, so equally did he dispense his favours among them.

When he had given some orders in his house, he walked out to visit his family, and enjoy the sublimest instance of the happiness of power, in making all who were subject to it happy, by the unaffected tenderness with which he enquired after their welfare, and returned their caresses, on his entering every cottage.

The appearance of these females was most different from the delicate sensibility that softened the beauties of *Amelia*,*[79] or the fire which animated the charms of *Olivia*; but custom, that reconciles all things, had made them agreeable to him, especially as no comparison could there be made to their disadvantage; and the honest readiness with which they met his addresses, the warmth with which they shared his joy, amply overbalanced any imaginary defect in feature or complexion; any ignorance of those affected arts of coyness, which overacted often pall the taste for long expected pleasure.

As his women did not expect his visit so soon, he found them engaged, according to their different inclinations, either in the management of their domestic œconomy, or in such amusements as custom had made pleasing to them. The occupations of the former kind were necessarily confined within a narrow circle, from the circumstances of their lives; but in the latter, fancy, sole sovereign of the scene, asserted her unbounded rule, and sported in variety of forms, many of which I soon had an opportunity of seeing.

As my master proceeded in his patriarchal progress, he met a considerable number of the females of his family, with such of the neighbouring men, as from age or idleness were unfit for more useful employments, assembled together under a spreading tree,

---

79 Johnstone's note here directs the reader to I.I.IV. See 1.33-43.

that grew before the door of one of their cottages, dressed out in
their gayest apparel, and engaged in different kinds of diversions.
At the sight of him they all arose, and would have desisted, but
he prevented them; and not only made them resume their sports,
but also sat down himself, in the midst of the company, to be a
spectator of them.

It seems it was a custom among them to meet frequently
thus at each other's cottages, for the pleasure of enjoying their
favourite amusements to more advantage together, and displaying
their *finery*, to set off which, no art nor care was neglected on these
occasions. They dressed themselves in their best blankets, which
were covered all over with patches of various colours to make
them look more gaudy. Their heads were adorned with plumes of
feathers. Strings of glass-beads were rolled around their arms and
legs. Their toes were loaded with rings of pewter and brass; and
their necks and faces were carved with figures of birds and flowers,
and painted of various hues.

I see your laughter moved at this description; but that proceeds
from narrow prejudice, and want of rational reflection, on which
it would appear that all useless ornaments are equally just objects
of ridicule, whether made of silks, and laces, or parti-coloured
rags; whether bits of glass, or pearls and diamonds. Think, I say,
but for a moment; and you will see that in reality there is nothing
more absurd in wearing one kind of metal, or upon one part of
the body, than another, *rings of brass*, for instance, *on the toes*, than
golden on the fingers; in *carving the skin*, than *boring the ears*; or *in
painting the face blue and green*, than *white* and *red*. The same vanity
is the motive of all, and all produce the same effect of admiration;
as in things equally unsupported by reason, custom and caprice
bear equal sway. The difference in the means therefore makes
none in the end; at least none to the disadvantage of the persons
of whom I speak, as it certainly is more absurd to lavish treasures,
that might be so much better employed, to a worthless purpose
which cheaper bawbles would answer as well.

The amusements, in which they were engaged, were as
whimsical as their dresses. Some skipped about, describing various
figures in their motions, till want of breath and weariness obliged
them to sit down. Others, and these the greatest number, were

employed in chucking shells or pebbles from the brook, into holes dug in the sand, for prizes of bits of tin, or brass, which game they applied themselves to with the greatest eagerness and anxiety, and many were so expert at it, as to strip their antagonists of all their hoards, often indeed not without the assistance of chicanery and deceit: And a few of the eldest, and those who had nothing to stake at play, gathered up and down into little sets, and entertained themselves making remarks upon the rest, not always dictated by good-nature or truth; while the mistress of the cottage busied herself in adjusting ceremonials, settling her company at their several amusements, and serving them with milk, or broth, and tobacco, the fatigue of which office she never repined at, as her consequence was established by the number of her guests.

Though mere amusement was the obvious end of these meetings, other objects were generally pursued, and other consequences produced by them. Intrigues were commenced, and often completed; and trifling as the prizes were for which they contended, emulation and avarice agitated the passions, and set the competitors together by the ears, till they almost clawed out each other's eyes.

Their sports were at length beginning to take their usual turn. The tempers of the losers became soured; and the detection of some *deep* strokes of play gave rise to altercations, which would soon have been followed by blows; but my master interposed his authority, and put an end to their disputes, when the party broke up; some retiring to keep the assignations they had made in the warmth of their inclinations, and the rest to calculate their winnings, or devise schemes for retrieving their losses, at the next meeting; and my master having singled out the happy favourite of that night, repaired with her to his own habitation, without any of the rest taking offence, or even particular notice of the preference, as they had it in their power to supply their loss elsewhere.

I have observed your astonishment at this whole scene, especially at my master's hardiness in expecting to be happy among a number of women, and attempting to keep them in order together, when one, in your opinion, is more than any man can manage; but what will it be, when I tell you that that number often amounted to hundreds; and that he never had recourse to any kind of severity, in his conduct to them?

To comprehend this, it is necessary for you to consider, that most of, if not all, the uneasinesses which embitter the life of man arise from an officious intrusion to the uneasinesses of others, or an overweening partiality to himself, that makes him expect treatment, which he does not give, and take offence where none is meant him, for matters not worth his being offended at; an observation that will hold in every state, public and private; among *governors*, as well as *governed*.

His rule then was never to take part in their disputes among themselves, nor offence at their infidelity to his bed, of which he himself set them the example. This disarmed them of that *perverseness which is the sex's most offensive weapon*. They remained constant to him, because they were not restrained from being otherwise, whenever they pleased; nor did they trouble him with their disputes, because they saw he would not be troubled at them.

CHAPTER IV

Chrysal's master is honourably rewarded for his services. An unexpected meeting with one of his country-women, introduces an uncommon remark on a common matter. The lady gives an odd instance of conjugal love; and refuses the civil offer of *Chrysal's* master, for a natural reason. *Chrysal* changes his service.

THE very next morning his people assembled before his door, in readiness to obey his commands, when he led them directly in quest of the enemy, sharing himself in all their fatigues, and teaching them to despise danger by his example, so little did he know the duty of a general.

It would be tiresome to enter into a particular description of an expedition, carried on among wildernesses and deserts, and consisting chiefly of ambuscades and surprises. It is sufficient to say that he was successful in all his enterprizes, reason and presence of mind serving him instead of experience, in the regular art of war; and courage well supplying the place of discipline in his men.

Such services could not miss of reward from a just and judicious

Sovereign. His power was enlarged; and he received those marks of favour and distinction, which were originally instituted to excite virtuous emulation, and set the seal of honour on successful merit;[80] though like most other human institutions, they too often produce the contrary effect, and reflect only disgrace, from being bestowed contrary to their intention, and on unworthy objects.

As he was preparing the way thus for the motions of the main army, whenever the general should think proper to let it move, some of his people brought before him an *European* lady, whom they found wandering in those unfrequented wilds, her guide having mistaken his way.

Such a situation necessarily entitled her to his compassion and assistance; but he soon felt himself still farther interested in her favour, when he found she was a native of his own country, and of a family not entirely unknown to him, before he came to fix his abode in this distant part of the world.

There is not a stronger instance of the force of that attachment, called in a larger sense *patriotism*, than the instinctive affection which persons of the same country, though utterly unacquainted before, feel for each other the moment they meet in a strange place. My master instantly called her his dear country-woman, and embracing her with the tenderness of a brother, led her away to his own tent, which he resigned to her, as the best accommodation he could give her; and then went and ordered every thing that had belonged to her, which his men looking upon as fair prize had taken and divided among themselves, to be restored, promising to recompense the captors himself.

As soon as she had adjusted her appearance, in some better manner, she went to desire my master's company, for he had told her that he should not come without permission, for fear of intruding improperly upon her; and on his expressing wonder what could have brought her thus into the midst of those deserts so far away from every *European* settlement, she gratified his curiosity with the following account, which was often interrupted by sighs, tears, and every expression of the most poignant grief.

---

80 For defeating French forces at the Battle of Lake George, Johnson "became a war hero, rewarded with £5,000 from Parliament and a baronetcy from the crown" (DNB).

Her husband, (she said) who had been an officer of distinguished rank in the *English* forces, had fallen in one of the defeats they suffered in the beginning of the war, before *England* had exerted herself in such a manner as to entitle her to success; the news of whose death affected her so extraordinarily, that she resolved to brave all the fatigues and dangers of so long a voyage by sea, and journey through uninhabited deserts in time of war, for the melancholy pleasure of one last view of his dear remains, which she had accordingly obtained, though not so much to her satisfaction as she could have wished, the body being in a state of putrefaction, not possible to be approached without disgust and abhorrence; nor to be distinguished from any other mass of corruption, when she had caused it to be dug out of the grave, in which it had been buried on the spot where he had been killed, among the other victims of the day; and was now returning home, when she had happily been found by his people.

Though my master was as much unversed in the regular rules of politeness, as of war, good-nature taught him the essentials of one, as reason had of the other. He heard out her story, though not without pity and contempt at the extravagance and folly of it; and consoling her with some general remarks on the error of indulging immoderate grief, for things not to be remedied, offered to send her under a sufficient escort to his own habitation, where she might remain in safety, and have the conversation and attendance of his women, till the conclusion of the campaign, when he would convey her himself to the next sea-port, in order to her returning to her own country.

Though she would have looked upon any attempt to console her, as the highest affront, in another situation, her present circumstances made her think it not proper to shew any resentment of it to him: besides, there was something in his appearance, that some how made it less disagreeable from him, than it would have been from any other person; and would possibly have influenced her to accept of his offer, had not the mention of *his women* alarmed her delicacy, and set her virtue on its guard.

Resolving therefore to have this cleared up, before she would give any direct answer to his offer, she expressed her high sense of his kindness in the politest terms; and entering into a general conversation, among other questions of mere curiosity, asked him in a careless manner, whom he meant by *his women*, and in what capacity they served him?

Such a question was more than he desired, though he had inconsiderately laid himself open to it. However, as he thought no delicacy could justify deceit, he answered her directly and without preface, that they served him in the natural capacity of women, while they pleased to continue with him; nor did he desire any other service from them.

Though she was a good deal disconcerted at this answer, she had the address not to seem to understand it, in hopes that he would take the hint, and explain himself in a meaning less offensive to her modesty; to give him an opportunity for which, "I presume, Sir," (replied she) "you mean that they wait upon your lady, or perform the other domestic offices of your family, in which women servants only are employed?"

"No really, madam," (answered he) "that was not my meaning. I have no lady for them to wait upon; nor do they live so immediately in my own family, as to have any domestic employment in it."

"How, Sir! Are you not married?"

"Not particularly to any one person, madam."

—"That's very strange!" (said she, pleased at having gained so material a piece of intelligence, and resolving to pursue the conversation). "That is really very strange. And pray, Sir, are these ladies *Europeans?* I suppose" (sighing heavily, and wiping her eyes) "they are the unhappy widows of such officers as have fallen in the service, to whom you have shewn the same politeness and humanity, as I now experience from you."

"I am sorry, madam," (answered he, to satisfy her curiosity at once, and put a stop to questions which began to be troublesome) "to be obliged to undeceive you in an opinion so favourable to me; they are all native *Americans*, by whom I have had children; and in whose unfeigned affection, and easy complying tempers, I find such satisfaction, that I never shall quit them to attach myself solely to any one woman, however superior to them in the advantages of beauty and education; not, indeed, that they want qualifications to raise both love and esteem, as you will find when you have been some time among them."

This, which was too plain for her to affect not to understand it, instantly put an end to the pleasure she had begun to find in his conversation, and determined her as to his proposal. "I am much obliged to you for your civil offer, Sir," (said she, bridling up her chin,[81] and making him a formal courtesy)[82] "but I cannot accept of it. I have not the least desire for the conversation of *Squaws*, and am in haste to leave this savage place; for which reason I shall take it as a favour, if you will send some of your people to guard me to the next *English* settlement to-morrow morning. At present I am quite exhausted with fatigue, and want some rest, if the distress of my heart will permit me to take any."

This thought recalled the remembrance of her loss: She burst into a flood of tears; and my master withdrew, after finding that his attempts to console her only aggravated her grief, and gave offence to her delicacy.

Unversed as he was in the ways of the polite world, he was too well acquainted with the ruling principles of the sex, which in every state are the same, not to see through this change in her behaviour; but the discovery had no other effect, than to confirm him in his contempt for such hypocritical levity. Accordingly, finding she continued in the same mind next morning, he made the best provision he could for her journey, and sent her away with a sufficient guard, forcing upon her a purse of gold, (*in which I was*) to defray any accidental expence, for which she might be unprovided, in case she should not directly meet a ship ready to carry her to *Europe*.

81 "To hold up the head" (Johnson), "expressing pride, vanity, or resentment; to assume a dignified or offended air or manner" (OED).
82 "The reverence made by women" (Johnson). A curtsey.

CHAPTER V

Chrysal's mistress gives some striking instances of female consistency. She
is cured of her grief by a person of accomplishments as extraordinary
as her own. The advantage of comparative excellence. *Chrysal's*
mistress marries, and he changes his service for that of an old master.

As soon as my mistress found herself out of sight of my late master,
she gave vent to that indignation and rage of disappointment,
which she had thought proper to suppress while in his presence.
"Insensible brute!" (said she) "Not quit his odious *Squaws* for any
woman! And to have the rudeness to tell me so to my face! It shews
his gross, low taste, for which such animals are fittest."

Then pausing for some moments; "What a charming figure!"
(continued she, sighing softly) "Such a size! Such strength and ease
in every motion! And then the manly beauty in his looks! Had I
but the polishing[83] of him! I was too hasty, I should have waited to
insinuate myself into his heart by degrees. I could not have failed
of success. My husband was as strongly attached to another when
first I undertook him. Oh! dearest, best of men! Never shall I meet
your fellow! Never shall another possess your place in this faithful,
wretched heart."

A flood of tears here interrupted her meditations, which were
often renewed in the same strain during her journey, and always
ended the same way.

On her arrival at the sea-port, she had the mortification to find
that she must wait some time for a passage home, all the ships
which were there, having sailed a few days before.

But her vexation at this disappointment was considerably
lightened by the conversation of several companions in it,
particularly that of a chaplain of a regiment, who had taken such
offence at the immorality of the army, and the uncomfortable way
of living in those savage countries, that he had hired a substitute, at
a cheap rate, to do his duty, and was returning home to enjoy a life

---

83 Making "more elegant or cultured, or improving something or someone"
(OED).

more agreeable to the delicacy of his character and inclinations, and exert his talents to more advantage in paying court to his patrons, than in reforming soldiers or converting savages.

Extremes are never lasting: The violence of my mistress's grief had been too much for nature to support, and was beginning to abate of itself, when my late master awoke another passion, that would soon have supplanted it; and though he did not pursue his advantage as far as he might have done, he had opened her heart, and inspired a warmth ready to receive any other impression.

As the chaplain's function, and her rank, not to omit the accomplishments of both, seemed to point them to each other as the most proper companions, it was not strange that they should soon grow intimate, nor that their intimacy should be insensibly improved into a tenderer passion. They made *tete a tete* parties, at games which no one else in the place knew how to play with them. They talked of all the places of pleasurable resort in England, and of the amusements pursued at them: and they raised their own consequence in the eyes of each other, by boasting of acquaintances with persons they knew only by name.

Such uncommon accomplishments were not without effect. Each took the tales of the other upon credit, because their own met the same complaisance; and found a pleasure in being deceived by one whom it was an equal pleasure to deceive.

But this was not the only thing that advanced their mutual influence upon each other. All human excellence is but comparative. Though far from being beautiful, they were the nearest to being so; though far from being well-bred, they knew most of the common ceremonies, in which good-breeding is by many thought to consist, but which really are the encumbrances of it, of any persons there; and consequently appeared to enjoy those advantages in the highest degree. They regulated the assemblies, they laid down the rules of play, they made fashions; in a word, their opinion was the law in every matter of polite amusement and concern.

Thus *cut out* for each other, it was impossible for this accomplished pair not to come together. They were accordingly married, not more to the grief of their respective admirers, than the joy of their rivals, the bride forgetting her grief for a dead, in the arms of a living husband, and the happy bridegroom pleasing himself with the thought that the high accomplishments of his lady would increase his interest with his noble patrons.

To crown their happiness, in a few days after they were married, an *English* man of war put in there, in its way home, the captain of which politely offered them their passage. Such an opportunity was not to be missed: they accepted his offer with the greatest joy, and in return made a *party* and entertainment for him, when he won *me* from my mistress at a game of *brag*,[84] the only game indeed at which he thought himself a match for her.

Though I had no reason to regret leaving her service, my present change gave me no great pleasure, as it wanted even the recommendation of novelty; my new master being the captain, with whom I had left the *Spanish* coast, who had at length been made so happy as to be ordered home.

CHAPTER VI

Chrysal arrives in *England*. His master is saluted by a sight not very pleasing. The history of the unfortunate hero of the day opens some mysterious scenes. *The obvious use of councils of war.*

(Chrysal's *master having in the course of his voyage home given offence to his officers, by his prudential regard to his own safety; to obviate any bad consequences which might attend their complaining to his superiors, he resolved to employ* Chrysal's *mediation in his favour, as soon as he should arrive in* England.—I.I.X. See 1.62.)

His arrival in *England* presented him with a scene that confirmed this resolution, and made him wish he had not been in such haste to return. On his entering the harbour, he found the boats of the men of war there drawn up around one ship, in which was displayed the dreadful signal of the execution of the commander.[85]

---

84 A card game "essentially identical with the modern game of 'poker'" (OED).
85 KEY: "Adml. Byng." John Byng (bap. 1704, d. 1757), sentenced to death for commanding an ill-fated, poorly-conceived mission to save Minorca from French invasion. From the fall of the fortress in June 1756 until Byng's March

The sight appalled his soul, conscience anticipating the stroke of justice, and taking this as an omen of his own fate.

He had not time to brood over these gloomy reflections long, when an officer came on board him with an order to attend the execution in his boat, along with the other captains, which he obeyed, in a state of mind scarce less unhappy than that of the criminal.

As soon as the bloody work was done, he waited on the chief commander, where the melancholy, in every face he met, was far from relieving the anxiety of his mind. He could have no pleasure in such company. When he had answered a few general questions of course, he went away to the ship of a captain of his intimate acquaintance, to learn some account of this shocking scene, for he had not had resolution to make any enquiry about it; nor even to attend to the conversation of every one around him, which would have explained the whole.

After mutual congratulations on their meeting, my master signified his curiosity, which his friend promised to gratify *over their bottle*, as soon as they should be alone after dinner.

Accordingly, when *the coast was clear*, "You desire information in an affair" (said he) "that has given our corps the deepest wound we have ever received. The circumstances are many, and mysterious; but I will strive to give you a notion of it in as few words as possible, for it can be no pleasure to either of us to dwell upon such a subject.

"In the beginning of the war, soon after you went out to *America*, the unfortunate man who has this day fallen a sacrifice to the humour of the times, was sent out with a fleet to counteract the schemes of the enemy, and relieve a fortress of ours which they were then besieging.[86] (This was the purport of his *public orders*; but

---

1757 execution, "Minorca completely dominated politics" (DNB), and the trial was breathlessly covered by the London press; Walpole wrote that "no history was every so extraordinary, or produced such variety of surprising turns" as the trial of John Byng. The hero of Voltaire's *Candide* likewise witnesses Byng's execution, and is given a tongue-in-cheek rationale: "in this country it's good to kill an admiral from time to time to encourage the others."

86 KEY: "Minorca." In March 1756, Byng was promoted to Admiral and sent to protect Fort St. Phillip in Minorca from possible invasion. The Admiralty, however, headed by Lord Anson (see 1.78 and 1.122-27), refused to believe the French would

it will appear to you presently, that he must have received *private* ones, of a very different nature, from those who at that time had the conduct of affairs.)

"Instead of making the expedition necessary to have carried his orders into execution with effect, he trifled away the time here, in such a shameful manner, using every frivolous excuse he could devise to delay his departure, that the voice of the public was raised against him; and it was found necessary to appoint another to the command in his place, in order to silence their clamour; but unfortunately for him, he sailed the very day before his appointed successor was to have set out to supersede him.

"The same dilatory conduct threw a damp upon every thing he attempted to do. He seemed resolved upon nothing; but though he was invested with the fullest powers to act as he saw proper himself, called councils of war to deliberate upon every the most trifling occasion, that he might have the sanction of their advice to excuse his neglect, and often direct disobedience of his orders; for you well know, that *a council of war always speaks the sense of the commander*.

"One instance of his proceeding in this manner will be sufficient to justify this remark. He had been ordered to call at another fortress in his way,[87] and take from thence a reinforcement for the garrison of that which he was sent to relieve. On his arrival there, instead of demanding that reinforcement peremptorily, as his orders empowered him, and making the expedition, which the urgency of the occasion required, he shewed such indifference to the enterprize by his delays, and expressed such diffidence of his success, that the commanding officer[88] took the alarm; and

---

actually attack. After needless delays and outfitted with too few ships, Byng took nearly a month to reach the British fort at Gibraltar, where General Thomas Fowke was to contribute additional troops for the defense of Minorca. When Fowke balked, Byng sailed onward without reinforcements. Byng further failed to land troops at the fort, and again failed to engage the French fleet when meeting them on route. Concluding there was little the British fleet or reinforcements could do to prevent the surrender of Minorca, British forces abandoned the mission and returned to Gibraltar. Admiral Byng was arrested, court-martialed, and finally executed by firing squad at noon on March 14, 1757.

87 KEY: "Gibraltar."

88 KEY: "Genl. Fawke." General Thomas Fowke (d. 1765), governor of Gibraltar.

following his example, called a council of war to consider whither he should send it, which on mature deliberation he absolutely refused, on account of the danger of weakening his own garrison, in case it should be attacked; whereas, it was notorious that could never happen, if this unhappy man did his duty, as the force he had was sufficient to keep the command of the sea, and prevent any such attempt. But far from urging this, he quietly acquiesced in the officer's excuse, and sailed away without the reinforcement, for which alone he had been ordered to stop there.

"On the same principles, when at length he came in sight of the place, the siege of which was pushed with the greatest vigour, he excused his sending any relief to it, on a pretence of the danger of entering the harbour, as if any military operations could be free from danger, and sailed away to seek a fleet of the enemy, which was coming to assist the siege, and which he came up with sooner than he wished.

"An engagement now was unavoidable; but still he had it in his power to prevent any effect from it, which he notoriously did, by trifling away his time in vain unnecessary *manoeuvres*, and pretending to come to action at a distance too great for him to do any thing.[89]

"The enemy, whose interest it was to avoid an engagement, in which their most sanguine hopes could not promise them success, availed themselves of this conduct, and made their escape; after having, from the superiority which his *keeping aloof* in this manner gave them, treated very roughly a part of his fleet that had advanced with less caution, and come really to action.

Fowke justified his refusal to supply Byng with reinforcements by claiming he was given contradictory sets of orders. As reported in the *Gentleman's Magazine*, he was found guilty at court martial in August 1756, and sentenced to suspension from service for one year. King George II, however, "observed, That if he was unfit for service for *one* year, he certainly was so for ever," and expelled Fowke from the armed forces.

89 When battling the French fleet, Byng gave unclear signals to his captains, and the rear division of his fleet did not engage. The Admiral justified his actions by claiming he was attempting to avoid the missteps of Thomas Mathews (see 2.79). Byng's jury eventually found him guilty of the charge that "he did withdraw or keep back, and did not do his utmost to take, seize, and destroy ships of the French King, which it was his duty to have engaged."

"This served him as a pretence for calling a council of war next day, by the advice of which, instead of pursuing the enemy, who had evidently fled from him, or making any attempt to relieve the fortress which was besieged, obviously the first object of his being sent out, he returned directly to the other, from which he was to have taken the reinforcement, as I mentioned before, to defend that from the danger brought upon it solely by his own conduct, leaving the former, deprived thus of every prospect of relief, to take its fate: and giving up the honour of his country by flying from an enemy, whom he might have vanquished, and who had fled from him before."

CHAPTER VII

Continued. Consequence of the foregoing conduct. An extraordinary sentence attempted to be reversed in an extraordinary manner, and by as extraordinary persons. The reason of this; and why it miscarried. More mysteries. Just fate of the *Bunglers*, who left their poor *tool* in the lurch; with the consequence of this affair to a certain corps.

"THE consequence of so strange a conduct was, the nation took fire, and with one voice demanded satisfaction for such a sacrifice of their interest and honour. He was therefore not only deprived of his command, but also sent home a prisoner; and after suffering every indignity and abuse which the rage of a licentious populace broken loose from all bounds could suggest, brought to his trial, found guilty of *neglecting to do all in his power to destroy the enemy*, and for that crime has this day suffered the sentence of the law; a sentence not more unexpected by him, and extraordinary in itself, than in the manner it was passed; and afterwards attempted to be reversed by those who had passed it, when they reflected on the danger of establishing a precedent, that might one day come home to themselves.

"For persuaded (perhaps by their knowledge of the true motives of his conduct) that nothing more was meant by the trial than to amuse the public, they resolved to act their parts in the farce, and found him guilty, as I have said, of such a part only of the charge against him, as common sense could never conceive punishable with death,[90] it being impossible to acquit him absolutely of the whole, without involving themselves in his guilt, by which means they expected to save both his life and their own credit. But such *trimming*[91] seldom answers; *the tables were now turned*; and it was resolved to carry even this lame sentence into execution, with the utmost severity.

"Alarmed at a measure so contrary to their expectations, his judges were driven to their wit's end; and from a provident regard to *themselves* left nothing unattempted to save *him*. They retracted, as far as was in their power, their own judgment! they petitioned the ministry! they applied to the whole body of the legislature. They prayed! they expostulated! they wept! but all was in vain.[92] His fate was determined; and they only drew upon themselves that contempt, which such inconsistency deserved.

"From this general account of his conduct it must have appeared to you, that he acted by *secret* orders, directly opposite to his *public* ones, as no man however prostituted in principle, however infatuated by fear, (neither of which, it was well known, was his case) could otherwise possibly have acted in such a manner, the inevitable consequences of which were disgrace and death. But if any doubt should remain on your mind, from the inconsistency of man's actions at different times, the least attention to the following circumstances will effectually remove it.

"Repeated informations of the enemy's design upon that place had been sent to those in power for a considerable time before;[93]

90 Under the inflexible Twelfth Article of War, Byng's verdict merited execution. The captains and admirals trying him, however, "considered the mandatory punishment too severe" and sent a unanimous plea for mercy to the Admiralty (DNB).
91 "Balancing between opinions or parties so as to remain in favour with both sides" (OED).
92 "Numerous intelligent and humane people," including Voltaire, Walpole, William Pitt, Francis Dashwood and Admiral Keppel, "earnestly tried to prevent Byng's execution." Indeed, excepting King George II, few of those in political or naval command wanted Byng executed. "A noisy populace," however, shared the King's view that Byng was a coward and deserved death (DNB). Byng was likely sacrificed in deference to public opinion.
93 KEY: "Mr. Fox, Sect. State." Henry Fox (1705-74), Secretary of State at the loss of Minorca and the subject of the first four chapters of Volume IV. The

but no notice was taken of them to reinforce the garrison; or even order the officers, regularly belonging to it, to attend their duty, till the siege was actually begun; when this unfortunate man was sent, but so late, that the common impediments of contrary winds might very possibly have delayed him so long as to defeat the design of his going, even had he exerted himself with the greatest ardour.

"Had it also been really intended that he should reinforce the garrison, a force proper for that purpose would have been sent directly from home, without subjecting him to the further delay of stopping for it at another place, where it might not be spared, as proved to be the case.

"And lastly, had he not had secret reasons, which he thought sufficient to justify his conduct, it is not to be imagined that he would have wasted the time before he sailed; that he would have accepted the refusal of the commanding officer of the fortress, from which he was to have taken the reinforcement; that he would not have attempted at least to throw some relief into the place; and that he would not have fought the enemy's fleet, when he had the fairest prospect of defeating it; for the tenor of his former life acquitted him, as I have observed, of all suspicion of cowardice, or traitorous correspondence with the foes of his country.

"His conduct at and after his trial confirmed these remarks. Depending on support from those in power, he neglected the only measure prudence could have suggested for his defence, which was to have retorted the charge of his miscarriage upon his very accusers, and perplexed the cause with such a variety of matter about *disobedience to signals, and breach of discipline*, as to blind the world and bewilder his judges, so that they should be glad to have acquitted him, if only to be rid of the plague of the enquiry; a method which experience had shewn to be effectual, in as flagrant

---

administration of Fox and Newcastle (then Prime Minister) had failed to act on several warnings the French would attack Minorca, including letters sent by Minorca's commander, William Blakeney. Common sentiment held that "the Newcastle administration cast Byng as a scapegoat to hide its own negligence" (DNB); Admiral Augustus Hervey, for example, wrote in his journal that Fox "artfully conducted" a plan with the King, Newcastle and Anson "to sacrifice Admiral Byng in order to screen themselves from the just resentment of the people for the loss of Minorca and other infamous misconducts."

a case as his.[94] And even after he was condemned, his behaviour proved that he expected a pardon to the last moment, for a crime which he had committed in obedience to their orders. Why he did not produce those orders, in his vindication, must have been, that they were only *verbal* ones; which in the blind lust of ministerial confidence and favour, he had been weak enough to take.

"The reason of his being so basely deserted is too obvious. The administration of those who had employed him, had been such a series of blunders, (not to call it by a severer name!) that they had not only been supplanted by another set,[95] who promised better things; but were also obliged to give it up, *as a sin-offering*, to the rage of the people; as protecting, or pardoning him would have implied a participation of his guilt: And in this light the other party viewed it so strongly, that they exerted all their strength to have saved him, in hopes of being able by his means to gain a clue, to guide them through some of those labyrinths of iniquitous and false policy, which they suspected, but could not otherwise detect, to the entire overthrow of their rivals.

"This so absolutely reversed the whole scene, that they who would have supported, now found themselves obliged to crush him, in their own defence, which, as it was the most popular measure, they were still able to do.

"There is but one thing more necessary for me to add: and that is the motive for their giving him such secret orders; which, as far as reason can judge in such dark, confused mysteries, must have been this.

"Provoked at the repeated insults and injustice of the *French*, the ministry here had precipitately plunged themselves into a

---

94 KEY: "Adml. Lestock's." The acquittal of Richard Lestock (1679-1746) for misconduct at the Battle of Toulon (see 2.79, note 61). A parliamentary inquiry and court martial cleared Lestock, placing blame instead with his commander, Admiral Thomas Mathews. Public opinion and the fervent pamphlet-war surrounding the case, however, found it unthinkable that Lestock could be cleared for failing to fight "and the admiral cashiered for fighting." Modern-day historians agree "there is every sign that the exoneration of Lestock was arranged" (DNB) and that the sacrifice of Mathews was politically motivated.

95 KEY: "Mr. Pitt." William Pitt. See 1.302-305. The loss of Minorca prompted the resignations of Newcastle and Fox, and brought Pitt to power as Secretary of State.

war,[96] without being prepared, or even determined to pursue it; and then like a parcel of children who have exhausted all their strength and resolution, in one spiteful assault, stood in a state of stupefaction, utterly at a loss how to proceed or retreat; till roused at length by the preparations and menaces of the enemy, they unluckily blundered in their fright upon the wretched expedient of letting them take this fortress, that for the recovery of it they might have a pretence for giving up to them those places about which the dispute began; and so *botch up* a peace any way, to get rid of a war they found themselves unable to manage.

"The consequence of this notable stroke of policy was, the spirit of the people was inflamed to such a degree by this disgrace upon their arms, that they have pushed on the war with a resolution little short of madness; and the scheme, which the ministers had so wisely laid for their escape, only sealed their ruin.

"This, my friend, is a short but just sketch of this unfortunate affair, to which I shall only add one circumstance to prove what I have said of his being *sacrificed to the humour of the times*. The officer who commanded in the fortress which was besieged,[97] and who in the defence of it had betrayed a want of every qualification necessary for such an office, *but courage*, and had even let that be overruled by the instances of his officers, who were tired of

---

96 KEY: "Captures before the Declaration of War." French and British forces had been fighting in North America for years before the official declaration of war in Europe. In 1755, British forces seized Forts Beauséjour and Gaspareaux on the frontier between Acadia and Nova Scotia.

97 KEY: "Genl. Blakeney," seconded by other keys. William Blakeney (1672-1761), Lieutenant-Governor of Minorca and commander of Fort St. Philip during the French siege. After Byng's promised reinforcements failed to arrive, Blakeney, "after seventy days' defence, surrendered on the honourable terms that his garrison was to be transported to Gibraltar, and not made prisoners of war." He received no blame for the loss of Minorca, although several pamphlets criticized his actions, and contemporary satire contrasted the unfair treatment of Byng with Blakeney's accolades. A 1756 biography depicts him as honest and brave, "a soldier of the soldiers, always living among them, enjoying his punch as well as any of them, and beloved by them" (DNB); and the account of his life which appears in the *Gentleman's Magazine* for that same year commemorates his gallant "defence of *St Philip*, in which he was infamously abandoned to the enemy, with a garrison known to be insufficient to man the works, after he had by repeated letters sollicited a supply."

fatigues and dangers from which they saw no prospect of relief, to surrender it at last, without any absolute necessity, was loaded with honours of every kind,[98] in reward of a merit merely negative at best; that is, for not having done the very worst in his power, and surrendered it at first, without making any defence.

"I have thus gratified your curiosity, in the best manner in my power. If I have made any mistakes, they are not those of intention; but have proceeded from the inability of reason to trace such mysterious actions to their real motives. One observation though, I know I cannot be mistaken in, which is that this affair has given *a wound to our corps,* (as I observed before) *which it can never recover.* For after such an example, what officer, of any rank, can expect to escape should he neglect to do his duty in the fullest manner, however powerful his private motives to the contrary may be?

"For my own part, I cannot say it yet affects me much. I am poor; and therefore must push. If I ever have the good luck to be other, I know the consequence; and will rather quit the service, than hazard being shot, as I know must be any man's fate who shall hereafter be found to fail in the performance of his duty, from a prudential regard to the preservation of his life or fortune; however great that fortune, or powerful his family. And so *here's to you, neck nor nothing* is now the word."

The effect which this whole account had upon my master may be easily conceived. He *pledged* his friend though without *naming* the toast; and assenting to his remarks, by an heavy sigh, took his leave without saying a word.

---

98 Soon after his defense of Minorca, Blakeney was made a Baron in the Irish peerage.

CHAPTER VIII

Chrysal changes his service. He gets a view of a court of *civil judicature*,
on an extraordinary occasion. Some reflections out of the common
cant on the delays of the law. A whimsical application of an old story
produces the strange effect of putting a counsellor out of countenance.
The necessity of absolute power in some government; with a common
decision, by which nothing is decided.

"As soon as my master returned to his ship, he took *me* from his
purse, once more, and looking earnestly at me, for some moments,
'We must part!' (said he, with a sigh) 'we must part! but I hope to
good purpose. *Thou* only wast the cause of that conduct which
now gives me fear; exert therefore thy influence equally, where I
now send thee; and thou wilt excuse my fault, if it is one.'—

Tears, at the thought of losing me, here choked his utterance.
He gave me a last kiss, and sent me directly away, in company with
a considerable number more, to mediate his peace.

As the delicate nature of this transaction required some
address, he entrusted the management of it to his purser, who had
convinced him by many instances, of his sagacity in the methods
of obtaining an influence over the great."*[99]

My new master's road leading through a city, where a matter of
great moment was under judicial determination, he waited for the
event to gratify a natural curiosity.

The affair was this. A *fore-mast-man* in a *guard-ship*, lying in one
of the neighbouring harbours, had by repeated misbehaviour in
going clandestinely on shore, contrary to the express orders of his
captain,[100] provoked him at length to give him *a dozen at the gang-
way*, in order to terrify others from following his example.

---

99 Johnstone's note here directs the reader to 1.62.
100 KEY: "Cap. Hamilton." The identity of this captain is unclear, as is the
lawsuit to which the chapter refers. These kinds of cases, however, were common
in the period. According to N. A. M. Rodger in *The Wooden World*, "officers were
often prosecuted by their men," and lawyers specialized in such suits. Although
the Articles of War "stated specifically that offences committed on shore were

Instead of being reclaimed by this punishment, the fellow persisted to misbehave in such a manner, that the captain, who was remarkably humane in his disposition, discharged him from the ship to avoid the pain of punishing him any more.

This was just what the wretch wanted. Accordingly he went directly to a prostituted, *pettifogging* attorney, who had before set him on the scheme; and employed him to sue the captain at law, for an assault, in punishing him in the harbour, where he had no power so to do.

In a country governed by laws, they must regularly take their course, in every instance however flagrant in its particular circumstances.

After all the preliminary delays of practice, which grievous as they may in some circumstances be to an individual, are yet the safety of the public, the affair was now brought to a legal decision. You are too well acquainted with *the forms of the law* to require a minute account of all which were observed in this case. But there was one incident which I cannot pass over.

As this was a matter that importantly concerned the interest of the navy, the rulers of it had ordered all the captains of the *guardships*, in the harbour where it had happened, to attend the trial, in order to inform the court in the usages of their service.

One of those,[101] who had never seen a court of *civil judicature* before, but was a man of natural good sense and some reading, having listened to the unintelligible pleadings, and gross exaggerations of *the counsel* on both sides of the question, especially those *hired* in the prosecution, till his patience was quite exhausted, at length arose, and having obtained permission from the judge to speak, addressed himself to the court in these words:

"I am sent here by those, to whom the King has entrusted the conduct of his navy, to explain the nature and rules of our service to this court, in case I see any danger of their forming a wrong judgment of it, from inexperience in a matter so much out of their way.

---

cognizable at court martial as if they had been committed at sea," the authority of a captain in the harbor was ill-defined by law.

101 KEY: "Lord Colvill." Perhaps Alexander Colvill (1717-70), Lord Colville of Culross, made Admiral of the British fleet in 1762.

"The little gentleman[102] yonder has spent so much breath, and shewn such great reading on the subject, that I imagine it is proper for me to make him some answer, which I shall do in as few words as possible, being not half so *long-winded* as he. But first I must beg leave to tell him a story, to conform to rule.

"I have read in a book, (for I perceive that common sense signifies nothing here, if not supported by a quotation, it matters not whether to the purpose or not!) that a certain philosopher, having declaimed one day for a considerable length of time before *Alexander the Great,* at the head of his army, on the duties of a general, the Emperor turned about to *Parmenio,*[103] one of his generals who stood near him, and asked him, what he thought of his speech?—'*Sire,*' (answered *Parmenio*) 'my opinion is, that *I never heard a fool talk so learnedly.*'

"I make no applications. All that I say on this occasion is, that I am sure that gentleman has never been at sea; and consequently knows nothing of the service, on which he has been haranguing with such vehemence and elocution. He has expatiated most pathetically on the injustice of inflicting corporal punishment, without a legal trial and condemnation; and flourished on the danger of such an invasion of liberty. These to be sure are fine words; but I much doubt whether they are properly applied on this occasion. The most perfect form of government is allowed to be *absolute despotism,* as best calculated to work its effects without delay. In all the communities in this world, I doubt if there is one, where immediate obedience to the command of the governor is so indispensably necessary to the safety of the whole, or where individuals are so insensible to every other motive to obedience but fear, as in a man of war.

"I have myself the honour to command a ship, in which I have

---

102 KEY: "Mr. Pratt, afterwards Lord Camden." Charles Pratt (1714-94), Earl Camden, who became Attorney General in 1757, then Lord Chancellor in 1766. He was a longtime friend and ally of William Pitt. Pratt reappears in *Chrysal* in Volume IV, in relation to the arrest of John Wilkes (see 2.293), and was also Crown Prosecutor in the trials of Florence Hensey (1.264), John Shebbeare (2.293) and Lord Ferrers (1.287-89).

103 Parmenion, a powerful and accomplished general during the reigns of Philip II and Alexander the Great.

five hundred men under me, the greatest part of whom, (I am sorry to say it) are the *out-casts* of human nature, as from some unhappy circumstances is, and perhaps must always be the universal case in our service. Now as instances daily occur, in which a moment's delay or hesitation to execute my orders, though attended with the greatest difficulty, or most imminent danger, must evidently hazard the loss of the ship, and every life in her; I desire that gentleman to inform me how I am to act, should one of the men, whom I order, suppose, to cut away a yard that's broke in the slings, refuse to go aloft, and tell me I have no right to punish him, till he is regularly tried and found guilty! Shall I admit of such an answer, to be an example to the rest? Or shall I punish him with such severity on the spot, by my own mere authority, as to terrify any other from imitating him? The answer to this plain question will determine the affair under consideration. If it is said that in the present case the ship's being in the harbour makes a difference, let us suppose her on fire there, and that difference will vanish. In a word, if the absolute authority indispensably necessary for carrying on our service in some instances is attempted to be abridged in any, it will of course be at length disputed in all, and the service ruined. All that can be done is to be cautious not to trust it in improper hands."

This method of reasoning changed the face of the affair. The counsellor hung down his head, and slunk out of the court. The fears which had been entertained for public liberty vanished; and the jury simply *found the fact*, but left *the point* of law to be determined by the judges; so that after all this expence and trouble, matters remained in the same state of uncertainty as before, to the great joy of the lawyers.

CHAPTER IX

Chrysal's master joins a remarkable set of company. Their characters. *Chrysal* changes his service. Account of the enterprize on which his late master's companions were going; with the convincing arguments they used to procure obedience to their commands.

(The purser having on his arrival in London parted with Chrysal *regularly, in the execution of the commission entrusted to him by his captain;* Chrysal, *now in the shape of a Guinea, after several changes of service, and a variety of curious adventures, has fallen into the hands of a* Physician *and* Author; *who, having shewn him many of the mysteries of the latter profession, proceeds to introduce him into new scenes.—I.I.XIX. See 1.112.)*

Happy in the contemplation of his own abilities, and the pleasing prospect they opened to him, my master[104] proceeded to *figure* as usual in his variegated sphere. Accordingly he descended from his *aerial citadel,* and going out *to visit his patients,* repaired directly to a tavern, to join a set of *critics,* and *choice spirits, souls of sentiment and fire,* who were going that evening upon an expedition that was to immortalize their names.

This was no less than to assume the modest power of making laws that should affect the property of a number of their fellow subjects; the execution of which they were resolved to enforce by the mild and equitable means, which the respectable legislature of the mob always use to enforce obedience to their decrees.

Those who were honoured by being taken thus under their immediate command, were *the actors of plays* and *interludes,* of which, as the works of *genius,* and calculated for the entertainment of *the idle,* they claimed the sole and absolute rule.

You conclude from this, that they must have been persons of learning, and large fortune, whose affluence gave them leisure to attend to subjects, which their education qualified them to judge of; but the contrary was the fact. They were either *blanks in the creation,* whom a superficial smattering of letters had filled with

---

104 KEY: "Dr. Hill." John Hill, first encountered in Volume I. See 1.102-12.

such an opinion of themselves,[105] as to make them look with contempt upon every exertion of industry as beneath their dignity, though at the same time they were barely able to subsist without it, by all the little shifts of œconomy; or tradesmen,[106] almost absolutely illiterate, who from a preposterous ambition of hiding an ignorance that was not any reproach to their station, set up for the arbiters of taste, on the strength of a set of phrases picked up at random, and of which they knew not even the meaning; and neglected the business by which they were to earn their bread, in order to make a shew of knowledge that could be of no use to them.

When this illustrious set had sufficiently conned[107] their several parts, in the great enterprize which they were going to undertake, and raised their resolutions to a proper pitch by wine, they prepared to adjoin to the scene of action, the theatre; and calling for a *bill*, I was *changed* by my master to pay his *club*, and directly borrowed from the landlord by one of the leaders of the party, who *changed* me again at the door of the theatre, to pay for his admission.

These changes of my service however did not prevent my

---

105 KEY: "Mr. Fitz Patrick." Thaddeus Fitzpatrick, journalist and critic. He appears in the *Town and Country Magazine* as Theatricus, a "constant attendant at the playhouses" and "a first-rate theatrical critic," whose judgment could determine "the success or failure of a new piece, or a young actor." Fitzpatrick's longtime rivalry with David Garrick led to the half-price riots of 1763, the subject of this chapter. After Garrick discontinued the traditional practice of half-price admission after the third act, Fitzpatrick and his followers roused support at local coffeehouses, then fomented an uprising at Garrick's theatre, where "the benches were torn up, the glass lustres were broke and thrown on the stage, and a total confusion ensued" (*Daily Advertiser*). Riots again erupted a month later at Covent Garden theatre, then managed by John Beard, where the damage, estimated at £2000, "was the greatest ever known ... all the benches of the boxes and pit chandeliers broken, and the linings of the boxes cut to pieces." Fitzpatrick and his coterie are satirized in Garrick's *Miss in Her Teens* (1747) and *The Fribbleriad* (1761), which dwell on his pomposity and effeminacy, and in Charles Churchill's *The Rosciad* (see 2.263), where he is "a six-foot suckling, mincing in Its gait, / Affected, peevish, prim and delicate."

106 KEY: "Mr. Bourke." According to Sir Walter Scott, a shopkeeper and "another leader of the rioters." Percy Fitzgerald's *Life of David Garrick* (1868) names Fitzpatrick's "henchman" as a Mr. Burke.

107 Studied; fixed "in the mind. It is a word now little in use, except in ludicrous language" (Johnson).

seeing the process of this extraordinary affair. On the contrary; as I now belonged to the whole theatrical community in general, I had an opportunity of getting a full insight into the nature and mysteries of every part of that profession.

I see you desire to know my sentiments on a subject that has been canvassed by the ingenious of all ages. Such a curiosity is natural, and shall be gratified at a proper time; but at present I must not interrupt the account of this transaction.

From the manner in which those self-made legislators had talked, when together, of every circumstance in the management of a theatre, and profession of an actor, you would have concluded that they were going to overturn the whole present system of the stage, and institute another on principles directly opposite, according to their own ideas of perfection.

But that was not the case. Among all the errors and abuses, against which they declaimed with such vehemence, they thought proper to attack only one, which they thought most interesting to themselves in particular. This was the right, which reason and law gave the performers to fix the price of their own labours.

In the infancy of the stage in *London*, before it had been brought by much labour and expence to such a degree of perfection as to attract the attention of the public, it had been the custom, after a certain part of the representation was over, to admit persons for less than was paid at the beginning.

The obvious reason of this was to allure company of any kind thither, and take the most they could get, rather than keep the house empty. But when the passion for seeing plays arose to its present height, this expedient appeared to be no longer necessary, and therefore was disused; a change which those who conducted the entertainments of the theatre justified by alleging the enhanced salaries of the actors, and the improvements made in the machinery,[108] and decorations of the stage since the time when that custom was introduced, which they said required reimbursement, by a method that could not justly be taken offence at, as *none were obliged to go who did not approve of the terms*.

Such a measure was most alarming to these men of taste,

---

108 Stage apparatus (OED).

some of whom denied themselves the pleasure of going to the beginning of the performance *because they were not able to pay the full price*; as the others *could not get from behind their compters before it was half ended*; and for these good reasons, both thought it the highest grievance to have a custom abolished that had been so convenient to them.

Accordingly, as soon as the performance began, they all arose, and without any respect to the rest of the audience, interrupted the players in the most outrageous manner, nor would desist, till the managers should promise to redress the grievance which affected them so severely, and take half-prices as before.

This was too flagrant a violation of justice to be submitted to, so suddenly. The managers therefore refused; upon which *these redressers of grievances* gave a loose to their resentment, at such an instance of disobedience to their authority; and tore the house to pieces, doing more damage to the proprietors, than their own entire worldly substance could repair.

CHAPTER X

The ruinous appearance of the scene of action supplies matter for mirth to those whose trade it is to laugh at every thing. The point carried against law and reason. Enquiry into the cause of this. The rise of the prejudice against the profession of an actor.

WHEN these men of genius and public spirit had thus gallantly accomplished their enterprize, they marched off in triumph, denouncing a repetition of their resentment, should their orders not be obeyed.

The appearance of the house, after this ravage, and the looks of the actors when they ventured to creep out of their hiding holes, seemed to realize the mimic scenes usually exhibited there. All was havoc, desolation, amazement, and affright. Crowns, sceptres, candlesticks, and broken benches were jumbled together: Sovereigns, and sweepers, lords, link-boys, duchesses, and cinder-wenches joined in one common lamentation of their fate.

This, however, lasted not long. Their hearts were not formed

of stuff for grief to make a deep impression on: Nor were they
so unaccustomed to the rubs of life as to be dejected at any
mischance. Their concern therefore wore off with their fright;
and one of them, resuming his character of turning every thing to
ridicule, marched with solemn pace and rueful countenance up to
the motley ruins now collected into a heap, and with some droll
variations, apt to the occasion, *spouted* over them a tragic speech,
in all the emphasis and trick[109] of woe. The humour instantly ran
through them all. Mirth grinned on every face; and they vied in
cracking villainous jests on each other's *undoing*.

But the managers[110] had suffered too severely in their property
to be in so merry a mood. They consulted among themselves, and
with the sages of the law, what was proper for them to do, to obtain
redress for such injustice, and prevent the menaced repetition of
it. But all was to no purpose.[111] Law gave way to licentiousness;
and they were obliged to submit to the most intolerable of all
tyrannies, *that of the mob*.

You are surprised that such things should be, in a country
governed by equal and established laws. In speculation it must
seem strange; but the least acquaintance with life would reconcile
you to inconsistencies still grosser. There is something however
in the circumstances of this case, which deserves attention, and
makes it not improper to trace to their origin the prejudices from
which such injustice could proceed.

When the system of Divine worship, which is now professed
in these parts of the world, was first proposed to mankind, the

---

109 "Characteristic expression (of the face or voice)" (OED).
110 KEY: "Garrick & Beard." David Garrick (1717-79), manager of Drury Lane
Theatre from 1747 until his retirement twenty-nine years later; and John Beard
(*ca.* 1716-91), who from 1761 to 1767 was manager of Covent Garden Theatre.
From his sensational debut as Richard III in October 1741 to his final bow in 1776,
Garrick was a London celebrity and a vital figure in eighteenth-century theatre,
balancing a talent for "virtuoso display and inspirational improvisation" onstage
with savvy business acumen and public relations in his managerial role. Beard, "a
charming, cheerful, and polite man with excellent social qualities and a handsome
appearance" (DNB), was a popular singer and actor.
111 According to newspaper accounts, four men were arrested after the riots. The
charges, however, were eventually dropped.

human mind was a slave to superstitions, which were a disgrace to that portion of reason given for its direction.

By a perversion, of which man alone is capable, the celebration of those superstitions, though professedly designed in honour of the Deity, was attended with *games*, and *scenical interludes*, in which the grossest immoralities received the sanction of religion, and were practiced openly as pleasing to him. This was done to attach the passions of the multitude; and satisfy their curiosity with sensible representations, in order to prevent their making rational enquiries into the grounds of those superstitions, the principles of which were subservient to the policy of the ruling powers.

A religion instituted on purpose to reclaim man from immoralities and superstitions, and restore him to the dignity of his nature, necessarily struck at every thing that conduced to their support: Accordingly the persons appointed to propagate it exerted all their endeavours against those games and interludes, both as a part of the superstitious worship which they wanted to abolish, and as in themselves subversive of moral virtue, by the vices which they exhibited to imitation, heightened and made still more alluring by every incentive art and pomp of expence.

For this purpose, reason as well as religion supplied ready and powerful arguments; but not content to wait for the slow effect of these, they strove to prejudice those whom they could not persuade; and to obviate the imitation of their example, raised an abhorrence to the persons of all concerned in such representations; casting them off from the rites of religion, and declaring them unworthy both of the protection of the laws, and the common privileges of society:[112] A method that in one respect defeated its own design; as it could never reclaim the offenders, however it might deter others from following their example.

Nor did they stop here. By an error too common in the heat of argumentation, they concluded *from the abuse, against the use* of the stage, and branded with the mark of reprobation all future actors for the faults of the present.

---

112 The contentious relationship of Britain's stage with its pulpit was longstanding. In 1642, under the influence of the Puritans, English Parliament banned London theatre. The ban remained until 1660, at the restoration of Charles II to the throne.

CHAPTER XI

Continued. The common consequences of excess of zeal. The professed
intent of the theatrical representations defeated by this absurd
prejudice against actors. The vices against which this prejudice is
levelled, in reality the effects of it; with the means of remedying this
and other abuses.

HOWEVER the occasion might there seem to justify this excess
of zeal, when the cause ceased, the effect should in reason have
ceased also; and these general censures have been repealed.
The superstitions which were the foundation of the first charge
against the stage have been long abolished; nor are the absurdities
and immoralities which gave offence to reason and virtue any
longer practised there. On the contrary, the professed intent of
theatrical representations at present is to insinuate instruction
under the pleasing appearance of entertainment,[113] to encourage
virtue by example, and inculcate the practice of it, by shewing
the evils inseparably attendant on vice; to regulate the passions by
displaying the danger of indulging them too far, and to put folly
out of countenance by holding it up to ridicule.

Now as experience has proved the stage capable of answering
these great ends, what can be more injudicious than to attempt
to bring it into disrepute? What more unjust than to consign to
infamy those who exert the finest powers of the human mind and
body, to accomplish this end in the most pleasing manner? Yet such
is the absurdity of man, that while persons of the most exalted
rank and sacred character not only frequent the theatre, but
also compose works to be represented on it, and evidently value
themselves more on possessing the abilities requisite to compose
them, than on all their other distinctions in life, those from whose

---

113 The idea that drama's purpose is "to instruct and to delight" is found in
the work of Aristotle, Horace, and Samuel Johnson. Didacticism became an
especially pronounced feature of eighteenth-century theatre, particularly after
the Licensing Act of 1737, and the emphatic purpose of theatre during the century
was moral instruction and improvement.

actions such compositions receive their force and beauty, are held in disrepute, and subject to the severest disadvantages only for acting them. If it is no disgrace *to write a play*, why should it be any *to act it?*

It is true the consequences of this prejudice are not so severe here as in other countries, but still they are such as reason is ashamed of. If actors are not *literally* excluded from the protection of the laws, they want support to avail themselves of that protection, as in the case which gave rise to these reflections! if they are not *actually* (*for literally they are!*) excluded from the rites of religion, they want encouragement to participate in them!

I see you are ready to object to the utility of the stage, the faults in many of the performances exhibited upon it; and to justify the disrepute affixed to the character of an actor, from the general immorality of their conduct in private life, as if it arose solely from their profession. But a moment's reflection would suggest answers to both these objections.

If there is any improper exhibition upon the stage, surely the blame should fall on those who have a legal power to prevent such abuse of the institution of it! If the actors are immoral in their lives, should it not be considered that they are prejudged from their profession, and deprived of one of the strongest inducements to virtue, that is *reputation*, before they are proved to be guilty of vice.

The consequence of this is, that too few enter into the profession, till after they have lost their reputation, or are driven by mere necessity; by which means they reflect that disgrace upon it which they are thought to suffer from it; and as they are sensible that they are precluded by this prejudice from all possibility of recovering or preserving it by the most careful deportment, they become desperate, and proceed till they even lose the sense of unavailing shame.

Whereas, if a different conduct was observed to them! if the brand of reprobation was taken off, and the profession established in that credit, which the abilities indispensably necessary to eminence in it deserve; Genius would be no longer damp'd by apprehension of reproach: More persons of good character would not scruple going on the stage, as they could preserve it there; nor vice seem to receive encouragement from public favour, *because from this circumstance unhappily too often entangled with merit*; but the life of the actor would reflect the sentiments of the poet, and enforce them to imitation by example.

Nor would it be difficult to work this important effect. All necessary would be to refuse admission on the stage to all, *notorious for vice of any kind*; to banish from it *such as should become so after, however eminent in their merits*; and *to support the profession by the civil power*, against the tyranny of the mob, so that the lives and properties of all concerned in it should be secure from suffering such licentious outrage, and injustice, as no other subjects are exposed to; and as are equally a reproach and insult to good government and common sense.

Nor need it be apprehended that this would make them insolent, or slacken their endeavours to please. Their very being depends on public favour, the bare withholding of which is punishment sufficiently severe; as ambition to acquire it will make them exert their utmost abilities, and always observe proper humility to the arbiters of their fate. They know that if they are neglected, they cannot live: On the contrary, it would enable them to rise to greater merit in their art, as they would no longer be under the wretched necessity of prostituting their own judgment to please the gross taste of their tyrants.

Many other arguments might be alleged against this grievous and shameful abuse, but what I have said is sufficient to convince candid reason; and with prejudice it is in vain to argue.

CHAPTER XII

The system of policy by which *Chrysal's* master governed his state. Account of his methods of parrying poets. The reason why so few new plays are acted. Enquiry into the present state of genius. The general motives for writing plays preclude them from success. Managers and poets equally in fault in their dealings with each other.

THE day after this great affair was *thus equitably* settled, on *the treasurer's* making up his week's account, I came into the possession of the *manager*, who having some occasion for money, put *me* into his pocket.[114]

The measures of my new master's government in his little empire were the strongest burlesque on the policy of the world, the greatest sovereign in which had not more intrigues *of state* to manage, than were continually carrying on about him, from the ambition, envy, and jealousy of the several candidates for his *royal* favour.

But all this bustle did not embarrass him in the least. He had the address to *play off* one party against another; and *by never engaging himself particularly to any, was able to manage all*. A method, by the bye, that might suggest an hint not unuseful to politicians in an higher sphere.

But the part of his conduct that was most curious, and gave me the greatest pleasure, was his manner of *parrying* the attacks of the *authors* who were continually bringing him their works for representation on the stage, of which I had an opportunity of seeing many striking instances.

As it is evidently the interest of the manager of a theatre, to exhibit those performances whose merit is most likely to gain the approbation of the public; and as no man, who is capable of writing a piece proper for exhibition, can be supposed to want judgment to know whether it has that merit, you may naturally think that there could not be much difficulty in the intercourse between them; but human actions are not always to be judged of from the strongest appearances of reason.

The representation of a new piece necessarily puts the manager to some expence, and much trouble. If you add to this the natural anxiety about success, *for merit is often rejected by caprice, or personal prejudice*, you will not wonder that he should be cautious what he brings upon the stage; and prefer acting old ones, unattended with these inconveniences, while the public will bear the repetition, and does not peremptorily demand new.

This is the real reason why so few new pieces are performed; and not any decline of poetical genius to produce them; it being certain that there are as many good plays written now, as at any

---

114 Flyleaf annotations in one volume specify that the manager is David Garrick. See 2.126, note 110.

former point of time. But the matter is this. All the good ones of those times lie together before you, and raise your opinion to the happy days which produced them: But if you consider the long intervals between, and the innumerable bad ones which appeared along with them, but are now lost in the wreck of time, you will find that you have not so great reason to complain of the present decline of genius, as you may have imagined.

I do not by this mean, that every one who pretends to write is possessed of that genius; or that all the pieces offered to the stage are proper for representation. On the contrary, many who want every qualification indispensable to success in such attempts, make them every day in defiance of reason; and strive to obtrude upon the public works which are a reproach to common sense.

The motives of this are obvious. Whenever a man is at a loss how to spend his time, or wants to raise a little money, down he sits, without more ado, and writes a play. The consequence of this is, that the very reasons which made him turn poet, necessarily preclude him from success. *Idleness* prevents that care, that *limae labor*, which alone can make a performance proper for public representation; and *distress* depresses the imagination; and hinders its rising to that *happy boldness*, which is the essence of poetry.[115]

It appears from hence, that if the managers of theatres from interested motives are often to blame for rejecting *good* pieces; poets (or those who would be thought such) are much oftener culpable for offering them *bad* ones. The difference of opinion unavoidable on this account occasions the difficulty in their intercourse. But in this the contest is not equal. The word of the manager is decisive; while the poet has nothing left, but to vent his resentment in unavailing (and often unjust) complaints and abuse, in which those who have least right are always loudest; for enamoured with the beauty of their own offspring, like the Ape in the fable, they throw dirt at all who presume to find fault with it.[116]

---

115 *Limae labor*: the "labor of the file," or the smooth polishing of a literary work. The phrase appears in Horace's *Ars Poetica*. *Happy boldness* likely also originates with Horace, in the *Epistle to Augustus*.

116 Aesop's fable of "Jupiter and the Ape," in which an ape foolishly asserts her ugly child is the most comely of the animals, then insults the others for disagreeing with her.

But severe as it must be to suffer this, it is not the greatest difficulty the manager has to encounter with them. Not satisfied with the civil refusal of affected delays and excuses, they must have a direct answer, which they controvert with all their power, and oblige him to support by such arguments as must give him pain, if he has either politeness or good-nature; though after all, instead of convincing them, he only gets theirs and their friends ill-will, and arms all their tongues against him.

It is not to be doubted but the *evasions* which managers use to *shift off good* pieces are as grossly offensive to moral propriety, truth and candour, as the arguments of authors in defence of *bad* ones can possibly be to reason; but as I did not happen to be witness to any instances of them, I shall confine my account to the latter.

CHAPTER XIII

Chrysal's master sits in judgment on some pieces offered to him. A poet of fashion enters. The arguments by which he supports his work against the objections of Chrysal's master, who makes some curious dramatical strictures. The poet driven from his last retreat, the interest of his great friends, by the common cant of the house's being full for the season, departs in a rage, denouncing their resentment, which Chrysal's master shews his reason not to fear the effects of.

The important morning after I came into the possession of the manager was big with the fate of many a poetical performance, the authors of which were appointed to come there for his decisive answer.

Accordingly, as soon as he had breakfasted, he repaired to his tribunal, where he had been waited for, some time, by one of those aspiring genius's, who sacrifice the solid happiness of independence, to the vain ambition *of being well with the great*: submitting to their capricious humours for the honour of a nod in public places, or an invitation to their tables; to enhance their welcome at which, and consume time they know not how to make better use of, they fall upon this wise expedient of turning poets.

When they had gone through all the formalities of polite

address, and taken their seat with proper ceremony, the poet opened the business. "Well, Sir," (said he with a smile of self-complacence) "you have perused that trifle! what is your opinion? Heh! don't you think it will do?"

"Sir," (answered my master, with the smooth simper of a courtier) "you do it injustice by calling it a trifle! the piece has a great deal of merit; and reads very prettily in many places; but I fear it is not quite so proper for the stage!"

"How, Sir! not proper for the stage! pray, Sir, where does the impropriety lie? Several persons of the first rank have read it, and found no such thing. *His Grace* said it abounded with the *vis comica*. Lord *Tastely* was charmed with the *Attic salt*; and *Sir Courtly* admired the elegance of the diction.[117] Pray, Sir, where then can the impropriety lie? They are allowed to be judges."

"Pardon me, Sir, I do not presume to call their judgment in question, in the least. But—a"—

—"And why then should you hesitate to receive it? They will support it with all their interest."

"That, Sir, I do not doubt. But—still, Sir,—the town"—

—"The town, Sir! and pray what of the town? Is the judgment of the town to be put in competition with theirs?"

"No, Sir! by no means! but still the town is a very formidable and arbitrary judge; and will not admit its authority to be disputed in such matters as this."

"And pray, good Sir! what objections can the judicious town, or you, its learned advocate, make?"

"Sir, you impose a very disagreeable task upon me! I had much rather be excused."

"I do not in the least doubt that, Sir; but my friends insist upon a direct answer. Either receive the play, or say why you will not."

"Sir, I should be sorry to give offence to any gentleman; but since you insist upon my opinion, Do you not think, Sir, the plot is too—too—too domestic? Are not the intrigues and tricks of servants too low a subject for polite entertainment?"

"How, Sir! have you any objection to servants? Do not they

---

117 *Vis comica*: comic power or force. *Attic salt*: "refined, delicate, pointed wit" (OED).

make a principal part in all our modern comedies? Are the *Jeremy's, and Scrubs, and Phillis's*,[118] and a thousand others to be rejected because they are servants?"

"No, Sir! but consider they are not the principal characters; nor does the plot turn upon them. They come in, as it were, by accident; and indeed except in the instances you have mentioned, and perhaps a very few more, they had much better be left out. It shews a grossness of taste to stoop to them for entertainment."

"And do not I introduce the masters, and mistresses too, as well as the servants? Are there not country-squires, and town fops, and fine ladies?"

"Yes, Sir! you do introduce them, but in a subordinate light; and merely to be the dupes of their servants, without any business, or importance of their own."

"And pray, Sir, in what other light do most masters appear? Hah! hah! hah!—Well then it seems all your objections are to the fable.[119] You have nothing to say against the sentiments and diction."

"The sentiments, Sir, may be very proper; and the diction suited to them; but you must be sensible that the former objection affects them all equally. The characters are too low; and the sentiments and diction consequently too coarse."

"Sir,—Sir,—Sir,—I shall not enter into any farther arguments with you. *His Grace* bids me tell you he insists upon your receiving it; or giving him such reasons as he shall think satisfactory, which must be very different from those insignificant cavils."

"His Grace need not exert his authority to influence my obedience. The least hint of his pleasure were sufficient; but unluckily I am engaged for the whole season! quite *full*."

"*Full!* why did you not tell me so at first?"

"Because you insisted on having my opinion."

"Very well, Sir! I shall let his Grace and all my friends know how you behaved. Let me have the play! impertinent, insolent, ignorant puppy!" muttered he, as he went out.

"So" (said my master, as soon as he was gone) "I have now made him my enemy forever. As for his *noble friends*, they are above

---

118 Stock names for servants in eighteenth-century plays.
119 The series "of events which constitute a poem epick or dramatick" (Johnson). The plot.

troubling themselves about any thing of the kind, and give him leave to mention their names, only to get rid of his importunity."

CHAPTER XIV

Continuation. *Chrysal's* master rejects the work of a poet for his ignorance of the laws of the drama. More dramatical strictures. The poet modestly insists that his play is refused only because it wants the interest of the great; and goes off in a huff. Another poet repulsed for his attachment to the laws of the drama. Arguments against these laws. The poet refuses to conform to the present taste; and makes an appeal. One more poet refused only for wanting every poetical talent. Remarks on something that affects more than care to own it. *Chrysal* changes his service, on an occasion not common.

THE last poet was scarce down stairs when a footman *announced* the entrance of another.

My master did not think it necessary to observe so much ceremony with him, as he had done with the former, but told him directly that he could not receive his piece.

Such a sentence struck the poet *all of an heap.* He was unable to speak for some moments; but recovering himself at length, "Not receive it, Sir!" (said he) "you surprise me. Pray, Sir, why so?"

"I am very loth to find fault, Sir!" (answered my master) "But you seem to be utterly unacquainted with all *the laws of the drama.*"[120]

"The laws of the drama! they are but art; I write from nature. These laws have been long laid aside. *Shakespeare* wrote without laws."

"So much the worse. But he is a dangerous example to imitate. The local, temporary laws of the ancient drama are laid aside, it is

---

120 The "unities," neoclassical rules for drama, derived from Aristotle's *Poetics*. The first (the unity of action) stipulates a play should have one main plot; the second (place) that the stage should represent one physical location; and the third (time) that all action should fit within a 24-hour period. That "Shakespeare wrote without laws" was often repeated in the eighteenth century, reiterated by Samuel Johnson in the *Preface to Shakespeare* and by Voltaire, who thought the playwright a "barbaric genius."

true; but not the immutable, general laws of propriety and reason. Your fable is unconnected, improbable, and unaffecting."

"How, Sir! unaffecting! Can the fall of a mighty empire be said to be unaffecting?"

"No, Sir! But the description of it most certainly may, if not drawn with judgment and force. And then your characters are ill supported; and your sentiments and language lost in the clouds."

"What, Sir! can the sentiments of Kings and Princes be too sublime?"

"There is a wide difference between being sublime, and swollen out of nature."

"But what objection can you make to the language? Is it not raised with *epithets*, and *metaphors*, and all the figures of poetry?"

"Good Sir! poetical figures in poor language look like embroidery on a blanket. They only make its poverty ridiculous. Besides your *stalking in their stilts*, betrays you into many a stumble in the dirt. Your figures frequently fly in the face of common sense, and break through every rule of grammar."

"Well, Sir! I shall consider of these particulars. The great objection I have heard made to modern plays is their want of business: But this can never be charged to mine. There is a *ghost*, and a battle; and a king dethron'd. Business enough and enough, I am sure."

"Ghosts and battles, Sir, it is true, are sometimes introduced with success; but then it must be by a master in the art, else they have a very contrary effect."

"I apprehend that the aim of tragedy is to work upon the passions. In this I believe you cannot say I have fail'd. The distress is truly great."

"Distress when out of character loses the appearance of reality, and becomes ridiculous. A king in an alms-house, and a queen begging from door to door, are images which sink into burlesque."

"It is very well, Sir! you may say what you please, but I am satisfied it is not want of merit in my play that makes you refuse it. You daily act much worse. If it had been recommended to you by some lord, you would have found none of these faults; but merit may starve without interest to support it now-a-days. This is fine encouragement to genius truly; and the public is like to be well entertained while such men have it in their power to refuse every thing that does not happen to please themselves."

Saying this he snatched up his play, leaving my master to please himself with the prospect of being *criticized upon in a news-paper*, and pulled to pieces in a scurrilous pamphlet.

He had not time to indulge these reflections long, when another of his clients attended his levee.

As soon as he was seated, "I have read over your work with great care;" (said my master) "and am sorry to say, I think it improper for the stage."

"Pray, Sir, why so?" (answered the poet, with an air of importance) "It is written strictly according to the rules of the drama; and enriched with the sublimest sentiments of the ancients."

"Sir, I am sensible of its merit; as well as of the great learning of the author: But the taste of the times requires entertainment of a different kind."

"Surely compliance with a vitiated taste will not justify the breach of rules, taken originally from nature, and established for so many ages."

"I neither dispute the original justice, nor the antiquity of them: But I apprehend that the latter in a great measure destroys the present force of the former. The customs of mankind, the part of nature that comes within the province of the drama, are so changed since the establishment of those rules, that it would be most absurd to exact obedience to them now. Besides, may it not be said, without violation of the respect due to antiquity, that experience in a great length of time may have made many improvements in those rules. The infancy of every art is weak."

"But whatever change may have happened in the customs of the world, truth still remains the same, and the genuine sentiments of nature cannot displease."

"Very true! but still they may not always be received with equal pleasure, in the same garb. Unimpassioned sentiment, however just and sublime, works not the effects designed by the drama, whose aim is to convey instruction and pleasure at the same time, by an immediate address to the passions."

"Is it possible, that you can be an advocate for the irregular monsters, which at present dishonour the stage?"

"As for irregularity, I look upon it to be but an imaginary defect. Though even if it were otherwise, I am the servant of the public, and obliged to find entertainment for their taste, be it what it will. If you would but conform"—

—"No, Sir! that I never will, against reason and the ancients. I see you are prejudiced, and therefore shall not argue with you any longer. But I shall not acquiesce in silence. I will publish the performance, without being discouraged by your refusal, and appeal to the judgment of the learned."

He then marched off with a stately pace, and my master looking after him, "There again" (said he, shrugging his shoulders) "I shall now have the ghosts of *Sophocles*, and *Aristotle*, and all the doughty ancients raised to haunt me."

As he said this, a person entered whose whole appearance spoke distress. He approached my master bowing lowly, and trembling with anxiety as he spoke: "I have made bold to wait upon you, Sir!" (said he) "but if you are not at leisure, will call another time."

"Pray, Sir, sit down;" (replied my master, with a smile of encouragement) "I have looked over your work, and am concerned that it is not in my power to receive it; as I should be sincerely glad to serve you. But in this, it is not possible. I must be plain with you.—You seem to want every poetical talent."

"I thought, Sir," (returned the poet, scarce able to collect spirits enough to speak to him) "that the business of tragedy was to work upon the passions! I depended entirely on the distress."

"Very true, Sir! But there are other passions, beside pity, to be applied to; nor is poverty a proper distress to work upon them. Severe as it is to be felt, it affects very little in representation. The upper ranks of life know not what it is; and those who do are desirous to keep the thought at a distance; and conceal a knowledge they are ashamed of. The mind must be properly prepared to feel for another. The description of a famine would affect but little after a feast."

This came too home to the unhappy poet. He burst into tears; and was departing without being able to make any reply. My master felt his distress; though he could not receive his play, as he knew that an audience would pay no regard to his circumstances, nor give up an evening's entertainment to relieve an author's indigence; and waiting on him to the door, slipped a couple of guineas into his hand; when it fell to my lot to change my service.

I had never experienced my own influence on the human heart so strongly, as on this occasion. The poet kissed the hand of his benefactor in a rapture too big for utterance; and forgetting for a moment all his distresses, went to a coffee-house and *changed* me to pay for his breakfast; "where I was immediately *borrowed* at the bar, by an officer, who was going to dine with his general, and wanted money to give his servants." I.I.XX. See 1.112.

CHAPTER XV

Chrysal's master engages in a genteel amour. A delicate way of refining pleasure. His mistress persuades him that she has poisoned him, and herself. His situation at hearing this. Striking proofs of medical skill with the advantage of a regular course of practice. An exemplary instance of charity and forgiveness diverts the doctor's attention to the murderess.

(Chrysal, *after having seen several striking scenes, in the course of an extensive circulation, is at length carried to an horse-race, where he is initiated in some of the mysteries of the turf.*)

"It was on a sporting bet, on one of the bye-matches, that I was *lost* that evening to the nobleman, as I said, in whose possession I happened to remain till the end of the meeting." II.I.XIV. See 1.300.

As it was late in the evening when my master arrived in *London*,[121]

---

121 KEY: "Ld. Orford." George Walpole (1730-91), third Earl of Orford and Horace Walpole's nephew. Walpole's letters chronicle Orford's development from a spendthrift wastrel, "the most ruined young man in Europe," into a raving, suicidal lunatic; Orford ended his life insane, surrounded by his mistress, several physicians, an apothecary and "rascally," inept servants. Horace Mann referred to Orford as "the dissipator of all he could lay his rapacious hands upon to squander among whores and parasites." Indeed, when Walpole temporarily took over the management of Orford's estate, his debts amounted to more than £44,000. He was "the most selfish man in the world," wrote his uncle, who "disgusted every friend he had by insensibility, and every friend he might have had, by insincerity." Horace Walpole became fourth Earl of Orford upon George's death in 1791.

he resolved to indulge himself for that night in the embraces of a tender-hearted female, whom he *picked up* in the street, (for he was no way nice in his amours), as he walked from the inn, where he alighted, to his own house, in order to stretch his legs.

Nothing more than common occurrences passed upon this occasion. When his lordship had made his mistress *nobly* drunk, *by the way of refining his pleasure,* the delicate pair went lovingly to bed together, where waking about midnight, he was surprised to find her cold, and lifeless in his arms. After some fruitless efforts to move her, he started out of bed in a fright, and called up all his servants; who perceiving that she was not actually dead, took such pains to recover her, that she at length opened her eyes, and staring wildly around her for some moments, "Where am I?" (said she) "Are these the regions of the damn'd? For thither only can such self-murdering wretches, as I am, go."—Then seeing his lordship, whose curiosity had brought him to the bed-side, "and are you dead too?" (continued she, wringing her hands and weeping most passionately) "O why did I not confine my rage to myself? Why did I add your murder to my own, to plunge my soul still deeper in perdition?"

This surprised all present. The servants, who were indifferent whether it was true or false, imagined she only raved, and doubled their efforts to bring her to herself, soothing her with expressions of tenderness, and telling her she was not dead, but would soon be very well: But my master was too nearly concerned to think so coolly of the matter.

"What is that you say?" (said he, trembling in horror) "What is it you say about murder? There is no one murdered here."

"How!" (answered she, fixing her eyes eagerly upon him) "Is it possible, that I am still alive? And that you also live? It cannot be! the poison which I swallowed this night, and in which you shared too largely, cannot have missed of its effect. But soft: its operation now begins! that pang!—oh!—that pang bespeaks the near approach of death!—O mercy!—O cry for mercy on your sins!"

"What poison?" (interrupted he, terrified almost to distraction) "what poison have I shared in? Speak! tell me directly, or"—

"Spare your threats, my lord," (said she, with a composure in her looks and manner that persuaded every one present she was in her senses) "spare your threats to a wretch whom death will soon deliver from your power; and forgive a crime, that proceeded from despair. Wearied of the miseries of this life, I this night resolved to put an end to it, and for that purpose, though on another pretence, procured a dose of poison from a Chymist's apprentice, who, on giving it to me, said it was sufficient to kill twenty of the strongest men alive: And this poison did I take an opportunity to put into the last bottle of wine, when you went out of the room, determined to sacrifice one man to my revenge for the injuries I had received from the sex: Though after I had done it, my heart relented; but you insisted on my drinking, and fear of your resentment prevented me from making a discovery, that would have saved us both from this unhappy"—At these words, she fell into convulsions so strong, that every one who saw her thought she was really in the agonies of death.

The situation of my master, at this sight, may be easily conceived. He instantly felt every pain that poison could produce; and falling on the floor, roared aloud in anguish of mind and body, lamenting his untimely fate, and confessing all the sins of his life, to the servants who stood around him.

As soon as they had raised him up and carried him into another room, a dawn of hope arose at his finding he did not immediately die. "What!" (exclaimed he) "is every one combined against me? Am I to perish for want of assistance? will nobody even call me a physician? Perhaps I might yet be saved, were proper means applied! will nobody call me a physician?"

On his saying this, every one was running to obey him, the sight of which threw him into new distress. "O wretch that I am!" (exclaimed he) "and so I am to be left alone! to perish for want even of a drop of water! is it not enough for some of you to go; and not all to desert me in this base, this barbarous manner?"— This seemed to restore them to their senses; and accordingly, while some went to call the doctors, the rest stayed to take care of him.

Where the carrion is, the crows will soon be gathered together. He was immediately surrounded by half the meagre faces of the faculty, (for as he had not named any one in particular, his servants to shew their care had summoned all they knew of) who taking the account he gave them of his being poisoned for truth, proceeded

instantly to practise upon him every method they had ever heard
of being used in such a case, in hope that some one of them might
take effect. He was cup'd,[122] bled, and blistered; vomited, glystered,
and purged, in the space of two hours; the doctors sagaciously
discovering new symptoms of the poison, every new remedy they
tried.

When they found that beyond their expectations he had
strength enough to out-live all this, they put him into bed, and
covering him up warm, to take a sweat, comforted him with hopes
of his recovery, in consequence of their skill and care.

While they waited *patiently* for this important crisis, some of
them happened to think of the poor murderess, who had been
neglected all this time, and now lay in a swoon, the convulsions
having gone off, as her strength failed.

On hearing her name mentioned, his lordship to shew his
Christian charity, and prove the sincerity of the repentance and
amendment which he vowed in case his life should be mercifully
spared, desired that they would do something for the unhappy
creature, if she was still alive. This was sufficient to attach their
compassion and care. They answered with one voice, that it was
a pity to let her perish, without even attempting to save her, and
praising his lordship's goodness, prepared to try some experiments
upon her also, if only to do something for their fee.

CHAPTER XVI

The recovery of the murderess opens a new scene. She clears up the
    mystery, less to the satisfaction of the doctors than of their noble
    patient, who rewards her liberally for her good news; and sends them
    off without their errand. Reflections on some genteel matters. *Chrysal*
    changes his service.

Their practice upon this new subject, however, was cut short by
a success more speedy than they desired; their first operation of
bleeding bringing her directly to herself.

---

122 A medical practice in which a glass cup was placed "upon the skin, to draw
the blood in scarification" (Johnson).

As soon as she perceived what had been done, and recovered strength to speak, "Good God," (said she) "what is the meaning of this? Who can have been so inhuman as to bleed me, when it is known to be ruin in my disorder?"

"In your disorder!" (said one of the doctors, with a contemptuous frown) "what disorder? Have you not poisoned yourself? and what is still worse, his lordship also; who now lies in the same desperate condition with you, and has from his unmerited goodness directed us to take this care of you; though if we can save you from this death, it must be to suffer one more ignominious."

"I poison myself!" (interrupted she, raising herself up in the bed) "I poison his lordship! What can you mean by this? I understand you not; and am innocent, even in thought, of any such crime. Explain yourself therefore; and do not sport with the misery of a wretched creature, who has more real distresses than she is able to bear, without the addition of imaginary guilt."

This amazed them all. They stood looking at each other for some moments, wrapt in reflections not the most pleasing, on the consequences that might attend their precipitation in treating his lordship in the manner they had done, in case what she said should prove true. At length, on her repeating her entreaties, one of them condescended to inform her of every thing that had passed, dwelling particularly on the desperate condition his lordship had been in, and the various methods they had used to relieve him.

Weak and dispirited as you must suppose her to have been, she was scarce able to refrain from laughter at this account. "A desperate condition he must be in now indeed;" (said she) "whatever he was in before! but if you will give me leave to slip on my gown and go to him, I'll soon complete his cure."

This was a step so contrary to all rules of practice, that they could not permit it. On the contrary, one of them observing the impropriety of listening to the ravings of a person, whose head must certainly be distracted by the effects of the poison, they all took the hint, and were actually going to hold her down by force, in order to proceed in their experiments upon her, which you may think would not have been the more merciful, for what she had just said.

But she was delivered from this discipline, by the appearance of his lordship, who on one of his servants carrying him the pleasing news of what she said, had found strength enough to run to her, and throwing himself on the bed, "O my dearest girl!" (exclaimed he, clasping his arms around her neck) "am I not then a dead man? Tell me, tell me the truth, directly! am I not a dead man?"

His haggard looks, and the bandages and flannels in which he was wrapped all over, convinced her of the truth of what the doctors had told her he had suffered. Shocked at the thought, she held up her hands in a supplicating posture, and imploring his pardon for what she had been the involuntary cause of, informed him that she was subject to fits, which attacked her with double violence whenever she drank to any excess, as his lordship had compelled her to do that night, much, he must have been sensible, against her inclination, had she dared to refuse him; and that when she was in those fits, which lasted till the effects of the liquor went off, she was apt to rave, and speak every extravagance and inconsistency that could come into a disordered head.

The manner in which she spoke left not the least room for doubt. All his fears were instantly removed, his joy at which obliterated the remembrance of every thing he had suffered in mind and body, and he not only forgave her, but also made her an handsome present in recompence for her happy news.

But his doctors met with a very different treatment. He reviled them in the severest terms for their ignorance and presumption in putting him to such torture, and tearing his constitution by such violent means, before they were certain of his ailment; and without permitting them to allege in their vindication his assertions of what he felt, and entreaties not to leave any thing unattempted, that they thought might possibly relieve him, ordered them to be turned out of doors, without giving them a farthing for all their trouble.

I have seen that you were surprised at his lordship's indelicacy, and disregard to his health, in having an amour with a creature in so low a state of infamy and wretchedness, as to walk the streets to offer herself to casual prostitution; as well as at her expressing herself in a manner so much above her appearance and circumstances. But the least acquaintance with the world would easily account for both.

When once a woman falls from chastity, the characteristic

virtue of her sex, the descent to this lowest degree of human misery is natural, and seldom, very seldom, fails to come of course. The kept mistress, who this day shines in brocade and jewels, and rattles about in her chariot, will in a few months spend the night in the streets, for want of an habitation to hide her head, and without clothes to shelter her from the inclemencies of the weather, when the novelty that first recommended her is worn off; *for no prosperity that is not established on virtue can last.* Theirs indeed is of all the most fleeting; the vice which is their support affecting their own conduct by example, and making them lavish profusely, what they get from profusion.

Such had been the case of this female. She had been entitled by birth and education to better hopes; but vice had blasted all, and left her only the reflection of what she might have been, to aggravate her present wretchedness.

As to him! his health possibly was in a state not worthy of regard! and for his delicacy, the indiscriminate vague intercourse of the sexes effectually destroys that, as well as the sentimental attachment, which refines the desire of rational beings, and distinguishes it from the gross appetite of brute animals, so that in general nothing farther than the gratification of that appetite is now sought; and as that can be effected by any one object, as well as another, whether it is found in a palace or a brothel makes no difference, with those who profess themselves men of pleasure. The sex is all they seek, without regard to any qualifications; and consequently, when their appetites are gratified, they desert the objects of them with the same indifference as they took them.

But to return to my master. It was some time, as you may imagine, before he recovered the effects of this affair; but I remained not with him so long. The doctors, in revenge for the treatment they had met with, blazed[123] it abroad, with the addition of every ridiculous circumstance they could invent. This brought all his acquaintances to have a laugh at him upon the occasion; to one of whom he *lost* me that afternoon on a bet, at a race, between two of the *maggots*, which they found in the nuts they cracked after dinner.

123 Published, made known; "spread far and wide" (Johnson).

CHAPTER XVII

Chrysal's master goes to be admitted into an extraordinary society. Some
reflections not suited to the taste of the times. Rise of this society. A
description of a monastery, with an account of its members, and of
some of its rules.

THE next morning after I came into the possession of my new
master, he set out upon a party of pleasure of a most extraordinary
nature.[124] This was to be admitted into a society, formed of a
number of persons of the first distinction, in burlesque imitation
of the religious societies which are instituted in other countries.

I have already told you, that I shall not give any opinion in
religious matters. But whether the original institution of such
societies was right or not, as the motive of them was the worship
of the Deity, any attempt to turn them into ridicule most certainly
must be wrong; the mind of man seldom being acute or attentive
enough to distinguish between matters, which to appearance are
so intimately connected as the mode of worship, and the object
of it; but generally involving either in the disregard affecting the

---

124 As the Key later makes clear, Chrysal's master is John Montagu, Earl of
Sandwich, whose storyline will resume in Volume IV (see 2.199). Sandwich was
an especially notorious member of the Monks of Medmenham (also known as
the Franciscans, the Knights of Wycombe and the Hell-Fire Club), "a gentleman's
club for feasting, drinking, and fornication, the meetings of which might be
enlivened by fancy dress and travestied religious rites." Medmenham is the
"extraordinary society" of this chapter. *Chrysal* became the unlikely foundation
for a teetering stack of breathless, hyperbolic, and misinformed accounts of
the order, each exaggerating its precedent, until by the early twentieth century
the Monks were avowed Satanists, devoted to necrophilia, incest, orgies and
sacrifices. It is far more likely, however, that the Society was not dissimilar to
many other such clubs of the day: "whatever rites, carnal or profane, that might
have enlivened their meetings, the monks' serious and continuing concerns were
probably feasting, drinking, and politics" (DNB). The mockery of religious rites
was in all likelihood only play-acting, the sex and drinking were not atypical
for gentlemen of their age and rank, and the members' eventual exposure was
motivated not by moral opprobrium but by political interest.

other. In the present instance indeed, the disregard was designedly
levelled at both alike.

To give you a proper notion of the scene in which my master
was going to act a capital part, it is necessary to trace the whole
from its original.

A person of a flighty imagination,[125] and who possessed a
fortune that enabled him to pursue those flights, cloyed with
common pleasures, and ambitious of distinguishing himself
among his companions, had resolved to try if he could not strike
out something new, that should at the same time please his own
taste, and do honour to his genius.

The mere gratifications of sense, in their utmost extent,
not answering his design, he had recourse to the assistance of
imagination to enhance them. The great *butt*, against which
men of pleasure play off all their wit, is Religion. Their reasons,
for a practice so gross, are obvious. As the voice of conscience
will sometimes intrude upon them, so as to pall their highest
pleasures, in the very moment of enjoyment, their first endeavour
is to silence it, which they find by experience cannot be done so
effectually by any other method, as this of taking off the respect
paid to Religion, from which conscience borrows the terrors, that
make its admonitions so unwelcome. Beside, they think it shews
their superiority over the rest of mankind to laugh at what they
are afraid of; as it is also convenient for their character of wit, to
exert it on topics, where it is safe from being rivalled by men of
real understanding.

---

125 KEY: "Sir F. Dashwood. Ld. le Despenser." The infamous Francis Dashwood
(1708-81), Baron Le Despencer, founder and eponym of the Franciscans. His self-
cultivated reputation as rake *ne plus ultra* later hampered his political career; he
"made powerful political enemies," such as Charles Churchill and John Wilkes,
"whose attempts to discredit him were facilitated by the manner in which he
flaunted his lecherous proclivities" (DNB). After Wilkes exposed the Society
in the popular press (see 2.152, note 130), the public imagination construed le
Despencer "as a blaspheming, libidinous rake that had used the restored abbey
to engage in black magic, outlandish orgies, and obscene parodies of the rites of
Rome" (DNB). Dashwood's reputation as lecher, and his social and political ties
to Sandwich, are caricatured in Hogarth's *Sir Francis Dashwood at his Devotions*:
Dashwood, dressed as a monk, serenely gazes at a recumbent, naked woman,
while in his halo can be seen the features of Sandwich.

CHRYSAL 149

These weighty considerations determined him to season his scheme as high as he could with impiety, in order to make it be the better relished. Accordingly, after due deliberation on a matter of such moment, he at length hit upon a plan that pleased him.

In the middle of a large lake upon his estate there was an island, the natural beauties of whose situation had been heightened by every improvement of art. On this island he erected a building exactly on the model of the monasteries,[126] which he had seen in other countries; and to make the resemblance complete, there was not a vice, that he had ever heard imputed to the inhabitants of them, for practising which he did not make provision in his. The cellars were stored with the choicest wines; the larders with the delicacies of every climate; and the *cells* were fitted up for all the purposes of lasciviousness, for which proper objects were also provided.

Thus far the ridicule, however criminal in itself, may seem to have been designed only against those societies of human institution: But it was beneath his genius and spirit to stop here. Nothing less would satisfy him, than to attack the very essentials of the Religion established by the laws of his country, and acknowledged by every serious person in it, to be divine.

For this pious purpose, when every thing was prepared for their reception, his next care was to find a fraternity proper for the place. But in this, his rank and course of life made him not long at a loss. He selected from among his intimates a number equal to that of those who had been at the first chosen to inculcate the Religion which he designed to ridicule, whose names they assumed, as he with equal modesty and piety did that of the divine author of it:[127]

---

126 KEY: "Medenham Abbey." In the early 1750s, Dashwood and his circle rented the ruined medieval abbey of Medmenham, a village on the Thames, then augmented the structure with "a ruined tower, a small cloister, and stained glass to create a picturesque riparian summer retreat. Over its entrance was the inscription from Rabelais's Abbey of Theleme: *Fay ce que vouldras*," or "do what you will." Walpole visited Medmenham in 1763, afterwards writing, "each member has his cell, in which indeed is little more than a bed. They meet to drink, though the rule is pleasure, and each is to do whatever he pleases in his own cell, into which they may carry women" (DNB).
127 According to Wilkes, the Franciscan inner circle was constituted of thirteen members: Dashwood (the founder) plus twelve apostles. General membership,

And to supply any decrease in this number by death, or desertion from the terrors of reflection, he instituted an inferior order of as many more, chosen also with the greatest caution and regard to the latitude of their principles, their fortunes, and mirthful accomplishments.

The probationary office of these latter was to attend upon their superiors in the celebration of their mysteries, which were all performed in the chapel of the monastery, where no other servants were ever permitted to enter, on the most common occasion, as the very *decorations* of it would in a great measure have betrayed their secrets, the ceiling being covered with emblems and devices too gross to require explanation to the meanest capacity; and the walls painted with the portraits of those whose names and characters they assumed, represented in attitudes and actions, horrible to imagination.

Nor was their care to keep their mysteries impenetrably secret confined to this exclusion of common servants. The diffidence of conscious guilt made them even distrust each other, till bound to secrecy by oaths and imprecations, receiving their force from the Religion thus abused by them: An absurdity common among men associated for the most flagitious purposes.

But strong as the power of superstition is over weak and wicked minds, (for nothing but the grossest superstition could make them think oaths in such circumstances binding!) their secrecy was secured by a still stronger motive, which was fear.

They were sensible that even suspicion of such vices would forever exclude them from the society of all those, whom in despite of themselves, they could not help holding in respect; and that so outrageous an insult upon the laws was liable to punishment from the secular power, though they might by their interest evade the direct effects of which, yet the imputation would make them so obnoxious to the people in general, that they could no longer

---

however, was certainly larger in number, although many may only have visited once or twice. Records are scant, but members—in addition to Wilkes, Sandwich, and Dashwood—included the poet Paul Whitehead, George Bubb Dodington, and Thomas Potter, son of the Archbishop of Canterbury. Others said to be Franciscans, although evidence is less solid, were John Manners, Lord Orford, William Douglas, William Hogarth and Charles Churchill.

hope to enjoy any of the lucrative employments of the state, if
their resentment did not arise still higher, and make them take that
punishment into their own hands! and these fears prevented the
secrets from being divulged even by such as had resolution enough
to desert the society; as they imagined the stain could never be so
effectually expunged, as to secure them from those consequences.

The rites of this society, and the ceremonies observed upon
admission into it, will be best explained by the account of what I
saw my master perform on this occasion, when he was a candidate
for the higher order, having already served his noviciate in the
lower.

CHAPTER XVIII

Chrysal's master arrives at the monastery. The manner of his being
   admitted into the society. Character of his competitor. The method he
   took to revenge the society's injustice in preferring *Chrysal's* master to
   him. The mirth of the company disturbed by the entrance of *the devil*,
   just as he was invoked by *Chrysal's* master. The effect of such a visitor
   upon the company. The *devil* fixes upon *Chrysal's* master in particular,
   and makes him squeak.[128]

IT was about four o'clock in the afternoon when my master arrived
at the verge of the lake, where he no sooner made the concerted
signal, than a boat was sent to ferry him over.

On his landing in the island, he went to the monastery, where he
found the society just sitting down to dinner, at which he took his
place among them. When they had made a short meal, and drank
their spirits up to a proper pitch, they retired to their respective
cells, to prepare for the solemnity they were going to celebrate.
My master then clad in a milk-white robe of the finest linen, that
flowed loosely round him, repaired at the tolling of a bell to the
chapel, the scene of all their mysterious rites, and knocking gently
thrice at the door, it was opened to him, to the sound of soft and
solemn music.[129]

---

128 "To break silence or secrecy for fear or pain" (Johnson).
129 In the *Nocturnal Revels* (1779), which purports to have been written by one

On his entrance he made a most profound obeisance, and advancing slowly towards a table that stood against the wall, in the upper end of the chapel, as soon as he came to the rails, by which it was surrounded, he fell upon his knees, and making a profession of his principles, nearly in the words, but with the most gross perversion of the sense of the articles of faith of the religion established in the country, demanded admission within the rails, the peculiar station of the upper order, where the superior and eleven of the fraternity (the twelfth place was vacant, and now to be filled up) stood arrayed in the habits of those, whose names and characters they profaned by their assumption.

When he had finished, another candidate advanced in the like manner,[130] and making his profession also preferred the same claim; as there were more who had a right to do, but discouraged by the superior merit of these two, they had declined their pretensions for this time.

The brotherhood having heard the competitors with attention, retired to the table, and kneeling around it, the superior repeated

---

of the Franciscans, initiation is similarly described: "the ceremony of admission is performed in a Chapel allotted for that purpose, upon the tolling of a bell, accompanied with solemn, plaintive music." Each candidate approaches the inner circle of monks, "makes a profession of his principles, and requests admission within the rails, the appointed station of the original twelve members, arrayed in the clerical habit." Finally, votes are collected by the superior, and the candidate with a majority is elected.

130 KEY: "Mr. Wilkes." John Wilkes (1725-97), radical journalist and politician. He was an early member of the Monks of Medmenham but became *persona non grata* around the summer of 1763, roughly when Sandwich joined the order. In 1762, Wilkes founded the *North Briton,* a political weekly dedicated to attacking the new ministry of the Earl of Bute, the Scottish favorite of George III. Once Dashwood became Chancellor of the Exchequer in the new ministry, Wilkes excoriated Dashwood as an inept tool of Bute, and social ties between the two ruptured completely. In late 1763, during Wilkes's prosecution for seditious libel for publishing the *North Briton* 45 (see 2.278-303), Dashwood seconded Sandwich's condemnation of Wilkes for publishing the *Essay on Woman.* Wilkes retaliated by publishing an *exposé* of the Franciscans, and Sandwich and Dashwood were branded and satirized as hypocrites, the entire affair ballooning into "one of the major scandals of the age" (DNB). Wilkes, who was famously, hideously caricatured by Hogarth in "John Wilkes Esquire," was indubitably a womanizer, libertine and blasphemer, but he was also a talented scholar and a keen proponent of civil liberties, particularly freedom of the press.

a prayer, in the same strain and manner with the *profession* of the candidates, *to the Being whom they served* to direct their choice to him of the two most worthy of his service.

The superior then proceeded to take the suffrages of the rest, with the same mimic solemnity; when my master being found to have the majority, his election was exultingly attributed to immediate inspiration, and he was accordingly admitted within the rails, where he received *the name* and *character* which he was to bear in the society, in a manner not proper to be described, every the most sacred rite and ceremony of Religion being profaned, all the prayers and hymns of praise appointed for the worship of the Deity burlesqued by a perversion to the horrid occasion.

In this manner the evening was wasted till supper-time, when they sat down to a banquet in the chapel, in honour of the occasion, at which nothing that the most refined luxury, the most lascivious imagination could suggest to kindle loose desire, and provoke and gratify appetite was wanting; both the superiors, and the inferiors, (who were permitted to take their places at the lower end of the table, as soon as they had served in the banquet) vying with each other in loose songs and dissertations of such gross lewdness and daring impiety, as despair may be supposed to dictate to the damned, in both which my master shone so unrivalled as to bear down the superior sprightliness, wit, and humour of all the rest; and compensate for the want of every companionable merit.

But while they were in the height of their festivity, an affair happened that interrupted it for a time, and shewed their resolution, particularly that of my master, in a proper light.

The person,[131] who had that day been his competitor for the honour of admission into the higher order of the society, possessed the qualifications, which he wanted, in the most eminent degree. He had such a flow of spirits, that it was impossible ever to be a moment dull in his company. His wit gave charms to every subject he spoke upon; and his humour displayed the foibles of mankind in such colours, as to put even folly out of countenance.

---

131 KEY: "Ditto." Many commemorate Wilkes as wonderfully witty and charming in company, although Walpole disagreed: "I saw no wit: his conversation shows how little he has lived in good company, and the chief turn of it is the grossest bawdy."

But the same vanity which had first made him ambitious of entering into this society, only because it was composed of persons of a rank superior to his own in life, and still kept him in it, tho' upon acquaintance he despised themselves, sullied all these advantages. His spirits were often stretched to extravagance to overpower competition. His humour was debased into buffoonery; and his wit was so prostituted to the lust of applause, that he would sacrifice his best friend for a scurvy jest; and wound the heart of him, whom he would at that very moment hazard his life and fortune to serve, only to raise a laugh; in which he was also assisted by a peculiar archness of disposition and unlucky expertness of carrying his *jests into practice*, as he proved upon this occasion.

Though he disdained to decline the late competition, as the others did, he had been well aware that my master's higher rank in life would carry the point in dispute against him; for which injustice he resolved to revenge himself in the most signal manner.

For this purpose he had contrived the night before to bring into his cell a great *Baboon* which he had provided for the occasion.[132] When the brotherhood retired to their cells after dinner, as I have told you, to prepare for the ceremony, he availed himself of the office of keeper of the chapel, which he then filled, to convey this creature, dressed up in the fantastic garb, in which childish imagination clothes devils, into the chapel, where he shut him up in a large chest that stood there to hold the ornaments and utensils of the table, when the society was away. To the spring of the lock of this chest he fastened a cord, which he drew under the carpet that was on the floor to his own seat, and there brought the end of it through a hole, made for the purpose, in such a manner that he could readily find it; and by giving it a pull, open the chest, and let the *Baboon* loose whenever he pleased, without being perceived by any of the rest of the company.

Accordingly, when they were all in the height of their mirth,

---

132 Wilkes's simian practical joke is almost certainly fictional, although the DNB holds that Dashwood brought a baboon to Franciscan meetings, to which he "was accustomed to administer the eucharist." A similar trick is played, using a bear skin, in Ned Ward's account of the "Atheistical Club" in *The Secret History of Clubs* (1709).

on my master's kneeling down, and with hands and eyes raised towards heaven, repeating an invocation in the perverted phrase of Holy Writ, to the Being whom they served to come along them, and receive their adorations in person, he pulled the cord, and let the animal loose; who, glad to be delivered from his confinement, gave a sudden spring upon the middle of the table.

The effect which the sight of such a visitor had upon them, may be better conceived than expressed. Their attention had been so fixed upon what my master was saying, that they perceived not from whence he came; and his appearing so critically at the invocation, and in such a shape, made them conclude he was *the Being invoked*.

Terrified out of their senses by the thought, they all roared out with one voice, *The Devil! The Devil!* and starting from their seats made directly toward the door, tumbling over one another, and oversetting every thing in their way.

In the height of this uproar and confusion, *the Baboon* frighted at the effects of their fear, happened to leap upon my master's shoulders, as he lay sprawling on the floor, who turning about his head and feeling the shock, saw the animal grinning horribly at him, and concluded the Devil had obeyed his summons in good earnest, and come to carry him bodily away.

Driven as he was to despair by this thought, he strove however, in the instinctive impulse of self-preservation, to shake off the invader: but he, instead of loosing his hold, on his repeated efforts, only clung to him the closer, clasping his paws around his neck, and chattering with spite at his ear. This completed the caitiff's distress. Every shadow of spirit failed him, and conscious guilt suggesting to him the meaning of this unintelligible jargon, he attempted in the blindness of his fear to move the very Devil to pity, by his pathetic wailings and supplications.

"Spare me, gracious Devil!" (said he) "spare a wretch, who never was sincerely your servant! I sinned only from vanity of being in the fashion! thou knowest I never have been half so wicked as I pretended; never have been able to commit the thousandth part of the vices which I have boasted of. Take not then the advantage of that vanity; but judge me only from my actions. I knew not that thou wouldst have come, or I should never have invoked thee!

leave me therefore, and go to those who are more truly devoted
to thy service. I am but half a sinner. My conscience always flew
in my face when I committed any crime! my heart gave the lie
to my tongue, when I gloried in my vices; and I trembled at the
damnation I affected to brave! O spare me therefore, at least for
this time, till I have served thee better. I am as yet but half a sinner."

CHAPTER XIX

The *Devil* is degraded to a *Baboon*, and his appearance well accounted for,
   which restores the mirth and courage of the company, and particularly
   of *Chrysal*'s master, who exerts himself to recover his character. The
   appearance of the be-deviled *Baboon* is traced next day to his introducer,
   who, at the instance of *Chrysal*'s master, is expelled the society for
   presuming to ridicule their rites. Farther consequences of this affair
   make the superior break up his monastery, and build a church.

WHILE my master was making this essay of his eloquence upon
the Baboon, the person who had brought him there took the
opportunity of the consternation the whole company was in, to
open one of the windows unperceived by them for the animal to
make his mistake, which he no sooner saw, than he made directly
to it, giving my master an happy release.

Before he could get clear off though, one of the company, who
was bolder than the rest, having mustered resolution to raise his
head, got a full view of him, and perceiving what he was, just as my
master concluded his supplications, "Your prayers are heard!" (said
he, starting up and speaking as soon as a burst of laughter gave him
utterance) "your prayers are heard for this time; and that Devil of a
great *He-baboon*, that's just gone out of the window, despising *half a
sinner*, has spared you till you are fitter for his service."

At hearing these words, they all arose from the floor, where
they had lain sprawling on top of one another, and looking in
amazement at him who had spoke them; "Courage, my friends!"
(said he) "this is but a false alarm! our *master* is not so ready to
come for us when we call him, or we should none of us all be here
now. How *a Baboon* though should come here to scare us out of

our little wits in such a manner, the Devil may tell you, if he will, for I cannot; but I'll swear I saw one go out of that window."

"And I'll swear, too, that I saw him come in at it;" (replied the author of the mischief, who saw no way to escape detection, but by preventing farther enquiry by this bold lie) "as I just then happened to look about to see from whence the wind came, that blew upon my poll."[133]

This eclaircissement satisfied them all! they instantly set the room to rights, and plastering up their broken shins and noses, sat down to conclude their carousal, resuming their former strain, in which they all exerted themselves in an uncommon manner, to wipe off the disgrace of the late *squeaking*, particularly my master, who *out-did his usual out-doing* in profaneness, blasphemy, and wickedness of every kind, to recover his character, and convince them he was more than *half a sinner*.

They held in this hand, till nature sunk under the fatigue, when they retired to sleep off their debauch in their *cells*; where, as I said, proper provision had been made for them, to reduce the theory of the day into practice, in the intervals of rest.

Though the affair of the *Baboon* had passed off so cleverly while their spirits were in such a flurry, when they came to enquire more coolly into it next day, the whole trick came out. It had been impossible to convey him into the monastery, without the privity of some of the servants, who had all so often *felt the jests* of this gentleman, that they were glad of an opportunity of being revenged upon him now, by making the discovery.

This account, confirmed by some circumstances in his behaviour, which they had not attended to at the time, plainly pointing out the guilty person, the superiors adjourned directly to the chapel to consult how they should proceed on so delicate an occasion. For though they had always highly approved of such *wit*, when *practised* upon others, they looked upon the application of it to themselves in the most heinous light, especially in such an instance as this, the consequences of which had exposed them to the contempt of each other, by detecting their *weakness*, and shewing that the guilt in which they gloried was only feigned.

---

133 "The head" (Johnson).

Mortifying as it was to their vanity, the thought however that the case was general, afforded them some consolation. However, to remedy the effect of this, and prevent a repetition of the like disgrace, it was proposed, after mature deliberation, and much learned argument on the question, to bury what was past, by a solemn act of amnesty, and make a special law, whose observation should be enforced *by an oath*, that no member should ever after presume to attempt exercising his wit upon the society, in any manner, or by any means whatsoever; on taking which oath, and asking pardon upon his knees, at the door of the chapel, the offender should be forgiven.

To this proposal they all assented, except my master, who for private reasons thought the latter part of it much too mild for so flagrant a crime. He had long cherished a secret grudge against the other, who not only often pointed his wit against him, in a manner that he could not digest, nor knew how to resent, it being as polite as it was keen, but also put him constantly to the expence of double wickedness, the only qualification in which he could possibly shine, to avoid being totally eclipsed by him: His desire of revenge also was strongest on this occasion, as he had suffered the deepest disgrace.

Accordingly he exerted all his eloquence, to shew *the enormity of the crime of attempting to turn any of the rites and ceremonies established by the laws of the society into ridicule;*[134] the letting of which escape without adequate punishment, he said, would argue weakness and want of spirit in them, and must end in the ruin of their authority; for which weighty reasons he proposed that the offender should be directly expelled the society in form, as the only effectual way to vindicate their dignity, and prevent others from offering it the like insult for the future.

This gave the affair a new turn. They all took fire at the thought of their dignity's being insulted, and expelled him that moment, without even waiting to hear him in his own defence. But he soon had the satisfaction of seeing himself amply revenged.

The care they took to keep every thing they did secret, had

---

134 Johnstone's italics here may well be capitalizing on irony. During Wilkes's later prosecution for seditious libel (2.278-303), Sandwich castigated him and the *Essay on Woman* for similar reasons.

long awoke the curiosity of the neighbourhood, who were the more severe in their guesses, the less able they were to guess right. But the affair of the *Baboon*, whom the servants got sight of, before he could be caught, and whether misled by his dress, or misrepresenting by design, gave out to be *the Devil*, was no sooner known, than a formal story was propagated over the whole country, that the end of their meeting was to worship the Devil, to whom this chapel was dedicated, and who had *often* been seen among them, in variety of shapes.

Scandal always meets easy credit. The story was believed by many, and repeated by more as if they believed it, never losing any thing in the repetition; till such an universal alarm was raised among the people (who are content to infringe the precepts of Religion, without denying its authority) that the superior, whose seat was in the neighbourhood, found it necessary to dissolve the society, and effacing every trace of it, convert the building to the better use of a pleasure house, in which he entertained all his neighbours in general, whenever he was in the country: Beside which, he also built a church on an eminence near his house,[135] that answered the double purpose, of convincing the populace of his regard to Religion, and of making a beautiful termination to a vista, which he had just cut through a wood, in his park.

I have anticipated these circumstances to satisfy your curiosity; as I have also omitted many, and softened more particulars in this account, which were too horrid to have been represented in their proper colours.

---

135 KEY: "High Wycombe Church," seconded by other keys. In 1763, Dashwood completed his renovation of West Wycombe church "in a picturesque Italian style." Many surmised the renovations were a cynical attempt to restore Dashwood's reputation: "Temples which built aloft in air," wrote Churchill, "may serve for show, if not for prayer."

CHAPTER XX

A further account of the rules of the convent; with some striking
instances of œconomy. A seeming inconsistency accounted for, from
a principle not sufficiently understood. Some remarkable effects of
vanity. Reason of the abuse of wealth.

You are astonished how such scenes of debauchery and excess
could be supported, either by the fortune of the entertainer, or the
constitutions of his guests; but this shall be explained.

To prevent satiety or fatigues, these meetings were never
protracted beyond a week at a time; nor held oftener than twice in
a year; by which frugality of pleasure, they were always returned
to with the keenness of novelty: And as for the expence of them,
that was defrayed jointly by the whole community; (the superior
contributing nothing more than any other member, except the
first cost of building the *convent*, which he thought himself amply
recompensed for, by the honour of having struck out the plan); and
regulated by the strictest œconomy; the slaves of their lusts being
sent back to the brothels, from whence they had been brought,
and the servants of their luxury discharged, at the end of every
meeting; and no more retained for the rest of the year, than an old
man and woman who took care of the place.

To you who have supported the dignity of your nature, by
preferring the pleasures of that reason, which was given to
distinguish man from brutes, to those of sense, which they enjoy
in common with him, the picture of this whole scene must appear
overcharged[136] and irreconcilable with the great principles of human
action, which always propose some *good*, either present or future,
however the judgment may err in the thing proposed. But more
acquaintance with life would solve this difficulty to you.

The general motive for attempting to turn Religion into
ridicule has been already explained. But as some are seen to give
into this practice, who seem to cultivate their reason with most
success; and whose actions, and even inclinations, appear not to

___
136 Excessive, inflated (OED).

have the remotest tendency contrary to moral virtue, it may be proper to account for such an exception.

The first principle of action, impressed by nature on every thing that lives, is *self-preservation*. From this, *brute* animals, which *by necessity* proceed regularly in the course prescribed for them, never swerve: But the *rational* animal, man, bewildered in his own imaginations, by the abuse of that *liberty*, which was given him to enhance the merit of his obedience to the dictates of *reason*, often substitutes another in its place, by whose impulse he acts in direct opposition to it.

This is *vanity*; the real source of that ambition, which courts danger, and plunges with open eyes into destruction, however speciously it may be disguised under the pompous titles of love of glory, and regard to the public good; as well as of most of the extravagancies and absurdities which puzzle superficial observers, and make them presumptuously impeach as a defect in the work of nature, their own neglect and perversion of its laws.

A particular enquiry into the effects of this *suppositious*[137] principle, many of which, as I said, are blazoned as the brightest virtues, while more are acknowledged to be the most atrocious crimes; or how nearly such virtues and crimes, proceeding thus from the same source, may be allied, though curious and interesting in itself, is not necessary here. It is sufficient to observe that its power is able to break the force of habit, reconcile contradictions, and confound the essential difference of things; to cope with *prejudice*, and overrule the *infirmities* of nature.

This it is, for instance, that makes the *constitutional* coward, who trembles at the thought of danger, and would see his country ruined, rather than draw his sword in its defence, *fight duels* for a doubtful punctilio of empty ceremony; the *superstitious* wretch, who finds *omens*, in *spilled salt*, and *crossed straws*, and *sees Goblins* and *Devils* in the dark, profess infidelity, ridicule Providence, and dare the wrath of heaven, by insults and bravadoes; and lastly, this it is, that makes the hoary Sage, whose life has been regulated by the strictest principles of morality and religion, while passion

---

137 "Not genuine; put by a trick into the place or character belonging to another" (Johnson).

might have rebelled against them, commence Libertine in the impotence of old age, and glory in vices he has lost the power to practise. Of the justice of these remarks, the members of this society, of which vanity was the cement, as it had been the origin, afforded the most glaring proofs.

You wonder what there could be to be vain of, in such an association! but you do not reflect, that vanity is never the result of real worth. The false glare of public estimation reflects it from the vilest and most reproachful objects.

The institutor of this society was *admired* for every polite accomplishment, every power of pleasing in conversation; and the first set he chose were all of the same cast. This, with their rank and fortunes, and above all the mystery of the institution, which set curiosity on fire, and gave imagination room to form the most flattering ideas of it, made admission into it an object of universal ambition, as it seemed a proof of every member's meriting the same character; and when once admitted, a vicious fear of ridicule made too many ashamed to quit it; and even they, who did, were precluded from discovering any thing that might deter others, by the secrecy to which they were sworn.

There is one thing more, which from the particular circumstances of your own life affects you more than any other, in this account. This is the folly and ingratitude of lavishing the blessing of wealth to the dishonour of the donor; and with so little regard to its real use. But this, as has been the case in other instances, proceeds from want of better acquaintance with life.

It has been remarked by travellers, that in those parts of the earth, where the blessings of nature are bestowed with greatest liberality, the people seem least sensible of them; and are sunk in the grossest vice; as if reason and virtue were incompatible with the good things of this world.

The reason of this remark holds with respect to wealth in other countries. Provided to profusion with every thing they want, the rich look no farther than to the gratification of their appetites and passions; as the means to procure which are in their possession, they acknowledge no obligation to the power which first gave, and still preserves the enjoyment of them: but on the contrary, affect to shew their independence, by prostituting it to purposes, directly contrary to his declared pleasure; and this causes that abuse of wealth, which generally mars the blessing, and makes the gift of it so dangerous.

CHAPTER XXI

Account of the members of the society. The history of the superior. The particular qualifications by which he arose in life. Success in a private instance encourages him to try his talents, in a higher sphere, from which he soon descends with disgrace. A striking inconsistency in his character.

I SEE you desire to have some account of the several members of so extraordinary a society. When the great lines which distinguish the characters of mankind are marked by virtues, or even by superior abilities, that dazzle superficial observation, by the splendour of their effects, and pass for such, however different in the tendency of their exertions, the delineation affords pleasure; but on the contrary, when those lines are all distorted by vice and folly, and distinguished from each other only by different modes and degrees of them, the contemplation is a pain; and to paint them a task so disagreeable, that nothing but an impartial regard to truth could make it be undertaken. However your curiosity shall be gratified.

As the *convent* was dedicated to pleasure, you may imagine that play made a part of their entertainment. Contrary indeed to the scheme of all other parties of pleasure, it was not the first object of their meeting; and only served to fill up the intervals between other pleasures, which nature without some respite could not support in such excess. The circulation however, even in this *piddling* for mere amusement, gave me an opportunity of taking a view of all their characters; such of which as contained any thing worthy of your notice, for you must not expect it from them all, I will give you some general sketches of.

As the looks of a man are generally a comment on his heart, I will place the whole company in your view, as I have done on other occasions, to assist you in forming a proper notion of their characters. At the head of the table sits the superior.[138] You see

138 KEY: "Sir F. Dashwood." See note 125.

every eye is expressively fixed upon him, in admiration at the vivacity, humour, and wit in all he says, while by an art peculiarly happy, he alone seems unconscious of his own pre-eminence.

These talents, which from the intoxication of present applause, are much oftener of prejudice than advantage to the possessor, by diverting from more solid pursuits, proved the foundation of his exalted rank and fortune; because always directed by the deepest and most delicate address.

The first instance, in which this address was displayed, was in his own family. He had a distant relation[139] who had spent his youth in such busy scenes, as left not time for his imagination to wander in search of amusement. To a mind accustomed to be wound up to such a pitch, the charms of a conversation like his were a relaxation, irresistibly engaging. He insinuated himself insensibly into his favour, and by seeming to have nothing in view, but his pleasure, led him as he pleased himself, not only into all the lengths of his own libertinism, so as to be a member of this society, when the decline of life, at least, should have suggested more serious thoughts; but also at his death, to reward his complaisance with a much larger portion of his fortune, than he had any claim to from consanguinity or the preference of reason.

Such success encouraged his ambition to higher attempts. Introduced by the same qualifications to the acquaintance of *the great*, he not only gained their favour by them, but also imposed them upon them for abilities of an higher class so far, that being secure of his subserviency to their designs, they admitted him to a share of their power.[140]

---

139 KEY: "Late Ld. Westmoreland," seconded by other keys. John Fane (bap. 1686, d. 1762), Earl of Westmorland, politician and Major-General in the British army. Fane was the uncle and guardian of Dashwood, whose father died while he was still at Eton. The two became good friends and political allies, and Westmorland is often named as a member of the Franciscans.

140 KEY: "Chancellorship of the Exchequer." Made Chancellor of the Exchequer in 1762, Dashwood proposed a new budget financing the nation's naval debt through a tax on cider. However, his speech on the matter was so poor, wrote Walpole, "with so little intelligence or clearness, in so vulgar a tone and in such mean language, that he said himself afterward: 'People will point at me, and cry: There goes the worst Chancellor of the Exchequer that ever appeared!'" The domestic cider duty inspired a public furor; Wilkes devoted an issue of the *North*

But in this he had deceived himself as well as them; as he found to their disappointment and his own extreme confusion, upon the very first trial of his political talents, when he shewed in the strongest light the difference between the abilities requisite to raise a laugh, and rule a nation.

He had sense enough however to see his mistake, before it had involved him in any consequences, from which he could not recede without danger as well as disgrace; and prudently sacrificing his ambition to his safety, he turned off all with a laugh, and returned to the enjoyment of those pleasures for which nature seemed to have so particularly designed him.[141] Whether that enjoyment is as sincere and undisturbed though, as should appear from his looks and conduct, is a point not so certain, as you may be apt to imagine.

The principles, on which this society was originally instituted, and from which it has never deviated, *the professed ridicule of moral Virtue and Religion*, should seem to have proceeded from an utter disbelief of a Deity; or at least, a fearless defiance of his power; but contrary to this, there starts not at his own shadow a more abject slave to superstition, and all its foolish fears, than he was at the time of his instituting it, and still remains.

Such an inconsistence requires explanation to you, whose notions of life are formed solely from rational speculation.

Briton to the controversy. Dashwood's pursuant reputation as an incompetent was commemorated in the *Town and Country Magazine* in 1774, which counted him "amongst the small number of those, who have not only declared their ignorance of the offices they filled, but that they were totally disqualified for them, and that, so far from being political arithmeticians, they could not cast up a common sum in addition."

141 Dashwood resigned as Chancellor in 1763. Afterward, "he regularly attended the House of Lords, but his interest in high politics began to wane and he rarely spoke in debate" (DNB).

CHAPTER XXII

Continuation of the history of the superior. The inconsistency in his
  character accounted for. The reason of his being sent early to travel for
  education. Political principles all necessary to be attended to, in a tutor.
  The method and effect of his tutor's care to instruct him in Religion. A
  frightful story gives rise to a frightful dream, which is interrupted still
  more frightfully. A tremendous apparition terrifies him into a swoon.
  Account of the apparition.

THE political principles of his family being in avowed opposition to
their Sovereign,[142] the earliest care was taken to instil the same into
him; and the ripeness of his parts and genius flattered them with a
promise of his future consequence in the state.

For this purpose, before reason should have time to be convinced
by experience of the injustice and danger of such designs, he was
sent abroad to be educated in a country, where every object should
concur to prejudice him against the laws and constitution of his
own, and the opportunity of personal intercourse confirm his
attachment to him, whose interest he was intended to promote.

The public conduct of his life has sufficiently shewn the success
of this scheme: as an incidental circumstance in the execution of it
will also account for the inconsistencies in his private character.

The religious principles established in the country, whither he
was thus sent for education, and the political ones it was designed
he should assist to establish at home, were so intimately and
essentially connected, that it was impossible to find a tutor for
him sufficiently attached to the latter, to answer the purpose of his
family, who was not also at least secretly inclined to, even if he did
not openly profess, the former.

But this made no difficulty. Religion is in reality the thing least
thought of, however pompously it may be professed in political

---

142 Westmorland, Dashwood's uncle and guardian, played "a leading role within
English Jacobite circles during the late 1740s and early 1750s," and was a favorite
of Frederick, Prince of Wales, the eldest son and political rival of King George II.
Later, Dashwood and Westmorland were "Frederick's principal representatives in
negociations to form a broad-based opposition" to the ministry in power (DNB).

schemes. They scrupled not therefore to commit his tender mind to the influence of such an one, regardless what impressions he might make upon it, beside those they desired: An opportunity which he did not fail to take advantage of.

Accordingly as soon as the tutor and his pupil were settled in the place of their designation, the former began his design, by displaying on every occasion the excellence and importance of the ceremonies and rites of the Religion professed there, as the objects most likely to strike the levity of youth, always complaining with a contemptuous concern of the want of such in that of his own country; not choosing to speak more directly at first, for fear of giving him any alarm.

But artful as this method was, he had the disappointment to see it did not succeed so well as he could wish. Though from the manner of his pupil's earliest education, it was easy enough to sink his own Religion in his opinion, yet some circumstances rendered the raising of any other in its place, a matter of more difficulty, than might have been obviously apprehended. His natural quickness and turn for ridicule made him see every thing in the most disadvantageous light, at the first glance, at the same time that his dissipation and levity prevented his attending to the abstruser arguments, often necessary to establish the credit of matters of such importance beyond the reach of rational doubt; so that all the pains his tutor was piously taking to enlarge his faith, threatened to work the contrary effect, of making him an infidel.

Alarmed at this, the tutor, whose bigoted credulity had swallowed every fiction of superstition, had always some miraculous story of a *judgment* or *apparition* ready to refute the scoffs of his pupil, and confirm the truth of whatever he himself advanced. The constant repetition of such tales, which he plainly showed his own belief of, insensibly made such an impression on his pupil's imagination, as persuaded him of their possibility at least, if he was not absolutely convinced of the truth of every thing in proof of which they were alleged; and filled him with fears, for which a good foundation had before been laid in the nursery.

When his mind was thus prepared to catch at every terror, his tutor took him one day to see the exhibition of one of those miracles, which are said to be wrought at the shrine of a contested saint;[143] and which really weaken the credit of the Religion they were devised to support.

The absurdity was too striking to escape his observation. He turned it into the most poignant ridicule,[144] in spite of all his tutor's pains to defend it; who finding that his arguments had no effect, had recourse to his usual proof of an *apparition*, which he dressed up in every colour and circumstance of horror, to make it have the greater weight.

His pupil took not more than usual notice of the matter, while light and company diverted his thoughts; but when he went to bed, and found himself alone, and in the dark, the whole flashed upon him in all its terrors, heightened in every instance, by the liveliness of his own imagination.

What he felt in such a situation may easier be conceived than expressed. He covered up his head with the clothes; and lay sweating and trembling till his mind was wearied with dwelling on the same thoughts, and he sunk into a kind of slumber.

But this was far from giving him relief. He was no sooner asleep, than imagination, now in her own empire, placed him in the midst of the scene, which had just before been so elaborately described to him by his tutor, from the contemplation of which he was delivered only to suffer still more severely; being awakened by sounds uncouth enough to startle, at such a time, the most resolute mind unacquainted with them.

Such a continuation realized all the horrors of his dream. He started up; and turning in the instinctive curiosity of affright to that part of the room, from whence the sounds still continued to come,

143 KEY: "Abbé Paris." François de Pâris (1690-1727), French Jansenist and Deacon of Saint-Médard, whose tomb was the site of multiple purported miracles, including instantaneous cures and inexplicable convulsions. At the height of the hysteria, writes B. Robert Kreiser in *Miracles, Convulsions, and Ecclesiastical Politics in Early Eighteenth-Century Paris*, "the tomb and the area surrounding it were sometimes completely covered with shaking and writhing bodies"—the so-called *convulsionnaires*—and thousands were flocking to the site from across France.

144 Le Despencer's irreligion abroad is seconded by Walpole's memoirs. One oft-repeated example claims Dashwood "secreted himself in the Sistine Chapel before the penitential scourging ceremonies of holy week and emerged from the darkness at the most sacred part of the ceremony, lashing out severely with an English horsewhip" (DNB).

saw four glaring eye-balls fixed upon him, at the same time that a voice distinctly articulated, but in a tremendous tone and language which he did not understand, thundered directly in his ear.

The darkness, which prevented his seeing the bodies, to which those eyes belonged, and his ignorance of the import of the sounds, only added to his fright by giving room to imagination, not only to form the most horrible conceptions of them, but also to apprehend them still more horrible than he could conceive. He was not able to support such an attack; but giving one helpless shriek, sunk back in a swoon.

His tutor, who lay in the next room, and had been awakened by the same sounds, but was not so much terrified at them, both because his mind was not so well prepared for terrors, and that he was acquainted with their cause, heard him shriek, and knowing his voice, ran to him, imagining he was engaged in a conflict, in which he might want assistance, with the *cats* which he heard in his room; for from two of those animals, which finding the window open, had chosen it for the scene of their amours, had those dreadful sounds proceeded.

CHAPTER XXIII

Continuation. Behaviour of the tutor on finding his pupil in a swoon. He recovers; and terrifies his tutor by mistaking him for a saint. Charity begins at home. The tutor sagaciously guesses at the meaning of the mistake; and piously resolves to improve it. The pupil's full and true account of the apparition, with the tutor's honest addition to it. His repentance, and conversion. His tutor moderates his zeal for weighty reasons. He relapses; and his tutor for private reasons divulges the whole affair. The method he took to invalidate the story.

You may judge how he was affected at seeing the person, upon whom all his hopes of wealth and preferment were founded, in such a situation. Awkward at the best, he now knew not how to attempt giving him any assistance, nor had even the presence of mind to call any one who could, so great was his embarrassment and confusion. Nature however soon delivered him from his distress, and restored his hopes, by the recovery of his pupil.

As soon as he came a little to himself, he stared wildly round him for some moments, and then fixing his eyes upon his tutor, who still stood gaping in amazement at him, he mistook him, from his being in his shirt, for the Saint that ran in his head, his imagination still continuing the former scene, and holding up his hands in a suppliant posture, as he lay trembling on his back, "O mercy, gracious Saint!" (said he) "Have mercy on my youth! never will I again presume to ridicule any of the sacred rites of Religion! never will I admit a doubt of any thing it commands me to believe! O mercy! mercy."—Saying which words he fainted away again.

This address, one word of which the tutor did not understand, threw him into a fright almost as great as that of his pupil. He stood for some time stupefied by astonishment, till the cold reminding him that he was in his shirt, care for his own health conquered every other concern, and made him go to put on his clothes before he attempted to do any thing for the other.

While he was dressing himself, he considered what his pupil had said, with rather more attention than his fear had permitted before, and recollecting the subject of their conversation the preceding evening, concluded that heaven had made use of some supernatural means to subdue his infidelity, the impression of which remaining still upon his mind had occasioned his mistaking him in the manner he did, for a Saint; (for that he should be terrified to that degree by the screaming of the cats, never came into his head) and piously resolved to contribute his assistance to the deception, by taking no notice that he had been with him before, or even denying it, if he saw occasion.

With this intention, he returned to his pupil, determined though not to disclose his suspicion, till the other should make some discovery to direct him more certainly how to proceed.

His pupil, who was just come to himself, knew him directly now he was dressed, and catching his hand eagerly as soon as he came within his reach, "O my dearest, my best friend!" (said he, pressing it to his lips) "What have I suffered since I saw you? How dearly have I paid for the profaneness, and infidelity of which you have so often reproved me, with pious and paternal care. But never will I be guilty of the like again. I resign myself implicitly to your direction; and will from this hour believe every thing you require me."

His tutor, after giving him some spiritual comfort, and encouraging his perseverance in this pious resolution, desired to know what had been the happy occasion of it; to which the other answered, that *some little time after he went to bed, the room was suddenly enlightened in a manner not to be described, when the apparition, of which he had given him an account the evening before, stood before him wrapped in blue flames, and breathing smoke and sulphur; and calling to him in a voice that appalled his soul, denounced heaven's vengeance against his infidelity, which he was just going to put into execution, when the holy Saint, whose miracles he had so impiously turned into ridicule, appeared all robed in white, and circled round with glory; and interposing between him and the spectre, the latter gave a shriek that shook the room, and then vanished in a flame of fire; upon which the Saint turned to him with a look ineffably benign, and exhorting him to repentance, gave him his benediction, and disappeared.*

Ready as his tutor was to believe every thing that exceeded belief, when alleged in the cause of Religion, the circumstance of his own having been mistaken for a Saint, staggered his faith in all the rest, and made him for once justly conclude that the whole miracle was no more than a fiction of that fear with which the screaming of the cats struck him in his sleep, for now he plainly traced the effects of their voices.

However, far from undeceiving him, he improved upon the thought; and as soon as his pupil concluded his tale, with a grave face and solemn air added a sequel to it, of equal truth, but dictated by a very different degree of veracity; the former being deceived himself, and having eked out the illusions of his fear, as distracted imagination suggested to him; whereas the latter aggravated those illusions, by untruths premeditately devised to confirm that deception.

He said, *that grieved at the danger with which an unhappy prejudice of education threatened the spiritual safety of one so dear to him, instead of lying down to rest, he had fallen upon his knees, and poured out his soul in prayer and supplication to heaven to enlighten his (pupil's) mind, and convince him of his errors, in which holy exercise he had continued*

ever since, till this moment, when in the impulse of a persuasion, which
he now perceived to have been divinely inspired, that his prayers were
heard, he came to satisfy himself of the reality of so miraculous an event,
for which he begged him to join in returning immediate thanks to heaven,
and the blessed Saint, who had wrought it.

This completed the deception of his pupil, so far as to make
him believe the truth of some parts of his own tale, which he
was not altogether so certain of before. He arose therefore, and
reconciling himself to the faith of his tutor, by the strongest and
most full professions, dedicated the remainder of the night with
him to prayer and pious conversation.

In the first heat of his devotion, he was for making the whole
affair public, and openly joining himself to that Religion, whose
truth was thus confirmed to him. But his tutor moderated the
fervency of his zeal, sensible that such a step would not only
defeat the political designs of his friends, which must be carried on
under a masque, and in whose success his own wishes were most
warmly interested; but also overturn his own hopes of being well
rewarded for the care of his education, by a church living of great
revenue, that was in the gift of one of his pupil's relations, who
had promised it to him, as soon as the incumbent, then sinking
under all the infirmities of extreme old age, should die: For his
religious principles never interfered with his interest.

For these most weighty reasons, though as you may imagine
he communicated only the former, he prevailed upon his convert
to be content with the private practice, without the profession of
his new faith, till he should in the fullness of time be so happy as to
contribute his assistance to the great event, which should establish
it in his own country.

Such an argument could not fail of effect upon one who found
the fervour of his devotion cool so fast, that in a few days the
whole matter was entirely reversed, and his practice as libertine
as ever, though fear of seeing any more spectres restrained his
professions within more decent bounds. For so deeply was the
dread of them imprinted on his mind, that to this day he dares not
sleep by himself, or be a moment alone in the dark: Though his
tutor soon after his return home divulged the whole affair, as far as
it affected not himself, with the addition of many circumstances,

if possible still more contemptibly ridiculous than the true, to
revenge his procuring the living for one of his raking companions,
and ingratiate himself with a particular enemy of his, from whom
he expected a recompence for so pleasing a piece of scandal; to
invalidate which was one of his pupil's motives for instituting this
society.

CHAPTER XXIV

Account of the members continued. History of one who turned libertine in speculation, after he had lost the power of being so in practice.
How this happened; the force of literary vanity; and the reason why
it is stronger than any other. Instances of the advantages reaped from
encouraging genius. A new method of flattery is successful where all
others had failed, and by a master-stroke makes vanity gain a signal
triumph over virtue.

AT the right hand of the superior you see one,[145] whose example
should be a warning to mankind never to be off their guard against
the allurements of vice, while there is any possibility, however
remote and improbable, of their falling into it.

While youth might have pleaded in excuse of passion; and the
busy application of manhood extenuated any speculative errors
in opinion, his conduct had been regulated by the strictest regard
to the principles of moral virtue, and the precepts of Religion.
But in the evening of his days, when all that heat and hurry give
place to cool reflection, and the serenity of the prospect more
than compensates for its approaching close, the whole scene was

---

145 KEY: "Lord Melcombe." George Bubb Dodington (1690/91-1762), Baron
Melcombe, who was over sixty when he became a Monk of Medmenham. Despite
"soaring, if buffoonish, aspirations to rank among the foremost whig grandees,"
Dodington "remained a political lightweight, a slightly ridiculous larger than life
character, blinkered, vain, and with little principle" (DNB). Walpole deemed him
"remarkable for his wit and want of principles," and, like many since, faulted
Dodington for political opportunism and side-switching. His vanity, portliness
and ambition were a favorite target of satirists: he appears in Hogarth's "Five
Orders of Periwigs" (1761), Churchill (2.263) called him a "swollen bullfrog with
lascivious face," and Lord Chesterfield (1.94) wrote, "God made Dodington the
coxcomb he is; mere human means could never have brought it about."

wretchedly reversed, and his setting sun overcast, with a cloud of vices most blameable in any stage of life, but aggravated ten thousand-fold in his, to which they were unnatural.

I have told you before that vanity was the cause of a fall, so reproachful to humanity: The manner though of its operating upon one, who seemed to be removed so far beyond its reach, is worthy of attention.

In no instance is the power of vanity so tyrannically exerted over the human heart, as when it arises from an opinion of literary merit. The reason is obvious. Real learning is the most effectual check to vanity, as it shews the instability of its foundation. When therefore any thing that makes pretence, however falsely, to that name, seems to administer to its support, it instantly looks upon itself as above control.

Though early engagement in the activer scenes of his country's service had prevented his making any great proficiency in the more abstruse pursuits of speculation,[146] his natural inclination to them, directed by a taste formed by the best education, made him embrace all opportunities of patronizing every advance in science and improvement in the finer arts.

The liberality with which he indulged this inclination soon marked him out to the attacks of every needy adventurer in the trade of letters. Projectors consulted him on their schemes. Poets submitted their works to his correction. His virtues, among which munificence was never forgot, were the inexhausted theme of panegyric; and dedications declared to the world his abilities and knowledge.[147]

Adulation so gross was an affront to reason. He rejected with

---

146 Dodington's political career was lengthy and varied, but the "activer scenes" may refer to his stint as envoy at Madrid, where he "ably represented Britain's commercial interests and renegotiated several vital agreements with the Spanish court" (DNB).

147 Dodington was a friend of Voltaire and the patron of many, including James Thomson, Edward Young and Henry Fielding. Thomson's "The Seasons" mentions him by name, and he is the dedicatee of Fielding's "Of True Greatness" and *Jonathan Wild*. Samuel Johnson and Alexander Pope, however, refused his advances, and Dodington was originally the target of Pope's "Epistle to Dr. Arbuthnot": "Proud as Apollo on his forked hill / Sat full-blown Bubo, puffed by every quill."

just contempt the praises to which he knew himself not entitled; and was superior to the flattery, which compassion for the flatterer often made him seem to pay for. Happy had he always preserved the same delicacy!

Among the crowds of parasites, who lay in wait thus for his favour, was a person, whom idleness seduced to prefer this abject state of dependence to the pursuit of a liberal profession, which he had been bred to: A baseness aggravated by his possessing every qualification necessary to have made him eminent in any state.

This man,[148] who had so thoroughly studied the human heart, soon saw that any direct attack upon his patron would prove ineffectual. He therefore struck out a new scheme, the depth of which secured it from detection, though at the same time, the difficulty of carrying it into execution would have discouraged any one, less anxious for success, and confident of his own abilities. He disguised the strongest flattery under the masque of the most cynical bluntness, and candour; and instead of praising all he did, and echoing in assent every word he spoke, he missed no occasion of differing in opinion with him, declaring he thought that being, who could debase the dignity of his nature so far as to give up his judgment to another, from any other motive than rational conviction, unworthy of the name of man.

A behaviour so singular necessarily attracted the notice of his patron, as the manner in which it was carried on soon won his favour: For in all the debates of any moment, which this champion for liberty of thought held with him, he managed with such

148 KEY: "Dr. Thompson." Perhaps Thomas Thompson, critic and quack doctor, who claimed to be physician to Frederick, Prince of Wales. His clients also included Alexander Pope, Henry Fielding, and Dodington, who kept him on retainer for room, board and £50 a year. He warrants an unflattering mention in the memoirs of dramatist Richard Cumberland, who avers that "a more dirty animal than poor Thompson was never seen on the outside of a pigsty," illustrating the assertion with an anecdote: when Thompson "cried out one morning at breakfast to have the *muffins* taken away, Dodington aptly enough cried out at the same time to the servant to take away the *ragamuffin*." Paul Whitehead, minor poet and fellow Medmenhamite, extolled him in his "Epistle to Doctor Thompson." Marginalia in another edition, however, suggests this is Thomas Potter (1718?-59), pamphleteer, politician, son of the Archbishop of Canterbury, and a fellow Monk of Medmenham. Potter was a close friend of Wilkes, and very probably the author of most of the *Essay on Woman*.

delicate art, as to lead him (his patron) to confute him, though frequently contrary to the opinion with which he had originally set out: In trifles indeed, where being foiled could reflect no disgrace, he proceeded not with that caution, but often gained a victory, for which he laughed at himself when it was won.

But with others he observed not such moderation. Be the subject what it would, he exerted all his powers, (and great as I have said they were) till he silenced at least, if he could not convince his adversary, over whom he then triumphed in all the insolence of superiority.

Such a method could not fail of success! his patron, sure of coming off with honour, sought every opportunity of entering into debate with him, and contracted an esteem for one who as he thought had thus discovered to him his own abilities, while every one else declined entering into a contest, which always involved them in disgrace.

Encouraged by this success, he boldly ventured upon a stroke, the event of which was to decide his hopes. In gratification to his own depraved taste, he had written a treatise in which the grossest libertinism was set in so advantageous and alluring a light, and the arguments against it evaded with so much plausibility and true wit, as were almost sufficient to put virtue out of countenance, and debauch its sincerest votaries.

The contradiction between such principles, and the practice of his patron, through his whole life, would have deterred any one less enterprizing and experienced in the weaknesses of human nature, from disclosing them; but he had lately made some discoveries, which emboldened him even to push his designs much farther, than owning himself the author of that book.

While the vigour of life had enabled his patron to persist in busier pursuits, he had despised the flattery paid to his literary merit; but as soon as the infirmities of age rendered him unfit for such employment, he with a natural partiality gave the preference to that pre-eminence, which he thought still within his reach, and affected to slight all the fame that was not founded on the nobler labours of the mind.

This was a sufficient direction to the parasite. He immediately shewed his book with a mysterious air, to several of his patron's friends, giving them broad hints at the same time, but under the seal of secrecy, that he was author of it. There is no way so effectual as this to spread any story. One whispered it to another, till in a few days the whole town was in the secret.

The hints and allusions which were every hour thrown out to the patron, on this occasion, perplexed him not a little, as he knew not what they meant. A secret though in the possession of so many could not possibly remain long such to him. One of his acquaintances, provoked at the seeming affectation of his not understanding his hints, told him the whole affair.

Much as he was surprised at the account, vanity would not let him suppress it by a direct negative, as the book was mentioned in terms of the highest praise. He answered with the coy evasions of modesty, the most effectual admiration, and shifted off any farther discussion of the subject, till he should be better informed.

Accordingly the moment his friend left him, he sent for the author of the report, and charging him with it, desired to see the performance which he had done him the honour to father upon him.

The parasite, who took his cue from the looks of his patron, was far from denying the charge. He presented him the book without hesitation; saying with his usual bluntness, that if it was not actually written by him, it was literally written from him, being nothing but what he had frequently said upon those subjects; and therefore might without any injustice be asserted to be his.

The advantageous manner in which the patron had heard the book spoken of prevented his making any reply till he should have read it, when he was so struck with the various beauties of it, that vanity subdued all his virtue, and deprived him of the power of denying it. "If the sentiments are mine!" (said he, blushing at his own baseness, as he spoke) "I am obliged to you for placing them in so advantageous a light; and think I ought to decline sharing in an honour, so much of which belongs to another."

Such a repulse was no way discouraging. The parasite repeated his assertion that the whole was genuinely his, both in words and sentiments, as indeed he knew not any other, whose they could be; and insisting that he had no more merit in the affair, than barely that of writing them down, a liberty for which he begged pardon, appealed to his former conduct to acquit him of so mean a piece of flattery, as giving to another the honour of a work which had not its equal.

It is not difficult to persuade a willing mind. The patron could no longer deny what was so clearly proved; and what his own conscience bore testimony to, against his false modesty. All that remained was to act in such a manner, that his practice should not contradict this declaration of his principles; and so raise a doubt of their authenticity.

But after having made the first step, he found no difficulty in this. He directly changed the whole tenor of his life. He laughed at morality, ridiculed Religion; and professed vices he was unable to practice: And lastly, to complete his character, procured admission into this society, which, as I said, was the proof of every polite accomplishment and qualification; where he nods, as you see, over the grave, as insensible to the mirth and pleasures enjoyed by his companions, as of the despicableness and danger of his own situation.

As for this parasite, his end was gained. From that moment he commanded him as he pleased, sharing in the enjoyment of his fortune while he lived; and sure of such a portion of it, if he survived him, as should sufficiently supply his appetites, the only use for which he desired a fortune.

Chrysal; or, The Adventures of a Guinea

Volume IV

VOLUME IV, BOOK I

CHAPTER I

Chrysal continues the account of the members. The history of a
remarkable person is given for a remarkable purpose. His pleasures
bring him into distress, from which he extricates himself by making
them subservient to his interest, and gets into a good *keeping*. Not
content with the mother, he casts his eye upon the daughter also, but
is disappointed, and forced to take up with a share of her fortune, for
procuring her in marriage for another. He resolves to be *a great Man*;
and for that purpose breaks with his *Keeper*, when he has got from her
all she had to give.

ONE of the most specious arguments alleged against the obligation
to virtue, is the success that is often observed to attend the violation
of it, in the general pursuits of the world. Of this you see the
strongest instance which this age has afforded, in that man[149] who

---

149 Henry Fox (1705-74), Baron Holland of Foxley. Fox first entered Parliament
in 1735, where he rose to positions of power and merit: Secretary at War in 1746,
and in 1755 Leader of the House of Commons and Secretary of State, under
Newcastle (see 1.304). The military disasters of the Newcastle-Fox administration,
however—particularly the loss of Minorca and the execution of Admiral Byng
(2.108-17)—resulted in the ministry's collapse in 1757. After some reshuffling and
wrangling for power among Fox, Newcastle and Pitt, a Newcastle-Pitt ministry
emerged, and Fox settled for a lucrative but comparatively powerless position as
Paymaster of the Forces. As Fox's bitter rival Pitt collected military victories and
public acclaim, Fox's unpopularity "became increasingly obvious and galling,"
and "anger and cynicism began to eat away at Fox's character." After George
III replaced Pitt and Newcastle with the new ministry of John Stuart, Third
Earl of Bute, Fox became Leader of the House of Commons, then effectively
purged his former political rivals—revealing, as wrote Cumberland, the "bitterest
revenge and inhumanity" (DNB). Further scandals—such as Fox's misuse of
public moneys in his position as Paymaster and his being made Lord Holland in
exchange for pushing the unpopular 1763 Peace of Paris through the House of
Commons—tarnished his reputation further, shaping Fox's legacy as "one of the
most desperate tools of a wicked administration" (*Town and Country Magazine*,
June 1769). Chesterfield seconds the unflattering characterization: Fox "had not
the least notion of or regard for the public good or the constitution, but despised

sits at the left hand of the *superior*, wrap'd up in the consciousness of his own importance, and smiling contemptuously at the company around him, while they believe he is joining in their mirth.

A particular account of his life would lead into too great a length. It would seem a satire on mankind, rather than a detail of the actions of one man. However, as a short sketch of it may be of advantage, by unveiling this mystery in the conduct of heaven; and proving the insufficiency of the highest prosperity to confer happiness, even in the hour of attainment, when that prosperity is not founded in, and procured by virtue, I will just run over the great heads of his story, with that brevity which the disagreeableness of the subject naturally dictates.

The opening of his life gave no prospect of his present exalted station. Pleasure in every licentious excess soon dissipated a small patrimony; and he was hardly entered into man's estate, when want, of his own earning, began to stare him in the face.

The peculiar cast of a man's mind is in nothing more strongly shewn, than in the expedients he has recourse to, in order to extricate him from difficulties. Instead of quitting the vices which had brought him into this embarrassment, he resolved on the first alarm to build his hopes of fortune on them, by pursuing them in a different manner. Experienced in all the mysteries of intrigue, he knew that age and deformity will purchase pleasures, for which youth and beauty expect to be flattered, if not even paid. Unrestrained therefore by any scruples of honour or conscience, he directly determined to fix upon some wealthy female of the former class, and never doubted making her passion repay him manifold, what he had expended on the gratification of his own.

I see the abhorrence with which the mention of such a scheme strikes you. Venal prostitution in the female sex, though cut off from every other method of prolonging a wretched existence, is the lowest state to which it can sink. What then can be said of a man, who, uncompelled by such irresistible necessity, voluntarily gives up the dignity of his nature, and hiring himself to be the slave of lusts, which are a disgrace to it, contentedly eats the bread of infamy and vice? Language yet wants a name for such baseness.

---

those cares as the objects of narrow minds."

This hopeful scheme was no sooner formed, than carried into execution. As his character gained him easy access to all such as were proper for his purpose, he immediately singled out an old dowager,[150] in whose disposal the dotage of a dying husband had left the accumulated wealth of several ages of successful industry. Such a quarry engaged all his attention in the pursuit. He paid his addresses to her, though destitute of every thing that could raise natural desire, with so much assiduity and warmth, that she readily received him into her good graces; and *in return for the pleasure she found in his conversation*, lavished her fortune upon him with a profusion that even exceeded his hopes.

From the principle on which he set out, it may be judged that he did not neglect to improve such an opportunity of repairing his broken fortunes, and laying up a fund for a future day, out of the overflowing of her untimely fondness. But unbounded as her generosity was, he was far from being content, while any thing farther remained possible to be got from her. Beside the great wealth which was directly in her power, a very large estate was by family-settlements to descend to an only daughter,[151] whom she had by her husband. As soon therefore as her modest lover had got possession of the former, his heart yearned for the latter also, with as much greediness, as if his wants were only increased by his acquisitions.

---

150 KEY: "Mrs. Horner." Susannah Strangways-Horner (1689-1758), a married woman twice Fox's age when she met him in France in 1728. By some accounts, Fox became her devoted friend and protegé; in others, she was his mistress. Walpole calls her "rich Mrs. Horner, who kept Mr. Fox," and Lord Chesterfield summarized their relationship in a witticism: Strangways-Horner was "a very salacious English Woman, whose Liberality retrieved Fox's Fortune, with several Circumstances, more to the Honour of his Vigour than his Morals." Walpole's letters confirm the two fell out, although upon her death Susannah Strangways willed her estates to Fox.

151 As one reader's notes indicate, "Lady Ilchester"—that is, Elizabeth Strangways-Horner (1723-92), Susannah's daughter, who married Fox's elder brother, Stephen Fox-Strangways, Lord Ilchester. The marriage took place in 1736 when Elizabeth was only thirteen, and against the wishes of Susannah's husband, Thomas Horner. Gossipmongers seized on the event. Wrote Lord Gower, "The Town is at present very much entertained with little Ste Fox's wedding, who on Monday night last ran away with the great fortune of Miss Horner, who is but just thirteen years old and very low and childish of her age."

But though he was seldom long at a loss for means to accomplish any thing he had in view, as he was under no restraint from principle in the choice of them, there was an obstacle in his way here, which all the fertility of his genius could not surmount. This was his connection with the mother, the nature of which he well knew would never let her consent to a scheme destructive of itself; for he had no fear of her making opposition from motives of honour or virtue to any thing that did not clash with that, as he found none in his own conscience even to this, though contrary to the first principles of nature.

Since he could not therefore get the daughter's whole fortune, by marrying her, he resolved to exert his influence on her mother to give her to some person of his choosing, who should divide it with him, as a recompence for making the match. For this purpose, he pitched upon a near relation of his own,[152] who readily gave into the scheme, though possessed himself of a fortune that placed him above the necessity of stooping to such meanness. The consent of the guardian mother, as he foresaw, was easily obtained. She was happy in having such an opportunity of proving her regard for him, as well as of removing her daughter out of his reach, his attention to whom, while his first project was in his head, had not escaped her jealous notice.

His share of the prize, added to his other gains, made him now a man of considerable fortune, and fired him with an ambition of making a figure in the state. To accomplish this, the natural turn of his mind suggested it to him to marry into some family, the interest and splendour of which might drown the obscurity of his own original, and assist his hopes. Nor did he apprehend any opposition to this scheme, from the same quarter that had defeated the former. He had now gotten from her all that she had to give; and the same principle which prompted him to be the hired drudge of her loose desires, made him find no scruple to leave her service, when she was no longer able to pay the wages of it.

Nothing is easier than to make matter for dispute. On her

---

152 KEY: "Ld. Ilchester." Stephen "Ste" Fox-Strangways (1704-76), Fox's elder brother, the husband of Elizabeth Strangways-Horner, and for some years the lover of John Hervey (1696-1743), Lord Hervey.

expressing her resentment, with the haughtiness which she thought the circumstances of the connection between them gave her a right to assume, as she had on many occasions before, at something he had done with design to provoke her, his *sensibility* took fire, and in just indignation at treatment so improper for *a man of honour* to submit to, he bound himself by the most dreadful imprecations to shake off so intolerable a yoke forever, and so flung out of her presence.

Her surprise at a behaviour, so different from what he had ever shewn before, suspended her resentment, and she waited with impatience for a repetition of the blandishments with which he had been accustomed to sooth her anger. But what was her astonishment to find, that instead of making any advances of the kind, he had actually withdrawn himself from her house. This alarmed her. In the arrogance of her former superiority, the loss of which she was not yet sensible of, she sent him a peremptory summons to attend her directly. But her commands had now lost their weight, and she received a refusal, the more cutting for being couched in cool, equivocal politeness. This drew on him an epistolary torrent of upbraidings, expostulations, and at last of the most tender entreaties; but all were equally ineffectual. He pleaded his rash vow, lamented the cruel obligation of it; and as she began to be softened by this address, hinted at a sense of religion, and even distantly recommended it to her, as the best consolation under the crosses and afflictions of life.

Such sentiments from him could mean nothing but sneering insult. In that light she took them. However, as the nature of the affair made it improper for her to open her mind too explicitly, she resolved to play his own game back upon him, and affect to be convinced by arguments, of which she hoped to take advantage, at a proper time, though in a manner very different from his intention in applying them.

CHAPTER II

Continued. He begins his scheme successfully by stealing a marriage.
His late *Keeper* makes an artful demand of all the presents she had
given him, which he answers as artfully. He advances in his scheme, by
steps exactly in his character, and gets into favour with a great person.
Chrysal makes some remarks on the origin of the affections of the
human mind, and the different manner of breeding men and horses,
with the consequence.

WHILE she was pleasing herself with this thought, he had carried
the most difficult part of his scheme into execution. The passion for
play, which marks the character of the present age, though it really
counteracts every social virtue, is yet the means of associating all
kinds and rank of people, who have, or even appear to have money
to play for. At meetings for this purpose, he had found means to
make an acquaintance with a nobleman,[153] who was so pleased
with his conversation, studied designedly to please him, that he
admitted him to an intimacy in his family, which he knew so well
how to improve with one of his daughters, that in despite of the
disparity of age and rank, he soon prevailed upon her to crown his
hopes by a private marriage, as the consent of her family could not
be expected.

As the immediate fortune of the lady could not be thought an
object of mercenary pursuit, when the first emotions of resentment
gave place to reflection, his plea of passion was admitted as an

---

153 KEY: "late Duke of Richmond." Charles Lennox (1701-50), Duke of Richmond
and Lennox, army officer, sportsman and politician. His daughter, Caroline
Georgiana Lennox (1723-74), was ardently wooed by Fox, and had been forbidden
to see the politician. Given an ultimatum from Fox, and concerned another union
might be arranged "without due regard for her feelings," Caroline eloped with
Fox on May 2, 1744. He was nearly forty; she was twenty-one. The event set off
a furor in London society, and Lennox "was immediately ostracized by her own
family and society at large" (DNB). Lennox was later partially reconciled with her
parents, however, and the couple seem to have loved one another sincerely: in his
"Character of Henry Fox," itself addressed to Lennox, Walpole wrote Fox loved
"one woman more than all," and that "the amiableness of his behaviour to her, is
only equalled by hers to him."

excuse for this violation of the sacred laws of hospitality; and his wife's father unknowingly completed his design, by exerting all his interest, which was very great, to advance him in the state.

The secrecy, with which it had been necessary for him to conduct this affair, and the rapidity of his success, prevented his late mistress from making any attempt to defeat it. As soon however as she recovered from the first stroke of her astonishment at the news of his marriage, she proceeded to put her scheme in execution. Accordingly she sent him compliments of congratulation on this happy fruit of his conversion, exhorting him to persevere in it; and professed her resolution to imitate his example; and dedicate the remainder of her days to the duties of virtue and religion; as a proof of which she proposed to begin by restoring to her injured daughter, as much as possible of the fortune which the confidence of her husband had left in her power, and she had unhappily lavished in pursuits, to the criminal nature of which he had opened her eyes.

As all that was not dissipated beyond recovery was what she had given to him, and her restoring it therefore must depend on his making a restitution to her first, he was not a moment at a loss for the drift of this extraordinary instance of penitence, nor how to treat the account of it. He immediately returned her an answer, congratulating her in his turn, with sincerity equal to her own, on her pious resolutions, the intention of which, he said, would make amends for the impossibility of carrying them into execution, any farther than by stinting herself to the indispensable necessaries of life, and laying up the rest of her large income to supply the place of the sums she had expended.

Such an answer necessarily drew on an explanation, and of course a demand of the several presents she had made him in the course of their dalliance, and knew he had laid up, as he lived at her expence all the time. This was no more than he expected. He replied therefore, without being in the least disconcerted, that he looked upon every thing he had received from her not as presents, but payment for the time he had devoted to attending upon her; and for that reason thought it inconsistent with that regard for justice, which is inseparable from true piety, for her to demand such a restitution, especially as she must be sensible that he could not now make it, without doing wrong to his wife, who had an undoubted property in every thing that belonged to him; and concluded with desiring that a correspondence which might be misunderstood, and so disturb his connubial happiness, might be dropped between them.

This sufficiently explained the motives of his conduct; and the despicable situation which she had brought herself to. However she was obliged to acquiesce with the best grace she could, without even the poor satisfaction of revenge; for he had taken care to insert in every paragraph of his letters such anecdotes of the connection that had been between them, that it was impossible for her to shew them in order to expose him, without exposing herself at the same time to the contempt and detestation of the world. From this time therefore all intercourse, beyond that of common civility, was broken off between them; though some consequences of their former connection, which happened even after her death, make one of the most striking parts of his story, as shall be observed in the proper place.

The first essays of a man's disposition indicate the rule by which his whole life will be conducted. The interest of the family into which he had thus stolen, had no sooner raised him to some degree of power, than he aspired to the highest; to attain which he resolved to pursue a method exactly in his character. This was to ingratiate himself, he regarded not by what means, with one of the first personages in the state,[154] whose interest he meant to make use of, as long as it could serve him, and then fly in his face to shew his independence. Nature had never endowed a man with qualifications fitter for such a purpose. He was every thing, to every man. The gay were struck with his wit; the grave with his solidity; while an appearance of candour and sincerity, that lulled suspicion to sleep, won the confidence of all with whom he conversed; all which powers of pleasing were, by a servility of disposition derived perhaps from a servile birth, prostituted to the

---

154 KEY: "D. of Cumberland." Prince William Augustus, Duke of Cumberland, Captain-General of the British army and Fox's political ally—particularly in his post as Secretary at War. Fox's passionate advocacy for the Prince in Parliament led to his identification, in the minds of the public, as the "political lieutenant" of Cumberland (DNB).

humour of those whom he desired to please, however contrary to his own.

I see your curiosity at my saying, that *the servility of his disposition might perhaps be derived from a servile birth*. You want to have the origin of the affections of the human soul explained, whether they are imprinted on it, at its first emanation, from the source of all existence, or received by traduction[155] from the immediate parents of the body, or only caused by the casual operation of external objects. But this, as I have said in other cases, is a difficulty that I am not at liberty to solve, as the question is not yet determined by the learned; though much ingenious reasoning has been displayed on every side of it. This only I shall say, that the practice of mankind seems to contradict the second of these opinions, who shew no regard to the dispositions of those on whom they propagate their own species, though they trace back the pedigree of a dog, or an horse, for many generations, for fear of any fault in the breed; the reason, you may perhaps imagine, why the *brutes bred with such care are found so much seldomer to degenerate, than the offspring of the greatest men*.

CHAPTER III

Continued. He practises a successful method for gaining the confidence of his new patron, which he turns to good account. History of the lover who succeeded him in the good graces of his late *Keeper*. He strives to prevent his taking advantage of his influence over her; and finding he fails in that, fools him into distress, which brings his life in his power. He slights many motives, which might have had weight with others, and takes advantage of the opportunity to get rid of him, and all farther trouble about him. He continues to dupe him, till the last moment when his eyes are opened, and all comes out.

As soon as he had insinuated himself into the pleasurable liking of his designed patron, by an unwearied exertion of all his powers of pleasing, he directly proceeded with the nicest art to improve that liking into an important confidence. He watched his every action,

---

155 "Transmission by generation to offspring or posterity" (OED).

word, and look, till he discovered the peculiar turn of his mind, to which he accommodated his own so implicitly, that the very faculties of his soul seemed to move only by the other's will.

They who are above deceit themselves, suspect it not in others. That self-love, which is inseparable from humanity, was easily imposed upon by such art. His patron liked himself in him; and insensibly came to think all reserve unnecessary with one, whose soul appeared to be only the shadow of his own. This soon gave him real consequence, as the numbers, whom interest or inclination attach'd to his patron, found it necessary to take the lead from him; and enabled him to grasp at every opportunity of engrossing power, and acquiring wealth, to supply those pleasures which he had quitted only from necessity, and returned to again the moment he had the means of obtaining them.

But all this torrent of success was not able to divert his attention for a moment from the smallest matter in which his avarice was concerned; as he gave the strongest proof in the following affair, to explain which I must look back to the woman, whose lavish fondness first raised his fortune, as it happened in consequence of his connection with her, though some considerable time after her death.

It is observed that habitual indulgence continues the passions proper to youth, after the fire that first supplied them is exhausted, and the end for which they were implanted by nature become impossible.

Old as this woman was, when our hero deserted her, and to appearance as incapable of feeling as raising desire, she had so long accustomed herself to the gratification of every sensual appetite, that she could not bear to live without a lover. The difficulty was, how to fix upon a proper object: for as interest was her only attraction, the first advances must necessarily come from her; and then her prodigality to her last had put it out of her power to make it worth the while of such another as she might like to supply his place. Precluded thus from much delicacy in her choice, necessity directed her to one of her own domestics,[156] something in whose circumstances pointed him out more particularly to her notice.

---

156 John Ayliffe, originally the servant of Susannah Strangways-Horner, who

There is not a more despicable instance of vanity, than being ashamed of the connections of nature, because of poverty, when that poverty is not the effect of vice. A far distant female relation had from this vanity bequeathed to her a very considerable fortune, to which this man should have been heir, had not the lowness of his condition, a motive sufficient to have influenced a generous heart in his favour, made her think it would be a disgrace to her to be succeeded by him; for which reason she wantonly deprived him of the inheritance of his ancestors, to give it to one who did not want it. Dispirited by such unnatural injustice, for which the Law afforded no redress, he was no longer able to pursue the industry that had hitherto been his support; and sunk into such distress, that his despair made him at length throw himself at the feet of her who enjoyed his spoils, to beg relief.

This happened critically at the time when her inclinations for a new lover began to get the better of her grief for the loss of the last. Softened by what she had herself so lately felt, she pitied his distress; and as all the tenderer passions are allied, that pity was soon warmed into such love, as she was capable of feeling. Accordingly, as she had taken him into her family, on his first application, she now entrusted him with the management of her affairs, to give colour for the further intimacy she had in view. The consequence was natural. He readily took hints, too plain to be overlooked; and she kept up *his assiduity in her service*, by some presents in hand, and grants of more, charged most of them indeed on the inheritance of his ancestors, which she had settled upon his predecessor in her favour after her death, till when they were not to take place or be discovered, to avoid his reproaches, as well as those of her daughter and her husband for such a repetition of her former follies; and because she did not choose to straiten her own circumstances, by the immediate payment of them. But these wages of vice, however welcome in his present indigence, proved fatal to him in the end.

The hero of my tale, who saw the rise of this new favourite, and knew from experience on what it must be founded, though she affected to attribute her notice of him to gratitude to his

---

according to rumor was Fox's replacement in her bed.

relation, and retributory justice to himself, gave him a genteel and profitable employment[157] under one of the many which he himself enjoyed in the state, professedly in compliment to her, but really to attach him to his own interest, and prevent his exerting his influence on her to obtain such grants as before-mentioned; for the turn of his own mind made him suspect every thing that was possible; and such is the partiality of man to himself, that he who has been ungrateful to all mankind, will yet expect gratitude from others.

Proud of this preferment, which raised his rank in life, and depending on the professions of friendship and promises which his new friend liberally made him, he thought proper at her death not only not to claim her grants for the present, to avoid breaking with him as he knew must be the consequence, but also to give up to him a particular gift, part of his own alienated inheritance, which he had received publicly from her, *as a reward for his services*, and trust to his honour for an equivalent return. But that return, when at length it was made, was so far from being equivalent, as his promises were from performance; nothing being more contrary to his intentions, than to enable him to support his claims to those grants, of which he had gotten notice, and judged from his own heart the reason of their being concealed. He continued therefore to feed him with promises, which led his vanity into expence, and encouraged him to embark in schemes that he had not a fund to execute, till he fell into distresses, to extricate himself from which he had recourse to means,[158] that laid his life at the mercy of this his supposed friend.

---

157 KEY: "Commissary of Musters." At the request of Susannah Strangways-Horner, Fox made Ayliffe a commissary of musters, in charge of "the food, stores and transport for a body of soldiers" (OED). His appointment was announced in the *Gentleman's Magazine* for 1750.

158 KEY: "Forging a lease." In 1758, Strangways-Horner died, leaving her estates to Fox. Aware that Ayliffe had significant debts, Fox granted him a lease on a farm in Wiltshire. Ayliffe, to raise additional money, mortgaged the estate, forging Fox's signature on the papers. Once Ayliffe was arrested for debts, his forgery was discovered, and he was tried, found guilty, and hung at Tyburn for the crime in 1759. His last words, addressed to the crowd, were "I am extremely sorry I offended Mr. Fox, so far as to make him bring me to this sad end." Popular sentiment saw Ayliffe as deeply wronged by Fox—likely due not to the facts of

There are some crimes, the consequences of which are so dangerous, that no punishment can be too severe to deter from them. One of the worst of these is imitating a man's *signature*, with a design to deceive. It perpetuates the violation of truth, undermines the security of innocence, and breaks that confidence which is indispensably necessary to carry on the concerns of life. But though no circumstances can, in a legal sense, extenuate the heinousness of this crime, there were some in this particular instance, which would have deterred any other man from the prosecution of it: it had been committed not with an intention of doing injustice to him, or any other, but to remedy for a time his injustice by raising apparently the value of the return he had made for the gift of their common benefactress, as I have before observed, nearer to an equality with it, in order to procure present relief from distress, of which he had been, in so many senses, the cause.

But all these considerations were of no weight with him, when put in competition with the conveniency of getting rid of one whom he doubly hated, for being privy to his iniquities, and interfering with his interest. He hesitated not a moment therefore to make use of an opportunity, offer'd beyond his hopes, and sacrifice him, under the specious appearance of paying obedience to the laws.

In this it was necessary for him to act with the deepest dissimulation, to accomplish his design in its full extent. But this was no difficulty to him. He professed pity for his misfortunes; and while he corrupted all, in whom the wretch placed confidence, to betray him, managed so as to seem to be compelled by law to appear against him, though he might with the greatest ease have avoided it, and buried the whole in silence. Nor did he stop here! his malice seemed to pursue him even beyond the grave; for instead of permitting him to prepare in peace for the approach of fate, he buoyed him up with hopes of a pardon, to earn which

---

the case, but because Fox's reputation was already thoroughly ruined. There are contemporary accounts, however, much kinder to Fox than Chrysal's; the *Annual Register* reported that Fox behaved "with a kindness and generosity not often found," sending Ayliffe "money and provisions" and paying for the forger's rent and physician during his confinement.

the deluded victim subscribed to every thing dictated to him to blacken his own character, and make void the grants, which he had purchased at so dear a rate; and in this infatuation he was kept to the last moment, to prevent his recanting; for which purpose, his nearest friends, and all who might have undeceived him, and administered comfort to his distress in the hour of anguish, were barred admittance to him.

But his eyes were opened on the verge of life, and in that awful moment when truth only is spoken, he revoked every thing he had been thus drawn in to say, and asserted the validity of the claims, which were the cause of his ruin; so that the whole scheme, laboured with such deep damnation to deceive the world, was defeated.

I see the horror with which you are affected at such a scene; and shall therefore close it with observing, that though he was permitted to perpetrate his crimes, divine justice prevented his reaping the fruits he proposed from them; as, beside the immediate price of his blood, it cost him more, than he earned by this complicated guilt, to stop the cries of the widow and orphan, and bribe venal defamation to silence, when it was too late, and the mystery of his wickedness was made known to the world.

CHAPTER IV

Continued. A view of his political character introduces a maxim not
   sufficiently attended to. He fails in a great stroke, and makes so many
   wrong ones, that he is kicked out of power, and forced to be content
   with profit, which he pursues through thick and thin. An unhappy
   event gives him an opportunity of shewing his ingratitude to his late
   patron, on the merit of which he raises to higher power than ever,
   which he wisely exerts behind the curtain, and leaves *his tools* to bear
   the blame. An account of the just fruits of so much success concludes
   his story.

You have hitherto seen him only in private life. I'll now give you a glimpse of his political character, which will convince you of a truth, for obvious reasons not sufficiently attended to, which is, that the ruling principles of the heart influence the actions in all capacities; and therefore that *it is impossible for a bad man to be a good minister*.

The power to which the confidence of his patron raised him was such as might have enabled him to effect either much good, or evil, had he known how to have used it to the best advantage. But his eagerness in the pursuit of his own views put him off his usual guard, and discovered his principles before it was too late to oppose them.

The most exalted minds are not exempted from human weaknesses. That of his patron was a thirst of power, though without a thought of using it in any improper manner. Some late services, of the highest importance, which he had performed to the state, suggested to our hero a scheme for riveting his interest with him still stronger, by procuring him a power which he knew would centre really in himself. Accordingly he exerted all his abilities and influence to wrest from the Sovereign an essential part of the incommunicable power of the crown, and vest it in him.[159]

Such an attempt instantly gave the alarm to every real friend, not only of the government, but also of him in whose favour it was professed to be made; who though they harboured no fear of him, did not dare to offer such an affront to their Sovereign, and give a wound to the political constitution of their country, which might be of most dangerous consequence in less safe hands. The design therefore was defeated; and instead of serving his patron, only instilled doubts of him into those who were not acquainted with the uprightness of his heart.

---

159 KEY: "Genl. of the Army for life." Per the key, this may refer to the Army Act, introduced by Fox to the House of Commons in 1749. Political opposition immediately attacked the Act as Cumberland's attempt to make his power over the army supreme and unquestionable, with the possible intent of seizing national power. An allusion to the Regency Crisis of 1751, however, is likewise possible. The death of Frederick, Prince of Wales, left the nation with an aging King George II and an heir apparent (the future George III) who was still too young to rule. Parliament saw heated debate, particularly between Pitt and Fox, over who should act as regent in the eventuality George II should die before his grandson came of age. Despite Fox's advocacy of Cumberland, Parliament eventually decided that in such a case the Princess of Wales should act as regent, though she would be subject to a council headed by the Duke of Cumberland.

Though the interest of his patron continued to support him for a considerable time after this, his whole conduct was such a series of blunders, (many of them so gross, that it was doing violence to probability to impute them to ignorance) that at length *the voice of the people was raised against him*, and he was obliged to give up all pretensions of power, and sit down with an employment of great, but mere profit,[160] which all his own solicitations, though urged with the abject importunity of a common beggar, even to shedding tears, and imploring compassion for his wife and family; all he had hitherto acquired having been squandered as fast as it came, on his pleasures, would not have procured for him, had not his patron sanguinely espoused his interest, even to the injury of his own, though on a discovery of his principles and private character, now too notorious to be concealed, he rejected him from his esteem, and refused to give any farther countenance to his ambition.

From this time he applied every power of his soul to amass wealth, which he had too many opportunities of doing in his present employment, the most iniquitous of which he never failed to improve to still greater iniquity, regardless of public reproach, and the distress of myriads, suffering under his injustice, whose cries and imprecations ascended hourly to heaven against him.

Riches give consequence, especially with those who sacrifice every thing to luxury. Though he had no public power, his personal influence over individuals in a short time became greater than ever, as he too soon had an opportunity of proving.

One of those events,[161] which shew the vanity of all human

---

160 KEY: "Paymaster of the Army." Fox served as Paymaster of the Forces from 1757 to 1765, a position he spent "speculating (quite legally) with the vast balances of public money that passed through his hands." By 1773, he owed the public more than £500,000, "and his unofficial profits as paymaster probably amounted to £400,000. Wealth on this scale was matched only by the opprobrium that followed in its train" (DNB). In 1769, the City of London presented a petition to George III accusing Fox of being "the public defaulter of unaccounted millions," and Fox's behavior would end his career "in a reputation for mercenary and rapacious self-interest totally at odds with the creed by which he tried, in all sincerity, to abide for twenty years" (DNB).

161 KEY: "Death of Geo. 2." George III's ascendency to the throne in 1760 resulted in a change in ministry: the new king thought the war "bloody and expensive," while the Pitt-Newcastle ministry insisted it was "just and necessary." Pitt and Newcastle soon resigned, Bute became new Prime Minister, and the new

designs, however wisely conducted and glorious in their end, threw the government into other hands. New men always adopt new measures, if only from an affectation of appearing wiser than their predecessors. In this change his late patron lost all influence, except that which *virtue establishes in the hearts of the virtuous*. This was an opportunity for shaking off the weight of obligation not to be missed by one of our Hero's turn. He not only deserted him directly in the basest manner, but also, to ingratiate himself with the present powers, fathered upon him the fictions of his own brain under the appearance of betraying his secrets, and made a merit of aggravating his ingratitude and perfidy by open insults, in hope of provoking him to some unguarded act or expression of resentment, which might give advantage against him, *by the common trick of applying to the master what is meant to the servant*. But for once, all his art failed. Confident in conscious innocence and merit, he disdained to give weight to such base machinations by taking notice of them; and receiving this ingratitude as a punishment for having placed his esteem so unworthily, looked down upon him with indignant contempt, nor was ever heard to honour his name with utterance.

Such a proof of his sincerity gained our Hero the confidence of his new friends,[162] to whose tottering power his personal interest was found a necessary support. But he lent not that support but on his own terms. Cooled by experience, he had learned that the name of power is always pursued by envy and ambition. He therefore wisely gratified the vanity of others with the dangerous shadow, while he reserved the substance to himself, dictating in safety, because in secret, all the measures for any mistake in which they were answerable.

In this situation you see him now. But such a series of success has been far from procuring him the happiness proposed in the pursuit. Recollection of the means embitters the end. The ingratitude and perfidy of one,[163] whom he had placed his whole confidence in, and

---

administration, with the assistance of Fox, settled the Peace of Paris in 1763.

162 One reader's notes suggest this is Bute, whose new ministry—once Fox had done "whatever was required of him in support of the government in the Commons"—made Fox Leader of the House of Commons (DNB).

163 KEY: "Mr. Calcraft." John Calcraft the elder (1726-72), whose "astounding

bound to him by the highest obligations, upbraid him continually with his own baseness to his patron, and make him afraid to place trust in any other; so that he lives in a state of constant suspicion and dread of all mankind, destitute of that friendly confidence, which is the cement of society, the comfort and support of life.

Nor is this the only wound that rankles in his breast! the unhappy victim of his avarice, murdered under the formalities of law, is never absent from his thoughts a moment. Conjured up by conscience, his spectre haunts his dreams. He *sees* him *in the dark.* He *hears* him *in the deepest silence.* Nor can the loud laugh of mirth and riot drown his louder voice in the midst of company. Hence that gloom which you see hang upon his brow; that consciousness of guilt, which gives a cast of horror to his very smiles.

Consider now the story of this man; and own with reverence and awe that *vice never wants an avenger; that wickedness is its own punishment.* Who would not rather be the apparent wretch, that wanders homeless through the world, fed by the cold hand of common charity, than he, with all his honours, power, and wealth?

The characters of the rest, except him who had been my master's competitor for admission into the superior order of the society, are not distinguished by any thing to make them worth displaying; I shall therefore leave them in the obscurity they deserve; as I shall reserve his for another place, where some new occurrences will shew it in a stronger light.

---

rise into wealth and power was due to the patronage of the unscrupulous Henry Fox," and who was thought by rumormongers to be Fox's bastard son (DNB). Fox secured Calcraft multiple posts, including Deputy Commissary of Musters, from which he made extraordinary sums of money. In 1764, the *Public Advertiser* estimated that Calcraft garnered £500,000 pounds through the position. In a "Tête-à-Tête Portrait" in *The Town and Country Magazine* for 1769, Calcraft appears as "Crafterio," whose "parasitic assiduity" amassed him "immense riches, squeezed out of the pittance of the poor soldiers and the still poorer half-pay officers." Calcraft betrayed Fox in 1763, re-allying himself with Lord Holland's rivals; according to the DNB, Calcraft's treachery robbed Fox "of his final defences against cynicism by wrecking what was left of his faith in human nature."

CHAPTER V

Chrysal leaves the convent. His master proceeds in character. He practises a new manner of courtship; and signalizes his talent for intrigue, by debauching the daughter of his friend. Her distress, when too late, gives him some slight qualms of conscience; but he soon recovers, and goes on in his enterprize.

IT was my fortune to leave this place, in the possession of the same person who had brought me to it.[164] The moment the meeting broke up, he flew to reduce into practice some part of the theory, which had been so well discussed among them. A person of distinguished learning and virtue,[165] who had taken great pains though to little purpose, with some part of the education of his youth, had observed of late, that he seemed to pay him particular respect, and was more frequent than usual in his visits at his house, where he behaved with a moral decency, very different from his general character.

The good man saw this with real pleasure, and attributing it to the influence of his own conversation, as vanity will find its way into the best hearts, gave him all the encouragement he could to come, in hope of working a thorough reformation in him. But he was deceived in that hope; and found, when too late, that he had cherished a viper in his bosom, to sting his heart.

Eusebius[166] (that was this person's name) had an only daughter,[167]

---

164 KEY: "Ld. Sandwich." John Montagu, Earl of Sandwich, "linked in gossip with a number of mistresses amateur and professional" (N. A. M. Rodger, *The Insatiable Earl*). The press capitalized on Sandwich's scandals by selling thinly-veiled accounts of his carnal exploits. He warrants a chapter in the *Nocturnal Revels* and is the devoted subject of *The Life, Adventures, Intrigues and Amours of the Celebrated Jemmy Twitcher* (1770).

165 KEY: "Dr. Sum," a name somewhat extended in another edition's key: "Dr. Sumner." Possibly the Reverend John Sumner (d. 1772), Headmaster of Eton and Canon of Windsor. According to Gray, in his notes to Charles Churchill's *The Candidate*, Sumner "had been Tutor to Ld Sandwich when at Eaton School."

166 Perhaps in reference to Eusebius of Caesurea (c. 263-339), a bishop and important historian of the early Christian church.

167 KEY: "Neice" [sic]. Probably Jane Sumner (d. 1766), John Sumner's niece, "a

on whose education he had exerted the tenderest care. She was now in that dangerous time of life, when ripened youth has given all the passions their full force, and reason not yet acquired strength to rule them. This danger though seemed less threatening to her than it is to most of the sex; nature, which had been most liberal to her mind, having denied those charms of face which too often prove a snare to the possessor; and the precepts of her father trained her in such principles of wisdom and virtue, as seemed a sufficient guard.

Such circumstances, exclusive of the obligations to honour not to infringe the laws of hospitality, (I add not virtue, for that has long lost all obligation in matters of this kind) would have prevented any other man from thinking of attempting her; but the pleasure of seducing innocence supplied every defect of beauty; and the difficulty of such a conquest doubled his ardour in the pursuit; as the triumph would establish the fame of his gallantry, which had never yet aspired beyond a servant wench; beside that the age and profession of her father secured him from the danger of personal resentment. Encouraged by all these equally powerful motives, the moment he saw her, he marked her out for the proof of his talents for intrigue; how to begin his attack though, so as to elude her father's vigilance, without alarming her virtue, was the question.

But he was not long at a loss. Difficulties, which appear unsurmountable to wisdom, are easily conquered by cunning, (and with this he was plentifully stored) because it will make use of means, which the other holds in abhorrence. In pursuance

---

common creature," wrote Walpole, "bestowed on the public by Lord Sandwich." According to Thomas Gray, after Sandwich deflowered her, Jane Sumner "professed herself a common *whore*," and was for a time kept by Sandwich as his mistress. Her brother, William Brightwell Sumner, paid MP William Skrine £10,000 to marry her in 1764. A somewhat more flattering picture of Sumner appears in the *Town and Country Magazine* for April 1770: "Miss S-mn-rs, afterwards Mrs. Sk——ne," was the "constant associate" of Kitty Fisher and a "great source of entertainment in Kitty's alliances, as she was not only a professed satyrist, but a woman of learning and an excellent companion." Betty Rizzo, in *Companions Without Vows*, suggests she was "a woman of beauty, wit, and cultivation," who despite having been debauched by Sandwich "had not repined overmuch at her lost respectability but took some pleasure in the freedom of 'the life.'"

therefore of a plan, which he soon formed, he cultivated the acquaintance of *Eusebius* with the greatest assiduity; and in all his visits to his house, turned his conversation entirely upon points of speculative knowledge, in which he professed the most earnest desire of information. *Eusebius* took the bait. As these were the usual topics of discourse between him and his daughter, he was pleased at her being present, whenever my master was with him, both for her information, and to give her an opportunity of displaying the advantages she had received from his care; for which purpose he often led her and my master into arguments, to which he listened with the highest delight, as she always had the better in them. Nor was she less pleased on such occasions, than her father. The modest deference, which my master constantly paid to her judgment, was so flattering to her consciousness of superiority, that she soon became fond of his company; at the same time, that the artfulness of his address to her, for he never shewed any other notice of her sex, than by a most guarded delicacy in his expressions, deceived the watchful care of *Eusebius* so effectually, that he never scrupled to leave his two pupils (as he fondly affected to call them) alone together, when any business demanded his attendance elsewhere.

As this was what my master had all along aimed at, it may be supposed he did not neglect to improve opportunities so favourable to his wishes. He always turned his conversation directly to such subjects, as were most likely to inflame the passions, on the gratification of which he expatiated with a particular warmth and luxuriancy of imagination, but in terms so well wrapped up, as to conceal the poison they conveyed. The effect soon answered his design. Subjects, proposed merely as points of speculation, gave her no alarm. And when such thoughts are once suggested, nature will lead them to her own ends. Her passions had been smothered, not extinguished; and were the readier to take fire for such restraint. She heard him, therefore, with pleasure, and slid insensibly into danger, the direct mention of which would have struck her with horror.

Matters were in this critical situation, when he returned from *the society*. The moment he alighted, he flew to the house of *Eusebius*, who unhappily was not at home. The conversation soon fell into its late course. There are some moments, in which nature will bear down all opposition. Though she had indulged herself in talking on such subjects, she meant nothing more. But he was too well versed in the practice to let her stop at the theory; and one unguarded minute murdered the peace of her future life, and blasted the fruits of all her father's care.

It is impossible to describe what she felt, when passion gave place to reason, and she became sensible of what had passed. Even he, hackneyed as he was in the ways of wickedness, could not stand it. He left her precipitately, and for the first time felt something like remorse. But these qualms lasted not long. His desires were rather raised than satisfied; beside that to have stopped here, without making his success public, would have disappointed perhaps the principal pleasure he had in view. He resolved therefore to seduce her from her father's house, that all the world might be witnesses of his triumph.

For this purpose he went to her the next morning, at a time when he knew *Eusebius* was usually engaged abroad. On enquiring for her, he was answered that she was not well; and was turning about to go away, when her maid, who from her own experience had suspected something of the cause of her mistress's illness, officiously ran to him, and told him she was in her dressing-room.

CHAPTER VI

Continued. *Chrysal's* master makes his triumph public, by seducing his new mistress away from her father's house. The manner in which he imposed upon them both to effect this; with the consolation he gave her for some natural consequences of his gallantry. His triumph is completed by her going upon the town, and her father's breaking his heart.

His intimacy in the family giving him a title to visit her there, he went directly up, where he found her in a condition that once more shook his resolution, and made him almost sorry for what he had done. She sat the image of despair! sleep had never closed her eyes! she had not changed the disordered dress of the day before;

and her face was so swollen with incessant weeping, that he could hardly believe it was she.

Her maid withdrawing *conveniently*, as soon as he entered, he threw himself at her feet in all the trick of woe, and imploring her pardon, lamented what had passed (for which he imprecated heaven's vengeance on his own head) in such passionate terms, as amid all her grief, alarmed her fear of his being overheard, for hitherto the secret was their own.

The first hint of this cured him of his penitence, and suggested to him how to proceed. He persisted in all the extravagance of grief; and acted his part so well, that forgetting her own distress for a moment, she was insensibly led to administer consolation to him. This was what he wanted! he at length seemed to be comforted by her arguments, which he gradually improved so far as to glance at a continuation of the guilty commerce, which he pressed for by the most rapturous professions of love, and the strongest vows of unalterable constancy and truth.

This was an attack, which she was no way prepared for! her heart was softened by grief; and shame for what was past precluded her arguments against a repetition. She hesitated however, silenced not convinced, till the voice of her father turned the scale. "O! save me from his sight!" (exclaimed she, wringing her hands) "save me from his sight! I'll go to death, to any thing rather than meet his eye."

"Nor shall you meet it," (answered my master, clasping her in his arms, and kissing away the tears that trickled down her cheeks), "I'll go this instant; and take him home with me as upon business, where I'll find means to detain him, while you pack up some immediate necessaries, and prepare to meet my *faithful valet de chambre*, who shall wait with a coach at the end of the next street, and conduct you to my country house, whither I'll follow you on the wings of love, and drown every disagreeable thought in rapture."

He did not give her time to answer, but rushed directly out of the room, and meeting her *ready* maid at the door, took his cue from her, who told him she had excused her mistress's absence from supper the night before, on a pretence of her being engaged in reading, as she said in the morning, that she had sat up so late she could not rise to breakfast.

Satisfied with these excuses, because he suspected nothing else, *Eusebius*, on hearing my master was above, was coming up to pay his compliments to him, when he met him at the bottom of the stairs. "I must give up arguing with that one," (said my master smiling, as he went forward into the parlour, whither he knew *Eusebius* would necessarily attend him) "who sits up studying all night. She has turned me out on a pretence of dressing; but I know it is to go back to the book at which I caught her; so that I shall make but a poor figure in the evening if you don't help me out. However, I'll try! I am not ashamed to yield to her! but come! I called so early to beg your company at my house, where I have something that will please you to consult you upon. I shan't keep you long, as I am obliged to go out before dinner."

To this *Eusebius* readily assented; and my master putting his hand under his arm, led him away, proud of such familiarity with a person of his rank, as unsuspecting as a victim to the altar. As soon as he got home, he gave the necessary instructions to his *trusty valet de chambre*, and then returning to *Eusebius*, amused him with imaginary schemes of reformation and œconomy in his family, and improvements in his house, till the return of his emissary let him know all was over. He then dismissed *Eusebius* with a smile of triumph, who went home, happy in his mind at the prudence and virtue of his conversation, the effects as he fondly imagined of his own care and example; the last time his mind ever knew happiness.

The moment he was gone, my master hasted after the deluded fugitive, whom he overtook just as she alighted at his house, the servants of which were too well accustomed to such things, to be surprised at the sight of a new face. The manner of their meeting may be easily conceived. On his side all was joy and triumph; on hers guilty confusion, shame and fear. However, repetition, though the highest aggravation of a crime, is yet less terrifying than the first commission; beside she had now gone too far to stop at any thing.

Three days he stayed with her, every moment of which was embittered to her by reflection, and seemed tedious to him from satiety and impatience to make his triumph known; and then left her on a pretence of business, with vows of immediate return, and going back to *London*, repaired directly to the tavern, where he had by letter appointed to meet all his associates, to whom he related the whole affair in such terms of exultation, as raised their envy, not so much at his possession of her, as the glory of such a triumph.

I see your anxiety to know the fate of the unhappy *Eusebius*, and his more unhappy daughter. Though I saw them no more myself, I had too many opportunities of hearing their story, the sum of which is this. *Eusebius*, on his return home from my master, found a note from his daughter, bidding him farewell forever, and desiring he would not take the trouble of making any enquiry after her, as she was unworthy of his care. The distraction evident in the style and purport of this note, too plainly shewed her ruin. This was an attack his heart was not proof against. He sunk down instantly in a swoon, in which he escaped some hours of misery before he recovered his senses.

The first exertion of his reason was to make enquiry after his daughter, but no one could give him any information, her maid who conducted having accompanied her flight. He then flew to his friend, my master, for counsel and assistance; for the goodness of his own heart would neither let him suspect him, nor desert her in the ruin into which she had fallen; but he was told at his house, that a certain nobleman of his acquaintance had called upon him the moment he left him, and taken him into the country for a few days. Every enquiry he could make after his daughter was equally unsuccessful, till my master's exultation made the whole affair public. This, if possible, gave fresh poignancy to his grief. He did not however desert the wretched victim of such villainy, but wrote to her directly to return to him, and hide her shame from the world in his bosom; but despair made her reject his offer.

As for her, a few days, in which my master left her to the comfort of her own reflections, discovered to her that his love had been injurious to her health, as well as to her peace of mind. What she felt at this discovery may easily be conceived. She wrote to him in the agony of her soul, to reproach such manifold baseness; but instead of an answer of excuse or consolation, received only a quack doctor's advertisement,[168] and a bank-note for a trifling sum,

---

168 Quack physicians of the period advertised their treatments for venereal disease in both posted bills and the periodical press.

enclosed in a blank cover. The same post brought her her father's offer of forgiveness and reception. The contrast was more than she could bear. She hurried back to town, where despair prompting her to revenge her folly on herself by still deeper ruin, she plunged into all the horrors of a life of common prostitution.

This filled the measure of her father's woe. He had no redress to expect in this world; and therefore resigning the punishment of his wrongs to the great Avenger, indulged his grief in silence, till in a few months it brought his grey hairs to the grave.

CHAPTER VII

"Chrysal's master pays his court to a great person, who seems not much to relish his humour, and expresses some unfashionable sentiments concerning polite pleasures. In the course of a regular progression, *Chrysal* comes into the possession of a Beau." History of a Beau, with a journal of his manner of life for one day. *Chrysal* changes his service, in a common way, for that of *a Lady of Fashion.*

"The next morning after my master's return to *London*, he went to pay his court to the Heir of the Crown, who was then at one of his country seats. Some public occasion had brought a concourse more than usual, in those retirements, to pay their duty to the Prince that morning. As my master was one of the last who came, as soon as his devoirs were ended, some of the company accidentally asked him what had kept him so late; on which, with an easy air of pleasantry he answered aloud, that he had been detained by a very whimsical affair: 'A certain nobleman' (said he) 'went into company last night, so *immensely* drunk, that having sat down to play, and lost five thousand pound, he quite forgot it this morning, and refused to pay the money, till some *person of honour*, who was unconcerned in the matter, should vouch his having lost it fairly; on which it was referred to me, and sorry I am that I was qualified to give it against him.'

"'How, my Lord! by being a person of honour!' (says the Gentleman he spoke to).

"'No!' (replied my master, with a significant smile) 'not so neither! but by being unconcerned in winning it.'—And then turning short to another, 'But have you heard the news, my Lord?' (said he) 'Mr. ———— caught his wife yesterday, taking a serious walk in *Kensington* gardens, with the gentleman whom we all know he forbad her keeping company with, some time ago.'

"A smile of general approbation encouraged him so much, that he concluded with saying, he wished he had himself been the happy delinquent so taken, as he doubted not but the gravest bishop on the bench would, were he to speak his mind honestly.

"The Prince had heard him without interruption; but as soon as he had ended, turning to a nobleman who stood near him, 'There can be no greater insult' (said he, with a determined look, and solemn accent) 'to a person, who is appointed to put the laws of a country in execution, than for any one to boast of a breach of those laws in his presence. *For my part, if I am ever called by Providence to that station, it is my invariable resolution, that no man, how exalted soever in rank, who lives in open violation of any law, human or divine, shall ever hold employment under me, or receive countenance from me.*'

"This rebuke dampened my master's spirits, as it struck a reverential awe into all present. He hung down his head; and in a few minutes withdrew quite abash'd. But he soon recovered; and to silence the jests of his companions, and shew that he was not to be brow-beaten out of his own way, he made one with them to spend the evening at a brothel-tavern, where he gave me to a pimp, who gave me to a whore, who gave me to a bully, who gave me to a pawn-broker, who gave me to a beau."*[169]

My new master was one of those cyphers in nature, who seem born only to make up the number of mankind. The poor pittance, which pride of family spares from the eldest son to save the rest from starving, had been just enough to purchase him a commission in the guards, in which he signalized his prowess on the parade, and talked as big, and looked as bluff[170] as the best, while

---

169 Johnstone's note: "As this conclusion of the foregoing character is so short, it is inserted to preserve the connection, and save the reader the trouble of referring." See 1.302.
170 "Big; surly; blustering" (Johnson).

his campaigns were confined to *St. James's Park*.[171] But the prospect of a war changed his note. The irregularities, and licentiousness of a military life now shocked his delicacy, and he exchanged for half-pay; and retaining only the convenient title of *captain*, resolved to push his fortune in the gentler way of matrimony.

For this purpose he directly commenced *beau*, as the fair sex is soonest caught by the eye, and when that is pleased, seldom enquires farther. Accordingly he now studied nothing but fashions, as all his care was to procure clothes to keep up to them, which the narrowness of his circumstances made so difficult for him to do, that his belly mourned many a time for the finery of his back. Nor was that his only difficulty. The very expence of going into company to display that finery was often as distressing to him as to procure it.

It was on an occasion of this kind, that I came into his possession. His shewy appearance, together with his *being one whom every body knew*, making him a convenient *faggot* to fill up those *musters*,[172] the only end of which is to shew the consequence of the *commanding officer*, by the numbers she can crowd together, there was hardly a genteel *route*[173] in town, to which he was not invited. Such a distinction was the height of his ambition; accordingly, having received a *card* to summon him to one the next evening, he was not able to resist the temptation of so favourable an opportunity of shewing himself to the ladies, though his finances were so low, that he had no other way to defray the expence of his chair, but by applying to such a place as this, *where distress is preyed upon by profession, and really aggravated under the deceitful appearance of momentary relief*; an expedient indeed to which he was well accustomed. As soon as it was dark, therefore, he came wrapped up in a horse-man's coat, and pulling a laced waistcoat out of his bosom, mortgaged it for three guineas, *one of which I was*.

---

171 One of the Royal Parks of London, and the place for fashionable men and women to see and be seen.

172 Faggot: "a person temporarily hired to supply a deficiency at the muster, or on the roll of a company or regiment; a dummy." Muster: "an act of counting or enlisting people into (esp. armed) service" (OED).

173 A play on words: both *route*, "the order to march," and *rout*, a "fashionable evening party" (OED).

When this weighty transaction was concluded, he returned home, and changing his dress repaired to a coffee-house at the court-end of the town, where he talked over the news of the day with all the significant airs and importance of *one in the secret*, confirming every word he said with the authority of *his cousin*, this lord; or *his friend*, that duke; till he *carelessly outstay'd all his engagements for supper*, when a *Welsh rabbit*[174] and three-penny worth of punch made him amends for the want of a dinner, and he went home satisfied.

Well as I was by this time acquainted with the inconsistencies of human life, I could not help being struck with the contradiction between the external appearance, and domestic œconomy of my new master. The former was in all the elegance of taste and affluence, while the latter was regulated by the strictest parsimony that nature could support. He lodged in an house, which opened into a genteel street, and had a back door into a blind alley, that served him whenever he chose to go out, or come in *incog*. Here one room up three pair of stairs (but the name of the street overbalanced that, and every other inconvenience) served him for every purpose of life, in most of which he ministered to himself, undisturbed by the company of any one but his hair-dresser, laundress, and taylor, at their appointed times. To all others he was constantly denied by the people of the house, who received all messages for him, and returned proper answers. But the manner of his life will be best described by the history of the one day I was in his possession, the business of every day being invariably the same.

As he had sat up late, it was near noon when he arose, by which *genteel* indulgence he saved coals, for the fire was never lighted till after he was up. He then sallied out *to breakfast* in a tarnish'd laced frock and his thick soled shoes, read the papers in the coffee-house *(too soon after breakfast to take any thing)*, and then walked a turn in the Park, till it was time to dress for dinner, when he went home, and finding his stomach out of order *from his last night's debauch*, and his *late breakfasting*, he sent the maid of the house for a basin of pea-soup from the cook's shop *to settle it*, by the time he had

---

174 Toast topped with melted cheese, butter and ale (OED).

taken which, it was too late for him to think of going any where to dine, *though he had several appointments with people of the first fashion.* When this frugal meal was over, he set about the real business of the day. He took out and brushed his best clothes, set his shirt to the fire to air, put on his stockings and shoes, and then sitting down to his toilet, on which his washes, paints, tooth-powders, and lip-salves were all placed in order, had just finished his face, when his hair-dresser came, one hour under whose hands completed him a first rate beau.

When he had contemplated himself for some time with pride of heart, and practised his looks and gestures at the glass, a chair was called, which carried him to a scene of equal magnificence and confusion. From the brilliant appearance of the company, and the ease and self-complacency in all their looks, it should have seemed that there was not one poor or unhappy person among them. But the case of my master had convinced me what little faith is to be given to appearances, as I also found upon a nearer view, that many of the gayest there were in no better a condition than he.

Having reconnoitred one another sufficiently to lay in a fund for remarks, and bandied about the common cant of compliments, the company sat down to cards, when the looks of many of them soon underwent a change. For *prudential reasons* my master always declined engaging in parties of this nature, but this night all his address could not excuse him. A lady,[175] *whom he had dressed at* for

---

175 KEY: "Ly. Mansel." The following chapters make reference to the lawsuit between Lady Mansell (d. 1761?), widow of Sir Edward Mansell, Baronet; and Sir Edward Vaughan Mansell, her nephew by marriage. It was "a very long affair, and it is not very clear," write C. A. Maunsell and E. P. Statham in their *History of the Family of Maunsell,* "what it was all about." A description of the case is included in the 1802 *Notes of Opinions and Judgments Delivered in Different Courts.* On his death, Edward Mansell left his estate to his wife, Lady Mansell. Edward Mansell only received his inheritance himself, however, based on some strict stipulations in his own father's will. Edward Vaughan Mansell, the nephew, claimed that since his uncle led "a very debauched life," and Lady Mansell, "long before her said marriage, was not only a woman of no family or fortune, but of ill fame," his uncle should never have inherited the estate to begin with. In 1757, the judges agreed with Vaughan, he was awarded his uncle's estate, and Lady Mansell's suit was dismissed. Later reporting in the *Annual Register* and the *Gentleman's Magazine,* however, suggests that the case was tried again in Chancery, and in 1759

a considerable time, happening to come late unluckily *wanted one*, and seeing him idle would take no apology. He complied therefore with the best grace he could, and invoking fortune with more fervency than he had ever prayed to heaven, *cut in*; when chancing *to fall against her*, her superior luck, or skill, aided not a little by his anxiety, soon stripped him of every shilling in his pocket, and sent him home in a pensive mood, to study *ways and means* for raising another supply; and, on this occasion, I followed the smiles of fortune, and entered into the service of the winner.

CHAPTER VIII

History of *Chrysal's* new mistress. She is brought into distress by her beauty, from which a lucky interview relieves her. The danger of arguing in favour of inclination against reason. Her friend puts her to school to learn manners, and afterwards marries her. His family shew impotent resentment, at which he is so enraged that he makes his will, by which he leaves her his whole fortune; and then dies. An uncommon instance of the good nature of the world.

THOUGH my late master had put the best face he could upon the matter, and excused his breaking up the party at the end of the first *rubber*, on a pretence of being taken suddenly sick, my mistress saw through him. "Sick indeed!" (said she, laughing) "hah! hah! hah! poor captain! I do not doubt but you are, and that at heart! I saw it coming upon you, ever since the first deal, when *I held four by honours!*[176] but I don't wonder at it. A full rubber was too much. Two guineas and an half are no trifle to some people!"

Two or three other visits, which she had to pay that evening, preventing her making a new party, she only stayed to tell the story of the captain's sickness to every one she knew in the room, who all joined in the laugh against him.

I see you are shocked at such an instance of insensibility; but if you will reflect a moment, you will find you have no reason.

---

was decided in Lady Mansel's favor.

176 That is, held the four highest trump cards: in whist, the ace, king, queen and jack.

Though poverty is attended with many real evils, yet when the worst of them are voluntarily encountered to gratify vanity, the pity, otherwise due to it, is justly turned into contempt; and the efforts used to hide it, which are always seen through, treated with ridicule and insult.

The morning after I came into the possession of my new mistress, she brought to conclusion an affair of a most extraordinary nature, which few women beside herself would have had spirit even to undertake. To explain it properly to you, it will be necessary to give you a short sketch of her story.

The gifts of nature are either a blessing, or a curse, according to the use made of them. My mistress was born in one of the lowest classes of mankind; the obscurity of her birth though seemed to be made amends for, by the endowments of her person and mind, which were such as raised universal admiration, from their first infant dawn. But these, tempting the licentious spoiler, like the beauty of a flower growing in the highway, lost their advantage, and proved her ruin, for want of proper care.

She had scarce passed her childhood, when one of those female purveyors for vice, who go about like their master, seeking whom they may destroy, to the disgrace not only of their own sex, but also of human nature, marked her out as proper for her purpose. There was no difficulty, either in getting her into her power, or seducing her mind. The poverty of her parents made them glad to part with her, without farther enquiry, to any one who promised to take care of her, only to be delivered from the expence of her support, as it had prevented their giving her the least education to form her manners, or inspire her mind with principles of virtue. Such a subject was exactly suited for so vile an agent to work upon. She took her home, dressed her up decently, and teaching her what account to give of herself, prostituted her, while she could make any profit of her, and then turned her adrift upon the world to live as well as she could, on the earning of sin and wretchedness.

I must not attempt to describe the life of a common prostitute! it is too horrible! she had run through the lowest scenes of it for some time, when fortune one night threw into her way one of those old debilitated debauchees,[177] who indulge in the speculation after they are past the practice of vice. Something in her air and manner, as she *picked him up*, struck him. He took her to a tavern, where he was still more pleased with her uncommon smartness and vivacity. "I am cloyed" (said he, to himself) "with the gross ignorance of the women of the town! I hate the impertinent airs of virtue, which those of better education give themselves! I'll therefore unite those qualifications, which separately please me in both, in this young creature, who can never offend me by pretences to virtue, at the same time that the excellence of her understanding will receive, and reward me with the fruits of, the best education."

There was novelty in the whim; and therefore he resolved to carry it into execution. He took her home with him, and sending for the most eminent masters in every part of polite education, put her under their care, and incited their application by most liberal promises of reward.

Young as she was, and hackneyed in every vicious habit, she had a sufficient sense of the change in her way of life, not to forfeit the advantage by any misbehaviour or neglect. On the contrary, she applied herself so closely to every thing taught her, and shewed a disposition so desirous of improvement in every sense, that her benefactor, proud of the discernment, which could discover such talents, under so great disadvantages, became enamoured of the effects of his own benevolence and care. "I have at length found" (would he say to himself) "what I have hitherto sought in vain, a woman that can make me happy! Her wit and understanding will enliven the hour of heaviness; while a false parade of virtue will never throw a damp on pleasantry and mirth. What though her birth is obscure! are we not all descended from one common stock? Is the blood of a peasant less pure, than that of a prince?— If she has taken a false step in the weakness of her youth, that should be charged to fate that led her into temptation, before she had reason to resist it!—But all these seeming disadvantages are now turned in her favour. Her experience in the ways of the world

---

177 KEY: "Sir E. Mansel." Edward Mansel (d. 1754), Baronet, who married Lady Mansel in 1740. See note 175.

will make it impossible to deceive her again. Her consciousness of the meanness of her own family will give her a proper sense of the honour of being admitted into mine; and save me from the intolerable plague of having her pedigree rung in my ears every hour. Her youth and luxuriance of constitution will also supply to our children the defects which too eager a pursuit of pleasure may have made in mine. Let those who are dependent on the world, regard its censure; I am above it, and will pursue my own happiness wherever it leads me."

There is nothing more dangerous, than seeking for arguments in favour of inclination against reason. Trifles, light as air, will be admitted as the weightiest proofs of that which is wished to be proved; and palliatives, barely possible, answer objections in their nature unanswerable. He had taken a liking to her! he had taken it into his head to secure the gratification of that liking, by marrying her; and a very little arguing with himself in this manner soon convinced him, not only of the expediency of such a marriage to his happiness: but also of the obligation he was under of doing that justice to her merit, and his own judgment. The consequence may be easily concluded. He married her, as he professed, in obedience to reason rather than to gratify inclination.

But the case was very different with the world, which, far from seeing the force of his arguments, laughed at him for being taken thus in a snare of his own making. His own family in particular beheld her with eyes perhaps not less blinded by interest, than his were by inclination; and depreciating the merit she really had, represented his marriage as the mere effect of vicious dotage.

Nothing is so ill judged as to shew impotent resentment. It only provokes a return of none effect; and makes a wound incurable which otherwise might have healed of itself. Incensed that they should presume to censure actions, which they could not control, he directly made his will, by which he gave away the inheritance of his ancestors from his own blood, leaving his whole fortune to his wife, as a testimony of his unaltered regard for her, and to shew his resentment to them; soon after which he died.

This was more than her most sanguine hopes could ever have risen to. She was in the prime of life; and possessed of a fortune to afford her all its pleasures. These advantages (and I should add her beauty, which was in the perfection of ripened bloom) naturally attracted a number of admirers of different kinds, and with as different views, who all thought themselves sure of her, from the circumstances of her past life. Needy adventurers (such as my late master) paid court to her fortune, in the matrimonial way; while her beauty attracted the most dangerous address of those, who meant no more than pleasure. But she was guarded against both. She had tasted something of the sweets of virtuous reputation, and knew the value of it too well to forfeit it entirely again by compliance with the latter; and her pride and experience set her above all the schemes of the former.

She lived thus for some time in the highest happiness, of which she had any idea; for she was a stranger to that false delicacy, which creates itself imaginary uneasinesses, and palls the enjoyment of present pleasures. She was admitted into good company, where her behaviour, if not absolutely approved of, was still received with good-natured allowances, as much better than might have been expected from the circumstances of her life; and she herself treated with tenderness to encourage her to perseverance, in so uncommon an amendment. But this happiness was too great to last long undisturbed.

CHAPTER IX

The common consequence of overdoing things. Her husband's relations find out a flaw in his will. The comfort of having good lawyers to keep up a client's spirits. For the advantage of having two strings to her bow,[178] she enters into an engagement of marriage, under an heavy penalty. The event of her law-suit shews the prudence of this precaution. She is cast; her lover flies off, and she sues him for the penalty of his engagement. He begs the money among his friends, and then by a nice finesse plays her own game back upon her, and flings her off with half. *Chrysal* changes his service.

IT daily happens, that men defeat their own intentions, by carrying

---

178 What we might call "covering her bases," having another option in line should the first fail.

them too far. Hurried away by his passions, her husband, in making his will, had exceeded the power vested in him by the law, and so by striving to give her more than he had a right, really gave her much less. But it was a considerable time before his family recovered sufficiently from the astonishment and confusion with which such a stroke overwhelmed them, to perceive this, and be able to pursue proper measures for taking advantage of it.

The first notice my mistress received of this affair, was by an offer they made her to refer their claim to private decision, in order to avoid the expence and trouble of a law-suit. But though the former part of her life had impressed her with horror at the very name of the law, she would not listen to such a proposal, without taking *proper* advice, the result of which may be easily judged.

Lawyers will never lose a good client for want of giving hopes. Hers persuaded her so fully of the justice of her cause, and gave her such positive assurance of success, that she resolved to spare no expence to obtain it. Though *right* and *wrong* are so essentially different from each other, they yet are sometimes involved in such intricacies, by the industry of those whose profession it is to distinguish between them, that it is difficult to know which is which. It was so in this case. They had raised such clouds, that reason could not see through them; and so every one was left to speak according to inclination.

While matters were in this situation, one of her admirers[179] thought it a proper time to push his fortune with her. His rank and expectations in life raised him above the necessity of such a scheme; but avarice will stoop to any thing; and he would gladly have taken her, with all her faults, for the sake of her fortune, the certainty of her establishing her right to which he had taken care to be well assured of by sages learned in the law, before he laid

---

179 KEY: "Gen. Geo. Boscawen," confirmed by other keys. Perhaps General George Boscawen (1712-75), the brother of Admiral Edward Boscawen, who according to the *Gentleman's Magazine* was made Major General of the Army in 1758 and Lieutenant General in 1761. But the match seems unlikely; General Boscawen married Ann Trevor in 1743, and Lady Mansel was not widowed until the next decade. Another George Boscawen (b. 1745) was a Member of Parliament from 1768 to 1780, but he was not a general, and his connection to Mansel is likewise unknown.

siege to her. This however he was far from avowing. He pleaded the most disinterested love, and pressed for a return with all the ardency of desire.

But though she could not do so much injustice to her charms, as to doubt their power of inspiring such a passion, she positively refused to listen to any proposals of marriage, till her law-suit should be decided, *from a generous fear of involving him in inconveniences*, which her lawyers positively assured her could never happen; as he, *with equal generosity*, founded on the like assurances, offered to marry her, while it was still depending; whereas the truth of the matter was with both, that *he thought he could make a better bargain, as she knew she must a worse*, if it should be concluded till every thing was absolutely settled.

They had played this game upon each other for some time, when a diffident word dropped by one of her lawyers, as the day of decision drew near, determined her to change her system, and make sure of something for fear of the worst. Accordingly, the next time her lover visited her, on his repeating his professions of the violence of his passion, and offering as a proof of his disinterestedness to enter into a mutual engagement of marriage, as soon as the suit should be ended one way or other, under the penalty of a large sum of money on the refuser, she let herself be overcome by such an instance of sincerity, and taking him at his word, signed the engagement directly.

The event justified this caution; for after all the assurances of success, by which she had been led on by her lawyers to run into every expence they could devise, justice appeared so strongly in favour of her opponents, that she *was cast*; and a considerable part of the estate of her husband adjudged to return directly to his family, and the rest after her death.

Though what remained to her was more than sufficient to support her in the genteelest manner, she could not but feel at first a fall from so high hopes; but her spirit had been too well exercised in the beginning of her life, to yield long to any thing; and she had almost got the better of it, when something that piqued her resentment, roused her effectually. Among all the *friends*, who came on this occasion *to gratify the insolence of condoling her misfortune*, she was not a little surprised never to see the face of her lover. As she could not be at a loss for the mean motive of such behaviour, she might possibly have treated it with the contempt it deserved, had not necessity urged her to shew a warmer resentment.

The expences of her law-suit had involved her in debts (for she never lowered her living, depending on the assurances given her of success) which were now demanded with an importunity that perplexed her. This was just at the time when she took notice of the desertion of her lover. The urgency of her creditors therefore suggested it to her, to call upon him to fulfil his engagement of marriage, which his conduct convinced her he would forfeit the penalty rather than do, by which means she should punish him for his rashness, and extricate herself from her difficulties at the same time; for had she thought that he would fulfil it, there was nothing she would not have suffered sooner than link her fate to him.

There is something in a woman's calling upon a man to marry her, so contrary to those notions of delicacy, on which the superior class of the female sex value themselves, that perhaps no other woman of her rank could have prevailed upon herself to do it. But she had not been born in, nor bred up with expectations of that rank; her notions therefore were of a coarser complexion; and though she had learned the external modes of behaviour, *the trick of complaisance*, she had been put to school too late in life, to change her sentiments so far as to make her think it necessary to sacrifice so powerful motives as resentment and interest, to a delicacy that appeared to her merely fantastic.

The moment, therefore, the thought occurred, she applied once more to her lawyer; and by his advice wrote a letter to her lover, in which she directly claimed the performance of his engagement. But as this was no more than his heart told him he must expect, (for he would have done the very same thing himself) he was prepared how to answer her. Accordingly he wrote to her in the most artful manner, *excusing his not having been to wait upon her, since the fatal decision of her law-suit, on account of the pain he must feel at seeing her, when he had lost all hopes of ever calling her his; for as her generosity would not permit her to marry, while there was only a possibility of such a misfortune, he could not suppose, that her sense of honour and justice would now, when it had actually happened; and for this reason he desired that she would please to send him his engagement, not that it was of any consequence, as he would return hers, to whom he wished the highest happiness in every scene and view of life.*—Such a refusal was just what she wanted! she therefore instantly commenced a suit at law with him to recover the penalty of his engagement, which he had thus forfeited to her.[180]

The care he had taken himself, to make the engagement as binding as possible, precluding every hope of defeating her claim; and his knowledge of her temper convincing him that it would be in vain to attempt prevailing on her to drop it, now she had once begun, he had recourse to an expedient to extricate him from this difficulty, of the same mean kind with that which brought it upon him. Accordingly, though he was well enough able to pay the penalty himself, as he did not choose to fulfil his engagement by marrying, he put on a poor face, and went begging to all his relations for their assistance, pleading poverty and alleging the disgrace it would bring upon the whole family if he should be obliged to marry such a woman, whom he represented in the blackest colours, exaggerating every circumstance of her life. Though this might justly have been retorted upon himself, for ever thinking of her, they took pity on his distress, and raised the money for him, by a general contribution.

Such success encouraged him to hope for further, and try the force of his eloquence upon my mistress. For this purpose he desired an interview, which she had with much reluctance consented to give him, the next morning after I came into her possession.

I had seen vice and folly in a variety of shapes, but never did the human heart appear to me in so contemptible a light, as his upon this occasion. He began his attack with flattery, professing the highest respect, and lamenting in the most passionate terms, that the difficulty of his circumstances would not permit him to have the happiness of marrying her; and appealed to her generosity and justice, as before, for a release from an engagement, that it must be the ruin of them both to fulfil. But all was in vain. She scarce deigned to make him any answer; and that only to tell him, that

---

180 Reneging on a marriage contract, or "breach of promise," could be brought to legal action in common-law courts.

his professions and arguments were equally ineffectual to alter a resolution, which the baseness of his behaviour alone had made her take. Not quite discouraged though by such a repulse, he instantly changed his method of application. He threw himself at her feet, implored her compassion on his poverty, and offered, as the utmost it would permit him to do, to pay her down half the penalty directly, concluding with saying that if she refused to accept of that, he had no other resource, but even to fulfil his engagement, and marry her.

This was fighting the devil at his own weapons. The mention of marriage was a stroke she was not prepared for. Startled at the thought, therefore, as she knew not what despair might drive him to, she agreed to his proposal, and so they divided the money between them (for he prudently pocketed the other half himself, as he could not think of offering such an affront to his friends as to return any part of their bounty) and were equal gainers by a bargain, in which each out-witted the other.

Though what my mistress got fell short of her expectation, it answered the double end of gratifying her resentment, and paying her debts, on the latter of which occasions, *I left her service.*

CHAPTER X

Chrysal makes some out-of-the-way remarks on matrimony. Description and history of his new master. *Chrysal* vindicates his using a common expression. His master's first rise from a beggar to a foot-boy. He gains his master's favour, of which he makes the use natural to be expected from his first education. Some account of a relation of his *principal's*. The danger of giving advice. *Chrysal's* master insinuates himself into the *Colonel's* liking, and undermines the principal, in his regard.

I HAVE observed in the course of this account of my last mistress, that you have been shocked at the thought of a man's marrying a woman in her circumstances. To you, who view life only by the light of reason, it must certainly appear most unaccountable; but better acquaintance with the ways of the world would reconcile you to that, and many other things equally gross and shocking in speculation.

Marriage is a mutual trust of honour. A man's marrying a woman therefore who has lost her honour, is trusting his whole fortune to a bankrupt, who has no security to give for that trust; a fool-hardiness that must proceed either from a consciousness of having himself no honour to lose, a total disregard to the loss, or an affectation of acting on different principles from the rest of mankind, as a proof of being above their prejudices. Where her honour indeed has been lost to himself, justice makes it a duty upon him to repair her loss by marriage; but then that very marriage is a punishment for his crime, as it must want the essential happiness of confidence; for he will always be ready to suspect, that the disposition which betrayed her into error with him, may have the same effect with others. Nor is this suspicion unnatural.

I see you would argue from the habitual, avowed incontinence of man, that this trust of honour is not equal, and therefore cannot be obliging. But this is judging without duly considering the subject. Chastity is in its nature a virtue equally the duty of both sexes to observe, and with regard to society in general, the violation of it is equally criminal in both; but in those nearer connections of life, the interest of which is the more immediate object of human attention, the consequences of that violation in woman are attended with so much greater inconveniences than in man, that in respect to them, the crime is obviously less pardonable in her, than in him; and for this reason, *this virtue of chastity is made in a peculiar manner the honour of woman;* while *the honour of man* is placed *in other virtues,* from which she receives as much advantage, as he does from her chastity; and therefore the trust of honour is mutual and equal.—In distinguishing thus between *honour* and *virtue,* I speak according to the notions of mankind; in their own nature, there is no distinction between them.

There was something in the whole appearance of the person to whom my mistress *paid me away,* that made me expect to see a character of a cast, which I had not yet met with among mankind. His looks were sly, methodical and plodding. Practice had fixed upon his passive face the hollow varnish of a servile smile; and an overacted affectation of polite behaviour made his natural awkwardness truly ridiculous. But under all this, I could see a depth of design, and a latitude of principle equal to any *great* attempt, the success of which should in the opinion of the world determine the quality of that *greatness*, whether *villainy* or *virtue*.

The knowledge of his life, which is necessary to explain his character, and account for the principles upon which he acted consistently his manifold part, will be comprised in a few words. Sprung from the dregs of the people, and turned loose upon the world to shift for himself, as soon as he was able to crawl, he took his stand about the house of a person of business, where he hardly earned a morsel of broken victuals by running of errands, cleaning shoes, and such other offices, as are performed by those *servants* of *servants*.

I see you wonder at my saying he was sprung from *the dregs of the people*, as if difference of rank could make any alteration in the essential equality of human nature; but without entering into a discussion of *undetermined* points, on both sides of which much has been said with equal strength of reason, the best observation of the power of early example to impress those principles, which are to govern the future life, will sufficiently justify my using the expression here.

The patience, with which he was obliged to bear the cuffs and kicks of those worst of tyrants, who always wantonly revenge tenfold upon their wretched underlings, whatever they suffer themselves, taught him that hypocrisy and abject submission, to every thing that might in any way serve his convenience, which afterwards proved the groundwork of his fortune; as the example of his parents, who got their living by retailing to the poor the meanest necessaries of life, initiated him so early into every species of low fraud and chicane, that they became absolutely natural to him, and invariably ruled the conduct of his life.

He had been some time in this hopeful course of education, when an accident opened him an opportunity of shewing what a progress he had made in it. A brother of the person[181] about whose house he picked up the scraps that kept him alive, happening to

---

181 KEY: "Mr. Burgh." The identity of this figure and the impetus for this section remain unclear.

see one of the servants beating him unmercifully, interfered from mere humanity, and saved him. The marks he bore of his beating raised a curiosity to know how he had deserved it; when he gave so seemingly innocent, and pitiable an account of himself, and attributed the servant's cruelty so artfully to his having refused to do something for him, which was improper for him to do, that the young gentleman believed him; and taking compassion on his distress, admitted him into the family to wait upon himself, by which he was delivered from his dependence on the other servants, and protected from their future insults.

The humility, with which he behaved himself, in this first step of his advancement, his assiduity, and seeming attachment to his master, soon won his good opinion so far, that he dispensed with his attendance, and sent him to school, where he applied himself so closely, and made such a proficiency, that his master took him into his own business; in which his sobriety, diligence, and obedient temper gained his confidence so entirely, that as soon as ever he thought him capable, he admitted him into fellowship with himself, and absolutely resigned the management of his whole business to him.

It may naturally be supposed, that he did not neglect to improve such an opportunity of practising the lessons he had learned in his youth. He secreted the profits of all the business, which his principal was not indispensably obliged to be personally engaged in; he supplanted him with such as he could of his customers; he cheated of considerable sums of money such others, as long experience of his (the principal's) honesty had put off their guard with him; and took every occasion of insinuating to the world, under the most effectual disguise of friendly concern, and complaint, his negligence and incapacity; at the same time, that he professed to himself the most implicit respect and obedience, and seemed ambitious of shewing his gratitude and attachment by performing the same servile offices, which had been his first occupation about him.

But all this was trifling in comparison with the stroke he made against him, in his own family. There was a near relation[182] of his

---

182 KEY: "Cap. Wheeler of the Isis." Perhaps Edward Wheeler (d. 1761), Captain

principal's, who was indebted to his friendly assistance, for the first step of his rise to *the rank of a colonel in the army*. Nature had been lavish to him, in the endowments of mind and body; but pride marred the blessing, and turned them all to his disadvantage. Confidence in the external graces of his person made him neglect the improvement of his understanding, while an affectation of *singularity*, which is always assumed as a mask to hide real ignorance, made him set his own opinion in opposition to the established judgment of mankind.

As the conduct of such a man must necessarily be irregular, his relation and friend, my master's principal, exerted the authority of those characters, and frequently reproved him in the sincerity and well-meaning of his heart. The notion that this liberty, which when properly taken is the highest proof of regard, was assumed on the score of obligation, gave offence to the captious haughtiness of the *colonel's* temper, and estranged an esteem, which it ought to have confirmed.

This was an opportunity for my master to display his talents. He studied the temper of the *colonel*, and paid court to his caprices. He cringed to his haughtiness, bore his insults, and ministered to his vices, with an implicit submission to his superior sense and judgment, which he received as the only standard of right and wrong.

The contrast between this complaisance, and the superiority which *the colonel* thought his relation assumed by giving him advice, insensibly transferred to my master that regard, which his principal lost. As this was what he had all along aimed at, he omitted nothing to widen the breach by insinuations, so artfully conveyed as to aggravate the offence taken by *the colonel*, and yet if repeated would bear a sense directly opposite, and seem to spring entirely from friendly concern, should a reconciliation between them bring his practices to light. But an event, that he could not scheme for, removed every such apprehension, and riveted his influence beyond his most sanguine hopes.

---

of the ship *Isis*, who was killed in combat in the Mediterranean April 1, 1761. His death, "very soon after the beginning of the action," is reported in the *Gentleman's Magazine* for May 1761.

CHAPTER XI

Further account of the *Colonel*. *Chrysal's* master, in conjunction with
a female associate proper for his purpose, completes his scheme of
alienating the *Colonel's* regard from his family, of which he gives a proof
of a most extraordinary nature. A remarkable instance of *Chrysal's*
master's talents for a particular kind of wit, with a striking account
of the worthy manner in which he and his fair associate acquitted
themselves of the trust reposed in them by the *Colonel*.

VAIN of the beauty of his person, *the colonel* prided himself in an
opinion, that there was no woman whose virtue could resist his
addresses. This self-conceit, which the frailty of the lower class
of females had first given rise to, was confirmed by his success
with one,[183] whose fortune and education should have secured her
against his attacks. The glory of such a conquest satisfied his vanity;
and the pleasure of having her on his own terms so endeared her
to him, that he thought not of any other. One thing only gave him
concern about her; which was, in whose care he should leave her,
when the business of the *campaign* called him into the *field*.

But in this he was not long at a loss. The humble implicit
attachment of my master pointed him out as the person, in
every respect most proper for such a trust. To him, therefore, he
committed her at his departure, hugging himself in the happiness
of having such a mistress, and such a friend.

The nature of this trust necessarily brought on an intimacy
between my master and his *charge*. Intimacies between the sexes
are dangerous in any circumstances; but in theirs, where she could
not even make pretence to that virtue which could be her only
guard, the consequence is obvious. From this time, they joined
their interests, and laid their heads together to estrange him from
his own family, particularly my master's principal, who in case of
death had the first claim, from law and nature, to his fortune.

In carrying on this scheme, they played into each other's hands
with such address at his return, that when he was going to the

183 KEY: "Miss Stephenson."

next *campaign*, he made a will, by which he gave not only his own large acquisitions, but also the inheritance of his ancestors between them, in such a manner as plainly shewed a wrong mind, and supported his bequest with such reasons, as were an insult to the laws and religion of his country; at the same time, that they perpetuated the infamy of those to whom it was made, by arguing expressly in favour of the vices, which had gained them this mark of regard; and this will, the substance of which satisfied them for the circumstances, he left in the hands of my master.

In this situation matters stood between the three, when I came into his possession. When he had finished the drudgery of the day, he went as usual to spend his evening agreeably with his *charge*.

There was one species of what is called *wit*, upon his expertness in which my master valued himself not a little. This was telling a fictitious story with so grave a face, and corroborating it with such plausible circumstances as to raise the hearer's anxiety, and then to laugh at the easy faith that could be so *taken in*. Low as the merit of *such wit* was, at the best, in him it had none at all. His fictions were no better than downright *lies*, destitute of imagination, or humour, and corroborated with nothing but *new-coined oaths* and *imprecations*, fit to afford entertainment only to the damned.

With an essay of this kind he resolved to entertain his mistress this evening. Exerting therefore all his command of countenance, "My dearest love," (said he with a melancholy look, and deep-drawn sigh, as he entered the room) "I have received bad news, *blast my eyes!* there has been a battle, in which our fool"—

"Has not been killed!" (interrupted she, snatching the word out of his mouth), "that is bad news indeed; but another battle may afford better."

I see you are struck with horror at my repeating the imprecation he made use of on this occasion. Instead therefore of intermixing them with every period of his discourse, as he always does, I will in their place make a pause thus ————, which will serve as well, for he uses them in general, as no more than mere expletives.

"No!" (answered he, shrugging up his shoulders), "that chance is lost forever ————. He has received a wound ———— ——, which without endangering his life, has disabled him from further service, so that we shall be blest with his company ———— ————, for the rest of our lives."

"Cursed, you should say! But is there no way to be thought of, to prevent it? Could not proper application be made to the surgeons?"

"All is too late! his leg was taken off directly ————; and the danger entirely over, when the account came away; as you may see by his letter, in which he writes me word ——————————, that he hopes to be at home with us, in a month, to leave us no more. Eh! what have I done with his letter? ——————————It should be in this pocket! I certainly have left it behind me, in my confusion ————————. But you'll see it soon enough. He sends his love to you; and bids me tell you, he would have wrote to you, but was prevented by company, so that you see he cannot be in any danger ————————. But he'll make you amends. I see how every thing will be ——————————. He'll marry you, as soon as he returns ————————; that he may introduce you into his family, who will treat you with forced civility in order to get him into their hands again. I see very well ——————————how every thing will happen."

"No! that shall never happen! I hate themselves, and despise their civility. I had rather bear the sneers and insults of the world than that. Nor will I marry him, let what will be my fate! his insolent, capricious humour is scarce to be borne now; though he curbs it, because I am at my liberty to leave him. What would it then be, were I to be his slave for life? I had rather feign penitence, and throw myself on the compassion of my own family, than plunge into such misery. Marriage on any terms is a state I despise, but with him I abjure it."

This passion was such a triumph to my master, that he could keep his countenance no longer. "Hah! hah! hah! a fair *humbug*, damn me!" (said he, bursting out into an horse-laugh) "your humble servant, madam! I thought you could not be *taken in*. Hah! hah! hah! a fair *humbug*, damn me."

"*Taken in!*" (said she, vexed at being played upon, but more pleased that it was no worse) "how can you take delight in such a low-lived trick? If I could not shew my wit in a better manner, I am sure I would give up all pretensions to it."

"All pure spite and malice! But don't fret for it. Come! we'll kiss and be friends, and think no more of the matter! only remember not to brag another time that you cannot be *taken in* though! hah! hah! hah!"

Every thing being thus made up, their conversation for the rest of the evening was such as may be supposed between persons of their cast, and in their situation. They gloried in the success of their schemes upon their common dupe, *the colonel*; they formed plans for spending his fortune, should any lucky accident put an end to his life; they ridiculed the pride and self-sufficiency of which they had taken advantage; and concluded in their usual way, with proving in each other's arms *the justness* of his confidence in their fidelity.

CHAPTER XII

Chrysal's master receives an account of the death of the Colonel. He finds, after much deliberation, that he cannot fling his worthy associate out of the whole spoil, and therefore prudently resolves to share it with her by a marriage, of which he draws a comfortable picture. He urges his suit, and she strives to evade it by arguments consistent with both their characters. He carries his point in a particular manner.

BUT all this harmony was soon disturbed forever, by the accomplishment of the very schemes it was founded on, which was much nearer than they imagined. The first news my master received on his return home the next morning, was that *the colonel* had been killed in a late battle. This was an interesting event! he directly locked himself up in his closet, and taking out the will, though he had often read it before, studied every syllable of it over and over to try if there was any possibility for him to *fling* his own and *the colonel*'s common mistress, and get the whole fortune himself; but he had the mortification to find that this exceeded all his sagacity, and that the whole must stand or fall together.

After some, not the most pleasing, meditation therefore, "And so!" (said he, biting his nether lip, and turning up his eyes, with an execration, too horrid to be repeated) "I have been labouring all this while to get a fortune for this *brimstone!* A very pretty reward truly, for supplanting my best benefactor! it were better for me, that even he had it, than she; for then I might not only enjoy my share of it as it goes, along with him; but also very probably cheat him out of most of it, in the end. What though I am to have it after her death! may not she live as long as I? Beside, I have made away with the greatest part of the money, and so am liable to be *blown up* and undone, whenever she thinks proper to call it in; for I know too much of her to expect that she should shew favour to any one, when once in her power. No! that shall never be! I have it in my power to set aside the whole unnatural, nonsensical will, and I will do it, if she refuses to come into terms with me. Such a sacrifice of my own interest to gratitude and honesty, as this will appear, will gain me so great reputation, that I shall make a better fortune myself, in a little time; and as to what I have embezzled, I know by experience, that I can *sink* that upon my wise principal at a proper time, as I have done more before now; so that after all, I may find honesty to be the best policy, as the saying is. Well! be that as it will, I am resolved to be honest to myself first, and do that which shall serve my own interest best, without regard to proverb or opinion. Let me consider then! suppose I marry her; and so get possession of all at once. But the devil of it is, that I must take her into the bargain; and I know her too well for that, if I could help it. She may most likely serve me the same trick, with some body else, that she has served this fool with me; *once a whore and always a whore.* However, I must take my chance for that. Cunning as she is, she shall not cuckold me easily. If I am not a match for her, she must be able to outwit the devil himself; so happy come lucky, I'll e'en venture."

Having reasoned himself into this prudent resolution, he would lose no time; but went to her directly to carry it into execution. As soon as he met her, "I have brought you news now" (said he) "in earnest. News, that will be either good or bad, according as you take it."

"Psha!" (answered she slightingly) "this is more of your *wit,* I suppose. But for heaven's sake leave off making a fool of yourself, and teazing me. I am quite sick of such stuff."

"Strike me to the centre," (replied he passionately) "but I am

serious. I have this moment received an account, that *the colonel* is actually dead. He was killed in the late battle."

The look with which he said this, had more weight with her than all the oaths and imprecations he could utter; for much as he was master of his countenance, he could not conceal the agitation of his mind. "Dead!" (interrupted she, eagerly) "thank heaven! then all my fears are over."

"Aye!" (replied he dryly) "but it is well if your hopes are not also over with them."

"How? What do you mean? Has he not made a will, by which all his fortune comes directly to me? For heaven's sake do not torture me in this manner."

"Yes! he has made a will, it is true. But don't you know that the last letter I received from him revoked it, so that every thing goes now to his family, for he lived not long enough to make another after he received his wound; though that is no great loss to you, for from what he said when he was dying, it would not have been much in your favour."

"But did you not promise me, that you would suppress that revocation, in case any thing of this kind should happen; which you said you had it in your power to do, as your principal was fool enough to promise you, that he would never open any letters that should come directed to you from the army, as he had a right to do, by which means it had luckily escaped coming to his knowledge."

"Perhaps I may have said so! but do you think I have no more conscience, than to conceal such a thing; and rob a man to whom I am under so great obligations?"

"Conscience! For heaven's sake, I conjure you again, do not torture me any longer. Speak of conscience to those who do not know you. I have had sufficient proof, that your *interest* is your *conscience*; and this will surely determine you to serve me, as you serve yourself at the same time. Is not all to come to you at my death?"

"But what am I to do in the mean while? Come then! as you say you know me so well, I'll offer you a fair proposal, that shall make it my *present interest* (for that is what I regard) to serve you; and your *future interest*, on which you lay so great a stress, to serve me. Suppose, we join our interests in all things, and marry. By this expedient I shall come directly into the enjoyment of the fortune; and your children will inherit it."

"Marry!" (exclaimed she, starting in surprise) "what could put such a strange thought into your head, who know my sentiments on that unnatural state of superstition and slavery? No! that of all things, I can never come into. But, I see you are at your *humbugging* again. The professions, and oaths of friendship, you have so often made me"—

"Were all but wind," (answered he) "and have left no trace behind them. But this kind of talking answers no end. The whole depends on the one word, by which you answer me this short question, 'Will you marry me? Or will you not?' If you consent, I will secrete the papers, that set aside the will, and so we shall share the fortune between us. If you refuse, I will give them up to his family, who will directly defeat your claim, and then you may follow for your living that libertine way of life you appear so fond of; for I have no notion of damning my character in this world, and my soul in the next, to serve any other but myself. Consider therefore before you speak, as I will go directly from you to them if you refuse me."

Such a menace was not ineffectual to one who knew him so well. "Will nothing else satisfy you?" (replied she, bursting into tears) "No part of the fortune; and to continue as we are at present, man and wife in every thing but the cursed ceremony?"

"No! that ceremony is the very thing I want, and nothing else; because that only can give me a right to your fortune; for as to your person, I would not have you think I set any value on that! I have long since had enough of it: and for sharing the fortune, I am resolved I will have all, or none; and this is the reason, why I make you such an offer; for otherwise, I assure you, I hate marriage as much as you possibly can. So let me have your answer directly, for I will not trifle thus a moment longer."

The manner in which he said this left her no room to doubt his resolution. "Well then," (replied she, sighing) "if you will have it so, it must be so; and I consent because I cannot help it. But when is this blessed marriage to be solemnized?"

"As for that, I am in no more hurry than you. All I desire is that you will directly sign a promise of marriage, whenever I think proper to call upon you. I'll go this instant, and draw it up; and leave you to consider how much better this is for us both, than to have disagreed, and let all go to his family."

He waited not for a reply; nor was long before he returned with the deed, which she signed with evident reluctance.

CHAPTER XIII

Account of the methods which *Chrysal's* master took to obviate the effects of his principal's resentment, with the characteristic conversation that passed between them, on the former's avowing the Colonel's will. *Chrysal's* master overshoots his mark, and provokes his principal to do more than he ever intended. An uncommon instance of the justice of the world. *Chrysal's* master obliges the lady to court him in her turn, and at length marries her. The consequence of such a marriage, and fruits of the success of all their schemes.

THIS point being settled, the next thing was to produce *the colonel's* will, the thought of doing which gave him some alarm in spite of all his fortitude, as it would be throwing off the mask he had worn all his life, and declaring war with his principal, who he judged from himself, would not fail to publish to the world the meanness of his original, and the misery from which his compassion had raised him.

But such thoughts, disagreeable as they might be, could not divert him from his purpose. To disable his principal though as far as possible from carrying his resentment any farther than words, he ransacked all his papers, and took away not only such as related immediately to the private transactions between themselves, but also those of other people with whom they had been concerned in business, in order to distress his circumstances, and involve him in such perplexities as should lay him under a necessity of keeping fair with him. But this precaution, like many others dictated by the same spirit, occasioned the very thing it was designed to prevent.

The first news of the affair was like a thunder-clap to the family of *the colonel*. My master's principal, though, who in the course of law and nature, had the first expectations, as I have said before, could not believe it to be true, so high was his confidence in the honesty and attachment of my master. To satisfy however the importunities of his family, he came to him, and with a look of indignation at the baseness of such a report, rather than apprehension of the truth of it, "I am come" (said he) "to tell you a piece of news, I have just this morning heard, which is that *the colonel* has left his whole fortune between that jade, his mistress, and you; and that you were privy to his will, which he left in your hands when he was going abroad. But the latter part of the story makes me easy about the rest; for whatever his capricious temper might lead him to do, I am convinced you would have no hand in so base an affair, nor even conceal his having such an intention from me a moment. I see you are shocked at the scandalous imputation; but do not think I mention it, as if I believed it. I could not do you so much wrong."

The first impressions of youth can never be totally effaced. Though my master could lay schemes to cheat his principal, and revile him behind his back, he had learned to look at him with an awe, when a beggar about his brother's house, and afterwards his servant, that he could never after get over when in his presence. This awe, added to the confusion of conscious guilt, made him unable to make any answer for some moments, and had wrought that change in his countenance which the other took notice of.

As soon as he could collect spirits to speak, "I-I-I am obliged to every one, f-f-for their good opinion of me;" (said he, with his eyes fixed upon the ground, and faultering at every word) "and hope I shall not f-f-f-forfeit it, by accepting the favours of my friends."

"How! (interrupted the other eagerly) "what can you mean by that? You surely do not, cannot avow!"

"As for that, Sir!" (replied my master, plucking up a little more assurance) "what I avow or disavow is nothing to the purpose. I presume that my *most dear and worthy friend, the colonel*, had a right to leave his fortune to whom he pleased; and that whoever he has left it to has also a right to take it, without being answerable to your opinion, or that of any others who may be prejudiced by you; for the world will judge better, and be satisfied that he had sufficient reasons for what he has done."

"And so then! it is even so!" (replied the other, after a long pause) "and this is the return I meet for raising you from wretchedness, and admitting you to the first place in the esteem and confidence of my heart. *Cherish a viper in your bosom, and he will sting you to death.* But it is beneath me to upbraid you! I leave the revenge of my wrongs to your own conscience, and the justice of heaven; and from this moment disclaim all intercourse with you; nor shall my lips ever more utter your name, if I can help it. The sight of you is a pain to me! I will send a person to take my affairs out of your hands, and desire you will directly provide yourself another habitation! Unhappy for me was the day, when I first gave shelter to your misery in mine."—Saying this he turned away without waiting for a reply, and left the room.

This insolent behaviour (for so my master called it, as soon as the other was gone) was such an affront to *his honour,* as in his opinion cancelled all obligations, and justified every thing he had done, or could do against him. Giving vent to his resentment therefore in *a burst of blasphemous execrations,* he proceeded in the execution of his schemes, with this improvement, that to obviate the imputations of base dishonesty and ingratitude, which his own conscience told him his principal would publish to the world against him, he loaded him with every scandal that his inventive malice could suggest. But instead of answering his purpose, produced the very contrary effect, as it put him under a necessity of laying open things to vindicate his own character, which indignant shame of having placed his confidence so unworthily would otherwise have made him conceal; and in this instance the world was not dazzled by success, but directly paid his villainy with the infamy it deserved.

As for the lady, fashion made it necessary for her to put on all the mimicry of woe, in which she persisted most decently for the usual time; at the end of which she found her husband, that was to be, so slack in his addresses, that she was obliged to court him, as such an unsettled life was equally contrary to her interest and inclinations. This answered a double end. It gratified his vanity, (for he took care to make it known) and seemed to obviate the credit of the contract between them, should it ever happen to be discovered. Accordingly he kept off a little longer; and at length consented with the affected irresolution of a man of the most delicate principles and sense of honour.

As he only got a *legal* right by his marriage, to what he was already in possession of, he soon grew tired of the state, the circumstances of which, in his particular case, could not be very pleasing to any man. However, to avoid the evils of which he was most immediately afraid, he went to live in the country, where he admitted his wife to see nobody but those he approved, and in company with himself. Nor was he satisfied that his utmost vigilance could prove effectual, as he had had experience of the looseness of her principles, and her expertness in all the arts of intrigue.

Their situation, in these circumstances, may be easily conceived. Continual suspicions, quarrels, and recriminations aggravated their mutual dislike to the most rancorous hatred, and made their lives such a scene of misery, that they themselves looked upon it as a commencement of heaven's vengeance on their crimes; while all who knew them expected in horror that they would make that vengeance still more signally dreadful, by wreaking their hatred upon each other's lives, or their despair upon their own.

All the advantages, thus dearly earned, were an affluence disgusting for want of power of enjoyment, except in an external pomp that only mocked the misery within, and made the meanness it was designed to hide the more remarkable.

CHAPTER XIV

Chrysal's master designs to set up a coach; but wants a material article toward making a proper figure with it. He consults with an *Herald*, who gives him an elaborate dissertation, not the most pleasing to him, on *coats of arms*, and the modern methods of making them, in which he unfolds many curious mysteries, and undertakes at last, on proper encouragement, to make him a gentleman. *Chrysal* changes his service. Conversation between his new master and an *Antiquarian*. Curious arguments, by which he proves the genuineness and importance of certain relics of antiquity. *Chrysal* changes his service.

IN this age of delicacy and refinement the first thing thought of in genteel life is *a carriage*, which is so indispensably necessary to procure respect, that no eminence in science, no practice of virtue is held in esteem, where that is wanted. Sensible of this, my master resolved to bespeak one, the elegance and grandeur of which should prove his taste and magnificent spirit. One difficulty though perplexed him not a little in the design. This was his want of a *coat of arms* to decorate the outside of it, and display to the world his illustrious descent.

After much fruitless meditation on so important a subject, it occurred to him, that an *herald* must be the proper person to consult with upon the best means of remedying this defect. Accordingly he enquired for the most eminent in that way, and on the morning fixed for his attendance, prepared to receive him in such a manner as he imagined could not fail to inspire him with respect. He was lolling at breakfast in an elbow-chair;[184] dressed in a morning-gown of green damask, with a red cap on his head, the cambric lining of which was edged with a rich lace, that turned up over it, and crimson velvet slippers on his feet, one of which was extended on a cushion of the same materials, to give him the appearance of the gout, a disorder which he looked upon as an incontestable proof of his being sprung from a good family,[185] while his lady poured out his tea, and between every dish read a paragraph in a news-paper to entertain him.

As soon as the *herald* was shewn in, my master cast an eye upon his lady, and nodding majestically toward the door, she withdrew, and left him to his business. After the usual questions about the weather, and the news, my master at length entered upon the subject. "I understand S-S-Sir," (said he, faultering, and almost blushing in spite of his assurance) "that you have great skill in heraldry; and therefore desired to see you to consult about my *c-c-c-coat of arms.*"

"I do presume, Sir," (answered the herald with an air of importance) "to have some knowledge in that mysterious and sublime science, and hope I shall not wrong the character you have

184 An armchair (OED).
185 The illness was considered a sign of social distinction. "Gout," wrote Lord Chesterfield, "is the distemper of a gentleman, whereas the rheumatism is the distemper of a hackney coachman."

received of me, in any thing in which you are pleased to employ me. Hem! ahem! Pray Sir, what may be the nature of your present commands? I suppose you want to introduce into your own *coat*, the *bearing* of some branch of your family, which is fallen to you. There is nothing in the world easier to be done, that is by one, who, as I said before, understands the science. It is only dividing *the field* properly, and taking care that the *blazoning* of the different *quarterings*, of which all good families gain many in a long course in descents, may not be wrongly blended, as *colour upon colour, or metal upon metal*, which you must know is *false heraldry*; though I beg pardon, your *blazoning* is most likely in *precious stones*, the peculiar emblems of nobility with us.[186] But that makes no difference, as I will convince you, if you please to let me see your arms."

"Sir," (replied my master, still more confounded by this jargon) "that is not what I want. I would have an entire *n—n—new coat.*"

"O! I understand you, Sir! *you are the first of your family*; and want to *make arms* for yourself, as none of your ancestors have left you any! Why Sir, that too may be done; but it must be with judgment and care, as I said before, for fear of interfering with the *arms* of any other family. But you may trust me for that, Sir! half the *arms* you see cut such a figure about the town are of my devising. *The king may make lords and knights of whom he pleases, but it is the herald must make them gentlemen*; for what is any man without *a coat of arms?* Pray, Sir, what is your name? And of what profession was your father?"

"Wh-wh-why do you ask, Sir? I suppose there cannot be any thing material to your purpose in them?"

"Pardon me, good Sir, they are material, very material. A name, especially if it consists of many syllables, often gives an excellent hint; for much as your modern wits may affect to despise the mysterious learning of *Rebus's*, wiser antiquity held it in high repute, as you must have observed from the many illustrious *coats of arms* taken entirely from the name: and then knowledge of the profession of a gentleman's father is absolutely necessary

---

186 The blazons of "some *English* Armorists," explains the 1765 *Elements of Heraldry*, distinguished "the different degrees of Persons." Metals were used for gentlemen and knights; precious stones, noblemen; and planets were reserved for kings.

for many reasons. There are professions the implements of which are never *drop'd*, because the professions themselves are reckoned honourable, as there are also others, nothing related to which is ever *borne*, for the contrary reason. The son of a gentleman or admiral, for instance, will have his *arms* charged with implements of war; but *the son of a man who kept a chandler's shop* will never *bear* a lump of butter, or a bunch of candles, nor *the son of a taylor*, a pair of scissors or a thimble; for these would at once betray what is designed to be hid; and therefore it is absolutely necessary that I should be informed of these particulars."

"B-b-b-but Sir, can you not strike out something entirely new, without alluding to any name, or profession at all? I am willing to pay you well for your trouble, only let me have something elegant and grand."

"I understand you, Sir. I'll engage to please you. I'll *quarter you the coat of a crown'd head*[187] in an instant, without any body's being able to say a word against it. Leave it to me, and I'll engage to please you; not the richest *contractor* or *Nabob*[188] of them all shall make such a figure."

"And pray, Sir, what is your price, for a job of this kind?"

"Price, Sir, I never make bargains! let common mechanics do that! Gentlemen always make me a present when they bespeak their honours; and according to the value of that, my invention is either high or low."

"Well, Sir, it shan't sink on that account now. Here are ten guineas for you, as an earnest of what I will give, if I like your work, when it is done."

"Sir! you may depend on having *the highest arms* of any man in the kingdom. Your generosity shews that you ought to be a gentleman; and it shall be my fault if I don't make you one, in

---

187 KEY: "Fleur de Lys." The symbol, according to the 1747 *New Dictionary of Heraldry*, was "originally borne by the Kings of *France*, tho' tract of Time hath made the bearing of them more vulgar." It seems to have been indiscriminately used in Britain for the reasons implied in this chapter: "this Flower is become very frequent among us," the *Dictionary* continues, "in some Coats One, in others Three, in others Five."

188 Specifically, "a British person who acquired a large fortune in India during the period of British rule." In extended use, "a wealthy, influential, or powerful landowner or other person" (OED).

the sight of the world."—Saying this, he took his leave, *when I was heartily glad to go with him, being part of the price paid upon this occasion for the making of a gentleman.*

As soon as my *new* master[189] went home, he retired to his closet, and taking out the money he had just received, "Hah! hah! hah! no bad price for a little *daubing!*" (said he laughing, and chinking the purse). "I wonder how the fellow could be such an ass as to think that any thing in my power to do could make him pass for a gentleman! But let him have his way! his folly is my gain; and it is no more than justice, that one who has cheated the world so long, should cheat himself at last, and sacrifice the earnings of villainy to vanity! But hold! this is about the time my *Antiquarian* was to come. Let me see those *ancient manuscripts*, and *inscriptions which I had done last week!* upon my life, they look very well. The *canker*[190] upon this copper, and the *smoke* upon this parchment are as natural as they were the work of a thousand years; and these *scrawls* might pass even for the *spells* of the witch of *Endor*,[191] they have so little likeness to any marks made to convey thought, at this time. He is a very pretty fellow that did them, and deserves encouragement."

Just as he said this, the person he expected came, and entering without ceremony upon his business, "I called upon you, Sir," (said he) "to see those things you mentioned to me. If they are really what you describe, we shall not differ about the price, high as it is."

"I hope, Sir," (answered my master) "you have not so mean an opinion of my judgment, as to imagine I could ever think of imposing upon you. No, Sir! I know that to be impossible; even if I could be base enough to attempt it; and therefore would not mention any thing to you, that could admit of the least doubt to a person of your profound learning. As to the price, I could have

---

189 KEY: "Mr. Prestagi the Auctioneer." Prestage (d. 1767), of Prestage and Hobbs, Savile Row. In the *Daily Advertiser* appear announcements of items to "be sold at auction by Mr Prestage at his great room the end of Savile Row," including paintings by Titian and Reubens. Lady Ailesbury wrote to Horace Walpole in 1756: "I see in the *Advertiser* that there is going to be an auction of Mr. Pestre's furniture, which, if it really is his, as Mr. Prestage assures us, I imagine there must be some good things amongst it."

190 "Corrosion on the surface of metal" (OED).

191 The witch of Endor appears in 1 Samuel 28:7-25, where King Saul of Israel directs her to summon the ghost of the prophet Samuel.

had much more since I saw you; but I thought it but justice to their merit to offer them first to you, as there is no other collection in the kingdom worthy of them, and I am above rising in a demand I have once made, though infinitely short of their intrinsic value, as you will be convinced the moment you see them. Here, Sir, is the *manuscript*, which I had the good fortune to meet with as I was rummaging among some old records in our office, that had never been stirred since the reign of *Henry the Eighth*. The paper in which it was wrapped was so decayed, that it mouldered quite away so immediately upon its coming into the open air, that I had scarce time to read the contents, which were *that this parchment had been found in the tomb of Thomas a Becket, upon the breaking up of his shrine at the Reformation*,[192] and was laid up there, on account of its antiquity. That it must have been very ancient, even before his time, the colour and decay of the parchment would sufficiently prove, were there not other proofs still more convincing to them as have judgment to comprehend them. The shape of the letter shews its age. This manner of writing, as appears by comparing it with other ancient manuscripts, was introduced in the beginning of the second century of the Christian Era, and quite dropped by the middle of the third. Within that period therefore it must have been written. Its antiquity being thus fixed, the purport of it is next to be considered; and of that, and its importance, there can be no just room to doubt. This *spot* at the bottom of the parchment, though so much defaced by time, bears a strong resemblance to the impression of a *mitre*, and thereby proves that some bishop was the author of what was written over it, into which these four letters, M—A—T—H, fortunately so very plain, give the clearest light; for as they must have been part of the word ARIMATHEA, they prove that the opinion of *Joseph* of *Arimathea*'s having first preached the Gospel in *Britain*,[193] was known so early as in the

---

192 Thomas Becket or à Becket (1120?-70), Archbishop of Canterbury, who was murdered in his cathedral and revered as a Catholic saint and martyr for centuries after. His shrine, a popular destination for pilgrims (including those in Chaucer's *Canterbury Tales*), was destroyed in 1538 by orders of Henry VIII.

193 Joseph of Arimathea, who interred the body of Christ. Some early Christian historians reported he visited Britain—an idea debated with interest in the eighteenth century. Medieval legend associated Joseph of Arimathea with the

second century, and so decide that long-contested point; as, who can be such an Infidel as to doubt a thing given thus, as I may say, under the sacred seal of the *mitre*, and that so very near the time."

"Very true! but is it not as probable, that the design of this writing was to refute that opinion, as to confirm it?"

"My good Sir, if you allow weight to such trivial objections as this, you give up all the knowledge of an *Antiquarian*, which never amounts higher than to possible conjecture, without regard to probability even against him; for *conjectures such as this, founded on effaced remains of antiquity, are of much greater weight in the learned world, because they shew more learning than the plainest conclusions drawn from evident and complete records, as these are obvious to any common person.* But why do I mention these things to you, who understand them so much better than I pretend to do."

"I believe I do, Sir, know something of those matters; and was satisfied both of its antiquity, and importance, at the first glance of my eye; though I started that objection for mere amusement. But where is the fragment? I should be glad to see that also."

"Here it is, Sir;" (answered my master, taking a bit of broken copper out of a box, in which it was carefully wrapped with cotton) "this plate of copper was torn in the manner you see, from the head of a sepulchral monument on top of mount *Libanus*,[194] by a person who had been sent thither by a celebrated Society, on purpose to seek for such things; and at his return made me a present of it, as the most valuable acquisition he had made, out of gratitude for my having helped him to the job. Observe this *canker*, Sir! Much as it has been rubbed off in the carriage; the depth and colour of it shew, that it must have been some thousands of years in gathering. What the occasion of setting it up was, some particular circumstances direct to a conjecture sufficiently probable: you see this *hole*, which the canker has eaten almost through the copper, with this *stroke* turning up over it. This certainly is the remains of the figure of a lion, as is plain from these two *tufts* in the middle, and at the end of the stroke, which must have been the tail of it.

---

arrival of the Holy Grail in the British Isles.
194 Mount Libanus, mentioned several times in the Old Testament, was the ancient name for the Lebanon Mountains, now in modern-day Lebanon.

Now as the lion was the emblem of *Judah*,[195] it cannot be doubted but some great personage of that tribe must have been buried where this emblem was set up; a circumstance, that so clearly proves the antiquity of *coats of arms*, that I do not know how to think of parting with it, it affords such an illustration to a treatise I am at this time engaged in writing, on that sublime and difficult subject."

"Not part with it!" (replied the *Antiquarian*, returning it carefully into the box, and then cramming the box into his bosom) "you must get it first, my good friend, to part with it. Hah! hah! hah! a very pretty jest truly! you offer a thing to sale, and set a price upon it, and then you cannot part with it! a very pretty jest truly! Here is your money, both for the *manuscript*, and the *fragment*; and when you meet with any other such precious remains of antiquity, I shall be obliged to you to let me have the preference. Nobody will give you a better price."

Saying this, he reached my master a bank-note, which he took with an air of dissatisfaction; and while he was telling out change, "You do as you please with me, Sir," (said he) "this time; but the next, I shall be more upon my guard. I am glad, however, that it goes into so noble a *collection* of yours, where it will have justice done to its merit."

"Aye, Sir!" (answered the *Antiquarian*, with a smile of self-complacency) "I have been at some pains, and expence too, to make a *collection*; and have the satisfaction to think, that whenever I die, it will make as good a figure in a *sale catalogue* as that of most of my cotemporaries. I shall leave proofs behind me, that I have not spent my life in vain. What would I not give to hear the character which an able *Auctioneer* will give of me, upon opening the sale? I wish my good friend *Puff* [196] may out-live me, to have the job. There is no man sets forth the merit of any thing in such happy terms. He has words at will, as they say. What an high opinion will he raise of my learning, taste, and judgment? But that's right. You said you wanted this *fragment*, for a particular occasion! I am by

---

195 Per *Genesis*, the lion is the symbol of the Tribe of Judah, one of the original twelve tribes of Israel.

196 In its eighteenth-century sense, to puff was "to praise, extol, or commend, esp. extravagantly, unduly, or in inflated or unjustifiable terms" (OED).

no means averse to obliging you. You are welcome to quote it, as in my *collection*, suppose in this, or some such manner, *'as appears'* (proving what you have advanced before) *'by a most valuable, and rare antique fragment,'* (or whatever else you shall call it) *'in the most curious,'* or *'costly,'* or *'inestimable,'* or *'noble,'* (or perhaps all these) *'collection of my late most learned, and judicious, and indefatigable, and munificent friend,'* or whatever other titles of the kind your judgment and regard shall dictate to you."

"I am much obliged to you for the favour;" (returned my master, scarce able to restrain his laughter) "and shall be sure to avail myself of it, at the proper time, as also to do it in a manner, which, however short it may fall of your merit, will yet testify my high and respectful sense of it."—Saying this, he gave him the change of his note, *among which I was*, and sent him away happy.

CHAPTER XV

A modest method of seeking fame. *Chrysal's* master confirms himself in his resolution to gratify an unknown curiosity, by a great example. The judicious and learned manner in which he classed and entered his new acquisitions. Curious remark on the value of books. He goes to an auction, where he makes an extraordinary purchase. *Chrysal* changes his service, for that of the Auctioneer.[197] Specimen and effects of his new master's eloquence, learning, and judgment.

A MAN's spending his life and fortune, in buying up books of learning, and obscure remains of antiquity, only to make a great sale after his death, was a method of seeking fame more modest than I had hitherto met among mankind. As soon as my *new* master reached home, he went directly into his *Musaeum*, and taking out his rare purchases, stared at them for some time in a kind of stupid delight, till no longer able to contain it, "What an

197 According to one key, Abraham Langford (1711-74), the foremost auctioneer of the period and the basis for Mr. Smirk in Foote's *The Minor* (see 1.272). George Colman's *The Connoisseur* for 1756 refers to those "precious curiosities, as are frequently seen in *Mr. Langford's* Auction-Room," and Langford's "great auction-house" in Covent Garden is likewise mentioned in Eliza Haywood's *The History of Jemmy and Jenny Jessamy* (1753) and William Cowper's *The Task* (1785).

opinion" (said he) "will the world have of me, when all these come to be shewn for sale? I hope my worthy friend *Puff* will live to do me justice! What if I should beg of him to give me a specimen of the manner in which he will set them out? He cannot refuse me that gratification, in return for all the money he has taken from me, especially as I have told him that I design he shall have the job. Such a request is not improper. It has the sanction of one of the greatest names in antiquity to support it. *Cicero*,[198] the great *Cicero*, desired his friend the historian to let him know what he intended to say of him; and need I hesitate to follow his example? Whatever has the authority of antiquity must be right; and therefore I will go to him directly about it.—But hold! I must enter these articles in my catalogue first."

Then taking down an huge folio richly bound, and inscribed CATALOGUE, on the back and sides, in capitals of gold, he sat down to insert this valuable addition to his treasure; and opening the book with great deliberation, "What are the *heads*" (said he) "under which they are to be classed? Let me see! *Antiques!* no. That is for my *coins*, and *busts*, and *urns*. What is the next? *Ancient manuscripts*, and *fragments!* Aye! these are they. Let me consider now what are the titles!"—Then laying the forefinger of his right hand upon the tip of his nose, supporting his chin with his thumb, shutting his eyes, and leaning back in his chair, on the arm of which he rested his elbow, "How unlucky it was" (resumed he, after a long pause) "that he did not tell their names! I was ashamed to ask him directly, though I did as much, if he had minded me. But can't I make them out, from what he said? *A very antique manuscript*—no. That will not do. *Antique* is for works of art; *ancient* is the word here.—*A very ancient manuscript written by Thomas a Becket in the second century, and found in his tomb at the Restoration, proving that Joseph of Arimathea was an English bishop.*—Yes. That is it. And then for the *fragment*,—*a very ancient*—no, *antique*. *Antique* is the word for *fragments*, they are made by art; *a very antique fragment torn from a monument on mount Libanus, proving that some great person was buried there; and that a lion was the arms of Judah.*—Aye! these will do! I knew I could make them out. This is just the substance

---

198 Marcus Tullius Cicero, Roman philosopher, orator and statesman.

of what he said, but in fewer and better words. Titles should be short and pithy. *Multum in parvo.* Much in a little compass. Let me alone for hitting off a striking title. I have not been an *Antiquarian* so long for nothing."—Then conning them over twice or thrice to try how they sounded, he entered them in his catalogue, and putting the book back into its place, sat down to contemplate his own consequence in the learned world.

But sublime as this enjoyment was, his indefatigable industry would not permit him to indulge it long. "Hah!" (said he, starting, as upon sudden recollection) "that's right! the sale of those *Chinese characters*, brought over in the last fleet, comes on about this very time. It was quite out of my head; and I would not have missed of them on any account. They'll make a capital article; for the *Chinese* taste is coming into such great *vogue*,[199] that I suppose we shall soon learn their language; though I should be sorry to see that too, as it would lessen the value of my *Chinese* books; for *books are valued now the more for not being understood*, as I know by experience, having laid out many a pound in the purchase of such as I understand no more of, than if they were *Chinese*. But let those who know no other use of books but to read them, buy only such as they can read: I *collect* mine for another purpose, and a noble *collection* I will have, let it cost me what it will; I care not whether I die worth a groat beside. The fame of that is fortune enough for me."

Pursuant to this noble resolution he went directly to the sale, where he was so charmed with the *Auctioneer*'s learning and eloquence, that he out-bade every body, and carried off in triumph *the curious, the rare, the inestimable key, into all the mysterious, the profound, the sublime wisdom of that Prince of all Philosophers, Legislators, and Hierarchs, the divine* CON—FUT—SEE,[200] *and all his learned, and judicious Disciples and Commentators,* THE CHINESE CHARACTERS, in paying for which, *I changed his service for that of the Auctioneer.*

My *new* master proceeded for the remainder of the sale, to display his abilities in the same extraordinary manner; giving

---

199 Eighteenth-century fashion was marked by a fervent interest in *Chinoiserie*, far Eastern ceramics, textiles, furniture, and decor.
200 Confucius, Chinese social philosopher and the founder of Confucianism.

circumstantial accounts of things he knew nothing of; and
bestowing the most extravagant praises for excellencies of his own
invention, often inconsistent with each other, and with the subject
to which they were ignorantly attributed, with a confidence that
bore down doubt, and gained implicit credit with the gaping
crowd, in defiance to reason, and their very senses, till he led them
on by little and little to pay the price of such an imaginary value.[201]
But this will be best explained by an instance that happened just
after I came into his possession.

The sale of that day consisted *nominally* of the *collection* of a
Cheesemonger lately deceased, who had been *an eminent Antiquarian*,
and *Virtuoso*. I say nominally; because though the whole went
under his name, scarce the tenth part of it had ever been his, the
rest being *made up* from every quarter by my master. Among the
rare, *curious*, and *costly* articles exhibited on this occasion, was a
vessel of *Porcelaine*, of an uncommon shape, ornamented with
several odd and uncouth representations of animals, and some
figures not unlike the characters of a language.

"Gentlemen," (said my master, as soon as this was produced)
"You here see one of the rarest, and most valuable remains of
antiquity, ever brought into *Europe*. This *here* superb vase was the
identical cup, out of which the sublime emperors of *China* for
numberless ages drank the consecrated wine, on the day of their
coronation. It was found, gentlemen, among the treasures of the
Great *Mogul* by *Thomas Couli Can*,[202] when he dethroned that *there*
prince, out of the wreck of whose spoils, when they were lost
in passing the river *of the Indies*, it was saved by a *Chinese Nabob*,
from whom it was afterwards taken, together with his crown, by
that there *heaven-born* general, who made those effeminate, and
dastardly *Indians* tremble at the name of an *Englishman*,[203] and

---

201 The eighteenth century saw both the rapid growth of auction businesses
(including the founding of Sotheby's and Christie's), and the standardization of
the ascending bid or "English" auction method with which we are now familiar.
202 Nader Shah (1688-1747), Shah of Iran, and a military genius whose campaigns
created a great Persian empire incorporating Iran, Afghanistan, Pakistan and
central Asia. He crossed the Indus river to conquer Mughal India in 1738.
203 Readers of the popular press in Britain, who knew Nader Shah as "Thamas
Kouli Khan," followed his victories with great interest, and for some years it was
rumored the great general was actually a European. A letter in the *Gentleman's*

given by him as a precious token of his esteem, to the deceased, his very learned and curious friend. This, gentlemen, is in few words the whole full and true account of this here inestimable curiosity, every word of which can be proved by unquestionable authority. As for the vase itself, exclusive of all this, its own merits give it sufficient value. Observe these here figures, gentlemen; they are *Egyptian Hieroglyphicks,* denoting the duties of a sovereign, which those wise *Mandarines* always take care to instruct their emperors in. This here *lion,* for instance, signifies, that he must be courageous and valiant; this *fox,* that he must be wise; and so on. But the most extraordinary thing of all, gentlemen, is these here characters. They are a *talisman,* or *charm,* invented by *Mahomet*[204] to protect the owner of this cup from the influence of evil spirits. I do not presume, gentlemen, to stand up for the virtue of such things. The notion of spirits, I am sensible, is much exploded; and the religion of *Mahomet* cried down among us; but still, gentlemen, without entering into these here nice points, we all know that he was a great man, and *lived a great while ago,* which is sufficient to make any thing that was his, of great value to men of learning, who are above prejudice in these matters. But beside all this, these here characters are of the greatest importance, on another account; as they prove beyond dispute, that *the true method of writing the learned languages was without accents,* not one appearing, as you see, gentlemen, in this most original and authentick relick of antient learning, and so put an end to that there controversy, that has so long puzzled the world. It were presumption in me, gentlemen, to attempt putting a value on a thing that is invaluable. I will therefore set it up at what you please, as you are the best judges. This only I will make bold to say, that the best judge of all will have it, as he will give most for it; for too much it is impossible to give."

So just an account, and such judicious praise, could not fail of effect. The *Virtuosi* round him, satisfied that what he said

---

Magazine, 1735, assures "the Publick that he is a Native of *Ireland,* and that his real Name is THOMAS C'ALLAGHAN, the Name of a very ancient Family in this Kingdom"; and a writer for the *Daily Gazetteer* reported, on May 28, 1736, that other writers were claiming, "all at the same time, that he is a *Frenchman,* a *Fleming,* an *Englishman,* a *Scot,* an *Irishman,* and I know not what besides."

204 Muhammad, founder of Islam.

must be true, because spoken with confidence, and above their comprehension, vied with each other for the possession of so inestimable a treasure, till they *raised* it to an height, at which they themselves were surprised, as soon as the spirit of *bidding* began to cool, and they had time to reflect.

CHAPTER XVI

An unsavoury accident stops him short in his harangue. He turns off the jest, with another, and accounts learnedly for what has happened. The real cause and consequence of that accident. Reflections on auctioneering, and the causes of its success.

THIS was the time, for which he always reserved the highest flights of his eloquence, to raise that spirit again. Resuming therefore his harangue, "You pause, gentlemen," (said he) "only to consider how much farther you may *rise* with safety; for it is impossible that persons of your profound taste and judgment should disgrace them so much, as to let such a jewel *go* for so mere a trifle. Do not take my word, gentlemen, for its value. I may be mistaken, but you cannot. Examine it therefore yourselves. Observe the beauty of these here *unknown* figures! *read* these *unintelligible* characters; and smell the aromatic odour which the vase still retains, and ever will retain, from the quintessences of all the spices of the *Indies*, which used to be mixed with the consecrated wine. The perfume is almost enough to revive the dead."

Saying this, he went to smell it himself to lead the way to the rest, and putting the mouth of it to his nose, without taking off the cover, that the fragrance should not evaporate, as he raised his hand, a stream, that emitted a savour far from aromatic, gushed out into his face, and filled his mouth, as well as nose, with something more substantial than perfume.

It is impossible to describe his situation, at such a disgraceful accident. Surprise, shame, and loathing aggravated each other, and threw him into such confusion, as once in his life deprived him of utterance for some moments. As soon as he had emptied his mouth, and wiped his face, "Villain," (sputtered he, to his servant) "how has this happened? Whom have you let play me this base, malicious, low-liv'd trick?"

"S-S-Sir," (answered the fellow, as well as his struggle to suppress his laughter permitted him to speak) "I know nothing of the matter. I never left any one a moment alone among the things, but them there ladies, who I told you sent me out for a glass of *Ratifia*, t'other morning, and how could I have suspected their doing such a thing?"

"*Ratifia!*" (replied my master, who had by this time recovered his assurance, and knew the best way to turn off one jest is by another) "*Gin*, you should say; for if I can judge by taste, and smell, that is their liquor. I suppose they did it on purpose to revenge their sex upon *Mahomet*, for taking away their souls (I wish he had also taken away the filthiness of their dispositions!) by defiling so celebrated a monument of his learning and skill, in this nasty manner, Hah! hah! hah!"

The oddity of such a thought naturally made the company join in his laugh; but could not so far wipe off the disgrace which the defiled vase had suffered, as to make any more be offered for it, so that it was forced to be *knocked down* to the last *bidder*, at not much more than if it had been made of gold, at which the purchaser and my master were equally mortified, though for different and very unequal reasons.

As for the cause of this misfortune, it was really what the servant said. One of the ladies, who came to view the curiosities, having certain pressing occasions, feigned a pretence to send him out; and in the mean time made such use of this vase, being the first conveniency that came to her hand, as overpowered the scent of some spices, which had been put into it for the purpose.

It was fortunate for my master, that this was the last article in the sale of that day, as a spirit of ridicule could not be favourable to his business. As soon as the company was gone, he settled his accounts, and summing up the profits, "Why this is pretty well!" (said he, rubbing his hands and shrugging up his shoulders) "this does pretty well! Though if that damned accident had not happened," (turning up his nose, and spitting with loathing) "it would have been much better. The fools were in the humour, and wanted only to be kept up. However, I have not much right to complain upon the whole. That there *Jordan*[205] cost me five shillings, and I have sold it for fifty pounds. Much good may the judicious buyer make of his bargain. This is the happiness of a man's having his tongue *well hung*. A mealy mouth will never do in my business; which after all is the best going. I might have stood freezing behind a counter this month, and not make half this much. In the way of *fair trade*, as it is called, people have their senses about them, and stand to examine before they buy, but any trumpery will go off in this way."

I have observed your astonishment at the easiness with which my master succeeded in such gross imposition; but the reason of it is obvious. All mankind have an ambition of distinguishing themselves, one way or another; and generally choose that in which they have the least qualifications to entitle them to success, in order to hide their own deficiency. The coward, for instance, affects valour; the block-head knowledge; and the illiterate tradesman, who has made a fortune by plodding on in some illiberal business, taste and judgment in the abstrusest pursuits of learned curiosity, in which, as there is no fixed rule to judge by, caprice takes the direction, and opens an ample field for imposition.

As to the business of *auctioneering* in general, it owes the greater part of that success, with which my master was so pleased, to another cause. The desire of *buying bargains*, which governs every one who buys any thing, makes people crowd to those places where things are to be sold, not as in the regular course of trade, for what they appear to be worth, but for the most that can be got for them; and there emulation, dependence on each other's judgment, (*"those people know what they are doing, and would not bid so much, if it was not worth more"*) and the *oratory* of the auctioneer lead them by insensible advances, as their spirits rise, to give prices which they never meant to give, when they began to *bid*. That great bargains are often got at such places is true, but that is chiefly in a particular branch of the business, the mystery of which will be explained to you.

---

205 "A chamber-pot" (OED).

CHAPTER XVII

Chrysal's master is visited by a *Connoisseur*,[206] to whom he gives a short *receipt*[207] how to make his pictures sell, and makes some striking remarks, on the disregard people shew for their families, which send his visitor away in a huff.

My master was interrupted in his pleasing meditations, by the entrance of a gentleman, the sight of whom promised him the greater pleasure of carrying the subject of them into execution. After some judicious remarks on the taste of the town, and the present state of *virtu*, in the course of which each liberally complimented the other, "Pray, Sir" (said the gentleman) "how do pictures sell this season?"

"Never better, Sir" (answered my master) "pictures are every body's money now. A *good master* brings any thing; and what is more, I am convinced they will rise still higher, so that buyers have no time to lose. I have a sale next week, when you will see such prices as will astonish you. There are some things there that I know you will have, let the cost what they will, they suit your fine collection so exactly."

"Why, as to that," (replied the gentleman) "my mind is a good deal changed. I have taken it into my head lately to part with my pictures, and have therefore called upon you to desire that you will come in the morning, and let me know what you think they are worth."

"Worth, Sir! they are worth a great deal of money; which there is not the least danger but they will bring, if they are managed properly. There is more, Sir, in the management of a sale, much more than most people dream of, I assure you."

"I am sensible of that, Sir; and also of your abilities in such management, which you will have the best encouragement to exert on this occasion, as I propose selling the whole to you together, if we can agree."

This turn came so unexpected that it struck my master quite

---

206 "A judge; a critick: it is often used of a pretended critick" (Johnson).
207 "The means to be adopted for attaining some end" (OED).

down of the mouth, as he was sensible that he had overshot himself, and spoiled his market by saying so much. "It is very unlucky, Sir;" (answered he, changing his note directly) "that I did not know your intention sooner. I could then have divided them properly among the several sales of the season; but it is now quite too late; this here one next week is the last; and the catalogues for that are all made out, and dispersed, so that there is no possibility of *slipping in* a single article. Besides, the buyers have laid out all their money."

"Slipping in, Sir! I don't understand you. Do not you think my pictures are sufficient both in number and value to make a sale by themselves? I am sure I have more than once known you make noise enough about *collections* in no respect equal to mine. There must be some mystery in this, which I cannot comprehend."

"Very true, Sir! there are mysteries, as you observe, in all businesses; and perhaps in none more than ours."

"I am not enquiring into your mysteries. All I desire to know is, why after just telling me that pictures never bore so high a price as at this time, and that mine could not fail of bringing a great deal of money, you should so soon change your opinion."

"Pardon me, Sir! I have not changed my opinion in the least; and shall be very proud to serve you to the best of my abilities, in the way of a sale; but there is a material reason, why I must beg to be excused in buying them, to stand the hazard of it myself."

"I should be glad to know what that reason can be, for I must own I cannot conceive it."

"Why, Sir, it is a thing to be sure that may seem odd to you; but experience has taught us the truth of it. In short, Sir, it is your being alive."

"How! my being alive! What difference can my life or death make in the value of my pictures?"

"A very great one, Sir, I assure you. In all the course of my business, I never knew one instance of a sale's going *off* well, where the owner was living. People conclude that a person parts with pictures either through dislike or necessity. The former, you know, depreciates them at once; nor does the other much less; as people of fashion despise a man, and every thing belonging to him, the moment it is known he is in distress. Besides, an *Auctioneer's* tongue is *tied up* from saying any thing of a person's taste, and judgment, and all that, while he is living, it sounds so fulsome; and you are sensible that a good character of the *collector* often goes a great way in helping off a *collection."*

"The best thing then for a man to do on such an occasion, I presume, would be to shoot himself through the head! Hah!"

"Hah! hah! hah! You are pleased to jest, Sir; but to be sure it would be of great advantage. Curiosity brings all the world upon those occasions, and then a man has an opportunity of saying so many things, as *'that the deceased would not take ten times so much, if he were living;'* or, *'that the high price he gave for it caused the distress that made him kill himself;'* or a thousand other striking things of the kind. *I never have so much pleasure, as upon those occasions*, they give a man such room to shew himself. Indeed, if gentlemen considered the thing in time, more of them would take this method of delivering themselves and their families both from distress, and not defer it till all is gone, and the survivors can make nothing by their death; but few people take any care for their families now o' days. It is a bold push to be sure; though not so bad as *a man's shooting himself to win a wager* neither. I should beg your pardon, Sir, for speaking so freely; but as I know it is not your case, you cannot take offence; though even if I thought it was, I would not presume to recommend such a thing for the world. Every body is to judge for himself. I only give you my opinion what effect it would have."

"I understand you very well, Sir," (answered the gentleman, who had much difficulty to hear him out) "and in return for your opinion, will give you my advice, which is to consider better whom you speak to in this insolent manner another time, for fear of receiving such chastisement, as contempt alone prevents my giving you this moment."—On saying which words he turned about and left the room.

CHAPTER XVIII

Chrysal's master receives an agreeable summons. His encomiums on the
generosity of merchants, and account of the way many of them acquire
reputation for taste and judgment. He meets the merchant, who
consults him on a different branch of his business, from that which he
expected. *Chrysal's* master, in order to encourage his customer, gives a
large account of his own abilities, and opens some curious secrets in his
business. A bargain is struck, to the mutual satisfaction of both parties;
and *Chrysal* changes his service for that of the merchant.

WELL as my master was accustomed to rebukes, there was
something in the nature of this which disconcerted him so much
that he had not power to make the gentleman any reply. But he
was soon relieved from the trepidation into which it threw him,
by a message from an eminent merchant to meet him directly at a
neighbouring tavern. "Aye," (said he, adjusting his wig at the glass,
and putting on his cloak) "this is the thing! There is some difference
between treating with a good substantial citizen who will mind
what a man says, and your people of fashion, who fly into a rage
forsooth, if they can't have their own way in every thing. No
people part with their money so freely as merchants. They don't
stand higgling, and criticizing like the others. All they require is to
be asked a good price, and then they think a thing must be good of
course. Many a time have I got five times more from a merchant,
than I dared to have asked from a duke. I suppose he wants to
shew his taste next week at the sale; and has sent for me to tell him
which are the best pieces, and how much he may bid for them. He
is not the first citizen whom my instructions have made pass for
a man of taste and judgment. I love such pupils, and they pay so
well for their learning; and that more ways than one; for they buy
what nobody else would bid for; *it is only slipping a puffer*[208] *or two
of quality* at them, *enough of whom come sharking to every sale for that*

---

208 "A person employed to bid at an auction in order to raise the price or to
encourage others to bid" (OED).

purpose only, and they may be raised to any price. No people part with their money like merchants."

When he came to the tavern, he found the merchant waiting for him. After the compliments common upon such occasions were politely interchanged, "I desired to see you" (said the merchant, proceeding to business, though not without evident confusion) "on an affair that will convince you of my confidence in your abilities and honour. Trade, as you know, has been so dead for some time past, that there is no getting in a penny of money, without tearing people to pieces. Now as I had rather suffer something myself, than oppress any honest man, till he can bring his affairs about, I should be glad to dispose of some parcels of goods, even under their value, to raise money for present occasions, that is, provided it can be done in such a manner, as not to be known, as such a thing might injure a man's credit."

"Dear Sir," (answered my master, whose heart leaped with joy at the mention of such an affair) "never fear that; I'll engage to manage it so, that if every one who knows you, were to watch, they'd never even suspect the least of the matter. There is nothing easier, nor more common in the way of business; and it luckily happens, that I have the finest opportunity at this very time, that ever I have had in my life. I have a large sale under a commission, the very week after next, into which I can *hedge* a thousand or two, with the greatest ease and safety. Assigners never take notice of such things. We understand one another better than that. Many a worthy man have I enabled to hold his head above water, for years, by this method. To be sure, it must have an end some time; but then a man stands in fortune's way for a lucky hit, you know; and not only that, but also makes sure of so much good living in the mean time, and can be no worse at the last; and then, when all comes to all, and there must be a *blow-up*, it gives him an opportunity of securing something against a rainy day, as the saying is. As for its being discovered, there are ways enough to prevent that. *It is but entering them as sold, and I'll find a buyer, that shall never be heard more of.* Lord, Sir, if it was not for things of this kind, our business would be nothing to what it is. Half the sales you see every day in the papers, are made up in this manner."

"Well, Sir," (replied the merchant, who had listened to him

with attention, and seemed greatly affected at some part of what he said) "I presume you understand your business; and as I have no doubt of your honour, I shall leave the whole entirely to your management. Here is an account of the particulars, which I want to dispose of at this time. They are in a private warehouse, whither I have had them conveyed to be ready for the purpose, of which this is the key; and here is a bill of sale, which I will execute directly, as I have an occasion for two thousand pounds this very evening. You see there is value more than sufficient for double that sum, as you will be a better judge when you see the goods, but the rest can *stand forward* till they are disposed of; and the account made up."

"Really, Sir, I should be extremely glad to serve you; but I fear, I have not so much cash by me. However, if you please, I'll go with you, and look at the goods; and then I'll step home, and try what I can do."

Accordingly away they went together to the warehouse; where my master, being satisfied with the value of the goods, left the merchant, and hied him home directly with a joyful heart for the money.

"So!" (said he to himself, as he went along) "I thought what things would come to in the end! His coach, and country house! his wife's routs! and his own kept mistress have made quick work with him. I believe such men must imagine the rest of the world to be blind, or they would never go on at such a rate. I suppose he's preparing for a place in the *Gazette* to-morrow, or next day. But that is no affair of mine. I'll take care to make a safe bargain for myself; and let him look to the rest. *I am not to swear for him.* Of all the business in our way, I like this the best. A man can make up what account he pleases, without danger of its being disputed with him. All here is snug and secure. If I could but get jobs enough of this kind, I'd let who would chaffer²⁰⁹ for *toys*, and *daubings* with people of quality, who often *outsharp* us, in spite of all our experience."

By this time he reached home, where he soon made up the money, with the help of that and the former day's sale, without hesitating a moment at its not being his own, and taking with him proper persons to *attest* his bargain, and *new locks* to make sure of

---

209 "To haggle; to bargain" (Johnson).

it, returned to the merchant, with whom he soon concluded every
thing without scruple or delay on either side; and then paying him
on the spot, in bank-notes and cash (*among the latter of which I was*),
sent him away, as well satisfied, as he himself stayed behind.

CHAPTER XIX

Motive of *Chrysal's* new master for making such a bargain, with the many
and great advantages a merchant may make of being in the house.
A short sketch of an election. The curious method which *Chrysal's*
master took to evade the laws against bribery. He takes offence at the
unreasonable presumption of his constituents, and resolves to make
the most of the bargain he has bought from them, which by a singular
piece of management he proposes to make cheaper than they think.
Chrysal changes his service, for that of the idol of an inn. Some account
of *Chrysal's* new mistress. He quits her service, for a curious purpose.
An expedient to prevent the sale of poison for mind and body. *Chrysal*
again changes his service.

WHEN a man has fixed his mind upon gaining a particular end, he
slights any inconveniences which may attend the means. Though
my *new* master²¹⁰ was sensible of the loss he must suffer by his
bargain, the prospect of accomplishing the purpose for which he
made it, prevented its giving him any concern.

As soon as he got home, he gave orders to have his *equipage*
made ready for a journey into the country early next morning,
and then retiring into his closet for a few moments before he went
to bed, "At length" (said he, with a look of self-congratulation)
"I shall compass, what I have so long set my heart upon. What
an advantage it is to a merchant to be in the House! I can laugh
at *bailiffs* and *bankruptcies* for five years at least; and in the mean

---

210 In one reader's notes, "Shiffner." Perhaps Henry Shiffner (1721-95), an
importer of Russian iron and hemp, who campaigned to represent the borough
of Minehead in three separate elections from 1754 to 1761, although he had no
natural or hereditary tie to the borough. In the election of 1754, Shiffner lost,
then contested the results with suits both in Parliament and in courts of law; the
Gentleman's Magazine reports on one of the cases in September 1754. Shiffner won
the election of March 1761, though debt ruined him soon after.

time I shall have a thousand opportunities of making my fortune, by pushing boldly *in the alley*, now that all fears of the immediate consequences are over, or getting beneficial *contracts* with the government, or at least some genteel and profitable employment under it. A merchant may make many advantages of being in the House! Confound that prating fellow! I was once afraid that he *smoked* my design, he came so near some unlucky circumstances; but it was above his *cut*. All his schemes are common and low-lived. This of mine is a master-stroke. It is *playing deep*, to be sure! Fifteen hundred for my seat; and what with other expences, and the loss upon this night's work, as much more. It is playing damn'd deep. But it is too late to think of that now. I have *sported* many a thousand upon a worse chance in my time. At any rate, I can laugh at *bailiffs* and *bankruptcies*, for five years at least; what an advantage it is to a merchant to be in the House!"

Saying this he went to bed, where the advantages of being in the House still ran so strongly in his head, that he dreamed of nothing all night, but *bullying creditors*, and *cringing to ministers*; doing *jobs*,[211] and getting *contracts*, *places*, *and pensions*.

In pursuance of his scheme, he set out next morning with a splendid retinue for the borough he had in view,[212] where he managed matters with such judgment and generosity, keeping the whole town drunk from the moment he arrived, *according to the policy which permits a candidate to deprive his electors of their senses, in order to enable them to judge the better of his legislative abilities*,[213] that he was elected in preference to a gentleman, the munificence of whose family had for many generations been the chief support of the place,[214] and who himself spent his ample fortune in hospitality, and beneficence in it, but disdained to buy the votes of a venal crew on this occasion.

---

211 Using political office for private advantage; "a transaction in which duty or the public interest is sacrificed for the sake of such an advantage" (OED).

212 In marginal notes, "Minehead," a borough in Somerset.

213 As an expression of goodwill towards voters, it was customary for campaigners to liberally serve drink at elections.

214 Shiffner won the election of March 1761 with 287 votes to the 226 votes of Percy Wyndham O'Brien, Earl of Thomond. Thomond would be appointed to the office nine months later, after Shiffner's financial ruin.

As such a competitor naturally had every man of worth and honour in his interest, it had been necessary for my master to proceed with the utmost care and circumspection. Accordingly, instead of *directly giving* his voters money, he *lent* them the prices stipulated, on the *security* of their *notes of hand*, payable in a certain time; an expedient, in which he had a further view, than barely evading the laws against such practices.

Every thing being concluded, he was preparing to depart in triumph, when his *constituents* waited upon him in form, with certain *instructions* for executing the *trust* they had *thus reposed* in him. Though he looked upon this as such a bare-faced piece of insolence, that he scarce knew how to bear it, yet as he had not yet taken his seat, he received their *commands* with the politest *humility*, and promised the most faithful *obedience* to them. But they were no sooner out of his sight, than he changed his note. "Impudent, unreasonable scoundrels!" (said he to himself, giving vent to his indignation, as he walked back and forward in the room) "to talk of having reposed your trust in me, and pretend to give me instructions! I have *bought you*; and I will *sell* you to the best bidder, if he were the *devil*; and a bad bargain he will have of you, if he buys you as dear as I have. Though I have a stroke in my head to bring myself home, that you little think of. Those notes of hand, which you thought I took only to evade the law, shall be paid to the last farthing, if I am not *chosen* for nothing next election. You shall find you have no fool to deal with."

Just as he said this, he received notice that his coach was ready, and the landlord's daughter coming to wish him a good journey, he saluted her politely, and slipping a couple of guineas *(one of which I was)* into her hand to buy a ribbon, left the house like a man of honour.

I have not entered particularly into the circumstances of electioneering. They are too gross to give pleasure; and too well known to require repetition even to you. The effects, I mean immediately in the place, were such as reason may suggest to you. The electors, instead of making any advantage of the price, for which they had thus literally sold their consciences, liberties, and properties, continued to wallow in drunkenness, till every penny of it was spent, after which it was so long before they could settle rightly to work again, that it required a year's hard labour and starving to repair what they suffered by this *bout* of excess and idleness.

My *new* mistress was what is not unjustly called *the idol of an inn*. Endowed by nature with *prettiness* enough to entitle her to flattery, and sufficient *pertness* to make her a coquet,[215] on her return from a *boarding-school*, where her natural talents were so well improved by education, that she was thought fit to try her fortune in the world, she took her place in the *bar*, and flirted away with every gentleman that came to the house, in hopes of taking in some one of the number for marriage, as others in her way had done.

The first passion of the female heart is for *finery*, to the gratification of which girls seldom fail to apply all the money in their power. But though my mistress was very far from being insensible to this passion, another scarce less powerful with the sex took place of it this time, which was curiosity.

A young officer, who had lately been quartered in the house and made warm addresses to her, had said so many fine things in praise of a certain book, called *Memoirs of a Lady of Pleasure*,[216] that she resolved to see it, and for that purpose applied at a *circulating library* in the town,[217] the keeper of which told her, it was so *scarce* and *valuable* a book that he could not possibly procure it for her under a guinea.

High as this price was, she would have found means to raise it, so strong was her curiosity, had not the hurry of the *election*, which just then came on, taken up all her time. But every obstacle was now removed, and the very evening I came into her possession, she muffled herself up in one of her maid's cloaks, and went for it

---

215 "A gay, airy girl; a girl who endeavours to attract notice" (Johnson).

216 John Cleland's *Memoirs of a Woman of Pleasure* (1748-49), described by James Boswell as "that most licentious and inflaming book" (DLB) and now deemed "the most celebrated erotic novel in English" (DNB). The text, which details the sexual education of servant girl Fanny Hill, was banned for obscenity soon after its initial publication. It was, however, printed and circulated surreptitiously throughout the century and beyond.

217 Lending libraries, which proliferated in England throughout the century, were common targets for moralist outcries against the obscene tastes of the reading public.

as soon as it was dark, *when I was the purchase of her extraordinary bargain.*

I see you are shocked at the dishonesty and wickedness of my *new* master for hiring out at such a price, or indeed at any price at all, a book, whose obvious design (and which it is too well calculated to accomplish) is to supplant every principle of virtue in the youthful mind. But the blame rests not solely upon him. The excuse, which the poet puts into the mouth of the apothecary for selling poison, that *"his poverty, but not his will consented,"*[218] may with equal justice be alleged in palliation of a poor bookseller's vending impious or immoral books, the poison of the mind.

For this reason, as no penalty, however severe, may be sufficient to combat that necessity, the most effectual way to prevent the vending of *either poison* would be absolutely to prohibit all those, whose poverty might subject them to such temptation, from trading in *books* or *drugs* of any kind; as it is most certain, that if there were neither *poor apothecaries nor poor booksellers,* the sale of both vicious books and noxious drugs, would be much less extensive than it is, if it could not be totally suppressed; there being very few of the human species so entirely given up to a reprobate sense, as to murder either the soul or body of a fellow creature, merely for the pleasure of doing it.

It may be judged that I did not remain long in the service of this master. The next morning after I came into his possession, he came to *London,* where he laid out all the money he had in the purchase of a parcel of such books, as he thought most likely to suit the taste of his customers, without regard either to virtue, or religion, *on which occasion I changed his service for that of his bookseller.*

---

218 From Shakespeare's *Romeo and Juliet*: "My poverty but not my will consents," the Apothecary's defense for selling the poison which kills the eponymous characters.

CHAPTER XX

Account of *Chrysal's* new master. His heroic spirit and resolution to push for a pension or a pillory. Meeting between him and a poet, who turns the tables upon him. A curious method of forming a judgment of a work of genius. *Chrysal's* master is beaten out of all his art, and for once buys a book by quality, not quantity. The value of an author's name. *Chrysal* changes his service.

My *new* master was one of those aspiring genius's, whom desperate circumstances drive to push at every thing, and court consequences, the bare apprehension of which terrifies men, who have some character and fortune to lose, out of their senses. He was that evening to meet at a tavern, an author, the boldness and beauty of whose writings had for some time engaged the public attention in a particular manner, and made his numerous admirers tremble for his safety.

As he happened to out-stay his time, my master's importance took offence at a freedom, which he thought so much out of character. "This is very pretty truly!" (said he, walking back and forward in a chafe) "that I should wait an hour for an author. It was his business to have been here first, and waited for me; but he is so puffed up of late, that he has quite forgot himself. *Booksellers seldom meet with such insolence from authors.* I should serve him right to go away and disappoint him. But would that not disappoint myself more? He is come into such vogue lately, that the best man in the trade would be glad to get him. Well! if he does not do what I want, I know not who can! Fools may be frighted at the thoughts of a *cart's-tail*,[219] or a *pillory*, I know better things. Where they come in a popular cause, nothing sets a man's name up to such advantage; and that is the first step toward making a fortune; as for the danger, it is only a mere bug-bear, while the mob is on my side. And therefore I'll go on without fear, if I am not bought off. A *pension* or a *pillory* is the word."

---

219 The back of a cart, "to which offenders were tied to be whipped through the streets" (OED).

These heroic meditations were interrupted by the entrance of the author,[220] who throwing himself carelessly into a chair, "I believe I have made you wait" (said he) "but I could not help it. I was obliged to stay to kick a puppy of a printer,[221] who had been impertinent; as I am to meet company directly, so let me hear what you have to say."

"I thought, Sir," (answered my master, with an air of offended importance) "you had appointed me to meet you here on business; and business you know cannot be hurried over so soon."

"Don't mention business to me! I hate the very name of it; and as to any that can possibly be between you and me, it may be done in five minutes, as well as five years, so speak directly, and without farther preamble, for all your finesses could have no effect upon me, even if I would submit to let you try them."

"Finesses, Sir! I don't know what you mean! I defy the world to charge me with having ever been guilty of any. The business I desired to meet you upon, was about *a poem*, I was informed you had ready for the press, and which I should be glad to treat with you for."

"Well, Sir! and what will you give me for it? Be quick; for I cannot wait to make many words."

---

220 KEY: "Churchill." The Reverend Charles Churchill, made an instant literary celebrity by the success of *The Rosciad* (1761), a verse satire targeting the English stage. Churchill published the work at his own expense after printers refused to pay the twenty pounds he asked for it. Other satires followed, including *The Ghost* and *The Candidate*, an attack on the Earl of Sandwich. Indeed, many of Churchill's targets were likewise those of Johnstone. While Chrysal's hagiographic account testifies to Churchill's popularity at the time, his works would not last, eventual victims of their own topicality; as Samuel Johnson correctly prophesized, "being filled with living names," eventually the poems "would sink into oblivion." By the time Lord Byron wrote "Churchill's Grave," the poet was merely he "who blazed / The comet of a season," the defining symbol of "the Glory and the Nothing of a Name." Churchill famously appears as a drunken bear in a caricature by Hogarth, where in the bottom left corner of the print, Hogarth's pug urinates on Churchill's *Epistle to William Hogarth*.
221 In one copy's marginalia, "Dryden." Perhaps Churchill's printer, Dryden Leach, with whom Churchill came to blows in late 1764. *Lloyd's Evening Post* for October 26 reported that, after a public quarrel, Churchill "gave the poor Printer a terrible blow between his eyes, the marks of which he will carry about him for some time."

"What! before I have seen it! It is impossible for me to say, till I have looked it over, and can judge what it is, and *how much it will make!*"

"As to your judging *what it is*, that must depend upon inspiration, which I imagine you will scarcely make pretence to, till you turn *Methodist* at least; but for what it will make, here it is; and you may judge of that, while I go down stairs for a few minutes."— Saying which, he gave him an handful of loose papers, and left the room.

The first thing my master did, when left thus to form his judgment of a work of genius, was to *number* the pages, and *then the lines in a page or two*, by the time he had done which, the author returned, and taking the papers out of his hand, "Well, Sir," (said he) "and what is the result of your judgment?"

"Why really, Sir," (answered my master, after some pause) "I hardly know what to say. I have *cast*[222] *off the copy*, and do not think it will *make more than a shilling*, however pompously printed."

"What you think it will make is not the matter; but what you will give me for it. I sell my works by the *quality*, not the *quantity*."

"I do not doubt the quality of them in the least; but considering how much the trade is overstocked at present, and what a *mere drug* poetry has long been, I am a good deal at a loss what to offer, as I should be unwilling to give you or any gentleman offence by seeming to undervalue your works. What do you think of five guineas? I do not imagine that more can be given for so little; nor indeed should I be fond of giving even that, but in compliment to you: I have had full twice as much for two, many a time."

"Much good may your bargain do you, Sir; but I will not take less than fifty for mine in compliment to you, or any bookseller alive; and so, Sir, I desire to know without more words (for I told you before that your eloquence would be thrown away upon me!) whether you will give that; as I am in haste to go to company, much more agreeable to me than yours."

"What, Sir! fifty guineas, for scarce five hundred lines! such a thing was never heard of in the trade."

---

222 "To estimate how much printed matter will correspond to" a piece of manuscript copy (OED).

"Confound your trade, and you together! Here, waiter! what's to pay?"

"But, dear Sir! why will you be in such an hurry? Can you not give yourself and me time to consider a little? Perhaps we might come nearer to each other!"

"I have told you before, and I repeat it again, that I will have so much; and that without more words."

"You are very peremptory, Sir; but *you know your own value*; and therefore, in hopes you will let me have more for my money next time, I will venture to give you your price now; though really, if it was not for your *name*, I could not possibly do it; but to be sure *that is worth a shilling extraordinary I own*."

"Which is twelvepence more than yours ever will be, unless to the *Ordinary of Newgate*. But come! give me the money! I want to go to my company."

"Well, Sir! this is an hasty bargain; but I take it upon your word; and don't doubt but there is merit in it, to answer such a price. Satire, Sir! keen satire; and so plain, that *he who runs may read*, as the saying is,[223] is the thing now o' days. Where there is any doubt or difficulty in the application, it takes off the pleasure from the generality of readers, who will scarce be satisfied with less than the very name. That, Sir, is your great merit. Satire must be personal, or it will never do."

"Personal! that mine never shall be. *Vices*, not *Persons*, are the objects of my satire; though where I find the former, I never spare the latter, be the rank and character in life what it will."

My master had by this time counted out the money *(among which I was)*, which the author took without telling over, and then went to his company, leaving the bookseller scarcely more pleased with his bargain, than mortified at the cavalier treatment he had met in making it.

---

223 From the Old Testament book of *Habakkuk*: "Then the Lord answered me and said: Write the vision; make it plain on tables, so he that runs may read" (2:2).

CHAPTER XXI

Some account of the company to which *Chrysal's* new master went. His behaviour to a young female, who accosted him in his way home. He takes her to a tavern for an uncommon purpose, where he treats her uncommonly, and goes home with her from as uncommon a motive. Account of what he saw in her habitation, with the manner in which he behaved there. He takes another lodging for the whole family, where he leaves them abruptly, to save himself and them trouble.

THE company to which my *new* master was in such haste to go, consisted of a few persons, whom a similarity of temper had linked in the closest intimacy. With these he spent the remainder of the evening, in a manner which few would dislike, though fewer still could approve it; the spirited wit and liveliness of their conversation gilded the grossest debaucheries; at the same time, that the rectitude and sublimity of their sentiments, whenever their hearts could find opportunity to speak, made the vices of their practice still more horrible by the contrast.

They *broke* not up, as it may be imagined, till nature sunk under their excesses, when my master, as he staggered home, was accosted by a female, who had something in her air and manner so different from those *outcasts* of humanity, who offer themselves to casual prostitution in the streets, that his curiosity was struck, and he stopped to take more particular notice of her. She appeared to be about fifteen. Her figure was elegant, and her features regular; but want had sicklied o'er their beauty; and all the horrors of despair gloomed through the languid smile she forced, when she addressed him.

The sigh of distress, which never struck his ear without affecting his heart, came with double force from such an object. He viewed her with silent compassion for some moments; and reaching her a piece of gold, bade her go home, and shelter herself from the inclemencies of the night, at so late an hour. Her surprise and joy at such unexpected charity overpowered her. She dropped upon her knees, in the wet and dirt of the street, and raising her hands and eyes toward heaven, remained in that posture for some moments, unable to give utterance to the gratitude that filled her heart.

Such a sight was more expressive than all the powers of eloquence. He raised her tenderly from the ground, and soothing her with words of comfort, offered to conduct her to some place, where she might get that refreshment of which she appeared to be in too great want. "O! Sir," (said she, pressing the hand that had raised her, with her cold trembling lips) "my deliverer, sent by heaven to save me from despair, let me not think of taking refreshment myself, till I have first procured it for those, whose greater wants I feel ten thousand times more severely than my own."

"Who can they be?" (interrupted he, with anxious impatience) "Can humanity feel greater wants, than those under which you are sinking?"

"My father," (exclaimed she bursting into tears) "languishing under infirmities, acquired in the service of his country; my mother, worn out with attending on him, and both perishing of want, (heaven grant they are not already dead!) together with two infant brothers, insensible of the cause of their distress, and crying to them for a morsel of bread, which it is not in their power to give."

"Where can such a scene of wretchedness be hidden from relief? I'll go with you myself directly! but stop! let us first procure some comfortable nourishment from some of the houses, which are kept open at this late hour, for a very different purpose. Come with me! we have no time to lose."—With these words, he went directly to a tavern, and enquiring what victuals were dressed in the house, loaded her with as much as she could carry of the best, and putting a couple of bottles of wine in his own pocket, walked with her to her habitation, which was in a blind alley, happily for her not far distant, as weakness, together with the conflict of passions struggling in her heart, made her scarce able to go.

When they came to the door, she would have gone up first for a light, but he was resolved to accompany her, that he might see the whole scene in its genuine colours. He therefore followed her up to the top of the house, where, opening the door of the

garret, she discovered to him such a scene of misery, as struck
him with astonishment. By the light of a lamp, that glimmered in
the fireless chimney, he saw lying on a bare bedstead, without any
other covering than the relics of their own rags, a man, a woman,
and two children, shuddering with cold, though huddled together
to share the little warmth, which exhausted nature still supplied
them with.

While he stood gazing in horror at such complicated
wretchedness, his conductress ran to the bed-side, and falling on
her knees, "O! Sir! Madam!" (exclaimed she, in rapture) "Arise! I
have got relief from an angel of heaven!"

"Take care!" (answered a voice, the hollow trembling of which
was sharpened by indignation) "take care it is not from a fiend of
hell, who has taken advantage of your distress to tempt you to
ruin! for with whom else could you be till this time of night? But
know, wretched girl, that I will never eat the earnings of vice and
infamy. A few hours will put an end to my miseries, which have
received the only possible addition by this your folly."

"He must be such indeed," (interrupted my master, still more
struck with sentiments so uncommon in such a situation) "who
could think of tempting her in such circumstances to any folly.
I will withdraw, while you arise, and then we will consult what
can be soonest done to alleviate a distress, of which you appear
so undeserving."—While he said this, he took the wine out of his
pockets, and giving it to the daughter, went directly down stairs,
without waiting for a reply, and walking back and forward in the
street for some time, enjoyed the sublimest pleasure the human
heart is capable of, in considering how he had relieved, and should
further relieve, the sufferings of objects so worthy of relief.

By the time he thought they might have learned from their
daughter the circumstances of her meeting with him, and taken
some nourishment, he returned to them, when the moment he
entered the room, the whole family fell upon their knees to thank
him. Such humiliation was more than he could bear. He raised
them, one by one, as fast as he could, and taking the father's hand,
"Gracious God!" (said he) "can a sense of humanity be such an
uncommon thing among creatures, who call themselves human,
that so poor an exertion of it should be thought deserving of a

return, proper to be made only to heaven? Oppress me not, Sir, I conjure you, with the mention of what it would have been a crime, I could never have forgiven myself, to have known I had not done. It is too late to think of leaving this place before to-morrow, when I will provide a better, if there is not any to which you choose particularly to go. I am not rich; but I thank heaven, that it has blessed me with ability and inclination to afford such assistance as may be immediately necessary to you, till means may be thought of for doing more."

"O, Sir," (answered the mother) "well might my daughter call you an angel of heaven! You know not from what misery you have already relieved"—

"Nor will I know more of it at this time," (interrupted my master) "than that which I too plainly see. I will leave you now to your rest, and return as soon as it is day."

"Speak not of leaving us, Sir!" (exclaimed the daughter, who was afraid that if he should go away, he might not return) "What rest can we take, in so short a time? Leave us not, I beseech you! leave us not in this place!"—

"Cease, my child!" (interrupted the father) "nor press your benefactor to continue in a scene of misery, that must give pain to his humane heart."

"If my staying will not give you pain," (answered my master) "I will most willingly stay; but it must be on condition that our conversation points entirely forward to happier days. There will be time enough hereafter to look back."

Saying this, he sat down on the bed-side, (for other seat the apartment afforded none) between the husband and wife, with whom he spent the little remainder of the night, in such discourse as he thought most likely to divert their attention from their present misery, and inspire their minds with better hopes, while the children, all but the daughter who hung upon his words, comforted at heart with a better meal than they had long tasted, fell fast asleep, as they leaned their heads upon their mother's lap.

As soon as it was day, "Now, madam," (said my master, addressing himself to the mother) "I will go and provide a place for your reception, as you say all places are alike to you. In the mean time accept of this trifle" (giving her ten guineas) "to provide such necessaries, as you may indispensably want before you remove. When you are settled, we will see what further can be done. I shall be back with you within these three hours at most."

For such beneficence there was no possibility of returning thanks; but their hearts spoke through their eyes, in a language sufficiently intelligible to his. Departing directly to save both himself and them the pain of pursuing a conversation that grew too distressful, he went without regard to change of dress or appearance, to look for a proper lodging for them, where he laid in such provisions of every kind, as he knew they must immediately want. This care employed him till the time he had promised to return, when he found such an alteration in the looks and appearance of them all, as gave his heart delight.

"You see, Sir," (said the mother, as soon as he entered) "the effects of your bounty; but do not think that vanity has made us abuse it. These clothes, what we could raise on which has for some time been our sole support, were the purchase of happier times; and were now *redeemed* for much less than we must have given for the worst we could buy."—

"Dear madam," (interrupted my master, taking her hand respectfully) "mention not any thing of the kind to me, I beseech you. You will soon see such times again."—Then turning to her husband, "I have taken a lodging, Sir;" (continued he) "it is convenient, but not large, as I imagined would be your choice. I will call a coach to take us to it directly. If there are any demands here, let the people of the house be called up, and they shall be paid. I will be your purse-bearer for the present."

"No, Sir," (replied the husband) "there are not any. You have enabled us to discharge all demands upon us. People in our circumstances cannot find credit, because they want it."

My master would then have gone for a coach, but the daughter insisted on saving him that trouble; upon which he put the whole family into it, and walked away before them to their new lodging. It is impossible to describe what these poor people felt, when they saw the provision he had made for their reception. The father, in particular, could not bear it, but sinking into a chair, "This is too much!" (said he, as soon as a flood of tears had given vent to the fullness of his heart) "This is too much. Support me, gracious heaven, who has sent this best of men to my relief, support me under the weight of obligations, which the preservation of these alone" (looking round upon his wife and children) "could induce me to accept."—Then addressing himself to my master, "My heart is not unthankful" (continued he) "but gratitude in such excess as mine, where there is no prospect of ever making a return, is the severest pain."[224]

My master, who sought none, attempted often to give the conversation another turn; but finding that they could speak or think of nothing else as yet, he took his leave, promising to come the next day, when their minds should be better settled, to consult what more was in his power to serve them, having first privately taken an opportunity to slip a couple of guineas into the daughter's hand, to avoid putting the delicacy of her father and mother to farther pain.

---

224 While unverifiable, this anecdote of Churchill's charity was quoted at great length in the posthumous *Poetical Works of Charles Churchill* (1780), and informed later biographical accounts.

VOLUME IV, BOOK II

CHAPTER I

Chrysal gives some account of his master. Reason of his having been bred
to, and miscarried in a particular profession. Interesting remarks on the
different kinds of merit necessary to eminence in different professions,
confirmed by striking instances of their success in each. Natural
consequence of his being forced into a profession against his inclination.
He is compelled by distress to exert his abilities. Contradictions in his
character, and the particular turn of his works accounted for. He visits
his new family. Affecting story of an officer.

FATIGUED in mind and body from the debauch of the evening
before, and the height to which his tenderest passions had been
wound up by such a moving scene, my master went directly home,
and throwing himself on the bed, slept till next morning, without
disturbance from pain or reflection.

The contradictions, which I had seen in his character, prompted
my curiosity to take this opportunity of looking back to his past
life, to try if in the occurrences of that I could trace their cause.
Born in the middle rank of life, his parents were induced by the
dawnings of uncommon genius, which he discovered in his earliest
youth, to give him such an education, as might enable him to make
that figure in some of the learned professions, for which paternal
fondness flattered them that nature had designed him.

But however greatly he profited by his education, the end
proposed by it was far from being pleasing to his inclinations, which
the vigour of his mind and body turned to more active scenes. For
this reason, when he was to quit the pursuits of general learning
for those of some particular profession, his ardour cooled, and he
entirely lost that spirit of emulative ambition, which alone can
enable a man to arrive at eminence.

Such a falling-off could not escape the anxious observation of
his friends; but as it was not in their power either to remedy it,

or gratify his inclination in any other way, all they could do was to enter him into the service of religion, a profession in which though the greatest abilities and application of the human mind, are evidently and indispensably necessary, yet by the perversion of man, the least are required.

You seem shocked at the severity of this remark; but a moment's reflection will open to you the reason upon which it is founded. In every other profession, success depends upon an opinion of that knowledge which is called *merit* in it, because mankind see the necessity of such merit to attain the object of the profession. But in the church, the case is quite different. Every man thinks that he knows enough of religion to serve his own turn, and therefore gives himself no trouble about the knowledge of those who profess it, as he concludes that knowledge can be of no service to him; and therefore *success in the church depends not on a general opinion of merit, but on particular favour, which, for the reason given before, is not the necessary consequence of such merit*. An *attorney*, or *surgeon*, for instance, who is not thought to have some merit in his profession, will never be employed; but let him by any means get into the church, and curry favour with those in power, and he may rise to the first dignities of it, though he has no more merit in this profession, than he had in that, which he was forced to quit for want of bread. And this is the reason, why *they who have least abilities for any profession are packed into this*; and why *they again, who have the least of these, are generally most successful in it*; as consciousness of their want of merit makes them take most pains to gain favour.

The consequence of his entering into such a profession against inclination is obvious. An indignant sense of his own natural superiority to his superiors in station made him fall into the too common error of arguing from the *abuse*, against the *use*, and hold in contempt not only them, but also the very profession itself, in which they could have such success, and in which necessity alone obliged him to continue. He disdained to apply abilities which he thought above the end! He neglected duties, which he saw abused; and at length sunk into a state of listless indifference, in which he would have died in obscurity, had not distress roused him, and extorted an exertion of his abilities, which a mind soured by disappointment of its earliest hopes, and by domestic unhappiness after, turned to *satire*, with an asperity and strength, that made vice tremble in the bosom of the great, and folly hide her head in the highest places.

As this domestic unhappiness was the immediate cause of those parts of his conduct, which contradicted the general tenor of his character, justice requires that some account should be given of it. In the capricious levity of youth, he fixed his inclinations on a female, who had no other recommendation beside beauty.[225] Prudence would have forbidden a match, in which there was so little prospect of happiness, but men of great abilities too often think it beneath them to listen to her voice. He married her, though, in the phrase of the world, evidently to his ruin; the return she made him for which proof of his love, was infidelity to his bed. This is the deepest wound that can be given to an heart of any delicacy; it sharpens the sting of ingratitude with insult, by giving a preference, that reflects dishonour. He felt it so severely, that despair made him strive to drown the sense of it in wine, in the intoxication of which, he too often was guilty of what in a cooler moment his reason would have blushed at, and his principles abhorred; and this was the chief cause of that distress also, which, as I observed, forced him to exert his abilities, which he did with such success, as soon enabled him to quit a profession, that had not been his choice, and at the same time indulge the natural disposition of his heart, by practising some of the sublimest duties of it.

As soon as he awoke next day, he went to visit his *new* family, where the happiness that glistened in every grateful eye at his approach, made him happy. After some general chat, "It is my duty, Sir," (said the father) "to give you some account of myself, and of the cause of my falling into that depth of misery, from which your beneficence relieved me, that you should not think it has been lavished on objects altogether unworthy of it.

"I am descended from a good family, the fortune of which my

---

225 In 1748, at about the age of seventeen, Churchill eloped with Martha Scott. According to Walpole's *Paris Journals*, the two would "tire of each other" and separate *circa* 1760. She "went housekeeper to an officer and became his mistress, and Churchill fell into all his debaucheries, and grew the great poet he proved."

father dissipated in supporting a parliamentary interest for the ministry; the only return he received for which, and for his voice upon all occasions, was a small pension for himself, and a pair of colours in the guards for me, his only son, with promises indeed of farther provision, which were all forgotten when he died, happily for himself before the end of the parliament, which, as he had no prospect of being returned again, would have left him at the mercy of creditors, whom it was not in his power to pay.

"Though I was soon sensible that my best hopes died with him, I was so infatuated to a profession, the most pleasing to youthful idleness and vanity, that I laid out the little fortune of this best of women, whom I had married in my days of better hope, in the purchase of a company, in a marching regiment; at the head of which I flattered myself, that I should meet some opportunity, in the war just then broke out, of meriting further promotion. But I found the vanity of such a thought, when it was unhappily too late.

"After several years careful service, in the course of which I had sealed some degree of reputation with my blood, in several warm actions, without advantage to myself, or prospect of any to my family, who now multiplied the cares of life ten thousand fold upon my head, I was driven to despair to exchange my company, which I had bought, and therefore could have sold again, the price of which would at least have kept us from absolute starving, for an higher rank in a younger regiment, just then ordered upon an expedition, the object of which raised what was thought rational expectation of such profit, as should ease me from the anxieties that made life a burden.

"Allured solely by this expectation, I went accordingly. The expedition was successful. I did my duty. I was wounded in the course of it, to the extreme danger of my life. I entirely ruined my constitution by the severity of the climate; and on my return home was reduced to half-pay, without receiving so much prize-money, as defrayed the extraordinary expences of the expedition, and of the illness which I contracted in it; while those above me accumulated such wealth as if divided in any degree of proportion, would have recompensed the labours of us, who had literally *borne the heat and burden of the day*, and were now pining in discontent and misery, aggravated by a partiality so severely injurious.

"In this situation, I resolved to throw myself at the feet of my Sovereign, and implore relief from the known goodness of his heart. But his throne was surrounded by those, whose interest it was to keep the cries of his people from coming to his ears;*[226] and therefore, as it was necessary for me to make my errand known, I never could obtain access to him.

"The distress of this disappointment was still farther heightened by the *delays* in the discharge of that *half-pay*, which was now my only support; and the *draw-backs* it was subject to from the *fees of office*, even when it should come to be paid, which were such, that when I attempted to mortgage it, the wretch's last resource, to put off starving as long as he can, what I could get from those *vultures*, who fatten upon the sufferings of a soldier, was scarce sufficient to satisfy our present wants. How then could I look forward for a family, dearer to me than life? What could support resolution, when hope was gone? Mine was unequal to the trial; and I was beginning to meditate on putting an end to a life of such misery, without considering that the sufferings of those, for whom I felt so much more than for myself, must be still made heavier by such a base desertion of them, when heaven in its mercy visited my family with a violent fever, which freed me from farther fears for the future welfare of my three eldest sons, and with difficulty spared the two, whom you see before you. O! my poor boys! happier! thrice happier than us, whom you left behind! Excuse this weakness, Sir! nature will force the involuntary tear in spite of reason; for were they not the children of my love?

"During their illness, I lost every other care in my attendance upon them; nor omitted any possible means to preserve lives, for which my fears foreboded nothing but unhappiness; but though their deaths freed me from a part of those fears, they left a melancholy void in my heart, which was more painful, if possible, than any fear. But I was not long sensible of that pain. My children were scarce laid in the grave, when the fever seized myself with

---

226 Johnstone's note: "This reflection, *notoriously so groundless*, is alone sufficient to vindicate the author from any allusion to present times."

such violence, that I soon lost my senses, nor recovered them for above a month; and then only to feel the greatest wretchedness, that was ever heaped upon human creature.

"The expence of my children's, and my own illness, had not only exhausted all the money I had raised on the anticipation of my half-pay, but also obliged my wife to mortgage several of our best effects. Such a resource never escapes the watchful eyes of people who keep lodging-houses. Our landlady no sooner perceived it, than she seized upon the rest, and then turned us out, the moment I could be removed without instant death.

"In this situation, I must have perished in the street, had not a poor woman, whom my wife had been obliged to call in to her assistance when I sickened, shared with us her habitation, in which you found us, as she also did the earnings of her daily labour, till a chairman, who was carrying a beau to a ball, threw her down with such violence, for not making haste enough out of his way, that she broke her leg, and was obliged to be taken to an hospital.

"From that time we supported life by mortgaging the few clothes we had brought upon our backs, without one ray of hope to tempt us to look forward, till they also were all gone, and the misery of cold added to that of hunger. In this condition, we had been two days without tasting bread, or feeling the warmth of fire, calling incessantly upon death to put that end to our distresses, which a sense of religion, made stronger by my wretchedness, now prevented my daring to hasten, when my daughter stole out unknown to us to seek for charity in the streets, where she wandered without meeting any thing but insults, and solicitations to vice, till heaven directed your steps to her.

"Such was the reward of more than twenty years faithful and hard service, in which I had fought the battles of my country, in the opposite extremities of the globe, with honour, and been instrumental in making princely fortunes for the several commanders under whom I served.

"This, Sir, is the sum of my story, in which I have been as brief as I could, to avoid giving you pain. We are now your creatures. The lives we enjoy are immediately the gift of your benevolence; a benevolence, so critically timed, (for we could not have subsisted many hours longer without it) as to raise an hope, that Providence which sent you to our relief, will not leave its work unfinished, but save us from falling again into such misery, by means agreeable to its own wisdom and goodness, though impossible for us, in our present situation, to foresee."

It was some time before my master, who had listened to the officer's story with sympathetic attention, was able to speak. Recovering himself at length, "Fear not;" (said he, in a broken voice) "never was the righteous forsaken;[227] nor—nor—nor—. I have some friends, Sir, who may serve!—In the mean time take this," (reaching him a bank-note for twenty pounds) "I will not be refused! business calls me for a few hours; but I will see you again in the evening."—Saying this, he hurried away to hide his emotions without waiting for a reply, which indeed their gratitude left them not the power to make.

CHAPTER II

Chrysal's master carries him to visit an old acquaintance, who behaves in character, on hearing the officer's story, and surprises *Chrysal's* master with an account of his having turned *Patriot*. The general motive for such a step; with some remarks on the difference between practice and profession, in different instances. Insignificancy of private characters in attacks upon a ministry, and why. Reflections on the origin and use of *satire*, and the abuse of the terms *good* and *ill-nature*, with the reason why so many cry out against satire. *Chrysal* changes his service in a common way.

THE most intimate acquaintance my master had, was the person,[228] who had been competitor with a former master of mine, for

227 Psalms 37:25-26. As the lines appear in the 1761 *Book of Common Prayer*: "saw I never the righteous forsaken, nor his seed begging their bread. / The righteous is ever merciful and lendeth: and his seed is blessed."

228 KEY: "Mr. Wilkes." John Wilkes (see 2.152). A friend of Wilkes and his collaborator for the *North Briton*, Churchill likely also accompanied John Wilkes "to meetings of the scandalous Franciscans or Monks of Medmenham" (DNB). The two certainly shared prostitutes, and in one letter from Paris, Wilkes wrote to Churchill: "I long to introduce you here to the prettiest bubbies, and most pouting xxxx I ever kissed or made a libation to."

admission into the *higher order of* THE MOCK-MONASTRY.*[229] To him he went directly, and relating the officer's story, while it was still warm on his heart, asked his assistance to do something more effectual for his relief.

His friend was so affected with the melancholy tale, that it was some time before he could speak; but when at length he did, it was in a strain very different from what might have been expected. "And the girl was really so pretty!" (said he, with a look of inexpressible archness) "Well said, my good *Levite*.[230] I presume you satisfied your own appetites with her at the tavern, before you provided for those of her family, though you *sunk*[231] that part of the story, for fear I should want to come in for a *snack* with you. The concupiscence of you parsons is truly *catholic*, whatever your consciences may be, and would engross the whole sex, if it was not restrained; not indeed that women come within the meaning of the *Mortmain* acts;[232] as none do more good in their generation; and consequently are better represented to the state, than those who are occupied by the clergy."

"Why, what a sensual brute must you be," (answered my master) "to talk of satisfying appetites with a wretch just perishing of cold and hunger. But it is all affectation. If you had been in my place, you would have acted just as I did; for whatever airs your wicked wit may assume, I know your heart is strongly susceptible of charity."

"Charity! Hah! hah! hah! I expected that. It is always the burden of a parson's song. They make a cloak of it upon all occasions; and indeed if it will really cover sins, as they say, they are in the right to have it ready, for multitudes enough they have to take up every corner of it. But why can you not throw off the *cant* along with the *cloth?* However, that her hunger should not damp your desires any more, here" (giving him half a dozen guineas) "is my help to allay it."

"I will not refuse your money, for your own sake, in hope that your bestowing even this much so well may help to atone for some

---

229 Johnstone's note here directs the reader to 2.151-59.
230 "A priest: used in contempt" (Johnson).
231 Avoided "mentioning or alluding to" (OED), concealed (Johnson).
232 Acts preventing the inalienable possession of property by the church (OED).

of the thousands you have thrown away. But it was not with any view of getting it, that I spoke to you. Their immediate necessities are supplied. I want your assistance and interest"—

"My interest! Hah! hah! hah!—You apply to a person of great interest truly. Why, my very naming them would be sufficient to ruin their hopes forever. You don't know perhaps, that I have turned *patriot,* and *attacked the ministry.*"

"Patriot! For heaven's sake how long, and on what occasion have you taken this strange whim?"

"Whim! Pray, good Sir, speak with more respect of the noblest principle of the human heart. The thought came into my head the night before last; and as I do not love to lose time, especially in things of such moment, I gave it vent yesterday in the shape of a political pamphlet,[233] in which I have proved to a demonstration, that the minister[234] and all his friends and countrymen are fools, and rogues, and deserve to be hang'd."

"Is it possible that you can be serious! What in the name of common sense, could be your motive for taking such a step as this? I thought you had expectation of favour from them."

"What motive should any man of honour and honesty have, but the good of his country; their neglect of which has roused an indignation that will make them tremble."

"Or, in other words, they have disappointed your expectations,

---

233 KEY: "North Briton." Wilkes founded the political weekly *The North Briton* in June 1762 "to attack the new ministry of George III's Scottish favourite, Lord Bute. The very name was chosen to adopt a satirical guise of Scottish approval of Bute's take-over of England" (DNB). John Wilkes "wrote over half of the forty-five numbers issued; Churchill wrote ten or fewer, but he was editor of the whole and, according to Kearsley the printer, received all profits from the journal" (DNB).

234 Per one reader's annotations, John Stuart (1713-92), third Earl of Bute and Prime Minister from 1762 to 1763, who rapidly rose to political power with the coronation of George III. His administration was responsible for the declaration of peace with France. Although now seen as "an honourable, advantageous settlement," the terms at the time were viewed as far too lenient. After the peace was ratified in February 1763, "Bute was the most unpopular man in the country. Maligned, insulted, and manhandled wherever he went, he suffered threats of assassination, incurred the wrath of brilliant polemicists such as John Wilkes and Charles Churchill, and was lampooned in over 400 prints and broadsheets" (DNB).

and therefore you take this method of being revenged on them, and extorting for fear, what they would not do from favour; the general motive of modern patriots I acknowledge; but with what face you can pretend to the title, prostituted as it is, I cannot think, as your very name is a burlesque upon every thing that is serious."

"Pray, how so, reverend and grave Sir? If the most profligate sinner makes the best saint, as you say, why should not a moderate rake make a tolerable politician? I believe you will hardly attribute it to the superior excellence of the latter character; but the truth is, though it is impossible for me to profess political principles more contrary to my practice, than your *moral* practice is to your preaching, yet you would deny me the toleration which you avail yourself of, and have my words judged from my actions; not my actions from my words, as you expect your own shall be.

"But my private character, or practice, signifies nothing to this undertaking, which is to rip up the practices and characters, public and private, of a set of people who have obtruded themselves into a station that exposes them to envy, and every accusation against whom will therefore be received implicitly, without regarding who or what the author of it is. Not but there is sufficient room to attack those whose whole private lives have been such a continued series of vice and folly, and their public conduct of blunders and villainy, that it is impossible to say or think any thing bad enough of them, as I have already proved by incontestable instances in my pamphlet, and shall by many more in the course of the undertaking. If the tables indeed should turn, and I get into their place, then they may make the same use of my character, and perhaps not without effect; but at present it is quite out of the question. And now that I have opened myself to you, I expect your assistance, in return for my confidence."

"Assistance in politics! It is not in my power to give you any. I hate from my soul, every political system under the sun, as a jumble of folly and villainy, (I mean as they are carried into practice, not in their speculative plans) and therefore never could throw away a thought upon them."

"That signifies nothing. The assistance which I want, you are well qualified to give. While I detect their political blunders and villainy, you shall lash their private vices and follies, till we make them equally ridiculous and odious to every man of sense and virtue in the nation; a task that will give you the pleasing opportunity of indulging that *misanthropy*, which inspires the muse of a *satirist*, and is mistaken for virtue, because it rails against vice; for blazon it out as pompously as you will, nothing but *ill-nature* can make a man take delight in exposing the defects of others; and the more forcibly he does it, the more powerful must that principle be with him.

"And by the same rule, it is *good nature* that makes a man fawn upon folly, and flatter vice; and consequently whoever does it, is virtuous. A most judicious way of reasoning truly! now, on the contrary, I think it a much more just conclusion, that they who treat vice with tenderness approve in their hearts and would practice it, if they could; and that they who expose its deformities and dangers, really detest it, though they may sometimes, through human weakness, fall into the practice. But I do not wonder at your remark; it is an old and common one. All who are conscious that they deserve the lash, desire to lessen its force; and therefore derive satire from ill-nature, in order to obviate the application of it to the proper object; and fasten upon the satirist the fault which is in themselves. And this abuse of the terms *good* and *ill-nature*, is the reason why some have been provoked to call the former *folly.*

"But not to waste time in discussions, where prejudice only can find a doubt, I agree to your proposal with pleasure, and will hold folly up to ridicule, and brand vice to detestation, wherever you point them out to me, without regard to the rank or power of the person; or to any imputations of *misanthropy* and *ill-nature*, which may be levelled at myself, to shield against and blunt the edge of my satire; though I no more expect that I shall be able to reform the *moral*, than you the *political* conduct of the age. However, it is a duty to make the attempt, be the success what it will. But by the bye, are you not apprehensive, that your undertaking may be attended with danger? The people in power will certainly be provoked; and power, you know, has long arms, and will often reach over the fences of the law."

"I fear them not! I have friends who are able, and will defend the laws in me, while I keep within their fence; one of the principal of whom I expect every minute to call upon me, to communicate matter, and consult upon another stroke."

"Then I'll take my leave. You'll have things to talk about, which you will not desire me to hear. Conspirators against the state always choose privacy."

"Conspirators against the state! Our conspiracy, if such you call it, is for the state, against its worse enemies, traitors to the trust reposed in them, and fools to their own true interest, as members of the community."

"All this I'll grant; and yet it is well, if they do not find means to make themselves pass for the state, and of course, you for the traitors against it. They who have the power, can easily assume the name."

As he said this, a servant brought his friend a note, who upon casting his eye over it, "The gentleman I expected" (said he) "writes me word that he is not very well this morning, and therefore desires to see me at his house. If you are going my way, I'll *set you down.*"

"I thank you!" (answered my master) "But my ambition does not rise so high as that yet. I do not aspire to a pillory, or a prison, even in the cause of my country. Shall we see you at dinner?"

"Most certainly! but hold. Can you give me *change* for this note? I have not time to call upon my banker."

"I believe I can; but then it must be with the help of what you have yourself given me, for the officer; like other bankers, who make a parade of taking in charitable subscriptions, at the same time that they support their credit with the money."

"That's right! I'll mention him to the person I am going to. He has abilities to serve him effectually; and I am satisfied never wants inclination to do a generous action."—My master then gave him the change of his note, *among which I was*, and took his leave.

CHAPTER III

Chrysal sums up the character of his late master. Different opinions for and against the propriety and benefit of *satire*. The former supported by good authority. Reason of some inconveniences attending the indulgence of such a turn. Character of *Chrysal's* new master concluded from a former sketch. He waits upon his patron. Character of him, with his motives for such patronage. He gives striking reasons for objecting to some parts of *Chrysal's* master's pamphlet, which the other makes some weak attempts to vindicate. *Chrysal's* master enjoys the pleasure of tracing his own fame.

THE peculiar character of my late master made me feel regret at leaving his service till I should see more of him. His abilities did honour to the age and country in which he lived; and the exalted sentiments of virtue, which broke from him spontaneously, in the genuine effusions of his soul, gave sufficient reason to judge, that his conduct would be entirely ruled by it, and his talents exerted in the more pleasing and extensive way of recommending it to imitation by displaying all its advantages and charms, as soon as time should cool the fervour of his passions, and apply its lenient balsam to the sores in his heart, the smart of which first gave him that poignant turn, and drove him for relief to excesses that too often drowned his better reason, and led him into actions, which in a cooler moment he abhorred. In a word, his failings were the luxuriance of nature, as his virtues were her perfection.

As I have said that he turned his poetical vein particularly to satire, I see your curiosity to know my opinion of the propriety, and benefit of that manner of applying the powers of *wit*. But I have often told you, that I am not permitted to determine controverted points. Many with a plausible appearance of *good nature* decry it, as proceeding from a malevolence of disposition, and tending only to spread the influence of bad example by making it known, and harden people in vices they might forsake, if not made desperate by detection! Many with an appearance of *virtuous indignation* vindicate it, as terrifying from vice, by shewing it in its native deformity, and correcting folly, by putting it out of countenance; which latter opinion is supported by the authority of one of the most sensible and best men of his age.*²³⁵

But still the indulgence of this turn is attended with many inconveniences and dangers, if it be not guided with the greatest care. That imaginary superiority, which the power of making another ridiculous or detested flatters a man with, is so pleasing to the self-love inseparable from human nature, that it requires uncommon moderation to refrain from exercising it upon improper occasions, and makes him presumptuously conclude, that whatever happens to displease himself in any particular, is a just object of public ridicule and censure. An error, into which the impetuosity of my *late* master sometimes hurried him.

I have given you a sketch of the character of my *new* master upon a former occasion;*²³⁶ to which I have only to add here, that a wanton abuse of uncommon abilities inverted the end for which they were given, making them disgraceful to himself, and dangerous to his country, a licentious pursuit of every thing called pleasure having wasted his fortune, and driven him to the despicable necessity of prostituting them to any purpose, that might promise to retrieve his affairs.

The gentleman,²³⁷ whom he went to wait upon the morning

---

235 Johnstone's note: "Would the anachronism admit the supposition, the editor should imagine that the author here meant the writer of *Letters from a Persian in England*, &c. whose words are these, 'If all the edge of wit is turned on those who are justly the objects of ridicule, Wit is as great a benefit to *Private Life*, as the sword of the magistrate is to *Public*. Letter 40.'" The citation is from the 1735 *Letters from a Persian in England to his Friend at Ispahan*, "a series of fictional letters commenting on the manners and mores of Walpolian England" (DNB) by the author and politician George Lyttelton (1709-73), Baron Lyttelton.

236 Johnstone's note here directs the reader to III.II.XVIII. See 2.151-56.

237 KEY: "Lord Temple." While other keys here name William Pitt, this is almost certainly Richard Grenville (1711-79), Earl Temple, Pitt's brother-in-law and his "most steadfast and indispensable political ally and personal friend." Walpole went so far as to term him "the absolute creature of Pitt, vehement in whatever faction he was engaged" (DNB). Made Lord Privy Seal in 1757, he would resign from office in 1761 in solidarity with Pitt, both of them advocating a pre-emptive strike against Spain and opposed to peace negotiations with France. Temple was the principal backer of the *North Briton*, and financed John Wilkes's defense against the crown.

I came into his possession, was one who had served his king and country with fidelity and success, while he was permitted to follow the dictates of his own reason in their service; but gave up the empty and disgraceful appearance of acting in it any longer, on finding his judgment disregarded, and himself designed to be made only a cypher, to increase the consequence of another.

The indignation, however, which had prompted him to take this step, led him not into those unjustifiable lengths, which are too common on such occasions. He was faithful to his Sovereign, though he had lost his favour; and watched attentively over the interests of his country, though he was not permitted to promote them. The only instance in which his conduct could possibly be censured was his patronizing such a man as my master. But it is a maxim in human politics, that *the end justifies the means,* be they what they will. He wanted to be restored to his former power; and thought this man's exposing the insufficiency of those who had supplanted him in it, the most likely way to effect that purpose.

To this desire of power he was not stimulated by the usual methods of repairing a ruined fortune, or making a new family. His wealth exceeded his very wishes, and he already enjoyed the highest honours he could aspire to: all he proposed was the glory of his Sovereign, and the advantage of his country, which that enthusiastic ambition, from whence proceed the greatest actions, made him think himself the most capable, and wish to be the happy instrument of promoting.

By this gentleman, my master was received with that *civility* which is commonly mistaken for *esteem.* After some general chat on the occurrences and humour of the times, in which my master modestly took to himself the merit of the people's discontent at the ministry and their measures, as raised solely by his pamphlet, "I allow the good effects of it" (said the gentleman) "and greatly approve the principles upon which it is written; but I much fear that your zeal has transported you too far. You should of all things have avoided involving the master in your charge against the ministers;[238]

---

238 The *North Briton* 45, issued on April 23, 1763, attacked George III's speech to Parliament commending the peace with France. While Wilkes claimed to treat the speech not as the words of the King but as written by his ministers, namely Bute, George III was incensed and demanded the author's arrest.

because that alone can give them any advantage against you, and is therefore what they always feign, however unjustly, when they are attacked, in order to screen themselves behind him. Beside, the character of a Sovereign is sacred, and should never be treated but with the highest respect, especially when *the virtues of the man are such as would be respectable in any character.*"

Such disapprobation from his principal patron greatly disappointed my master, who was so little acquainted with his sentiments, as to think he bore resentment against his Sovereign for the loss of his favour, as well as against those who had deprived him of it, and consequently would be pleased with any thing, that might seem to reflect disgrace upon him.

Recovering himself however, before his embarrassment was perceived, "I imagined" (answered he, with his usual presence of mind) "that it was impossible to accuse me of disrespect to one, whom I have studiously sought every occasion of praising. As for what you take notice of, my charge is not *personally against* him, but *through* him, *against* those who had the baseness and insolence to abuse his *goodness* and *confidence* in such a manner; so that I think it is impossible to wrest it to the purpose you apprehend."

"I wish you may not be mistaken; but much fear that your argument will not have the weight you expect. Praise given with an air of irony is the keenest insult; beside, in this particular case, the praises you bestow upon his *goodness* are all at the expence of his *understanding.* However, do not be dispirited at what cannot now be helped. As I think your intention was not in fault, you may depend upon my countenance and support, let what will happen."

This comfortable assurance restored my master to his former spirits: not desiring however to continue the conversation any longer upon that subject, "I have this morning" (said he) "made no inconsiderable addition to our force. My friend, the poet, whose turn for satire I have heard you so much admire, has promised me to exert all his powers in our cause. He will attack the faults in their *private*, while I expose their public characters, and experience has shewn that it is easy to overturn the *minister*, when the *man* is made ridiculous, or odious."

"The former I'll grant you; but we have too many instances in contradiction to the latter, to build much upon it. However, his powers are great, and may do much, if he will take care to avoid the rock upon which you have fallen; and therefore I shall be glad to attach him seriously to us, especially as he does not seem to be utterly void of virtue, notwithstanding the libertinism of his conduct in some instances."

My master would not miss so favourable an opportunity of doing justice to the character of his friend. Accordingly he related the story of the distresses of the officer and his family, and his generosity to them, in so affecting a manner, that the gentleman directly gave him a considerable sum of money for their present relief, with a promise of providing for them himself, if he could not prevail upon those in power to do it.

Pleased with a success which he knew would be so pleasing to his friend, my master took leave of his patron, and set out to trace his own fame from one coffee-house to another, and enjoy the applauses, which the popularity and boldness of his attempt procured him from the multitude wherever he went; after which he repaired to his usual haunt, where he dined, and spent the evening, in his usual manner.

CHAPTER IV

Chrysal's master receives an unwelcome visit, at an unseasonable time. His extraordinary behaviour before his superiors. He is sent to prison. *Chrysal* makes some unpopular remarks, on certain interesting subjects. Consequences of his master's imprisonment, with an account of his behaviour in it.

CONFIDENT as my master was of his safety, he soon found that the fears of his patron were too just. He had scarce laid him down to sleep, when his bed was surrounded, and himself made a prisoner, by a number of fellows, who, under the sanction of authority, committed all the outrages of lawless ruffians, *breaking open his locks, rifling his effects,* and *searching into all his secrets.*[239]

239 Wilkes was arrested and his home was ransacked under the authority of a general warrant, which gave power "to make strict & diligent search for the Authors, Printers & Publishers of a seditious and treasonable paper intitled, the

It was in vain for him to expostulate with such people against so flagrant injustice, or claim the protection of the laws. They derided him, and all he could say; and having finished their work, dragged him away with insults and abuse, to a magistrate,[240] where he had the comfort of waiting a considerable time in such agreeable company, before his worship was at leisure to see him.

But this, though designed as an indignity, was of real advantage to him, as it gave him time to recover his spirits, and collect presence of mind for an interview of such importance. Accordingly when at length he was admitted to the dread tribunal, instead of shewing any dejection at the danger which seemed to hang over him, he behaved in a manner worthy of a better man, and a better cause. He asserted the violation of the laws in his person, with so much resolution, and appearance of reason, and returned the insolence of office with such contempt, answering illusively to the insidious questions put to him, and boldly demanding that right of being restored to his liberty, which was assured to every individual of the community by the essential principles of the constitution, that his *judges*[241] were startled, and more than once wished they had left him unmolested.

However, as there was no receding now, they concluded it to be their best way to go through with what they had begun, and bear down opposition with an high hand; with which intent they sent him directly to prison, in defiance to all he could say, where he was treated with uncommon severity, and the method which the law provided for his being restored to liberty eluded as long as possible, by finesses which power only could support.

North Briton Number 45." As it failed to specify the offenders by name, the warrant was technically illegal, although general warrants were routinely used. Public outcry over the case would lead to a direct ban of general warrants, clamorous attention to the ministry's abuse of power, and John Wilkes's enshrinement as a passionate defender of free speech.

240 KEY: "Ld. Hallifax." George Montagu Dunk (1716-71), Earl of Halifax and Secretary of State for the North, who issued the general warrant. Wilkes later successfully sued Halifax, winning £4,000 damages in 1769.

241 KEY: "Lds. Hallifax & Egremont." Halifax and Charles Wyndham (1710-63), Earl of Egremont and Secretary of State for the South. On April 30, 1763, Wilkes appeared before the two, who interrogated him, then committed him to the Tower of London.

I see your indignation at such an infringement of laws procured by the blood of myriads, and established by the most solemn engagements human and divine, for the security of the common rights of mankind. The part which every man feels in such sufferings, on a supposition that they may possibly one day fall upon himself, naturally interests you, as it did the multitude, in my master's cause. But when you come to examine coolly the manner of his being taken into confinement, which is what gives you such offence, it will not appear so contrary to reason and justice, the foundation, and as I may say, soul of all laws, as popular opinion may presume.

All power is delegated from the people for the mutual advantage of *governors* and *governed*. To support the use, and prevent the abuse of that power, laws are established by the consent of both, which are to be the rule of their actions. But as it is impossible for human wisdom to foresee and provide for every occurrence that may happen, there is essentially implied in the first trust a further power of applying *unprovided* remedies to *unforeseen* cases, for the safety and advantage of the whole.

If it be objected, that these remedies may sometimes be injurious to individuals, by being injudiciously or wrongfully applied, the answer is obvious. The sufferings of a few, are not to be set in competition with the safety of the many. Beside, if the remedies were never to be applied, where there was a possibility of a mistake, the evil might happen, in the time necessary for enquiry and deliberation. For, though *penal* laws are designed only *to prevent future by the punishment of past crimes*; yet where such crimes, if committed, will exceed the reach of punishment, and defeat the laws, the power of prevention must be exerted *earlier* to *anticipate* them before commission.

Without such a power, the trust of government would be imperfect, and inadequate to the end; as if no punishment could be inflicted *thus for prevention*, but by prescribed forms, human ingenuity, ever most fertile in evil, would devise expedients to evade it, till perpetration should secure impunity, as I said before, perhaps to the ruin of the state.

For these reasons an extraordinary power must have been implicitly given for extraordinary cases; or the good of the community, which is the end of government, cannot be obtained. If this power though should be abused, *the sacred spirit of the laws of your happy country will supply the inevitable defect of the latter,* and grant redress to the sufferer, when a proper time comes for enquiring into the circumstances of the case; a redress which was not provided by the people,*[242] the most jealous of their liberties of any who ever united themselves into civil society, who, sensible of the necessity of such a resource, made it a fundamental rule of their government, on any occasions of uncommon difficulty or danger, to entrust the whole power into the hands of some one person, whom they called DICTATOR, *as his word was to be the law,* without subjecting him to control in the use, or account for the abuse of it, when his power should be at an end.

As soon as my master's imprisonment was known, the populace all took fire. They made his cause their own. They looked upon him as a martyr in the darling cause of liberty. They insulted all government, and committed excesses every hour, infinitely more illegal and dangerous to liberty, than that of which they complained.[243]

In the mean time, his confinement was far from sitting so heavy upon him as might have been expected. Though he wanted the approbation of his own mind, and the *enthusiasm* of the principles he professed, to support his resolution, and encourage him to look forward with hope, levity of temper supplied the place of that resolution, and saved him from sinking under misfortunes, by making him insensible of their weight. He rallied[244] his jailors, mimicked his judges, cracked jests upon his own undoing, and turned every circumstance into ridicule, with such drollery and unconcern, as if he was *acting* the imaginary sufferings of another,

---

242 Johnstone's note: *The Romans.*

243 "Wilkite riots on London streets became a common phenomenon during the next dozen years" (DNB). In December 1763 the public attacked the sheriff at a burning of *The North Briton,* and Walpole reports in March 1768 that another mob in Piccadilly overturned carriages, chalking "Wilkes and Liberty!" on every available surface, "pelted, threw dirt and stones, and forced everybody to huzzah for Wilkes."

244 "To exercise satirical merriment" (Johnson); "to make fun of; to tease" (OED).

not *actually* suffering himself. How long he would have been able to support that spirit though came not to be tried.

CHAPTER V

Chrysal's master is visited in prison by his patron; and from what motives. His conduct on being set at liberty, and the consequences of it. Remarkable grounds on which he was set at liberty, with a conjecture at the reason of fixing upon them. *Chrysal* makes an enquiry into certain matters, much talked of, and little understood.

As soon as his friends obtained access to him (for the great severity of his confinement was the uncommon strictness of it) his patron went to see him. As I have taken notice of his disapprobation of what had brought my master into this scrape, you are surprised at his taking a step that seemed so inconsistent with his character. But *his motives for it did honour to the man*, however strange they may appear in the *politician*. He had admitted him to a degree of personal intimacy. He had approved of his engaging in a cause, to which he was himself attached most sanguinely, and he scorned to desert him in distress, occasioned by what he thought an error of his judgment, not a *fault of his intention*.

Beside the consolation to himself, the honour of such a visit was of the greatest advantage to my master's affairs; as it lightened the personal prejudice against him, and gave a good opinion of a cause, which appeared to have the countenance of such a man.

Intoxicated with the popularity he had thus acquired, which if rightly managed might have done great matters, he was no sooner at liberty, than he threw off all restraint, and ran into such licentiousness, as in a short time lessened its force, and lost him every trace of the good opinion of all who gave themselves time to think of the causes and consequences of such conduct. But his triumph was not long-lived.

He had been restored to his liberty, not as a right common to all the members of the community, on a supposition of the illegality of the manner in which he had been deprived of it; but in consequence of certain immunities,[245] annexed to a particular part of the legislature, to which he belonged.

Though the abilities and integrity of the magistrate[246] who made this distinction were unquestionable, some persons who looked farther than the present moment, imagined they could trace it to a cause not commonly attended to. He had on former occasions been instrumental in depriving some people of liberty in the same manner:[247] to have condemned that manner therefore now, as illegal, would have been condemning himself; at the same time, that upright obedience to the dictates of his present opinion, obliged him to set him free. Such a difficulty must have been distressing; but this distinction delivered him from it, and enabled him to save his credit, and conscience both; as those people had bore no part in the legislature, and therefore had not been entitled to such immunity.

I see your indignation arise at the thought, that in a country which boasts of being governed by *equal* laws, any one set of men should enjoy immunities, denied to the rest; but that indignation proceeds from viewing the manner in a partial light. In the country where your lot has happily fallen, the end of government is better secured by a division of its powers, than in any other under heaven. The great wisdom of those who made this division, appears in the provisions made to preserve each part in it, independent of the rest, the only means by which the division itself could be preserved.

Now as the *executive* power *necessarily* belongs solely to the prince, it was *equally necessary* to secure those who bore a part

---

245 KEY: "Privilege of Parliamt." As Wilkes was a member of Parliament, he could legally be arrested only for felony, breach of the peace, and treason—not for libel.

246 KEY: "Ld. chief justice Pratt." Charles Pratt (1714-94), Earl Camden, who on May 7 freed Wilkes on the basis of parliamentary privilege. The mob of supporters gathered in Westminster Hall erupted in shouts of "Wilkes and liberty!"

247 KEY: "Cases of Dr. Henry Shebbaire, taken upon Genl. Warrants when Mr. Pratt was Attorney General." As Attorney General, Pratt had successfully prosecuted Florence Hensey (see 1.264-66), Laurence Shirley (1.287-89), and Dr. John Shebbeare (1709-88), novelist and political writer, whose "widely read and politically influential" *Letters to the People of England* not only criticized ministerial policy, but advocated open revolution (DNB). Like Wilkes, Shebbeare was arrested on a general warrant.

with him in the *legislative*, from any undue execution of that power which might be attempted in order to break through that independence, and join the *legislative* to the *executive*; or in other words, *vest both powers absolutely, and without limitation in the prince*. And this was the reason of immunities, so much talked of, and so little understood.

If it be said, that these immunities operate also against fellow subjects, from whom there can be no such fear, and are sometimes (perhaps too often) abused to dishonest ends, the answer must be sought for in the depravity of the human heart, which will pervert the best institutions to the worst purposes, and make it necessary to preclude every exception, that it should not be extended to serve them. As for instance, if the meanest subject of the state had a right to claim the assistance of the civil power in every case, against any member of the legislature, while in his *legislative* capacity, that right might be suborned, or feigned by the *executive* power, in such a manner, as to overturn his independency, and prevent his discharging the trust committed to him: for which reason it is better that an individual should suffer (to suppose the worst) than an opportunity be given for ruining the whole community; according to the known maxim, that an *evil (which affects but one)* is preferable to an *inconvenience (which affects many)*. And this immunity, which is really the shield and safety of the state, can never be invaded, but from a design against the liberty of the state, nor absolutely given up, without giving up that liberty along with it; though the right may be waived in particular instances, which appear unworthy of the benefit of it. To actions criminal in their own nature, between individuals, or immediately dangerous to the state, it was never designed to be extended, as in such cases it would have been destructive of the end for which it was instituted.

While my master was running riot in this extravagant manner, some things happened which raised in his favour the indignation and pity of many who disliked the man, and disapproved his proceedings, because they saw him persecuted by unjustifiable means.

It may well be imagined, that I did not remain long enough in his possession, to see the conclusion of this affair; but as I had ample opportunity of being acquainted with it at the time, and see that your curiosity is interested in the event, I will continue the account here, especially as the principal occurrences in my next service, were connected with it in so particular a manner, that it is necessary to explain the one in order to understand the other.

CHAPTER VI

Chrysal's master takes a foreign tour. Remarks upon national reflections, and attacks upon private characters. *Chrysal's* master is called to an account for certain improper liberties, by a very improper person, whom he treats with uncommon propriety. *Chrysal* makes some out-of-the-way reflections on a question much canvassed to little purpose.

WHEN my master had in some measure exhausted the first flow of his spirits upon the recovery of his liberty, he made a short excursion abroad, as if merely for amusement, but in reality to provide a place of retreat, in case of the worst, as his apprehensions could not but be alarmed, whenever he allowed himself time to think.

I have observed that in the account he gave my late master, when he first told him of his attack upon the minister,[248] he said he had included in it all his *countrymen*. This he really had done on that, and continued to do, on all other occasions with a licentiousness unexampled; but which lost its force, and became contemptible, by sinking into scurrility.[249]

Attacks upon private characters, unless forced by necessity, or designed to serve good purposes, such as personal reformation, or caution to others, are literally *abuse*, and proceed always from a bad heart; but national reflections, as they can answer no good purpose of any kind, are abuse in every sense, and proceed equally

---

248 KEY: "Ld. Bute." See notes 130 and 234.
249 Wilkes fanned sentiment against Bute by appealing to anti-Scot prejudices. "The time is at length arrived," claimed the *North Briton* 3 of Bute's ascendency, that being of Scottish birth is "the best and most effectual recommendation to preferment in England." According to Sir Walter Scott, "When committed to the Tower, Wilkes requested of the Lieutenant, as a favour, to be confined in an apartment which had not been contaminated by the residence of a Scotch rebel. The officer regretted it was impossible to comply with his request."

from *folly* and *malevolence*. A *folly* indeed that is often punished by *fools*, who take to themselves that abuse, which belongs not to them in particular, and would pass by without lighting upon them, if not applied thus by themselves.

My master had not been long abroad, when a *countryman of the minister's* thought proper to call him to account for the liberties he had taken with his country.²⁵⁰ The absurdity of such a step in any man was still aggravated by the peculiar circumstances of this person, who had actually given weight to the severest part of the charge against his country, (indeed the only part that would admit of weight, the rest being, as I have said, nothing but scurrility) by engaging in the service of the enemies of its present government, and fighting their battles against it. Such an antagonist therefore was beneath the notice of any man of reason, and accordingly was treated so by my master, who on this occasion behaved with a moral propriety and prudence, much above the tenor of his general character. But his enemies beheld his conduct in a different light, and attributed to *cowardice* what was really the effect of *courage*.

You seem surprised at my saying that his declining to fight was the effect of courage! but reflect a moment, and you will see that it is *the motive of fighting*, and *not the mere fighting*, that constitutes true courage; and that the *fashionable courage* of venturing life for punctilios of imaginary honour is *real cowardice*, as it proceeds solely from fear of the false censure of the world; *and therefore, that to brave that censure in such cases is the highest courage.*

I would not be understood by this to declare absolutely against a man's fighting in his own cause, in all cases indiscriminately. Different circumstances make an essential difference in things which superficially appear to be alike. A man's venturing his life, as I have said, in vindicating *empty punctilios of imaginary honour,*

---

250 KEY: "Capt. Forbes." John Forbes of Skellater (ca. 1733-1808), a Scotsman who fought for France during the Seven Years War. William Beckford described him as a man of "excellent sense and much experience," who "speaks his mind with a manly openness" (DNB). In August 1763, while Wilkes visited Paris, Forbes challenged him to a duel. The account was widely covered in the press: "I let him know that I was a Scotch gentleman," wrote Forbes in an account for the *Gentleman's Magazine*, "and that, upon account of the scurrilous and ignominious things he had wrote against my country, I was determined he should fight me." Wilkes refused and placed himself under the protection of police.

or *in support of injustice,* is the highest and most ingrateful insult
to the author of that life, who has made the preservation of it the
first principle of action, and consequently an indispensable duty,
when it can be preserved without violation of those greater duties,
which he has thought proper to prescribe.

But as there are other things more valuable than life, because
without them life would lose its value, reason, which is the voice
of heaven, permits to hazard the lesser good for the preservation
of the greater, and this is the justification of war between different
states.

To prevent the evils which such a recourse between individuals
in the same state must be attended with, laws are established to
preserve those rights, and redress injuries, which they may offer
to each other; to these laws therefore it is an indispensable duty to
recur for such redress and preservation, where they are able to effect
them: but this duty does not seem to extend so far as absolutely and
indiscriminately to preclude the other method of a man's striving at
the hazard of his life to effect them himself, when the laws cannot
do it, as is too often the case, it being impossible for human wisdom
to make provision for every occurrence, which in the complication
and extensiveness of human action may require it.

An opinion, so contrary to that professed by all, who have
undertaken to discuss this subject, however consonant to the
sense of mankind in general, as shewn in their practice, should be
supported by the plainest and most convincing reasons.

A good name is the immediate jewel of the soul; it is the first
fruit and the reward of virtue: the preservation of it therefore
is indisputably worth hazarding life for, where the laws have not
sufficiently provided for its defence; as is the case in many of the
most delicate and tender points. If a man for instance is unjustly
accused of a fact that ruins his *good name,* at the same time that
the accusation comes not within the reach of any law from which
he may receive redress, can reason say, that he is not justifiable in
striving for that redress himself, and vindicating his good name at
the hazard of his life, when that life would be only misery without
it?

But here another difficulty occurs. Shall a man, it is said, put
himself upon a level with his injurer, and risque a second injury, in

seeking satisfaction for the first? This certainly is an evil, but must be submitted to, to prevent a greater.

If a man were permitted to redress himself absolutely without such a risque, the consequence would be, that partiality to himself would make him think every thing that should displease him an injury sufficient to merit such a redress, whereby murders would be multiplied to the reproach of humanity, and ruin of the state. But where this risque makes the redress attended with danger, people are cautious not to run into it, but on what they at least think good grounds.

Beside risquing life in an even scale is in some manner staking it upon the justice of the cause, and appealing to heaven for decision; and consequently success clears the character in general estimation; whereas killing insidiously, or without such equal risque, only confirms the first charge, on a presumption of consciousness, and aggravates it with the weight of new guilt. And this was the sense of mankind, till the remedy was perverted to such an excess as to become worse than the evil, and therefore necessary to be abolished, as far as human laws can abolish a general principle of action.

One particular though in the laws made to abolish it deserves remark; as it shews a striking instance of the sagacity with which human laws are often made. Killing a man, in a deliberate duel, be the cause ever so important, and utterly unprovided for in the law, is accounted *murder*, and made capitally criminal; but killing in a drunken broil, or ungoverned gust of passion, is only a pardonable offence, and called by the softer name of *man-slaughter!* Now if the makers of that law had but considered which action proceeded from the worst cause, and was liable to be attended with the worst consequences, from the possible frequency of it, they might perhaps have seen reason to reverse the case, and made the *latter* capital, and the *former* at least pardonable.

In a word, he who takes away the life of another, or loses his own, in a trivial or unjust cause, or where the laws of his country have provided him redress, is guilty of murder; whereas he who kills, or is killed in a cause of real importance, for which there is no remedy provided him by the law, sins not against the *spirit* of the law, however he may against the *letter*; and consequently seems to be entitled to an immunity from the penalties of it. This reasoning though respects only the reason of the law, and is by no means laid down as a rule for practice; it being the indispensable duty of a subject to obey the plain letter of the law, without presuming to oppose his private opinion to it, otherwise than by humble application to proper authority to have it altered.

CHAPTER VII

Chrysal's master's late conduct draws him into a new scrape, in which he comes off but second-best. He takes advantage of his misfortune to make his escape from a greater. He suffers the resentment of his enemies, as far as they can reach him; and meets from his friends the fate of all useless tools, after having served them with improbable success. A striking instance of the advantage of an upright judge, and equal laws. *Chrysal* changes his service.

THE opinion, that my master's having behaved in this manner proceeded from a want of spirit, soon laid him under a necessity of shewing the contrary. A person who was involved deeper than he chose to appear,[251] in his accusations against the minister, though he was known to be his creature, thought he might safely invalidate the credit of the charge, and curry farther favour with his patron, by denying it in terms of such abuse as should make the accuser infamous, on submitting to them, as he imagined he would.

But in this he found himself mistaken. The *captiousness of false*

---

251 KEY: "Mr. Martin." Samuel Martin (1714-88), Member of Parliament and Treasurer of the Dowager Princess's Household, whom the *North Briton* had called the "most treacherous, base, selfish, mean, abject and low-lived fellow that ever wriggled himself into a Secretaryship." During debate in the House of Commons, Martin called the anonymous author "a cowardly rascal, a villain, and a scoundrel." Wilkes wrote Martin to confirm his own authorship of the statement, and Martin challenged Wilkes to a duel in Hyde Park, where Wilkes was wounded in the stomach. To avoid arrest in case of Wilkes's death, Martin fled to Paris. "Wilkes has been shot by Martin," wrote Walpole, and "is reverenced by a saint by the mob, and if he dies, I suppose people will squint themselves into convulsions at his tomb." The duel is the subject of Charles Churchill's *The Duellist* (1764).

honour, that often passes for true resolution, *which is only the result of virtue*, was now piqued; and two beings (for it was impossible for the other to draw back) who called themselves rational, hazarded their lives in support of what neither could have supported by reason.

The event proved immediately unfavourable to my master, who received a wound that for some time seemed to threaten his life. But he soon thought the danger amply made amends for, by the pretence it gave him to put off from time to time the resentment of that part of the legislature to which he belonged, for the offence which had occasioned his being confined, and at length to fly from it, when he found it could not be any longer prevented by such finesses, from bursting on his head. Such a slight was an implicit acknowledgment of his guilt. He was therefore deprived of his part in the legislature,[252] and consequently of all the immunities annexed to it, and given up to the common course of the laws, for that and other matters, whenever he should be found within the reach of their power. Nor was this all! to shew still stronger disapprobation of his conduct, the breach of those immunities, upon which the magistrate had founded his discharge from confinement, was overlooked, and such offences as his excluded from their protection for the future.[253]

You cannot be surprised at his meeting such a fate. The tools of a statesman, however successful they may have been, are always thrown aside with neglect, the moment they have done their work; but when they fail, however blamelessly, or run into any error, though only from excess of zeal, the weight of the neglect is made still heavier, by heaping all the blame upon them. But what will you think, when I tell you, that unequal as he must appear to have been to such an attempt, in consequence, character, and abilities,

---

252 Badly wounded "in what many thought a plot against his life," Wilkes fled to Paris, refusing to attend further hearings in Parliament on account of his health. On January 19, 1764, the House of Commons "received evidence that Wilkes had published the *North Briton*, and so expelled him as unworthy to be a member, without a vote" (DNB).

253 On November 15, 1763, the House of Commons ruled that the *North Briton* was a seditious libel; nine days later, they concluded "that parliamentary privilege did not cover seditious libel, thereby exposing Wilkes to punitive legal action" (DNB).

he raised so threatening a storm, that the minister thought proper to retire out of its way; as all his friends apprehended they should have been obliged to follow him: a success, for which he was in a great measure indebted to the assistance of my late master, who represented their private characters in such colours, in his satirical writings, as will make their memories pay a dear price for their power, the poetical merits of his works, in which their names are branded with indelible infamy, ensuring their immortality. Such is the basis upon which statesmen found their greatness; and so easily is a jealous populace led away, by any thing that flatters their present humour.

I say not this, as deciding upon the merits of the disputes in which he was concerned. I think too meanly of human politics in general, to give my opinion in favour of any one scheme of them, in preference to another. They are all alike a jumble of villainy, and blunders. All I intend is, to shew on what a sandy foundation men who value themselves upon their wisdom, wear out their lives in anxious toils and dangers, to build their hopes; and what unworthy means are often made use of to overturn them, and work ends, reputed great, on purpose perhaps to humble man in his own eyes.

As for my master, he was no sooner removed out of the sight of the mob, whose idol he had been in such an extravagant degree, than he was entirely out of their mind, and the storm he had raised subsided so totally, as to leave no other trace behind it, but his ruin.

I have observed your anxiety, to know whether he ever obtained redress for the injustice done him in his property; and the injurious treatment he received when he was first apprehended, as I said that the fellows employed to take him, had under the sanction of authority committed all the outrages of lawless ruffians. The interest you take in the cause of such a man, can arise from nothing but your love of justice, *which should not be violated in the person of the most unjust.* It will therefore give you pleasure to be informed, that the laws of your country never shone with brighter lustre, than in this instance.

In despite of every artifice and effort which power and chicane could make use of to evade, or intimidate from the execution of them, (a striking instance of the latter of which was depriving his patron of every degree of power and honour, of which he could be deprived without regard to his great services and personal consequence, only for appearing in his cause)[254] an able and upright magistrate[255] supported them with such resolution and judgment, that he obtained exemplary redress for all he had suffered that could be redressed, as did several others who had been involved in the same circumstances, as having been employed by him.

In gratification to your curiosity, I have thus given you the general heads of his story. To have dwelt on the minuter circumstances, however curious in themselves, would have led me too great a length, beside that they come not within my design, as I was not directly in his possession when they happened. To return therefore now to the regular chain of my own adventures, I must go back to the time of my leaving his service, which was not very long after he had been released from his confinement.

Among the crowds that came to congratulate him upon this event, was a clergyman,[256] whose professions of personal attachment, and respect for his principles and abilities, were strained to such a fulsome height, as would have disgusted vanity itself.

My master saw through him directly, and played him off with humour peculiar to himself, till he concluded with telling him, that he had a work then in hand, upon the same scheme with his, which he intended to publish by subscription.[257]

My master, who knew the man, took the hint, in the proper

---

254 In retribution for supporting Wilkes, Lord Temple was dismissed from his position as Lord Lieutenant of Buckinghamshire, and the title was bestowed on Francis Dashwood.

255 KEY: "Ld. Ch. J. Pratt." On December 6, 1763, Chief Justice Charles Pratt "ruled in the court of common pleas that general warrants could not be used as search warrants" (DNB). Wilkes was awarded £1000 in damages by the jury.

256 KEY: "Mr. Kedgell." John Kidgell (c. 1722-80), Church of England clergyman and political writer; chaplain to William Douglas, Third Earl of March and later Duke of Queensberry; and author of The Card (1755), "a series of tales partly in epistolary form" (DNB). Walpole describes him as a "dainty, priggish parson, much in vogue among the old ladies for his gossiping and quaint sermons," and Churchill savages him in The Author as a "wretch from Sodom."

257 In publication by subscription, "the publisher or author undertakes to supply copies of the book at a certain rate to those who agree to take copies before publication" (OED). In other words, readers agree to purchase the book in advance to publication, instead of buying the book once it is published.

light of a modest way of begging, and *clapped* a couple of guineas into his hand, desiring to be inserted in his list, *upon which occasion I left his service.*

CHAPTER VIII

Reason of the joy with which *Chrysal* was received by his new master. Account of a curious, though not uncommon way of getting a living. Conversation between *Chrysal's* master and his guest. They compare notes on their different attempts in the literary trade. *Chrysal's* master is encouraged by his friend from his own example. A remarkable account of a certain matter, that made much noise.

THE joy my *new* master felt on the receipt of so small a sum, shewed the consequence it was of to him. He thanked his benefactor in terms of rapture, and vowing eternal gratitude and attachment to him, and his cause, departed with an happy heart. Nor was his joy without cause. He had invited an acquaintance to sup and spend the evening with him, and had neither money nor credit to provide any thing for his entertainment.

Despicable as the vanity of making invitations in such circumstances may appear to you, it was one of his chief resources, to support himself and his family; as he never invited any, but such as he expected to borrow much more from than it cost him to entertain them.

Your indignation at the mention of so mean a shift shews your happy ignorance of the ways of this populous place, in which there are numbers who keep up a decency of external appearance, and support life only by this method of raising contributions on their acquaintances, spending with one, what they have got from another, in order to get from him too, and so on; with this difference only from common beggars, that they seldom apply to the same person twice, and instead of praying for their benefactors with an appearance of gratitude, wherever they meet them, avoid their company, and are always seeking for new acquaintances, as quarry for them to prey upon.

On this errand he had sallied out this morning, but met with

such bad success, that he had been obliged to have recourse to the
subscription scheme, an addition which he had lately made to his
former plan. His joy therefore at my late master's generosity was
but natural. He returned home in high spirits, and giving his wife
half his prize to provide *two or three nice little things*, secured *me* for
future contingencies.

Every thing being thus adjusted, his guest,[258] who came
punctually at the appointed time, was received with all the
formalities and *airs* of *politeness* and *high life*. The conversation
before, and at supper, ran on the usual topics of the *weather*,
politics, and the *secret history of the day*; but when my master's lady
had withdrawn, and he saw his friend begin to palate his wine with
pleasure, (for he never made his push, till the heart was warm) he
took occasion from some *modest* mention the other made of his
munificence in the relief of merit in distress, to lament his own
inability to indulge that darling pleasure of his soul, as a proper
introduction to his business.

"I have wondered with much concern" (answered his friend)
"at your languishing so long in this obscurity. It is all your own
fault. Why do you not exert yourself? There is nothing which spirit
and diligence cannot conquer."

"Very true, my dearest friend!" (replied my master with a shrug
of his shoulders, and an heavy sigh) "But what can diligence or
abilities either do, when they cannot find employment. I have
offered myself to *ministry* and *opposition*, to *booksellers* and *news-
writers*, and all to no purpose: though indeed if it was not for the
assistance of one of the latter,[259] who now and then takes an *essay*,
or a *letter* from me, I should be utterly at a loss. So that what can I
do?"

"What! why any thing rather than be idle. If one thing won't
do, another may. There is not an article *in the trade*, which I have
not tried in my time, I *made bibles*, *magazines*, and *reviews*; *sermons*,

---

258 KEY: "Doctor Douglass." John Douglas (1721-1807), later Bishop of Salisbury,
critic, controversialist and historian, who assisted Samuel Johnson in the detection
of the Cock Lane ghost and would later edit the journals of Captain Cook.
259 KEY: "Mr. Leach, Printer." Dryden Leach, printer and publisher. Leach was
the first person arrested in conjunction with *North Briton* 45, although the issue
had in fact been published by Richard Balfe.

ballads, and *dying speeches;* and though all failed, I never lost my spirit. The miscarriage of one scheme only set my invention at work to strike out another. No man can have greater difficulties to struggle with, than I had: and yet you see I have got over them all."

"Yes! but my dearest friend, you had advantages! the countenance and assistance as such a patron as yours"—[260]

"Were just as great advantages to me, as your patron's are to you; and no more. I had the honourable advantage of *leading a bear,*[261] for a bit of bread; and betraying his secrets to his father and mother, for the hope of a church-living, which I should not have got at last; but that it was not worth selling."

"You astonish me! Don't you owe all your preferments, all your affluence, to the interest of your patron?"

"What I owe my preferments to is not necessary to mention; but my affluence I owe to a very different cause. *The detection of that impostor*[262] was the thing that made my fortune. I might have remained in my original poverty to this day, if it had not been for that."

"For that! Is it possible? I cannot conceive that the profits upon the sale of a pamphlet or two, (and that not a very extensive sale neither) could do such great things. My *novel,* I thought, bade as fair for a *good run* as any thing: it was *seasoned high* to the taste of the times, and yet it did very little more than pay."

"The sale! Hah! hah! hah! No, no! I did not depend upon that. My profit came in another way entirely."

"What can be your meaning? If it be not too great a secret, I should be much obliged to you to explain this matter. It may possibly be of service to me."

"Why, on that account, and as I think I can depend upon your

---

260 KEY: "Lord Bute." Douglas's relationship to Bute, if any, is unknown. Douglas's patron, as the next paragraph indicates, was William Pulteney, first Earl of Bath.

261 KEY: "Travelling as tutor to Lord Pulteney." In 1747, Douglas was introduced to William Pulteney, first Earl of Bath, who became his patron. The following year, Douglas accompanied "Bath's 'difficult' heir, Lord Pulteney, on a grand tour of Holland, Germany, and France" (DNB), where Douglas met Montesquieu and became very interested in the miracles at the tomb of François de Pâris.

262 KEY: "Mr. A. Hamilton Bowyer." Archibald Bower, exposed by Douglas as a fraud and a plagiarist in several pamphlets between 1756 and 1758. See 1.372-73.

honour, I don't much care if I do. If you are so much surprised at
my saying that I made my fortune by that pamphlet, what will you
think when I tell you farther, that I never wrote one line of it, nor
was I any more concerned in the sale than you, who knew nothing
of the matter? But not to perplex you with guessing at what it is
impossible you should ever discover! You can be no stranger to the
noise that *impostor* made when he first came here. While he did no
more than tell his own story, it was thought by his old fraternity to
be the best way not to give it consequence by contradicting it, but
let it die away of itself; besides, that possibly it might not have been
so easy to contradict it to any effect, while the persons concerned
were all living, and the facts fresh in every one's memory. But
when he went so far as to attack the whole body, and was evidently
undermining the foundation upon which they stood, by tearing
off the veil of antiquity behind which they hid themselves and
exposing all their mystery to light,[263] the matter became more
serious, and it was judged necessary to ruin his character in order
to invalidate the credit of his work, the merit of which made a
direct attack not only difficult, but also too doubtful of success to
hazard an affair of such importance upon it.

"For this reason heaven and hell were conjured up, and every
engine set at work to prove his story of himself false in every
particular, and make him appear the most complicated villain
that ever existed. But the credit of those who made this attack
upon him, was too low for it to have any effect, as their principles,
and the interested motives upon which they proceeded, were
sufficiently known; so that it only did him service, by shewing his
consequence.

"While they were considering how to repair this defeat,
necessity suggested to me the lucky thought of offering them my
assistance. I had already got some degree of credit by anticipating
time in the detection of two silly impostures,[264] the absurdity of

---

263 KEY: "Writing the History of the Popes." See 1.372, note 597.
264 KEY: "Lauder & Eliz. Canning." Douglas discredited other frauds than
Bower, including William Lauder (c. 1710-71), who had written a series of articles
in the *Gentleman's Magazine* accusing Milton of plagiarism, and the Cock-Lane
ghost. After reading Douglas's *Milton Vindicated from the Charge of Plagiarism*,
which called attention to Lauder's forgeries, Samuel Johnson forced Lauder to

which would soon have discovered them without my help. This gave weight to my offer: accordingly they readily embraced it; and desiring only the *sanction of my name*, (for which you may judge I was *well paid*) took all the trouble upon themselves.

"The reasons which defeated them, assisted me. Every thing *I was thought to say* carried weight, as *appearing to proceed* from the highest candour and attachment to truth, as nothing else could *naturally* be supposed to have made me take such pains to detect an imposture, so favourable to the principles I professed myself. The public also had got enough of his story, and was ready to listen to one against him. The consequence you know. His character was ruined with the public; and of course a prejudice raised against his work, which ruined that also, without the trouble of a regular confutation, which as I observed before, might not have been an easy matter: and now I hope the mystery is explained to you."

CHAPTER IX

Chrysal's master makes some striking remarks on his friend's account of this mysterious transaction, and draws inferences from it, not commonly attended to. He entertains his friend with a curious song, who makes an important hit, just in his own character, upon it. *Chrysal's* master boggles a little at first, at his friend's proposal, but is encouraged by his example to undertake it.

"I am much obliged to you, for such a proof of your confidence,"

---

confess, "apologizing for the offences listed by Douglas and revealing the other offences for which evidence was lacking" (DNB). Elizabeth Canning (1734-73), who claimed to have been abducted by gypsies and ruffians, received breathless coverage in the press and "became the centre of the most famous English criminal mystery of her century. The events and trials that followed her disappearance on 1 January 1753 excited Londoners for over a year and a half, bringing violent mobs on to the streets" (DNB). Among the "avalanche of newspaper articles pamphlets, engravings, and caricatures" (DNB) were works by Henry Fielding, who came to her defense with *A Clear State of the Case of Elizabeth Canning*, and John Hill, attacking her in *The Story of Elizabeth Canning Considered*. She was finally found guilty of perjury and transported to America. While Douglas was instrumental in the exposure of Bower, Lauder, and the Cock-Lane ghost, his role in the Canning case is unclear.

(returned my master) "particularly as it clears up some points to me, which I own gave me equal concern and surprise; and of which delicacy prevented my desiring an explanation from you. These were the manner in which that attack was made upon him, and the arguments and proofs brought in support of it, which were so *unfair, inconclusive,* and in many instances *contradictory*, that I was astonished any man of sense and honesty could make use of, or be influenced by them."

"Why, that is very true. Their zeal often overshot the mark to be sure. But that signified nothing. Set the public once upon the scent of scandal; and they'll hunt it like blood-hounds, through thick and thin. Nothing can be so gross[265] as to stop them. You may as well whistle to the wind to change its course, as speak reason to the people, when they have conceived a prejudice."

"But what is your opinion of that affair? Is he, or is he not, the impostor they would make him? For I confess, the arguments by which they would prove him one, are so far from answering their design with me, that *I think they prove the contrary, by proving nothing*; as it is natural to conclude, that if there were any better, such would not have been made use of. But you certainly must have had sufficient opportunities of being informed, in the intercourse you necessarily had with them."

"As to that, I know no more of the matter than you do, nor ever gave myself the trouble to enquire. All the intercourse I had with them, was only to save appearances, and get my money. Whether he was an impostor or not was the same thing with me. I was paid for seeming to prove him one; and that was all I cared for."

"But you continue to call him one still. Do they also pay you for that now?"

"No. I do that for my own credit. Were I to retract, all the scandal that has been heaped upon him *in my name*, would revert upon myself, so that whenever I mention him, I am obliged to do it in the old phrase. I know some *squeamish* people would have *scrupled* the whole; but that is not my way of thinking. I hold nothing to be so great a reproach as poverty, nor any thing a sin

---

265 "Stupid; dull" (Johnson).

that can get over it. And so here's my service to you. I wish you could hit upon such another opportunity."

"And if I would scruple to make use of it, may I perish in my present poverty; and I defy the devil to find an heavier curse."

The conversation then turned to more general topics, in the course of which, my late master naturally coming to be mentioned, "That's right" (said my master) "I have something to shew you that will give you pleasure.[266] You may remember I told you, that I am sometimes obliged to a printer of my acquaintance for *helping me to a job, in the letter or essay-way*. Happening to call upon him this morning, to try if he could take any thing from me, he shewed me this," (pulling a piece of greasy paper out of his pocket) "which I think really a curiosity. It is a *proof* of a bawdy-song, which the gentleman we have been talking of wrote,[267] and had a few copies of it printed for the amusement of his particular intimates. My friend got it from one of his journeymen,[268] who sometimes works for that gentleman, and says there are a good many more of them, which are all printed together in a ballad. You'll find it worth your reading. Nothing ever was so highly worked up. It gave me ineffable pleasure."

"If you can prove this to be wrote by that person" (said the other spitting, and wriggling in his chair, after having pored over it for some time) "your fortune is made! you know his enemies are striving to run him down by any means. Now this will give them so plausible an handle against him, that they will not fail to reward you liberally for the discovery. All you have to do, is to prove it plainly upon him."

"I am pretty sure that may be done;" (answered my master

---

266 KEY: "Essay on Women." The *Essay on Woman*, an obscene burlesque of Alexander Pope's *Essay on Man*, which Wilkes had collaboratively written with Thomas Potter.

267 KEY: "Mr. Wilkes." Wilkes intended the *Essay* only to circulate among friends, not to reach the eyes of the general public.

268 The initial proof sheet of the *Essay*, with corrections in Wilkes's hand, was first picked up by Samuel Jennings, a printer working in the shop of Dryden Leach, who used it to wrap some butter. Later, over a dinner of bread and butter, onions and radishes, Jennings shared the sheet with his friend Thomas Farmer. Farmer took the proof to his employer, William Faden (publisher of Samuel Johnson's *The Idler*), who finally shared the sheet with Kidgell.

with some hesitation) "But I—I—I—I hardly know how—I am under personal obligation"—

"Nay, if you let such things as that interfere, I give you up. What signifies *past obligation*, when put in competition with *present interest?* You know what my old antagonist says, that it is a rule among his former fraternity never to let any social or moral duties interfere with religion, of which he gives a remarkable instance in his own story. Now *my interest is my religion*; and every thing which interferes with that I abjure; as I have sufficiently proved. But I beg pardon, I would by no means press you to do any thing against your conscience, if it is so tender."

"Wrong me not, my dearest friend, by such an opinion: my conscience is as far from being tender, as yours can be. I was only surprised, that I had not myself seen what you mentioned. But now that your friendship has pointed it out to me, you shall see me pursue it as eagerly as you can desire. All I want is your direction! Leave the rest to me."

The remainder of the evening was spent in consultation upon the plan proper to be pursued, the forming of which my master submitted implicitly to the superior judgment and experience of his friend, who was so pleased with this mark of respect, and so sure of success, that on going away, he took a modest hint, and lent him five guineas, reminding him at the same time of the confidence he had placed in his honour, by disclosing his affairs to him, and enjoining him to secrecy.

CHAPTER X

Chrysal's master pursues his scheme, and violates moral honesty to
serve the cause of virtue and religion. He waits upon his patron, who
honestly refuses a character, to which he knows he has no right; but
undertakes the affair from a more prevailing motive, in which he is
remarkably assisted by another person, of less modesty, who pleads
the cause of religion and virtue in vain, till honour at length turns the
scale in their favour. *Chrysal's* master is disappointed of his hopes, and
makes use of an expedient in character, to escape from the just reward
of all his labours. *Chrysal* changes his service.

NOT to lose a moment's time, in a matter of such importance,
my master went next morning to his worthy friend the printer,
to whom he opened his scheme; and by his influence with the
assistance of a bribe, and promises of many more, he prevailed
on the fellow from whom the former paper was got, to betray the
trust of his employer, and steal the whole ballad.

The next thing was to make his honest acquisition known
to those from whom he expected the reward of his pious pains.
For this purpose he waited upon his patron,[269] and having with
difficulty gained access to him, on repeated messages of important
business, after the common cant of compliments, "I am come,
Sir," (said he) "on an errand, that I know must be agreeable to you,
as it will afford a signal opportunity of shewing your regard for
religion and virtue."

"Heh!" (answered his patron) "My regard for religion and
virtue! What the devil does the fellow mean! What regard have
I ever shewn for either in word or action, that should put such a

---

269 As several keys confirm, William Douglas, Earl of March and later Duke
of Queensberry (see 1.297-301). Kidgell shared the proof sheet with Lord March,
who had "been in secret consultation with John Montagu, Earl of Sandwich, and
probably with other members of the administration." They worked together to
secure a full copy of the *Essay* "so that the government could build a watertight
case against Wilkes for obscene libel" (DNB), and public monies were used to
bribe Wilkes's foreman for the full set.

thought in your head? If you are come to preach at me, you shall soon find the effects of your piety."

"Pardon me, Sir; I know you better than to be guilty of such presumption! What I mean is this. Fortune has favoured me with an opportunity of putting it into your power to establish such a character; and as I know most people are fond of the name, when it can be obtained without the trouble of the practice, I thought it my duty to acquaint you with it; especially as it will enable you, at the same time, to do a particular pleasure to your friends in power."

"Why, there may be something in that, as you say; but for the rest, I care as little for the name, as I do for the practice; and would not give myself a moment's trouble to get it; so be quick, and let me hear what you have got to say. I have *a match to ride* to-morrow against a gentleman for a considerable wager, and must see his groom this morning, in order *to settle matters with him*; beside which, I have an assignation with his wife, who expects me at this very time, so that I have not a moment to lose about religion and virtue."

My master, who knew him too well to attempt interfering with such engagements, politely wished him success, and then gave him in a few words, an account of the whole affair, only reserving to himself the honour of the thought, with which his patron was so pleased, that he promised to give him all the assistance in his power, *if it was only for the fun of the thing.*

Accordingly, as soon as he could spare time, from his own weightier concerns, he mentioned the matter to those more immediately concerned in it, who embraced the project eagerly, and rewarded my master with most *liberal promises* for his pains, of which they resolved to take advantage, in order to crush a person, either hated or feared by every one among them.

In the attack made upon him for this purpose, the principal part was undertaken by one,[270] whose regard for religion and virtue was heightened by a motive not the most consistent with either. This was the person who had been competitor with the culprit for *the*

---

270 Per one reader's notes, "Lord Sandwich." John Montagu, Earl of Sandwich, who had recently replaced Halifax as Secretary of State for the North—and inherited his predecessor's task of prosecuting Wilkes. See 2.152, note 130.

higher order of the MOCK-MONASTERY. In the account I gave you of that curious transaction, I observed that he cherished a secret grudge against the other, which was aggravated so violently by the disgrace he suffered on that occasion, that he had prevailed to have him expelled the society.*[271] Such an opportunity therefore as this, of completing his revenge, was not to be missed by one of his principles. Accordingly, though at the sight of the ballad he knew it to be no more than a collection of the songs, *which he had himself often bore a part in singing at the monastery, and some of the worst of which he had boasted of being the author of,* he inveighed against it with all the fervency and enthusiastic zeal of a modern fanatic, and displayed the danger of letting such an insult, upon every thing held sacred, go unpunished, in such strong and affecting colours, as afforded high entertainment to all who heard him, and were acquainted with his life.

But all his eloquence would have proved ineffectual to make such of his fraternity[272] as were not, like him, stimulated by private motives, give the lie to their own practice, in so flagrant a manner as to censure the theory of it, had not some particular expressions happened to affect the honour of one of them,[273] whom all the

---

271 Johnstone's note here directs the reader to III.II.XIX. See 2.158.

272 In marginalia, the "House of Lords."On November 15, 1763, while debate raged in the House of Commons over the *North Briton* 45, "Lord Chancellor Henley and then Bishop Warburton rose to protest the use of Warburton's name in a printed blasphemous poem. Lord Sandwich took over and began to read the poem aloud," then, "foaming 'with the violence of a Saint Dominic,' he declared, 'the blackest fiends in hell would not keep company with Wilkes, and then begged Satan's pardon for comparing them together'" (Arthur Cash, *An Essay on Woman*). The House responded with shock and laughter, in part because Sandwich's reputation as a rake easily rivaled Wilkes's. Dashwood claimed it was the first time he had heard Satan preach against sin, and Walpole said it had been read "with more hypocrisy than would have been tolerable even in a professed Methodist." The affair, which Walpole said fell "ten times heavier on Sandwich's own head than on Wilkes's," earned Montagu the sobriquet "Jemmy Twitcher," after a line in Gay's *The Beggar's Opera*: "That Jemmy Twitcher should peach me, I own surprised me."

273 KEY: "Bp. of Gloucester." William Warburton (1698-79), Bishop of Gloucester and religious controversialist, and friend of Alexander Pope and Samuel Richardson (for whom he wrote a Preface to *Clarissa*). Wilkes "grossly parodied the bishop's minute and pugnacious style of annotation in the notes to his notorious *Essay on Woman;*" said notes, attributed to Warburton, "were as

rest of course espoused; and *thus for once, honour turned the scale in favour of virtue and religion, too light by themselves*; and the ballad was condemned, as tending to debauch the principles of the people, though it was sufficiently known that it was not designed for publication, nor would ever have been heard of, had not this attack raised a curiosity about it.[274]

Through the whole of this important transaction, my master performed his part most cleverly, stopping at nothing that was thought any way necessary to bring it to effect. As soon therefore as it was concluded, he prepared to receive the reward of his labour, the enjoyment of which he had anticipated in imagination in every shape it could be given.

But it was not long before he found his hopes had been too sanguine. Instead of being rewarded immediately, as he had been made to expect, the job was scarce done when he could perceive the smiles of favour grow cooler upon him, as often as he went to pay his court to his patrons, in order to keep them in mind of their promises. A state of such uncertainty, severe enough upon any, was not to be borne by one in his circumstances. The expectations he had raised in the height of his hopes, had opened the mouths of all his creditors upon him, with an importunity not to be quieted; beside, that he had embezzled some public money[275] entrusted to him, a demand for which he expected every day, and knew he could not shift off for a moment.

Driven almost to distraction by such irresistible necessity, he had no recourse but to throw himself at the feet of the person

---

obscene as the poem itself" (DNB). In *The Duellist,* Churchill depicts Warburton as "A great Divine, as Lords agree, Without the least Divinity," and "A false Saint, and true Hypocrite" —"a curt dismissal with which many contemporaries would have concurred" (DNB).

274 The House of Lords charged Wilkes with blasphemous libel of Warburton, and he was tried for printing the *Essay,* even though the piece was never intended for public circulation. The final judgment of the court found Wilkes guilty, concluding the *Essay* was "more rank than the language of the most abandoned tongue in the lewdest scenes of prostitution" and "disgusting to every virtuous ear."

275 "Kidgell," notes one key, "was treasurer of a turnpike." Kidgell fled the country for Holland, "carrying with him the funds of the Godstone turnpike" (DNB), about £250.

who had appeared most sanguine in the pursuit of his scheme, and consequently been most liberal of his promises to him, and implore his assistance to extricate him from his accumulated distresses.[276] But they who will most readily avail themselves of villainy, always detest the villain. All the return he received was a cold profession of concern; and a shameless excuse of wanting that power to relieve him, which the caitiff[277] suppliant well knew he had.

A new misfortune often lightens the weight of those under which the mind was sinking before, by rouzing it from listless dejection, to an exertion of its powers. Such a disappointment of his only hope shewed him all the horrors of his situation; and made him instantly *cast about* how to escape from what he found he could not redress: instead therefore of betraying it, by his looks, which he knew were watched, he assumed an air of uncommon spirits, and telling every one that he had got a positive assurance of receiving the promised reward without any farther delay, he went to one of his tradesmen,[278] by that time he thought the news might have reached him, and taking up goods to a considerable amount, for which he confidently engaged to pay at a fixed and short day, no sooner got them into his possession, than he sold them privately at half price, and packing up whatever he could carry with him, fled beyond the reach of his creditors; and so proved how far his late conduct had proceeded, as he professed, from his high regard to moral virtue and religion.

The agitation and horrors of his mind, from the time he had resolved upon flight, till he had effected it, may be easily conceived. Whether the present safety it procured him gave him any lasting

---

276 Wilkes, "still the hero of ordinary folk" (Cash), was popularly seen as the victim of unfair intrigue and a corrupt administration. The public's wrath turned upon his accusers, including Kidgell, who tried to clear his name but failed; "his pleas of innocence were received incredulously. Many pamphlets abused and condemned him as a hypocrite priest and prostitute writer, who had publicly offended 'the cause of Decency' by his conduct" (DNB). Sandwich and March, his former allies, washed their hands of him. "Kidgell, the jackal," wrote Walpole, "completely blasted his own reputation; and falling into debt, was, according to the fate of inferior tools, abandoned by his masters."
277 Worthless, wretched, miserable (OED).
278 KEY: "A Bookseller."

relief, I had not an opportunity of seeing, as *I quitted his service* at the inn, where he took a post-chaise to get off; though it is most probable, that after the first hurry of his spirits subsided, a sense of the various villainies, by which he had brought himself to such a state of exile, embittered the very blessing of liberty, and kept his mind in slavery, though his body was free.

CHAPTER XI

Chrysal again changes his service. His new master is obliged to pay expedition fees,[279] to get over artificial delays. He and his mistress set out on a long journey, to do what might have been better done at home. *Chrysal* makes some interesting reflections on a most important subject. Story of *Chrysal's* master. *Chrysal* continues his reflections on the same subject, which he considers in a farther and most affecting point of view. *Chrysal* changes his service.

My late master had scarce decamped, when a young gentleman came into the inn, and ordering a *chaise and four*[280] to be got ready with the utmost expedition, gave my new master a bank-note to pay for it, *in the change of which he received me.*

The anxiety which my *new* master expressed to have the grooms make haste was a sufficient reason for them to practise every delay they could devise, in order to extort expedition-fees, at which they were so expert, that he was forced to give them almost as much as he paid for the chaise, before he could get it to stir.

When at length every thing was settled, he directed them to a particular place, where an hackney-coach[281] waited for him, out of which he received a young lady, with a couple of small bundles, and then bade the postilions[282] drive on; but they had no sooner got out of the town, then he changed his orders, and directed them to take another road. This occasioned a new delay. The fellows alleged

279 Money "paid for hastening the performance of any work" (OED).
280 A traveling carriage drawn by four horses (OED).
281 "A four-wheeled coach, drawn by two horses, and seated for six persons, kept for hire" (OED).
282 "One who guides a post chaise" (Johnson). The driver of a horse-drawn carriage (OED).

their being obliged to go where their master had ordered them, and no-where else; and made so many difficulties, that, as they expected, my master was compelled to purchase their compliance at their own price.

All obstacles being thus got over, he turned to the young lady, who sat trembling, and panting by his side, and embracing her tenderly, "Now, my dearest love," (said he) "all our fears are over. Should we be even traced to the inn, this turn will effectually baffle all pursuit."

"I wish it may," (answered she) "but I shall never think myself safe, till I am absolutely out of their reach, and all is over."

The conversation of lovers is agreeable only to themselves! The rest of theirs for two days, as they flew rather than travelled (for which expedition they paid sufficiently, every set of postilions giving the word to the next) will not bear repetition. As soon as they got to the end of their journey, they put an end to their most immediate fears also, by a marriage, which might have been performed with a much greater probability of success at home, had not a positive law prevented it.[283]

I see your surprise at my saying that a *positive law* prevented marriage, as the prosperity of the community depends in the first degree on the promotion of that state. But so it happens in human affairs, that the true interest of the people is not always the first object of the laws made for their government.

Though too general experience confirms this remark, it is necessary to explain the particular circumstance that gives occasion to it in this instance.

The first end of marriage is the propagation of the species, in the manner most agreeable to reason, and likely to produce the

---

283 KEY: "Marriage Act." The 1753 Marriage Act, proposed by Philip Yorke, First Earl of Hardwicke (1690-1764), which was "designed to prevent clandestine marriages, a matter of particular concern to the propertied classes" (DNB). Until the Act, neither prior notice nor parental consent was necessary to marry. The new law stipulated that consent must be secured for minors, and ordered "banns to be read for three Sundays in the designated church" before the ceremony. Pamphlets and periodicals of the period hotly debated the legislation, often to its detriment. An editorial in the *Gentleman's Magazine* held it would result in population decline, while increasing those licentious "vices, which the passions, not legally gratified, would produce."

happiness of the parties, as well as the population of the state. As the passions, which lead to this end, are strongest before reason has acquired strength to direct them, it is necessary that they should be subject to the direction of others who may be better qualified to discern and promote their interest. This right of direction naturally belongs to those who are most intimately concerned in that interest, as affecting a part of themselves; and hence, among every people upon the earth, however differing in other respects and customs, this right of directing the matrimonial choice has always belonged to the parents; till maturity of age may be presumed to ripen judgment, and so remove the necessity upon which it is founded.

But however evident this right is, the passions of youth so often rebel against it, that it was found necessary to enforce it by express laws. These laws though, the professed end of which is to make marriage happy, should never be perverted to the unnatural purpose of preventing it entirely, by clogging it with such unnecessary and unreasonable restrictions, as tend to subjugate not only natural liberty, but also the highest interest of the state, which depends upon population, to avarice, caprice, or pride of family in parents; or to views of interest in those appointed to supply their place.

The particular case of my master, which gave occasion to these reflections, was this. He was the younger son of a noble family, to the honours of which his rising virtues promised to add new lustre. Youthful inclination had first attached him to this lady, whose merits upon acquaintance confirmed that attachment, more than her very large fortune. Such a marriage could not fail to meet the approbation of reason and paternal prudence. Accordingly every necessary preliminary was agreed upon, when the sudden death of her father threw in legal obstacles which threatened to prevent it, at least for a longer time than youthful impatience could bear. For, as he had not actually signed to his consent, those to whom the care of his daughter devolved, thought proper to exert the right which the law gave them of objecting to the disparity between her fortune and that of her lover, and so break off a match evidently for their mutual advantage.

When the lovers found that all they could do to influence their compliance was ineffectual, they had recourse to this expedient (which the sage makers of the law had, perhaps inadvertently, left open) to evade it, by flying beyond its power;[284] and there solemnized a marriage, which should be valid at their return home, though entered into without any of the prudential cautions for securing happiness, which are customary on such occasions, and he had in vain offered to come into; so that the law, which was professedly designed to prevent inconsiderate and unhappy marriages, in its effect deprived this, and the many marriages of the kind, of the means for procuring happiness, which former laws, founded on reason, had provided for them.

It is not to be denied, but the evils, which were immediately alleged as the occasion of this law, called aloud for remedy; but whether the remedy provided by it did not introduce an inconvenience of worse consequence to the public than those evils, is not so clear a case. Whatever restrictions might have been thought necessary, in worldly wisdom, to prevent secret marriages, by which either the honours of families might be supposed to suffer diminution, or their fortunes fall a prey to mercenary design, where these considerations interfere not, such restrictions should never, in good policy, extend.

On the contrary, every impediment and delay, *not immediately proceeding from moral necessity*, should be removed; and the state of matrimony encouraged by such honours and advantages as should counterbalance the inconveniences of it, to persons labouring under circumstances of indigence; by which means the inferior ranks of the people, whose numbers make up the strength of a state, would be delivered from the difficulties and fears which at present deter them from entering into matrimony, to the heavy loss of the community, and the immediate ruin of such numbers of both sexes, whose natural passions, debarred from this, their only proper resource, lead them into such vices as defeat the end of their creation, and make them a reproach to humanity. How many infants would daily be saved from the most unnatural murder, to the ornament and advantage of their country, could the

---

284 As the law applied only to marriages solemnized in England or Wales, couples could evade it by marrying in Scotland.

wretched parents have saved their own shame by marriage? How
many females, who offer themselves in the highways to brutal
prostitution, perishing with cold, hunger, and disease, might have
been the happy mothers of many children, and performed all the
duties of their station in virtuous esteem, had not their being
hindered from marrying, *by impediments made by law,* betrayed
them to destruction?

As soon as my master had thus accomplished the end of
his journey, he set out on his return, to enjoy the fruits of it at
home. But I continued not in his possession to see much of that
mutual happiness which his marriage promised, *being borrowed*
from him on the road, by a gentleman of his acquaintance,[285] who
had been bubbled out of all his money at an horse-race, and was
now *fighting his way* to town, by running in debt at every inn, and
raising contributions thus on all he met, of whom he had the least
knowledge.

---

285 KEY: "Lord Deloraine." Henry Scott, Earl of Deloraine (1737—1807).
Though "descended from a most ancient and illustrious family in Scotland,"
wrote the *Town and Country Magazine* in 1770, "Lord D———ne" soon "gave loose
to a disposition which too frequently prevails in young men," spending his
youth gambling, drinking and whoring in Covent Garden. His self-indulgence,
"added to a violent itch for play," irreparably damaged his fortune "as well as
his constitution, ere he had compleatly attained manhood." An entire chapter is
devoted to him in the *Nocturnal Revels,* which asserted he had "figured upon the
horizon of gaiety and dissipation for upwards of twenty years," and Lady Mary
Coke's journal reports that in August 1766 he seduced and absconded with the
daughter of a gentleman of their acquaintance, "a young Lady of few scruples."
"His Daughter remains with Lord Deloraine," concluded Lady Coke, "where I
don't believe She will be long, as his Lordship soon tires of his Mistresses."

CHAPTER XII

Chrysal's new master strikes out an adventure. He is smitten with a girl in a travelling-waggon,[286] and changes his appearance to get admission to her. Account of the company in the waggon. A good-natured mistake of one of the passengers gives occasion for a broil, which is put an end to by an accident that does not mend the matter.

DISTRESSING as such a situation would have been to another, custom had made it so familiar to my *new* master, that he thought nothing of it, but travelled on with his equipage, as unconcerned, and ready to engage in any mad freak, as if his pockets were full of money. Nor was he long without an opportunity of indulging his disposition.

As he was rolling carelessly along, his chariot was stopped in a narrow part of the road, by one of those travelling-waggons, whose unwieldy weight gives them the privilege of taking place of their betters. Such a circumstance naturally made the travellers *in both carriages* look out, when he was struck with the uncommon beauty of a young creature in the waggon, whose charms in the first opening of their bloom gave scope to imagination to paint a prospect if possible beyond their present perfection.

Such a temptation could scarce be resisted by one who had reasoned his passions into the best subjection, much less by him who blindly obeyed them in, or rather stimulated them to their utmost excess. He no sooner saw, therefore, than he resolved to *have* her by any means. The first thing to be done, for this pious purpose, was to change his appearance, in order to get into her company, as the least suspicion of his rank would directly *blow* his design. But this was no difficulty. He was well accustomed to lay it down; and the meanest character in life sat as naturally upon him as his own.

Accordingly as soon as his chariot passed the waggon, he drove on furiously, till he was out of sight, when he alighted, and

---

286 "A covered vehicle for the regular conveyance of commodities and passengers by road" (OED).

changing clothes with one of his servants out of livery, ordered
them to leave the great road, and wait for him at an inn, some
miles distance across the country.

Thus equipped for his enterprize, he walked on leisurely, like a
common traveller, till he was overtaken by the waggon, the driver
of which *plied* him in the usual way to take a place, which after
some affected difficulties he agreed to. But the greatest difficulty
arose not from him. The waggon was already so full, that when
the driver mentioned taking in another, the passengers all cried
out against it with one voice. But his authority was too absolute to
be resisted. He fixed his ladder, and ordered them to make room,
barely condescending to say it was for a gentleman, who had been
taken suddenly ill, and wanted to go only to the next village. This
circumstance, though treated with brutal disregard by the rest, had
an immediate effect upon the tender disposition of his destined
prey, who squeezing closer to her mother, he crept into his nest,
and settled himself as conveniently as he could next to her in the
straw.

The company into which he had thus thrust himself, seemed
to be a representative of all the heteroclite characters of the
age. Beside the young female, whose appearance had attracted
him, and her mother, a plain good-looking woman, it consisted
of a mountebank-doctor and his zany,[287] a methodist preacher,
a strolling actor and actress, a fat ale-wife, a servant-maid, who
was going to *London* to repair a cracked reputation, a recruiting
serjeant, and two recruits, an outlawed smuggler, and a broken
exciseman.

Though my master could not at first view distinguish all their
different characters, some of them were so strongly marked, that
he promised himself the highest entertainment from the clashing
which he concluded must inevitably arise in such a group, and was
resolved to promote, upon the first occasion. But an accident soon
gave him that pleasure, without the trouble of planning for it.

As the weather was warm, and few of the company could be
suspected of the delicacy of changing their clothes often, it may

---

287 "One employed to raise laughter by his gestures, actions, and speeches; a
merry Andrew; a buffoon" (Johnson).

be supposed that every savour which arose among them was not purely aromatic. My master had not been many minutes in his place, when the various odours fuming round him, had such an effect upon his senses, that he undesigningly breathed a wish for a bottle of *spirits*.

As he had been introduced under the pretence of being sick, the ale-wife, who happened to be near him, mistook his meaning, and thought he wanted a *dram*, not once dreaming of any other use of spirits. Pulling out a flask therefore from under her coat, in the height of good nature, "Spirits!" (said she) "they are poisonous stuff. Here is what will do you more good by half!" Then drawing the cork, and taking a sup, to shew him that it was not poison, "Drink some of this," (continued she, reaching him the flask) "and I'll warrant it will *settle* you. It is right *Hollands*."

Before my master had time either to accept or refuse her offer, the actor, who sat between them, *smoked* her mistake, and intercepting the bottle, as she reached across him, cried out in triumph,

"Bravo, my queen! your gin from Holland pure,
  My stomach sooner than his head will cure."—

Then taking a large *go down*, or two, "Here, Belvidera,"[288] (added he, giving the bottle to the actress) *"in this friendly cup, drown all your sorrows!—Drink, as you love me, deep."*

His faithful mate could not disobey such a command. She took the bottle, and lifting it to her head, *"Thus to the bottom"* (said she) *"though it were a mile!"*

But she was interrupted in her intention by the smuggler, who lay at her feet, and no sooner smelled the dear liquor, than he raised his head, and perceiving what she was about, "Avast haling there," (cried he, snatching the bottle from her mouth) "or you'll pump the scupper dry."—And then going to put it to his own, "Hold," (said the exciseman, catching his hand with the same design) "I seize this in the king's name, till I know whether it has paid duty."

The mention of the word *duty* set the smuggler's blood on fire. "Duty! you shark!" (said he, grasping the bottle faster, and

---

288 The female lead in Thomas Otway's wildly successful Restoration tragedy *Venice Preserv'd*, first staged in 1682 and revived many times throughout the eighteenth century.

catching him in return by the throat with the other hand) "I'll seize you! damn my eyes and limbs! I'll pay you the duty, if you don't loose your hold this moment, you scoundrel! that I will."

Though he gripped the exciseman's throat so hard, that he could not return his compliment in words, he scorned to yield the prize without one effort. Giving a twist therefore with all his force to wrest it out of his antagonist's hand, though he could not succeed, he prevailed so far as to turn the mouth of the bottle downwards, by which means the contents were poured full in the face of the serjeant, who lay snoring on his back, with his mouth wide open.

Welcome as such a guest would have been in a proper manner, the intrusion thus unexpectedly was not so agreeable. He started up half suffocated; and belching his dose full in the face of one of the recruits, "Blood anouns! fire! and fury!" (sputtered he) "What's the meaning of this?"

Just as he said this, one of the wheels of the waggon came into a deep hole, with such a plump,[289] that though it did not absolutely overset, it tumbled all the passengers on top of one another; and instantly put a stop to the cries of the ale-wife, for the loss of her liquor.

The screams, oaths, and execrations of the whole company, on this occasion, would have given my master the highest delight, had he not been rather too nearly concerned to enjoy the *fun*, the fat ale-wife being thrown so full upon him, that he was unable to stir, though almost smothered, so that he could not help adding his cries to the concert.

---

289 "An abrupt plunge or heavy fall" (OED).

CHAPTER XIII

Chrysal's master experiences some comfortable consequences from the obliging disposition of the waggoner. He pursues his design, by paying common civility to his mistress's mother. Conversation and behaviour of the company. *Chrysal's* master, in the pursuit of his design, meets an adventure that cools his passion, and reassembles the company, when they are all like to be at a fault, till one of them luckily hits off the scent.

WHEN the driver had got his waggon out of the hole, and seen that all was safe about it, he came to know what was the matter with his passengers; and having *unpacked* them, my master had the pleasure to hear the young woman propose to her mother to walk a little way, till some, not the most agreeable, consequences of the late disaster should blow off, to which she readily consented, as he prepared to accompany them, both for the same reason, and in order to have an opportunity of making an acquaintance, which he found he could not so well do in the waggon.

But the waggoner was not in the humour to give them that indulgence. When they called to him to let them down, he answered surlily, that they had not above a couple of miles to their inn; and if he were to stop thus every moment, he should not get in, in time, and so without any farther ceremony whipped on his horses. This was a severe disappointment to my master, who soon grew so sick, that he could not hold up his head all the rest of the way.

But the qualms of his stomach did not affect his conscience, so as to make him in the least alter his design. On his arrival at the inn, he made a pretence of the compassion which the young girl and her mother had expressed for him, to attach himself particularly to them, and ply them with wine, by way of return, which false modesty made the mother take so freely, as gave him good hopes of success.

The conversation and behaviour at supper was strictly in the character of the company. The methodist made a long grace,

and talked of religion and temperance, while he eat more than
any two at the table, and his eyes were gloating at the servant-
maid, his fellow-traveller, who seemed to listen to him with great
complacency and attention. The actor mimicked the methodist
to his face, and lolled out his tongue at every one else, as they
happened to look another way. The actress spoke in heroics,[290] and
turned up her nose at every thing and every body. The smuggler
and exciseman sat growling at each other, as if they meant to make
a farther trial of their manhood. The serjeant talked of his exploits
in the wars, and proved his valour by an oath at every word, which
his two pupils listened to with looks of admiration, that shewed
they designed to imitate that part of his example at least. The ale-
wife lamented the loss of her gin, which, she said, she could not
replace with any like it on the whole road. In short, every body
eat and talked; and talked and eat together, except the girl and her
mother, who were quite lost in astonishment at a scene so new to
them, and my master, whose thoughts were too much taken up
with his own scheme, to mind any thing else.

Accordingly he stepped out when supper was ended, and
engaging the chamber-maid in his interest, by the present of half a
crown, she shewed him where his mistress was to lie, and promised
to settle all things in the manner most convenient to his designs, by
putting her and her mother in the bed next to the door, there being
two in the room, and placing in the other the servant-maid, who
paid for a bed to herself, as her modesty would not permit her to
sleep with a stranger.

As soon as the house was quiet, and my master thought the
wine which he had forced upon the mother had secured her, he
got up, and stealing in his shirt to the door of their chamber, found
it open, upon which he entered, and crept to the bed, where he
expected to find his mistress, without ever considering what must
be the consequence of surprising her in such a manner. Opening
the curtains therefore softly to feel by the difference of size on
which side she lay, he had scarce put his hand upon the clothes,

---

290 Heroic couplets, a typical verse structure in Restoration tragedy. An example
can be found in the preceding chapter: *"Bravo, my queen! your gin from Holland
pure, / My stomach sooner than his head will cure."*

when it was seized and gripped so hard, that he soon lost all thought of every thing but disengaging himself.

For this purpose, he made two or three efforts, but finding them ineffectual, and provoked at the pain his hand suffered in the struggle, he discharged a blow with the other full on the face of his antagonist, who springing directly out of bed, returned it with such usury, that my poor master fell sprawling on the floor, where he roared out murder with all his might, in which he was immediately joined by those who lay in the other bed, whose cries not only raised the house to his rescue, but also saved him from farther violence, his antagonist desisting to beat him, in order to make his retreat in time.

When those, who lay nearest, were assembled at the door, half clad, and worse armed with whatever they could catch up in their confusion, prudential regard to personal safety made them all stop short; every one finding some pretence to excuse himself from going in first, and pressing the post of honour upon his neighbour, till they at length raised their fears so high, that it was uncertain whether any one would venture in before day-light, though the cries still continued, had not the smuggler, who did not wake to join them at first, put an end to the debate. "Damn you all," (said he, snatching a candle from one, and a poker from another) "for a pack of cowardly lubbers! Will you stand *jawing* here, while the people are murdering?" Then rushing in, "Hallo!" (continued he) "what's going forward here, in the devil's name?"

The first object that presented itself to his view, when he entered, was my master, who was still upon the ground, unable, between fright and beating, to rise. Advancing to him therefore, "Hip, messmate!" (said he, giving him a kick on his naked posteriors) "What cheer? Speak, if you are alive!"

The entrance of light restoring my master to some spirit, he raised his head at this salute, and making an effort to get up, "I scarce know whether I am or not," (answered he) "I have been so beaten by that bitch of *Babel*; but she shall pay for it, if I ever recover."

The place where he was found, directing this accusation to the person in that bed, while some of them helped him up, the rest gathered round it, and asked the servant-maid, who lay there, what had induced her to treat the gentleman in such a manner? But the mention of her name saved her the trouble of a reply. Before she could speak, "It was not she!" (exclaimed my master) "I mean the old Beldam,[291] mother to the young Witch, whose baby-face brought me among you, and who lay in this bed. It was she who abused me thus; or rather some porter in woman's clothes, who passed for her, for no woman ever had such strength."

"I believe you must be mistaken, Sir," (interposed the exciseman) "the people you mean are lying quietly in the next bed, and seem to be as much frighted as you are hurt."

"How!" (returned my master) "did they not lie in this bed, next the door?"

"No," (answered the other) "Mrs. *Margery* lies here, as grave and demure, as a whore at a christening."

"Then the jade of a chamber-maid played me a trick;" (replied my master) "but who the devil lay with her? For I am sure she was never able to do what I have suffered."

"As for that!" (said the actor, who had all the while been peeping round the bed) "I believe it will be no hard matter to find it out. These breeches," (pulling a pair from under the bolster) "must belong to some body, and will certainly point out her bedfellow, if the lady, like a true Amazon,[292] did not wear them herself."

CHAPTER XIV

The advantage of a ready assurance. The methodist accounts curiously for what he has done; and turning the tables upon *Chrysal's* master, charges him with robbery, who is thereupon obliged to discover himself, but is contradicted by one of the company, who boasts of a curious acquaintance with him in his own character. He is luckily recognized by a footman, whose master extricates him from his distress, and makes out the mistakes that had caused so much confusion.

As the breeches were immediately known to belong to the

---

291 "A loathsome old woman; a hag" (OED).
292 "A race of women famous for valour," "so called from their cutting off their breasts, to use their weapons better. A warlike woman; a virago" (Johnson).

methodist, they marched away directly to his bedside, for he had not joined them, and asked him how he had come to use that gentleman in that inhuman manner, shewing him my master, whom they had dragged along with them.

"Who I?" (answered the methodist, affecting all the surprise of innocence, and determined to deny what he thought could not be proved). "Heaven forbid that I should use any fellow-christian ill. I engage not in such broils. My warfare is with the spirit."—

"And sometimes with the flesh too, I believe, doctor!" (interrupted the actor) "Nay it is in vain to deny it! do you know these breeches, doctor?"

"Breeches!" (exclaimed he, starting up in real affright, and fumbling under his bolster) "O they are gone! they are gone! I am robbed, ruined, and undone."

"No, doctor; they are not gone, as you see! But the question is, how they came under the young woman's bed's head, where this gentleman received this abuse."

"Let him answer that!" (replied the methodist, never at a loss for an impudent lie) "Let him answer that! all I know of the matter is this: Being disturbed in my rest, I then knew not, but now plainly perceive by what cause, I arose to pray, as is my custom, when hearing somebody go softly out of the room, I watched, as was my duty, to prevent any evil, and following the footsteps into another chamber caught a man in the very fact of attempting the virtue of some female, who lay there; upon which, expostulating with him upon the heinousness of such a crime, he flew at me so furiously that I could scarce defend myself from him, and if in the fray he received any hurt, he must charge it to himself, as he was the aggressor. But this is not the whole! I now perceive, that I was disturbed out of my sleep, by his stealing my breeches from under my head, which he accordingly took with him into the room of that damsel, and therefore I demand justice against him, for the attempt, as well as for any loss I may have suffered."

Saying this, he took the breeches out of the actor's hand, and searching the pockets, "It is too true!" (continued he, gnashing his teeth, and wringing his hands in a perfect agony) "It is too true! I am ruined and undone! I am robbed of all the money which I had collected in my pilgrimage to relieve the poor of the Lord.

Twenty golden guineas, besides silver and other monies. Let him
be searched! Let every body be searched this moment. I must have
my money! I must have my money."

As my master was a stranger to them all; and not blessed with
a face that could bespeak much favour, they began to give credit to
the charge against him, especially as the servant-maid corroborated
it, by saying that he had also been rummaging for her pockets,
when that worthy gentleman interrupted him (for women and all
were now gathered to hear the matter canvassed) and talked of
carrying him before a magistrate in the morning, that he might be
sent to jail.

At another time, such a scene would have given him the highest
pleasure, but he had no taste for *fun* now. Enraged therefore at
the iniquity of such a charge, and the insolence with which they
were proceeding to treat him, "Unhand me, at your perils, you
scoundrels;" (said he, telling them who he was) "Unhand me this
moment. As for that infamous villain, and his trull,[293] I charge you
to secure them directly, and send in my name for a magistrate.—
I'll make examples of them at least."

You may conceive with what surprise they were all struck at
hearing this. However, as he gave only his bare word for it, all were
not equally ready to believe him. "You, my friend *Scapegrace!*"[294]
(said the actor, coming and looking him full in the face) "No!
no, Sir! Say that to those who don't know him. I am his intimate
companion; his chosen among ten thousand. There is not a fine
girl upon the town but we have *bilked*; nor an house in the *hundreds
of Drury* where we have not *kicked up* a *dust* together.[295] He and I
are *Pylades* and *Orestes*;[296] sworn friends and brothers. No! no! that
stroke won't pass upon me."

---

293 "A low whore; a vagrant strumpet" (Johnson).
294 "A man or boy of reckless and disorderly habits; an incorrigible scamp. Often
used playfully" (OED).
295 Drury Lane, notorious for its brothels and streetwalkers. "Once going with
Mr. Winnington in his chariot through *Drury Lane*," writes Walpole, "I showed
him a board against a house, on which was written, 'Young Ladies Educated and
Boarded Here': he said, 'I believe they are boarded before they are educated.'"
296 In Greek mythology, Orestes was the son of Agamemnon and a member of
the cursed house of Atreus; he would kill his mother, Clytemnestra, to avenge his
father's death. Pylades was his close friend and companion, who in the version of

This made matters worse than ever with my master, adding ridicule to insult, which was poured upon him in such torrents from every mouth, that he could not speak a word in his own defence. But his distress lasted not long. The servants of a gentleman, who luckily happened to lie at the inn that night, being raised by the uproar, one of them knew my master through all his disguises. "By your leave there!" (said he, rushing through the crowd, and shoving aside some of them who had already laid hold of him) "Are you all mad, to use a gentleman in this manner?"—Then addressing himself to my master, "What is the matter, please your honour? I am sorry to see your honour in such a pickle. My master" (naming him) "is in the house, and will do you justice. I'll run, and call him up directly."

Such a testimony instantly turned the scale, and made those who were most insolent to him before, now most officious to pay him respect and attendance. Accordingly he was removed, without asking his leave, into his own room, where they were preparing to humanize his appearance, when the gentleman entered.

Much as my master was above the weakness of shame, he could not avoid feeling something like it, on being caught in such a condition. He was sitting on the side of the bed, covered only with the ragged remains of his shirt, which had been torn to pieces in the fray, daubed all over with blood and dirt, and beaten to such a degree, that he scarce retained one feature of the *human face divine*, which had not lost all likeness of the original.

The gentleman started at such a spectacle, and stopped short in doubt whether it could be he, till my master's voice satisfied him; when he gave orders to have every one concerned in the affair secured; and then seeing the poor sufferer taken proper care of, and put to bed, he proceeded to enquire into the matter, the circumstances of which appeared to be these.

The methodist having agreed with the servant-maid, his fellow-traveller, to have some *spiritual* conversation with her that night, she promised to lie in the bed next the door, and therefore after the chamber-maid had assigned them their quarters, as she had settled

---

Euripides married Orestes's sister Electra. The two appear in the work of several classical authors.

with my master, feigned some pretence to desire a change, which the others readily consented to. Accordingly as the methodist was secure of his reception, he came soon, and was got into bed to his *disciple*, when my master made his attempt, whose hand he seized in the manner I have related; and would have beaten him still more severely for his intrusion, had it not been for his crying out, upon which he retreated to his own bed in such an hurry, to escape detection, that he forgot his breeches, which he had taken with him for fear some of his chamber-fellows should search them, and rob him of eight or ten guineas that he had picked up in the course of his preaching about the country, and the actor had made bold to take as lawful prize, when they fell into his hands, and afterwards found means to convey to his wife, for more security.

Every thing being thus cleared up, the gentleman advised my master to drop the affair, as prosecuting it would only expose him still more, to which he willingly agreed, having no inclination for any farther trouble about it.

The methodist though was far from being so easily pacified for the loss of the fruits of his summer's labour in the vineyard, which he thought worse of than a thousand beatings, and was resolved to recover, if possible, in spite of all their scoffs and insults. But the detection of the other part of his history, had so entirely destroyed his credit, that he found it in vain to persist, especially as the actor offered to make oath that he had that very evening applied to him, to borrow a shilling to pay his reckoning. Cursing them all therefore in the bitterness of his soul, he changed his route, and went upon another preaching progress in order to retrieve his loss, in which pious work he prevailed upon his disciple and fellow-sufferer in shame, the servant-maid, whose pockets had escaped the pillagers, to accompany him.

By this time the waggon was ready to set out, when the rest of the company departed, except the actor and his lady, who were so tired of that vulgar way of travelling that they thought proper to continue their journey in the stage-coach; and my master, who was laid up in salves and flannels, and had lost both ability and inclination to pursue his enterprize any farther.

CHAPTER XV

Chrysal gives a striking account of his master. He arrives in *London*, and pays a visit to his mistress. His curious method of courting. His mistress makes him a present of half her fortune beforehand, in return for which he promises to marry her next day, and then goes to his girl. Difference in his behaviour to the two naturally accounted for. An uncommon guest at a wedding, with as uncommon a manner of celebrating a nuptial-night, shew a still more uncommon instance of matrimonial complaisance. *Chrysal* changes his service.

The singularity of my master's character gave me a curiosity to take a view of his life, while he was sleeping off some of the effects of his late adventure. He was born in a rank that supported the fair hopes of honour and advantage, which the first opening of his youth universally raised. But an error in his education blasted all those hopes in the bud, and drove him into every extreme of vice and folly, which it was designed to guard against.

The bad consequences which are seen to attend indulging the passions too far, often lead weak minds to attempt suppressing them entirely, without considering that the crime is only in the excess. The difficulty and pain of this attempt throw such a gloom over the whole appearance, as hides the native beauty of virtue, and makes it seem to be the source of unhappiness, to those who view it only in these effects, so as to terrify them from the pursuit of it.

On this error pretended enthusiasts have in every age founded their influence, by enslaving the mind to groundless terrors, which they never fail to turn to their own advantage. To the conduct of such blind and base guides, the mother of my master, to whom the sole care of his education had fallen by the death of her husband, implicitly resigned herself, and of course her son, in return for which they flattered her fanaticism and vanity together, with promises of breeding him up in the perfection of sanctity.

For this purpose, he was debarred from every innocent recreation, and harassed with studies improper for his age. His appetites were mortified by fasting; his rest was broken to chaunt hymns, and pray; nor was he allowed even to speak but in scripture-phrase; and all as the indispensable duties of virtue and religion.

Such a slavery naturally gave him so great an aversion to every thing that bore their names, that the moment he became his own master, he placed the supreme pleasure of his life in acting in contradiction to them, by every instance of expensive and vicious excess, in which he squandered away the inheritance of his ancestors, and broke his constitution with a rapidity that gave scandal to vice, put folly out of countenance, and made his name a bye-word in an age of excesses. And in this situation he was, when I came into his possession.

Though it was near noon before he awoke, the gentleman whose presence had so luckily relieved him the night before, waited to see him, when he completed his kindness by lending him money to defray his expences up to town, upon which he sent for his equipage, and set off without farther concern at what had happened.

On his arrival in *London*, he drove directly to the last place, which any other man in his circumstances would have thought of going to. This was the house of a lady of large fortune,[297] to which he had paid his addresses, since his extravagance had dissipated his own; and with this peculiar honesty, that he never even pretended a regard to herself.

---

297 KEY: "Hon. Mrs. Knight." The marriage announcement of Lord Deloraine to "Mrs. Knight of George-street, Hanover square," was reported in the *Gentleman's Magazine* for November 14, 1763. Deloraine's marriage to Frances Knight, the widow of the Honorable Henry Knight, son of Lord Luxborough, is commemorated in a "Tête-à-Tête Portrait" and the *Nocturnal Revels*. Both confirm it was a loveless marriage, engineered in an attempt by Deloraine to repair his squandered fortune. "Ambition was her motive," writes the *Town and Country Magazine*, "want and misery his excitements. Their hands were joined, but their hearts remained dis-united; and what is positively fact, he never bedded with her but one night; and having in the morning gained possession of all that she could dispose of, about noon he took a French leave, and never afterwards visited her." Frances Knight, now Lady Deloraine, "found it expedient to retire to a Convent in *Flanders*, where she some time since ended her days; which, probably, were shortened by reflecting upon her folly, and the mortification of having sacrificed every thing that was dear to her, for the empty whistling of a title." Henry Scott died without children in 1807, and the Deloraine title became extinct.

The success of such a courtship must appear improbable, but there is no accounting for the caprice of woman. She had taken a liking to him, which seemed to rise in proportion to the slights he shewed her, and was resolved to gratify, if only nominally, for she could expect no more, at the hazard of every happiness in life.

It may be supposed that the sight of him, in such a condition, struck her severely. She flew to him, threw her arms around his neck, and bemoaned his misfortune in the most passionate terms. But that was not what he wanted. Shaking her off, without feigning the least return to her fondness, "Psha!" (said he) "leave off this stuff; and let me know whether you have got the money, I told you I should want to pay off those debts of honour! If you have, and will also give me up the rest of your fortune without reserve, I'll marry you."

"Will you?" (exclaimed she, in rapture) "then you will have it, if it were ten times as much. Here it is;" (opening a bureau and reaching him an handful of bank-notes) "I *sold out* half my fortune to raise it, the very day you spoke to me."

"I wish I had known that," (said he, putting the notes in his pocket) "and then I might have made my excursion into the country longer. Farewell! I'll call upon you to-morrow evening, and conclude the job. Do you have the hangman and halter ready."

"What do you mean? I don't understand you."

"What should I mean, but the parson and the ring. Is not that an halter? And does he not hang us up with it for life?"

"But can't you stay a few moments! I want to know how you come in that condition!"

"It was only a scrape about a wench. I'll tell you the particulars another time. My girl would not forgive me, if she knew I was so long in town, without going to her."

"But will you certainly come to-morrow? I am afraid you will disappoint me, now you have got what you wanted."

"Never fear! I have not got what I want, while you have a shilling left in the world."

Saying which, he walked away without deigning to take any farther leave.

But his behaviour was not so cavalier where he was going. The moment he entered his mistress's room, she flew at him, not with the fondness of a dove. "So!" (said she) "what bawdy-house have you been breaking up now? You do well to come to me in such a pickle; but I'll see you damn'd before I take the trouble of nursing you."

"Don't be in a passion, my love," (said he, taking her into his arms, and giving her a kiss) "It is no such thing. I fell among a gang of foot-pads,[298] who abused me in this manner, because I made resistance."

"A very likely story truly, invented, I suppose, to excuse your not bringing me money! but if that is the case, you may go to the devil from whence you came. I'll not be troubled with your company."

"No, my dear! I never come to you empty-handed, let me do as I will elsewhere."—With these words, he pulled out one of the bank-notes he had just got from the other, and giving it to her, put her at length in a good humour.

I see your indignation at a man's acting in such a manner; but you could expect no other. The same baseness of temper which could treat the other woman with insult, naturally submitted to be insulted by this.

You imagine that his mistress must have uncommon attractions! to give her such power over him! You judge right. Hers were uncommon indeed. She had lost her hair and teeth in a salivation;[299] and was allowed to be the most profligate of her profession; charms sufficient to attach a man of his taste.

My master having thus happily made his peace, the loving couple sat down to their bottle, as usual; over which happening to mention his intended marriage the next day, her delicacy took such offence, that she positively refused to consent to it, till he promised not only that she should be present, but also to return and spend his wedding-night with her, to prove her triumph over the happy bride.

Accordingly he took her with him the next evening, and introducing her to the expecting fair one, "I have brought my girl"

---

298 "Highwaymen that rob on foot, not on horseback" (Johnson).
299 "The production of an excessive flow of saliva by administering mercury" (OED), "a method of cure much practised of late" in treating venereal disease (Johnson).

(said he) "to grace our nuptials. The dear creature insisted upon it; and you know I can't refuse her any thing."—The bride elect was so enraptured at the thought of her approaching happiness, that she had no sense of the insult, but received her with politeness, perhaps not without a mixture of pride on the occasion.

There are some scenes, the extravagance of which *beggars description*. I shall therefore only say, that the behaviour of the company was in character, during the ceremony and entertainment; at the end of which, the bridegroom alleging his promise to go back with his mistress, the convenient bride not only consented, but also proposed preparing an apartment for her, in her own house, to save him that trouble for the future, and procure for herself the pleasure of his company; a scheme that was actually carried into execution, while she had an house to receive her, which was not very long; a continuance of the same extravagance that had dissipated his own fortune soon dissipating hers also.

It may be imagined that I did not remain long in the possession of such a master. He *lost me*, the next evening after his marriage, on a bet, that he could repeat the *Lord's Prayer*, which he laid on purpose to lose, in order to prove how entirely he had got rid of the prejudices of education.

CHAPTER XVI

Chrysal makes some reflections, not likely to be much regarded. His master pays a love-visit to a young lady, whose father interposes unpolitely, and makes some out-of-the-way objections. *Chrysal's* master hits upon a scheme for getting over them. He proposes marriage on certain terms, which are agreed to, and the day fixed at a little distance.

I HAVE on former occasions given you a sufficient description how *people of fashion* spend their time in gaming-houses, where, though every meeting produces new misfortunes to some of the company, there is such a sameness in the manner as will not bear repetition, and must cloy any creature not absolutely under infatuation, or obliged to make a trade of it for bread, as neither of which was the case of my *new* master, he left the company early, to pursue pleasures more in his own taste.

In no instance are the contradictions in human conduct so strongly shewn, as in that of man to woman. He who would lose his life rather than violate the strictest principles of honour or honesty (as they are absurdly distinguished from each other) in his intercourse with another man, not only scruples not to study deceit, and practice the blackest and basest villainies against woman; but will even glory in the success of them, when accomplished, without shewing remorse in himself, or meeting reproof from others.

The reason of this is generally said to be man's partiality to his own cause, which as he has the power of judging in his hands, whether by usurpation or right, it matters not, makes him pardon in others the crime he would be glad to commit himself.

But without exculpating him in the least, woman bears an heavy share in the blame of her sex's ruin. I mean not here by her immediate consent in her own case, but by the countenance which she shews to the perpetrators of it, in that of others; it being as certain in fact, as it is gross and absurd to thought, that the surest recommendation to the general favour of women is the same of having ruined numbers of them.

Whether this proceeds from a vain ambition of triumphing over the triumpher, or an affectation of disdaining to espouse the cause of the fallen, as having forfeited the common regards of humanity, makes no difference in the consequence, whatever it may in the crime, as it opens an opportunity to the spoiler to extend his conquests often upon themselves, in the midst of their security; whereas, would women shew a true sense of the honour of their sex, by refusing every kind of intercourse with such as had ever violated it, man's partiality to himself would lose its effect, and all his designs upon them be restrained within the proper boundaries of virtue.

From the place where I came into the possession of my *new* master,[300] he went to pay a visit to a young lady of uncommon

<hr>

300 KEY: "Sir Chas. Coote KB." Charles Coote (1738-1800), fifth Baron Coote and Earl of Bellamont, variously called a coxcomb and a "person of disgusting pomposity" by his contemporaries. He is veiled as "Dorimont, the Hibernian

beauty and merit, whom he was violently in love with; that is, he was earnestly bent upon gratifying his desire for her, at the expence of her ruin; an enterprize for which he was eminently qualified, being possessed of all the advantages of youth, fortune, and address, and absolutely free from every restraint of principle, as he had proved on several successful occasions of the same kind. The reception he met shewed that he had made an interest in her heart; but all his experience in the science of intrigue could not elude the vigilance of her virtue for a moment, nor find the least opening for any attack upon her honour.

Such difficulties only redoubled his ardour. As he was considering therefore next morning how he should proceed, he was interrupted in his meditations by a visit from his mistress's father. After some time spent in common chat, "I have taken the liberty to wait upon you, Sir," (said the father) "about an affair, the importance of which, to my happiness, will apologize for any seeming unpoliteness in it. I have for some time taken notice of the frequency of your visits to my house, the honour of which I am justly sensible of, but not so far dazzled by, but I can see the motive of them through it; and therefore must for many reasons beg leave to desire that you will discontinue them."

"I—I—I don't understand you, Sir;" (answered my master, a good deal disconcerted at so unexpected an address) "I have no motive that I desire to conceal, or is any way inconsistent with the character of a gentleman."

"Pardon me, Sir," (replied the other) "I mean no such thing. But yet, what may be thought consistent with that character in

---

Seducer" in the *Town and Country Magazine* for 1786, where he appears as "a complet macaroni," ruled by vanity, whose "every appearance was gaudy and in the extreme of fashion"—a claim substantiated by Joshua Reynold's 1773 portrait of Bellamont, in which he wears an ostentatious, towering feathered headdress. The article seconds Bellamont's reputation as a seducer of women, and suggests Chrysal's account was, in some form, circulating as gossip in the period: "one amour, if report is to be credited, does not redound much to his honour. It is confidently said that he has denied a private marriage, but the probability is the charge was false, as every other circumstance of his life evinces a mind superior to such baseness; and indeed this accusation was not made till a matrimonial negociation had commenced between him and the sister of a noble duke." Bellamont would marry Lady Emily FitzGerald in 1774.

some things, may be very inconsistent with the happiness of a father. To be plain, Sir, I am not so unacquainted with the world, but I can see that all your visits are paid to my daughter; and as she is not upon a level with you, either in family or fortune, for a wife, I must repeat my request, that you will drop a pursuit, which must therefore have another view."

"You do injustice to your daughter," (returned my master, recovered from his surprise, and convinced that it was in vain to dissemble any longer) "to say that she is not upon a level with any man alive. I am above the vain pride of family; and as to fortune, my own satisfies me, without hazarding my happiness to seek for more."

"These" (said the lady's father) "are truly the sentiments of a gentleman, nor have I any doubt of the sincerity with which you declare them. But there are other considerations that make it impossible to carry them into execution. You and my daughter profess different principles of religion; and as I can by no means expect that you should change yours, so I hope she is too firmly established in hers, to quit them for any worldly honour or advantage."

This was a stroke my master was not prepared for. He acquiesced therefore seemingly, with the best grace he could, to avoid entering more explicitly into the subject, till he should have time to concert measures for getting over this new difficulty, for his honour was now piqued; and he resolved to stop at nothing, if only to punish the insolence of her father in presuming to forbid him his house.

Accordingly, after revolving a variety of schemes, he fixed upon one which he thought could not fail. Big with this hope, he went next morning to wait upon his mistress, notwithstanding the interdiction of her father, and finding her alone, after some moments of mutual confusion on the circumstances of such a meeting, "I—I—I—I am come madam," (said my master, hesitating, and blushing as he spoke) "I am come in consequence of what passed between your father and me yesterday, of which I presume he has informed you. It was never my design to disavow a passion, upon which depends the happiness of my life. I only waited till some particular circumstances should enable me to declare it with more convenience. But as he has made the discovery, that reserve is no longer necessary. If therefore, madam, I can be so happy as to find favour in your sight, all his objections I presume will be removed by my offering to marry you directly; on this sole condition, that our marriage shall be kept inviolably secret, till I have accomplished some affairs, to which you must be sensible the difference of our religions would be a prejudice. The ceremony shall be performed by any clergyman you please, in the presence of your father, and any other witnesses in whose secrecy we can confide, and every thing done that can convince you of the sincerity and honour of my attachment. Speak them, dearest madam, and make me happy, by complying with a proposal that has your happiness in view, equally with my own."

"I should be unworthy of the honour you do me," (answered she, the blush of true modesty heightening the charms of her beauty) "if I could let it interfere with superior obligations. When the approbation of my father gives a proper sanction to your application to me, you will probably find no great difficulty in making my inclination go hand in hand with my duty."

Her father just then entering, relieved her from the embarrassment of any farther conversation upon so delicate a subject; and she withdrew. But my master was under no such difficulty. Encouraged by a reply so favourable to his hopes, he directly repeated his proposal to her father, who promised him a decisive answer next morning.

As the manner of his reception left him no room to doubt of his success, he went again, at the time appointed, when the father gave his consent without difficulty, as did his mistress, stipulating only for a short delay, till she should return from the wedding of a young lady, her cousin, who lived at some distance in the country, and had engaged her to attend upon that occasion. As he could make no just objection to this, however disagreeable suspension of his hopes, he consented with a compliment, that his resolution was too firmly fixed for any time to make him change it, and then took his leave, exulting at the success of his project.

CHAPTER XVII

Chrysal's master is privately married. Not satisfied with one wife for love, he wants another for money. He proposes the matter to his wife, on whose refusal he discloses his grand scheme; in which, deep as it is laid, he has the mortification to find himself anticipated, and his own weapons turned upon himself. Consequences of this discovery. *Chrysal's* master takes a common method of silencing scandal. *Chrysal* changes his service.

THE smiles of hope make the sunshine of life; as the mind is then too intent upon the object in expectation, to see the inconveniences which afterwards embitter the enjoyment of it. The absence of his mistress, though considerably longer than he had apprehended, passed away pleasantly in the thought of his approaching happiness. As soon as he returned, therefore, he directly claimed the performance of her promise; to which all parties consenting, they were married by his own chaplain, in the private manner he desired.

Possessed thus of his wishes, his next care was to enjoy them, with the most convenience to himself. For this purpose, he took an house next to his own; and opening a secret communication between them, he removed her thither, as he could not take her directly home without declaring his marriage.

Mortifying as the mysterious appearance of such a situation must have been to her, she made no objection, but complied implicitly, in that and every thing else, as if she had no will but his. Passions merely sensual are soon sated. Though the resemblance of this intercourse to an intrigue heightened the pleasure of it, he had not carried it on long, when an opportunity of marrying to great advantage, in the phrase of the world, awoke his ambition, and gave his wishes another turn.

After some little conflict with himself, in which however the object in view proved too powerful for that in possession, he resolved to break the matter to his wife. Accordingly, as they sat together one morning at breakfast, after some expressions of uncommon tenderness, "The regard, which my dearest girl has always shewn for me," (said he, blushing at his own baseness as he spoke) "convinces me that she will not only take pleasure to hear of any thing to my advantage, but also forward it as far as may be in her power."

"I hope no action of my life," (answered she, surprised at his speaking in such a manner) "since I have been married to you, has given any reason to doubt either my duty or affection, that you should imagine such a preface necessary to introduce whatever you think proper to command."

"Very true, my dearest life. But—But—but there are some things, the nature of which requires delicacy, even to you, whose understanding is superior to the foibles of your sex. You know the young *lady Worthland!* I have received intimation that my addresses would not be unacceptable to her. Now as her rank and fortune would entitle me to expect the first honours in the state, I have that confidence in the attachment and love of my dearest girl, as to think that you will not oppose my interest."

"As how!" (replied she eagerly, alarmed at the hint, but unwilling to think so meanly of him as to understand it) "As how? What interest can you possibly have in her rank and fortune?"

"The interest which the law gives an husband. Possession! absolute possession of the whole."

"An husband? Good God! how can that be? Are you not already married?"

"True, my dearest life! But as that marriage is a secret, if it can be kept so, it will be no obstacle. You shall remain, as you are, the wife of my love; and I will only be the husband of her fortune."

"How you men, whose minds are stronger, take pleasure in playing with the weakness of woman? The very mention of such a thing even in jest, (for it is impossible you can be serious) strikes me with horror."

"In jest! I am serious upon my honour; and expect your immediate compliance, as a proof of your duty and affection."

"And can you mention honour in the same breath with such a base proposal? What a profanation of the word! But whether you are serious or not, I must be so on such an occasion; and therefore I declare that I never will sacrifice both honour and conscience, by giving what you are pleased to call a proof of duty and affection, but what would really prove that I had neither."

"This romantic spirit, child, much as you think it becomes you, is all thrown away. I am determined; and you must submit. But let me tell you, that on the manner of that submission depends your future welfare. If you comply properly with my proposal, I will make a settlement upon you, that shall exceed any expectations you could naturally have had in life, and remain your husband, in every thing but the empty name. But if you attempt making the least opposition to my will, I cast you off from this moment to beggary and shame; nor shall any late repentance ever bring me to receive you again; so consider the consequence before you rashly run upon your ruin; I shall expect your final resolution to-morrow."

"For that, you need not wait a moment. I fear no consequence that can attend my doing what is right. The duty of obedience, I have fulfilled in its utmost extent, by immuring myself thus, and forfeiting my good name to keep your secret; but while my conscience witnessed for the purity of my heart, I regarded not the present censure of the world, no more than I do now, from the same principle of virtuous resolution, your vain threats, for in such a light, the laws of my country enable me to hold them."

"The laws of your country, madam! Then claim their protection if you please; but you will find that they afford none to you. Such marriages as yours, between people professing different religions, are made void by those laws; and therefore if you think proper to depend upon them, I give you this notice, that you have nothing to expect from me, but what they shall procure you."

"And was this your motive," (returned she, with a spirit raised by indignation) "for desiring a private marriage? Impossible! you could not, cannot be so base. You only have a mind to try my resolution, which you shall ever find immoveable in this, and every cause of virtue and honour."

"Madam, I have no more time to trifle in this manner; therefore once more I desire you to let me know your final determination; for notwithstanding this behaviour, I still have such a regard for you, that I am unwilling to take an answer which must separate us forever. Think then, before you speak; and let my making you this generous offer, and preventing your exposing yourself in vain, teach you a return of proper gratitude."

"I want not a moment to determine between virtue and vice, infamy and honour."

"Then take the consequence; and blame yourself, when it is too late."

"I will; if any blame falls on me. And now that I see you are serious, in return for the notice you have so generously given me, I let you know, that I have obviated the advantage you flatter yourself you have over me, by conforming *legally* to your religion before I was married to you."

"Confusion! what is that you say? When, where did you conform?"

"When I went to the wedding of my cousin; as you will find upon enquiry, which I advise you to make, before you proceed farther in a scheme that can only expose you to worse infamy than that with which you threatened me."

"Infernal witch! Was this your love?"

"No; it was the prudence of my friends. My love could harbour no doubt of you; but they knew you better; and took this honest, wise precaution to guard against villainy, which I now am sensible they foresaw; and therefore, as you have thought proper to refer me to the law, I now tell you that I will immediately claim its protection, and declare my marriage, nor suffer any longer in the opinion of the world, by a secrecy that was enjoined for so base a purpose; by which I shall at least have the satisfaction of saving another woman from falling into the snare laid for her."

Saying this, she flung out of the room to conceal tears, which she thought would betray a weakness unworthy of her, and could no longer restrain.

The nature of my master's meditations on this discovery may be easily conceived. He cursed that foolish fondness, which had thus led him blindfold into his own snare; and damned all womankind, in revenge for being foiled at his own weapons by one of the sex.

When he had vented his rage in this manner for some time, a sudden gleam of hope flattered him, that what she said might possibly have been only the instantaneous suggestion of resentment and despair, without being really true. Pleased with the thought, he sent directly to make the proper enquiry, the result of which confirmed the defeat of all his designs. But this was not the only mortification he suffered. His wife, the moment she left him, went to her father, and discovering to him her husband's baseness, he supported her in her resolution of declaring her marriage, as the most proper means to prevent his forming any farther schemes against her.

The consequence is obvious. The public received such a curious piece of scandal with pleasure; and paid respect to his wife, if only to shew contempt for him; particularly the women, who made hers the cause of the sex, as he had precluded all farther designs upon himself, by marriage.

This though, however flattering to her vanity and resentment at the time, only widened a breach that she wished to close. His pride was piqued to disappoint her design, as she had his, and he left her to languish out the rest of her life in worse than widowhood, and repent of the folly of attempting to attach to herself a man who she knew had betrayed others of the sex.

As for my master, this detection made him desperate. He threw off every appearance of regard even to common decency, which he thought could no longer be of use to him, and determined to bear down scandal, by glorying in his vices; in the performance of which gallant resolution, he gave me to a stage-dancer, who gave me to an half-pay officer, who gave me to a tavern-keeper, &c.— II.I.XV. See 1.302.

CHAPTER XVIII

Chrysal gives an account of certain interesting occurrences. An extraordinary definition of a common word. Great expectations disappointed. The consequence of planning in the closet the operations of the field, with the origin of that sagacious practice.

(*Chrysal's master in the course of his journey from* Vienna *to* Lisbon, *falls in with one of the armies engaged in carrying on the war.*)

"The army through which my master was obliged to pass, as I have said, though paid by *England*, and the flower of it composed of *Britons*, was commanded by a *German* general, in disgraceful acknowledgment of the want of military merit equal to such a charge, in the natives."—II.II.XI. See 1.388.

SUCH an indignity to a people ever famed in war, and jealous of their honour, must appear unaccountable; but the web of human policy is woven in so mysterious a manner, as to reconcile inconsistencies still harder to be accounted for, on the common principles of reason.

When this army was first formed, the command of it was given to a *Briton*,[301] whose military abilities had in their opening dawn saved his country from ruin, and now in their meridian promised to raise his name to an equality in glory, with those of most renown, in the long list of heroes; but the wisdom of those measures by which the world is governed, defeated expectations so justly founded, and deprived his country forever of the advantage of such abilities.

As the professed design of this army was only to *observe* the motions of the *French*,[302] and defend the allies of *England* from their attacks, it was judged sufficient to make it barely of such

---

301 KEY: "D. of Cumberland." Prince William Augustus, Duke of Cumberland (see 2.21 and 2.188), Captain-General of the British forces, who was made commander of the Hanoverian Army of Observation in 1757.

302 The so-called "Army of Observation" of combined British and German forces, intended to protect Hanover from attack. See 1.388, note 620.

force as might effect that defence, with the assistance of those allies themselves. Though an inferior army may act successfully on the defensive in repelling an immediate assault upon itself, yet where its attention is extended to the defence of distant objects, the necessity of dividing such inferior strength enhances the disproportion, so as not only to defeat the design, but also often to involve the defenders in the ruin they were meant to avert from others.

The danger of such an event was evident in the present case, but some divisions in the *English* councils made it impossible to obviate it, by making the force of the army equal to the end it was appointed for; certain *patriots* having opposed the forming of any such army at all, with so plausible and popular arguments, that the sovereign was obliged to be satisfied for the present, with the shadow of one, as I may say, in expectation of being able to reinforce it, by degrees, as the *patriots* expected to make their compliance with such a measure, the means for gaining the end of their patriotism, that is, raising themselves to power.

You seem surprised at my calling men, who could act with such a view, and oppose a measure, which I have said to be founded on every motive of honour and justice, by the respectable name of *patriots*. But in this, as in very many other things, the name remains after the idea it was designed to represent is lost. *Patriotism*, that once meant the noblest exertion of disinterested virtue, by which every attention to private advantage was sacrificed to the public good, signifies now no more than an opposition to the measures of government, whether right or wrong, supported by such pretences as are most likely to inflame the passions of the people, till the governors are so embarrassed, as to be obliged to admit the patriots to a share of their power, when they directly throw off the mask for some other to take up; and do themselves the very things which they before declaimed against with such noise and vehemence. By this general description I do not absolutely preclude a few particular exceptions; nor deny the merit of some men, who even in modern times have deserved the name, in all the honour of its original meaning.

The nature of such a command, and the improbability of its success, would have deterred any man from accepting it, who was not actuated by principles so truly patriotic, as to make him disregard every other motive, for the mere possibility of serving his country.

As the abilities of the general often make up for the weakness of an army, the *Britons* under his command confiding in him, looked upon the superior force of their enemies with pleasure, as promising them the greater glory. Nor was this confidence without foundation; he had led them to victory before, when they scarce deserved the name of regular forces; and had since, with unwearied care, assisted their native valour with every advantage of the most judicious discipline. Under such a commander therefore, what might not such troops hope to do? But a difficulty still more distressing than the inferiority of his force disappointed all those hopes.

Military operations are so complicated, that every motion of an army requires a correspondent one, in that opposed to it. The obvious truth of this shews the sagacity of planning in the closet, the operations of the field. Particular objects indeed may be proposed; but the method of accomplishing them must be left to the judgment of the commander, as occasion may direct, it being absolutely impossible to foresee, and provide for all the instantaneous contingencies, which must make an immediate deviation from any system, that could have been laid down, indispensably necessary. Where this discretionary power is abridged, and the motions of a general marked out for him, it must be from the fault of his adversaries, if he performs any thing of consequence.

The first who introduced this scheme of shackling a commander were churchmen, who, puffed up by the power which their influence over the weakness of princes gave them, disdained to appear incapable of any thing; and therefore, as their want of military knowledge would not permit their undertaking the actual command of armies, they took this method of shewing their abilities and authority, by directing how the commanders of them should proceed; a method, however absurd in itself, so flattering to human self-sufficiency, that princes adopted it after, when age or infirmity prevented their leading their forces in the field.

CHAPTER XIX

Continued. The natural event of such a situation. The General, victorious
over himself, quits the pursuit of military glory for the practice of the
virtues of peace. Perfidy of the enemy justly punished. The army is
formed again under the command of a *German*, and a sugar-plum
given to the *English* to stop their mouths at such an insult.

DISTRESSED more by directions of this kind than even by the
weakness of his army, the *British* general took the field, rather in
obedience to his duty than from any hope of success, and literally
to *observe* the motions of an enemy whom he was not able to
oppose.

The event was as he foresaw. The enemy superior in strength,
and at liberty to seize every advantage, while he could only act
in consequence of orders given at a distance, and impossible to
be always proper, soon turned his attention from the defence of
others to the preservation of his own army. But even this, the
circumstances he was in made it impossible for all his judgment
and intrepidity to effect, though displayed in a manner that made
his name immortal, otherwise than by giving up the countries
he was sent to defend,[303] on the best terms he could procure, and
disarming his own troops.

Mortifying as such a necessity must have been to an heart
panting for glory, his conduct under it reflected more real honour
upon him than any victory gained against probability, at the
imminent hazard of the loss of his whole army could have done,
as it shewed that he was superior even to the desire of fame, when
clashing with the interest of his country.

But they who had driven him to this necessity, by disabling him
from pursuing the dictates of his own judgment, thought proper

---

303 KEY: "Convention of Closterhoven." Defeated on July 24, 1757, Cumberland's
forces effectively capitulated to the French at Kloster-Zeven on September 8.
George II was infuriated. He removed Cumberland from his post, lambasting
him for having "ruined his country and his army," as well as "his own reputation"
(DNB). Cumberland would never again assume military command, and Walpole
wrote that the King's response was "treachery to the best son that ever lived."

to view his conduct in another light, and censure in him their own errors. The honest indignation of conscious virtue could not brook treatment so disingenuous. In justice to himself, therefore, he resigned all military command; and quitting the profession of arms forever, devoted the remainder of his days to the practice of every virtue of peace.

As to the countries which he had been thus disappointed from defending, their troubles ended not so easily. The enemy, in the insolence of power, soon broke through the terms on which they had been given up, and treated the army that had submitted on the security of public faith, with every instance of the most flagrant injustice.

All obligations are mutual. The breach of one party therefore disengages the other. Provoked by such perfidy, the injured army joined the natives, and arose with all the fury of revenge upon their oppressors. Such attacks are not to be resisted. The tyrants were driven out of all their conquests;[304] and, to prevent their recovery of them, the army was formed again of force sufficient to accomplish the end proposed, and the command of it given to a *German* of proved abilities,[305] free from the restrictions which had made those of the late commander of no effect, his miscarriage having shewn the absurdity of them; and the *English patriots*, who had before opposed the raising any such army, having succeeded in their views of getting into power, and now aiding the design with all their influence; "though to palliate their disgrace, and to satisfy the jealousy of the *English*, they had the imaginary privilege of being immediately under a commander of their own,[306] and subject

---

304 In one key, "the French," who broke the terms of the Convention by attempting to disarm the disbanded troops. In retaliation, George II instructed the ministers of Hanover to ignore the Convention, and the conflict resumed. As Sir Walter Scott opined, "neither the laying down, nor the re-assumption of arms, was very honourable to Britain."

305 KEY: "Prince Ferdinand." Duke Ferdinand of Brunswick. See 1.388.

306 KEY: "late Duke of Marlborough." Charles Spencer (1706-58), Duke of Marlborough, who replaced the disgraced Cumberland as commander of the Hanoverian army. His death, soon after, led to George Sackville Germain's takeover of the post (1.388-91). Marlborough's refusal to let British soldiers be, as he put it, "cleavers of wood and drawers of water to the Hanoverians" prompted Pitt to declare him "general over all" in Hanover (DNB).

352 CHRYSAL

only to their own laws, in all things except the operations of the war, when they were of necessity to obey the *German* commander in chief."—II.II.XI. See 1.388-89.

APPENDIX

Index to the persons identified by the keys to Chrysal

GUISE, John   1682/3–1765
Army officer and art collector
I.I.XV   1. 83–84

HASTINGS, Selina   1707–1791
Countess of Huntingdon
II.I.XII–XIII   1. 286–90

HAY, Lord Charles (of Linplum) ?1700–1760
Major-General, arrested in 1758
III.I.XXI–III.II.I   2. 83–84

HENSEY, Florence   *fl.* 1748–1760
Physician and spy
II.I.IX   1. 264–66

HILL, Sir John   bap. 1714, d. 1775
Physician, naturalist, actor and writer
I.I.XIX–XX   1. 102–12
III.II.IX   2. 122

HOWE, George Augustus   ?1724–1758
Third Viscount Howe, army officer killed at Ticonderoga
III.I.XXI   2. 84–87

HOWE, Richard   1726–1799
Fourth Viscount Howe, later Earl Howe, naval officer
III.I.IV   2. 19–25
III.I.XVII   2. 68–77

HOWE, Sir William   1729–1814
Fifth Viscount Howe, army officer
III.I.XXI   2. 82–87

JERVIS, Sir John   1735–1823
Earl of St Vincent, naval officer
III.I.XVII   2. 68–77

JOHNSON, Sir William   ?1715–1774
First baronet, colonial official
III.II.I–IV   2. 90–105

KEPPEL, Augustus   1725–1786
Viscount Keppel, naval officer and politician
III.I.III–V   2. 13–23

KEPPEL, George   1724–1772
Third Earl of Albemarle, army officer and politician
III.I.IV–V   2. 16–25

KIDGELL, John   *bap.* 1722, *d.* ?1780
Church of England clergyman, novelist and political writer
IV.II.VII–X   2. 302–16

KNIGHT, Frances   *fl.* 1762–1765
Lady Deloraine
IV.II.XV   2. 334–37

KNOWLES, Sir Charles   *d.* 1777
First baronet, Admiral
III.I.I   2. 9

LANGFORD, Abraham   1711–1774
Auctioneer
IV.I.XV–XVIII   2. 243–57

LAUDER, William   *ca.* 1710–1771
Literary scholar and forger
IV.II.VIII   2. 306–307

LEACH, Dryden   *fl.* 1758–1768
Printer and bookseller
IV.I.XX   2. 263
IV.II.VIII   2. 304

LENNOX, Charles   1701–1750
Second Duke of Richmond and Second Duke of Lennox, politician and sportsman
IV.I.II   2. 186

LESTOCK, Richard   1679–1746
Naval officer, acquitted for misconduct at the 1744 Battle of Toulon
III.I.XX   2. 79
III.II.VII   2. 114–15

LIGONIER, John   1680–1770
Earl Ligonier, General
I.II.I   1. 113–18

LOWTHER, Sir James   ?1673–1755
Fourth baronet, politician and coal magnate
I.I.XVII   1. 95–98